Sixty-Four Goddesses

Reflections of Sacred Identity & Female Empowerment

B. Melusine Mihaltses

C.L.C., R.Y.T., M.M., B.M.

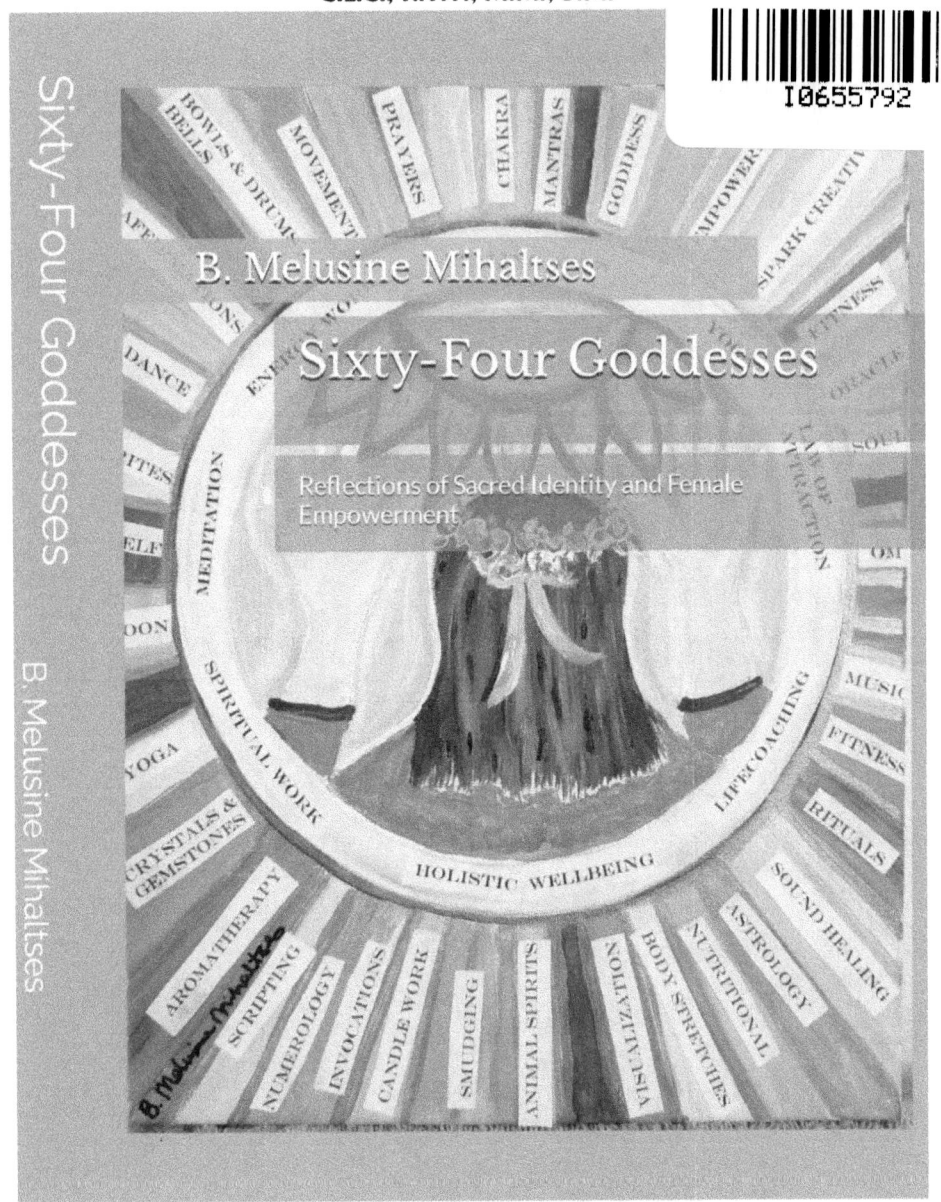

Feminine Divine Works
Schertz, Texas, U.S.A.
ISBN#978-0-9851384-6-2
LCCN# 2023914213

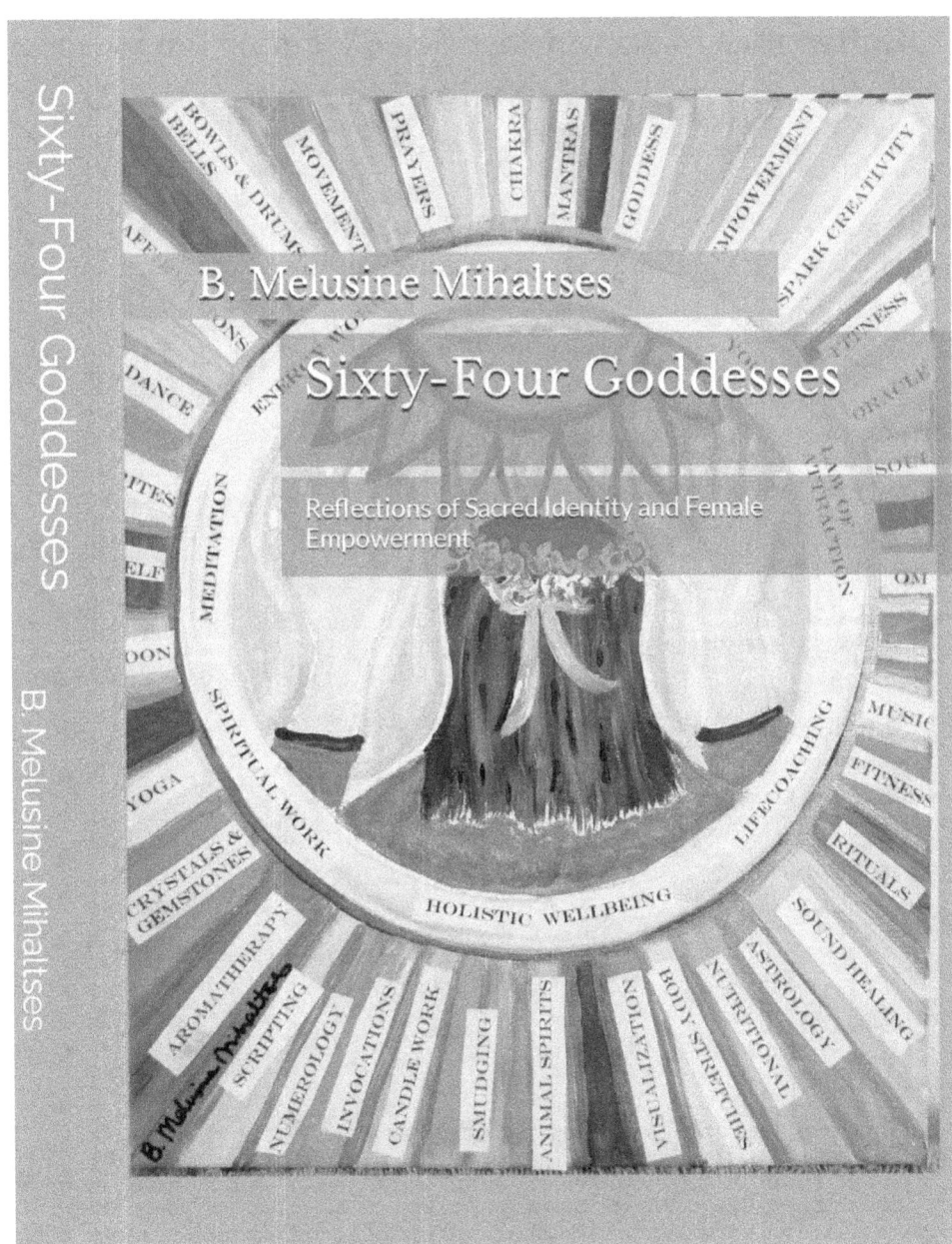

SIXTY-FOUR GODDESSES
REFLECTIONS OF SACRED IDENTITY AND FEMALE EMPOWERMENT
B. Melusine Mihaltses

C.L.C., R.Y.T., M.M., B.M.

ISBN#978-0-9851384-6-2
LCCN: 2023914213

SIXTY-FOUR GODDESSES
Reflections of Sacred Identity & Female Empowerment
B. Melusine Mihaltses
C.L.C., R.Y.T., M.M., B.M.

ISBN#978-0-9851384-6-2
Publisher: Feminine Divine Works
Schertz, Texas 78154, U.S.A
©B. Melusine Mihaltses
Year: 2023

Sixty-Four Goddesses
Reflections of Sacred Identity & Female Empowerment
© 2023 by B. Melusine Mihaltses

Published by:
Feminine Divine Works
P.O.Box 114
Schertz, Texas 78154
Femininedivineworks@gmail.com

©B. Melusine Mihaltses 2023
B. Melusine Mihaltses asserts the moral right to be identified as the author of this work.

Library of Congress Cataloging- in- Publication Data
Mihaltses, B. Melusine, 1970-
Sixty-Four Goddesses
Reflections of Sacred Identity & Female Empowerment

1. Goddess Mythology 2. Women Spirituality   3. Self-Improvement 4. Metaphysics 5.Life Coaching I. title

Includes bibliographical references
ISBN: 978-0-9851384-6-2
Library of Congress Control Number: 2023914213

Although the author and publisher have made every effort to ensure accuracy and completeness of information contained in this book. We assume no responsibility for errors, inaccuracies, omissions, or any inconsistency herein. Any slights of people, places, or organizations are Unintentional.

First edition
First printing, 2023
Cover Art by: B. Melusine Mihaltses
Text, poetry and photographs all by: B. Melusine Mihaltses
Interior Illustration and Original Art all by: B. Melusine Mihaltses

Printed and bound in the U.S.A.   LCCN: 2023914213

Sixty-Four Goddesses

Reflections of Sacred Identity & Female Empowerment

B. Melusine Mihaltses

C.L.C., R.Y.T., M.M., B.M.

Feminine Divine Works

Schertz, Texas, U.S.A.

ISBN#978-0-9851384-6-2

Books By B. Melusine Mihaltses

Gathering for Goddess,
A Complete Manual for Priestessing Women's Circles
978-0-9851384-4-8

***

Living Goddess Spirituality,
A Feminine Divine Priestessing Handbook
978-0-9851384-7-9

***

Goddess Grimoire Journal,
A Collection of Simple Prose and Spells
978-0-9851384-3-1

***

The Spellcrafting Coach,
A Metaphysical Guide to Revamp your Life
978-0-9851384-0-0

***

Major Arcana Goddess Living Tarot,
A Feminine Divine Works Creation
978-0-9851384-8-6

***

Feminine Divine Works Intuitive Oracle,
A Powerful Tool for Daily Insight and Inspiration
978-0-9851384-9-3

***

Feminine Divine Works Intuitive 70x Oracle Deck

***

Goddess Coaching Companion,
A Women's Guide to Magick, Protection and Empowerment
978-0-9851384-5-5

***

Goddess Inspired,
Artistic Offerings to the Sacred Feminine
ISBN #978-0-9851384-1-7

***

Revamped Goddess,
Coaching Yourself to a Better Life
ISBN #978-0-9851384-2-4

FEMININE DIVINE WORKS,
SCHERTZ, TEXAS, U.S.A

Sixty-Four Goddesses

Reflections of Sacred Identity & Female Empowerment
B. Melusine Mihaltses

ISBN# 978-0-9851384-6-2

Dedication

***

For those who seek to walk in
Their Divine truth....

****

SIXTY-FOUR GODDESSES
REFLECTIONS OF SACRED IDENTITY & FEMALE EMPOWERMENT
B. Melusine Mihaltses
C.L.C., R.Y.T., M.M., B.M.
ISBN#978-0-9851384-6-2

TABLE OF CONTENTS

INTRODUCTION

"There is no force equal to a woman determined to rise..." W.E.B. Dubois

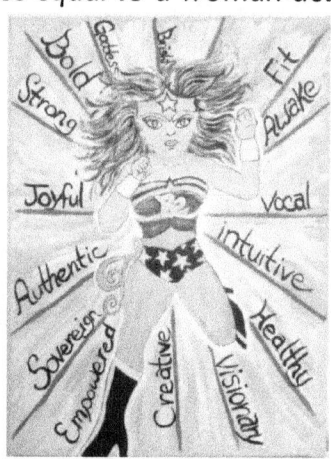

Present in every culture throughout various times in our history, around the globe, there has been indisputable evidence of the Sacred Feminine; better known as Goddesses. Today most Dictionaries, like The Brittannica Dictionary, define Goddess as, *"a Female God"* but also *"a Woman who is greatly loved or admired..."* Meriam's dictionary also defines Goddess as, *"a Female God"* and *"a woman whose great charm or beauty arouses adoration..."* Clearly the term Goddess is no longer just relogated to ancient myths & archetypes of our past but transcends into our modern language to potentially include every woman existing today.

The term Goddess is not meant to be sacrilegious, nor offensive, nor contrary to any preexisting religious belief we may have. It is meant to indicate the authenticity and value of our gender and points to our inherent gifts so often demeaned or disregarded entirely in our society.

This book endeavours to introduce a list of noteworthy Goodesses. Presented here are only sixty-four Goddesses, among the myriad known and still unknown througout our history. This collection of Goddesses, are a diverse representation from various cultures that have been instrumental in my own personal journey and, I believe, of great significance for most women.

No matter the era, or age or phase in a women's life, a glimmer into the Sacred Feminine & her Goddess myths offers us, as women, a window into our own capacity, strength and intrinsic value. Something changes within us when we start unearthing our ancestral lineage and Goddess connection. Our walk, self-talk, how we show up in this world, and in our own body, changes. Our purpose and our textile threads in this Universal tapestry gains telescopic clarity and who we are becoming takes on a different hue. It is as if something deeply lodged and ancient expands in our core the moment we are called Goddess and we indentify with her divinity. She is Internalize and remembered. We breathe life into her in our awareness and when she is awakened from within, we begin to walk with the opulent ancestral crown we never knew we possessed.

Discovering Goddesses and embracing the long forgotten aspect of our gender, inaugurates shifts in our psyche that changes everything, for we begin to walk and exist in our Divine Truth....

CHAPTER ONE
BALANCE
SHE WHO VALUES HER PEACE

"How people treat you is their karma; how you react, is yours… " Wayne Dyer

TARA

"Every action has equal and opposite reaction.
This is the law of the universe and it spares none.

TARA

The name *Tara* translates as, *"star or planet"* and it begins to paint a picture of this Universal, feminine deity. Tara is the Tibetan Buddhist Goddess of Compassion. She is a Goddess of immortality, physical prowess, benevolence, liberation, hope and a fierce protector and savioress of humanity. She is Mother of all the Buddhas and Mother of Liberation. Part of her name in Sanskrit means, *"to traverse or to cross,"* which speaks of crossing the stream of suffering or struggles. The Goddess Tara is also known as Arya Tara and Jetsun Dolma, in the Tibetan language. She is embraced by both Hinduism and Buddhism.

Her worship can be found and traced back to Bengal, Tibet, some parts of China and India, more specifically Aboriginal India and Hindu Jain. When we work with this Goddess we have to consider the two different regions she is associated most with and her distinct venerations in these cultures.

Tara is a Tantric Goddess in the Buddhist Tantric Religion. She is also venerated as a protectress and savioress of Humanity and a beloved Mother deity. As a Tantric deity, Tara is known to have five main forms represented by five different colors; although there are quite a few other aspects to Tara; in a Mandala she's depicted with 21 forms.

SITATARA	**White Tara**	**Compassion, Serenity, Healing**
SYAMATARA	**Green Tara**	**Peaceful, Protection, Enlightenment**
EKAJATA	**Blue Tara**	**Wrathful, Transmutation of Anger**
BHRKUTI	**Yellow Tara**	**Prosperity, Wealth, Wish Granter**
KURUKULLA	**Red Tara**	**Heroic, Swift, the Magnetizer**

The earliest mention of the Goddess Tara can be found in the middle of the 7th century. Her name is found amidst a Buddhist prayer in the *Subandhu's Vasavadatta*. She is described as the Lady Twilight, donning a red garment, devoted to the stars. Today Tibetan nuns and monks wear multi-layered robes made of this color red or deep maroon, mustard yellow/saffron and white.

The Goddess Tara belongs to the family of *Dhyani Buddha Amoghasiddhi, according to Buddhism*, and she is also more popularly linked with Bodhisattva Avalokitesvara. According to the well-known Tantric scriptures, Avalokitesvara heard the distress and lamentation of all the beings upon the earth. Humanity was beginning to mourn his imminent departure, as he journeyed towards nirvana. Upon hearing of mankind's pain, this Avalokitesvara sheds a tear of great compassion for all those he would leave behind suffering; from his tear, the Goddess Tara was born. It is stated she manifested from his tear and committed to staying upon the earth to serve humanity in all of their needs. Tara thus becomes the compassionate one and the savioress of humanity; who stays on earth to answer the prayers of her devotees. She is the Female Bodhisattva, viewed as the Mother of all Buddhas but in some traditions viewed as both offspring and companion of the Avalokitesvara.

For Tibetans, the Goddess Tara is seen as both queen and mother. She is the one born from a tear of compassion, highly revered as the Feminine Avalokitesvara. It is clear she is the beloved deity dedicated to answering the desperate prayers of humankind. Like the Chinese Goddess, Kwan yin, she is highly sympathetic and compassionate to her devotees. She is known as the "cheater of death" and can bestow a long life to her followers. There have been a plethora of writings exalting her answered prayers and documenting the numerous times she has intervened and helped her devotees.

She is known as the bringer of longevity, the rescuer of humanity and a Goddess deeply connected to life. She is not particularly called upon as a Goddess of fertility, although it is in her power to bless those who ask for that type of blessing. As a Goddess primarily connected with life and immortality, she is the one who preserves and guards our lives. Therefore she earned the titled, "cheater of death," and "prolonger of life."

In some parts of India, she was seen as the wife of *Brhaspati* who was abducted by Soma. In this context, she later gives birth to the Buddha, thus becoming Mother of all Buddhas. In Bengal, *Ramprasad Sen* (an 18th century devotee of Kali) wrote about Tara as a Hindu Goddess, almost synonymous with his beloved fierce patron Goddess, Kali.

In Hinduism, Tara is viewed very distinctly. She is indeed one of the *Mahavidyas*; the beloved Matriarchal deities and sacred mothers of humanity. Her appearance in descriptive Hindu sacred text and her rendered illustrations, reveals a Goddess that shares many of Kali's prominent characteristics. Tara is described in Hinduism as dark, wearing a necklace of head skulls, while Kali wears a garland of freshly chopped-off, gruesome, bloody heads. Tara is described with her disheveled braided hair, standing with one foot over a corpse, near a funeral pyre. Kali is described as naked, dark as night, hair disheveled as well, and standing over the corpse of Shiva. Kali is also near a crematory ground similar to the depiction of Tara. In this respect here, the Goddess Tara is embraced in Hinduism in her *Blue aspect as*, Ekajata or Ugra-Tara. You may also see her form as Red Tara, known as *Kurukulla*. Interesting to note, in Nepal she is embraced as Green Tara, better known as, *Khadiravani* Tara.

TARA'S HINDU & BUDDHIST SACRED MANTRA
"Om Tare tuttare ture svaha (or soha)…"
Translation: Om Tara, I pray, Oh swift one, so be it….

TIBETAN BUDDHISM
The introduction of Buddhism came to Tibet via India around the seventh century. Chinese Buddhism eventually also influenced Tibet later on between the 9th and 10th century. Buddhism and possibly the worship of the Goddess Tara, however, is believed to have started around 641CE. The Tibetan King Songstsen Gampo married two wives that same year and this helped unified Tibet. His brides were the princess Bhrikuti of Nepal and the princess, Wen Chang from China. Together they were credited for introducing the first king of Tibet to their spiritual practice of Buddhism. The king embraced Buddhism and had ancient Sanskrit scriptures translated and soon thereafter, Buddhist temples built. There are some writings of the time that claim the King's wives were different incarnated aspects of the Goddess Tara: Bhrikuti of Nepal was linked with Green Tara and Wen Chang of China, was linked with White Tara.

DEPICTIONS
Depictions of the Goddess Tara show her as a slim, energetic, playful and very beautiful young woman. She is almost always depicted in a happy, jovial disposition, wearing a royal crown on her head and dressed in regal garments. Upon one of her hands she will often hold a lotus flower and express a mudra with the other hand. As a benevolent deity she is always glowing in gold shimmering light and sometimes, you may even see her depicted sitting on the crescent moon or upon the sacred lotus. Obviously, her depictions are quite extensively varied and dependent on her exact aspect. It is of interest to note that her image is one that emits peace, joy, hope and vitality to her followers.

SACRED TEXTS
"The Homages to the Twenty -One Taras," and *"Tantra which is the Source for All the Functions of Tara, Mother of all Talhagatas,"* are among some of the many texts

revealing many of Tara's hymns; giving us a deeper glimpse into the many aspects and attributes of this beloved Female Bodhisattva.

HER RELEVANCE & OUR WORK

The Buddhist Tantric Goddess, Tara, also has a form known as Black Tara, Ugra-Tara, which is an aspect connected to power and mantra emanation. Our universe manifested from sacred sound, the Om, therefore this aspect of Tara is highly linked with divine creation and power. By far her most commonly known aspect is Green Tara. In this form she is known as Khadiravani. As Green Tara she gives courage to face our inner demons and fears. She helps us accept the truth of all matters and liberates us from delusions.

As Green Tara she protects us from Mara (the evil one/the Devil Tempter) and helps us transcend fears. It is Tara that gives us swift courage and helps us balance and differentiate what is real from the unreal. She clears our path from illusions and fortifies us on our spiritual journey. She helps us cross the stream of pain & struggle towards freedom.

Tara inspires us to live virtuously and pursue the attainment of the seven treasures or jewels in Buddhism. With Tara we pursue mastery of the seven virtues known as:

1. **Faith**
2. **Morality**
3. **Consciousness**
4. **Consideration**
5. **Learning**
6. **Generosity**
7. **Wisdom**

The Goddess Tara is beloved as "Mother Liberator," the one that helps us transcend all things. She frees us from the eight types of dangers or eight fears. According to Buddhist tenet, these eight dangers are:

1. **Pride**	**represented by the Lion**
2. **Ignorance and Delusion**	**represented by the Elephant**
3. **Anger and Hatred**	**represented by Fire**
4. **Envy and jealousy**	**represented by the Snake or Serpent**
5. **Fanatical, Wrong Views**	**represented by Robbers**
6. **Avarice**	**represented by Fear of Imprisonment**
7. **Lust, Desire, Attachment**	**represented by Floods**
8. **Doubt**	**represented by Demons or Ghost**

She is titled as *Arya -Tara* which means, Noble being. Clearly this Goddess has many attributes that we can further delve into. And, she could've easily been included in the chapter of Mothers and in the Chapter of Liberation but her message to us related to balance needed to be explored here. One of the reasons why she is included in this chapter is her message to us regarding our heart, the center of our being. Our heart is our treasure; within it we can find our point of balance and our personal altar. Therefore we walk with our sacred sanctuary contained, intact within our heart. The Goddess Tara reminds us to honor our hearts and live from this sacred place. She is yet another beautiful reflection of Goddess; exemplifying a powerful expression of the Divine Feminine for us women to draw our inspiration and strength from.

Today, the Goddess Tara continues to be a highly venerated deity across numerous countries, not limited to her initial birth place. She is yet another prominent example of how the Sacred Feminine is still very much alive and vitally present in our modern world.

SUNNA

SUNNA

Sunna is the benevolent Goddess of the sun in Norse mythology. She is seen by Scandinavians as holding a maternal role due to her nature as a sun deity. Known as the daughter of Mundilfaeri (his name means, axis mover), her brother, Mani, is known as the Moon God.

According to the myths, Mundilfaeri gave birth to two children and was so enamored by their beauty and light that he named them, the Moon and the Sun, respectively. Upon hearing of this, the Gods were not pleased and so they took his offspring and sent them up to the sky, to represent the Moon and Sun. These deities are often depicted, driving their chariot. Sunna drives a chariot of the Sun, while her brother drives the chariot of the Moon.

In ancient Norse mythology there are of two noteworthy wolves, named Skoll to and Hati. It was a common belief that these two wolves run after the chariot of the Sun and the chariot of Moon, always in an infinite attempt to devour these principal celestial bodies. Lunar and Solar Eclipses were often seen as the wolves actually succeeding at taking a bite out of the Sun or the Moon. According to Norse cosmology, the much feared end of the world, known as, Ragnarok, would one day manifest the moment these two wolves successfully devour the Sun and the Moon. There is an indication that the Goddess Sunna, will give birth to a daughter who is expected to take on her mother's role after the destruction of the world.

Most of what we known about Sunna comes from the Prose Edda, by Snorri Sturluson. In his 13th century writings he includes Sunna among the revered Norse Gods. As a Sun Goddess she is view as having healing attributes. She gives the earth much needed light and warmth, in the North, where the frigid climate is brutally endured. Her healing aspects can also be seen in Ragnarok, when she intentionally births a daughter, which she offers up to the Universe in order to sustain humanity after destruction.

While Egypt, Greece, and the Middle East region viewed the burning bright sun as both a destroyer and protector, in the north, it did not hold the same perspective. The sun did not have the same destructive, warrior like qualities, in the North. There were no consistent worries about rivers, or water sources, drying up, or crops being burnt and destroyed by the scorching hot sun. In Norse mythology, the sun was appreciated as a nourishing entity; melting away the icebergs, warming the bitter cold air and helping inhabitant of this icy terrain withstand the usual frigid temperatures. It is thus easy to understand how Scandinavia, Britain, Ireland and the Northern region could view the sun as a nourishing healing, Benevolent Goddess, like Sunna.

Wrong done, and injustices inflicted,
is paid back in the same coin.
No one has escaped Justice of the universe.
It is only a matter of time... " Anil Sinha

MA'AT

MA'AT

Ma'at is probably one of the oldest, most recognized deities in the Egyptian pantheon. She stems from the Old Kingdom (c.2680-2190 BCE) and the earliest mention of this Goddess can be found on the Pyramid text of King Unas in the 5th Dynasty (around CA 2375 BCE - 2345 BCE). *"Egyptian religion" by Siegfried Morenz, translated by Ann E. Keep page 275, 1992 Cornell University Press.*

Most of what we know about Ma'at is derived from the Egyptian *"Book of the Dead,"* a collection of funerary text, religious and magickal rites. Composed mostly in hieroglyphics or hieratic script, its original Egyptian title translated as, *"Book of Coming Forth by Day"* or *"Book Emerging Forth into the Light."* Its origins come from the Egyptian city of Thebes and can be traced to the first pyramid text of the 5th Dynasty (around 2400 BC). Kings and Pharaohs would often commission their own personal version of *"The Book of the Dead,"* later this practice was taken over by nobilities and those with status and the financial means to commission a personal funerary text rite. This text served as a guide for the dead transitioning into the afterlife via the journey through the Duat (the underworld). The numerous spells found in these writings were often painted and engraved on coffins, tomb walls, pyramids, and sarcophagi. Some of these funerary text, the more traditional ones, date as far back as the 3rd millennium BC but new Egyptian spells and writings were created as time went by and it was not uncommon to also reuse well established older, funerary text from this period.
"The Book of the Dead" is an extremely invaluable source for those seeking to understand funerary practices and beliefs, related to death and the afterlife in ancient Egyptian culture. In early times it was a text well consulted by many and today continues to provide much insight on a mysterious subject that still eludes so many of us.

Ma'at, or Mayet as she is endearingly called, is the Goddess of Truth, Justice, the Law and Divine Order. She is Goddess of Moral Integrity and a primordial Goddess of Righteousness. She is the judge of the dead in the halls of Duat, in the underworld. She is the personification of order and the law. Because she is considered a primeval deity, some debate whether she is a Goddess in actual human formed or simply the concept or female principle of order in the universe. She epitomizes the importance of justice for a thriving society, the importance of proper behavior, and fairness for the disadvantaged. She is in essence, truth embodied but she is more than the legislative; she is the cosmic law of the universe.

Her name in Egypt is synonymous with the word truth. Some scholars translate her name as literally meaning, *"that which is straight,"* a reference to her abilities to create order from chaos and provide the straight foundations necessary for the world to be built upon and exist in harmony. Even her hieroglyphics, an Ostrich feather, depicts this important aspect of the Goddess, with its straight lines, the hieroglyphics represents the Goddess of Justice.

Lady of Heaven, Mistress of the Underworld, Ma'at was often depicted with wings and this connected her to the pre-dynastic vulture deity of Upper Egypt; Nekhbet. Whether sitting, kneeling or standing, she is often shown dressed in the traditional Egyptian close fitted dress, in the color red or gold with a feather protruding from her head of solid black straight stresses. On one hand she holds the Ankhs, an ancient symbol of peace and on the other hand she holds a scepter, a symbol of power. Though many Egyptian deities are often linked with animals and are sometimes even depicted with an animal's head form, you will not find this to be the case for Ma'at. She is often represented as a beautiful woman, or an Ostrich feather or simply the very scales she would employed as she judged the dead.

As with most ancient deities there is some confusion regarding her parentage but we do know, from the ancient texts, her strong connection to Ra. The Egyptian Sun God, Ra, originally had two known daughters; Hathor-Sekhmet and Tefnut-Ma'at. The beloved Ma'at was considered the eye of Ra but also the heart, for it is the heart where moral judgment is made and this was her domain. Today, she continues to be the one who steers his boat, as he flies across the sky. It is Ma'at who guides the sun to set at night and rise every morning. She is the Goddess who controls the motions and patterns of nature in the Universe. She regulates the seasons, the stars, the planets and the waters upon the earth. Even the inundation of the Nile River, which was so important for Egyptians, falls under her domain. Ancient Egypt and its prosperous growth was heavily dependent on the water of the Nile river and naturally a Goddess who rules over the progression of the season and its sacred patterns found in the universe, would be responsible for these vital waters as well.

Ma'at existed since the beginning of time, according to Egyptian mythos, and cosmology. In the beginning there was darkness, the void, formlessness and chaos, as numerous cultures confirm and support in agreement in their respective folklores. In this chaotic, abysmal, boundlessness, which is found in so many varying myths explaining the earth's beginnings, there was also water and a cosmic egg floating upon the shapeless world. In the cosmic egg was the Kephera, the light, which remained hidden inside the darkness of the egg, until one day it was cracked open and unleashed upon the formless universe. In that very moment the world began to take shape; Shu, the atmosphere, manifested and soon thereafter Tefnut, as moisture, emerged, and through the space between these two, emerged the Sun God, Ra. According to Egyptian writings one of the first deities to manifest was the Sun God, Ra. Ra emerged from the Nun, the primordial waters and subsequently right then, the straightness to set the orderly foundation of the world was immediately necessary and thus, the Goddess Ma'at was called upon and she too emerged with Ra. Some scholars believe Ma'at gave birth to Ra, making her his mother, but more often she is considered one of his beloved daughters. Upon creation she is the one who organizes chaos and brings cosmic order into the universe. In this respect she is very similar to the Chinese Goddess, Nukua. In Ma'at's presence the natural laws of the universe exist and are enforced. She rules the movement of the stars and planets, the rising and setting of sun and the ebb and flow of the waters.

According to Egyptian cosmology, at this auspicious moment in the creation of the universe, there existed three Gods alone on the Solar Barque; the Sun God, Ra, Ma'at, Goddess of Divine order and her consort, the God of Wisdom, Throth. Ma'at was to eventually replace the God of Chaos and destruction, Set, and she becomes his antithesis.

And this reminds me of the Japanese myth related to Amaterasu, the Sun Goddess, and her struggles to eradicate the chaos of her brother, Susano-0, but I digress. These three primordial Egyptian Gods emerged and rode on the sacred *"Boat of a Million Years"* and together they helped to tame "Chaos." They organize the universe, bring balance, cosmic harmony, order and form into the world.

On a coffin inscription it states: ***"Tefnut is my living daughter and she shall be together with her brother, Shu; his name is life and her name is Ma'at...."***

Ma'at is sometimes associated with other Goddesses and Gods. She was considered an aspect of the parthenogenetically birthed Tefnut, the lion headed Goddess of Moisture, Dew and Rain. Tefnut was linked with Throth as his partner but so was Ma'at. The God of Wisdom and Knowledge, Throth, or Tehuti as he is also known, was considered Ma'at's consort. It is important to look at her spouse because in understanding him we can begin to understand parts of her. Some say they share similar attributes and they complement one another, as can be expected when two powerful deities are joined. Lord of Time, Throth was a Lunar Egyptian deity, attributed for inventing speech and writing. He reflects Ma'at's ideals and her finest qualities. In the *Papyrus Nebseni*, he is quoted as declaring that he brings Ma'at and her gifts to those who love her. His role as "bequeather" of Ma'at's most precious gifts becomes indisputable. It's important to note that Throth, the Lord of Wisdom, is also the patron God of Scribes. In ancient Egypt, scribes were exceptionally important. They were the ones that documented in writing; religious, political and social events of great significance to world history. In the *"Instruction of Amenemope,"* Egyptian scribes are encouraged to follow the ways of their Goddess, Ma'at, in their work but also in their personal lives.

The Ibis headed, Throth, who is credited for having invented Hieroglyphics, and also rules over learning and sciences (involving measuring and counting) reflects the best of her laws. She becomes known as his counterpart. In their unified light, all darkness is eradicated. Together they were credited for creating eight children, Amon, being the most famous of all of them. These offspring became known as the Chief Gods and Goddesses of Hermopolis. Thus, Maat and Throth became known as the ancestor Gods of Hermopolis and respectively mother and father of the Ogdoad.

"She adorns the breast of Throth"

Just as it is stated, Throth carries her on his chest with great love, the Kings and the Pharaohs of Egypt also held the Goddess Ma'at with the highest esteem. The Pharaohs were known as priest of Ma'at. She was their mystic sister and they too wore emblems, and personal symbols of the Goddess. They also carried with them ostrich feathers, to symbolize their commitment to represent her cosmic laws when asked to judge. Everyone, from the lowest of slaves, to the Pharaohs and Kings, all were considered instrumental for cosmic order and harmony, by the Goddess Ma'at. For Egyptians, there was a particularly strong belief that, lack of integrity caused disharmony not just in their personal lives but they also believed it had the power to reverberate into the cosmos; directly affecting nature, potentially causing global disasters; like plagues, earthquakes, droughts and famine upon the land.

Egyptian Kings were also zealously devoted to Ma'at and her tenets of truth and justice. Some would even add her name to their title to suggest an even stronger allegiance and devotion to the great Goddess, Ma'at. A King's decision always rested on Ma'at and her Divine righteousness and laws. In Egyptian theology there is a belief in a reciprocal relationship to deity, that as they give and provide to you, the devotee, so must you also give back to them; via offerings, worship, ritual, and songs etc.. Humans and the Divine cooperate and help one another exist in the universe and this is the balance and harmony of Ma'at.

"Lady of Heaven, Queen of the Earth,
Mistress of the Underworld" E.A. Wallis Budge....

Another very important function of the Goddess Ma'at is to judge the dead. The *"Egyptian Book of the Dead"* reveals the Goddess Ma'at is met by every person who has transitioned to death. She waits at Duat, the underworld, where the Jackal headed God, Annubis, leads the dead to meet their fate on her scales. In Ma'at's Hall it will be determined if the deceased person's soul may continue onward to meet the God Osiris and join the other Gods and Spirits into eternity.

With Throth by her side and the 42 Assessors of Ma'at, a life review for the deceased is inevitable in her Judgment hall. This is the moment of her truth, when the true heart of a person will be examined and weight. Ma'at, sometimes known as the scale herself, will weight a person's heart against her sacred Ostrich feather. A scale is presented and on one side rest Ma'at's ostrich feather and on the other side the deceased person's heart. All in Ma'at's Hall will watch as the scale will go back and forth trying to find its equilibrium and then in the end, reveal the deceased person's fate in the afterlife. If it is a balanced scale or if the heart appears lighter than Ma'at's ostrich feather, then that person will be met and embraced into the Hall of the Gods and immortality. They will go on to meet with Osiris, the Egyptian God of the Dead and the Afterlife. However, if the heart of the deceased person is heavy and out weights the feather, then the deceased person will have much explaining to do, for this will reveal a life lived poorly and sins, much too many, to be welcomed into the Hall of the Gods. The God, Ammit, the devourer, will ghastly lick her choppers in anticipation for what's to come next, as the deceased person will be sent to the deep recesses of the underworld, while its heavy heart gets hungrily devoured by hideously looking Ammit. Ammit, who was a smorgasbord grisly looking deity beholding the menacing snout of a crocodile, the mane of a lion and the body of a Hippopotamus, fed on those heavy sinful hearts of man. But before giving Ammit the satisfaction of a juicy meal, the deceased person will have a chance to come before the 42 deities of Duat, known as the "Assessors of Ma'at," to plead their case and recite the "42 Denials of Sins," also known as the "Negative Confessions." These writings derived from the *Papyrus Ani* found in chapter 125, of the *"Book of the Dead."* Below they are listed. *(Wikipedia.com)*

The "Forty Two Declarations of Purity" or "Negative Confessions"

1. I have not committed sin.
2. I have not committed robbery with violence.

3. I have not stolen.
4. I have not slain men or women.
5. I have not stolen grain.
6. I have not purloined offerings.
7. I have not stolen the property of the Gods.
8. I have not uttered lies.
9. I have not carried away food.
10. I have not uttered curses.
11. I have not committed adultery; I have not lain with men.
12. I have made none weep.
13. I have not eaten the heart.
14. I have not attacked any man.
15. I am not a man of deceit.
16. I have not stolen cultivated land.
17. I have not been an eavesdropper.
18. I have not slandered no man.
19. I have not been angry without just cause.
20. I have not been debauched the wife of any man, or God.
21. I have not debauched the wife of any man,(repeated addressed a god)
22. I have not polluted myself.
23. I have terrorized none
24. I have not transgressed the law.
25. I have not been wroth.
26. I have not shut my ears to the words of truth.
27. I have not blasphemed.
28. I am not a man of violence.
29. I am not a stirrer up of strife or disturber of peace
30. I have not acted or judged with undue haste
31. I have not pried into matters.
32. I have not multiplied my words in speaking.
33. I have wronged none, and done no evil.
34. I have not worked witchcraft against the King nor blaspheme.
35. I have never stopped the flow of water.
36. I have never raised my voice, spoken arrogantly or in anger.
37. I have not cursed or blasphemed the Gods.
38. I have not acted with evil rage.
39. I have not stolen the bread of the Gods.
40. I have not carried away the Khenfu cakes from the spirit of the dead.
41. I have not snatched away the bread of the child, nor treated with contempt the God of my City.
42. I have not slain the cattle belonging to the Gods.

From http://en.wikepedia.org/wiki/Maat--

Before Throth, Ma'at and the 42 deities, known as the "Assessors of Maat," (Their names listed in the Papyrus of Nebseni), the deceased person will have a chance to address his or her sins and hopefully, save him/herself from remaining in the darkest, place of the underworld, tragically ending his journey in the afterlife.

From the earliest of dynasties it was the Goddess, Ma'at who was well worshipped and today continues to reign powerfully in our collective consciousness. Ma'at is the standard by which we measure ourselves from. The heart must be free of weight for you to enter the hall of the Gods in the afterlife. Living by her laws of truth and justice, helped manifest an orderly thriving universe.

Though some compare Ma'at to the Hindu concept of Karma this is erroneous, as Karma implies that negativity is simply punishment for something done in a previous life. Early Egyptian doctrines would not have agreed in this belief, instead viewing the exact same negativity as proof of Ma'at's absence and indicating the need to supplicate her presence in order to make things fair and right. Early Egyptians and worshippers of Ma'at viewed misfortunes and catastrophic disasters as being caused by demons or spirits of the dead or being a direct result of falsities and inauthentic, unbalanced living, not by Ma'at herself. She was not viewed as a vindictive Goddess but rather as one who made things right, straight, fair and just. In this case she does not resemble the Hindu concept of Karma.

Recognized from the middle of the third millennium even earlier, Ma'at had many known Temples dedicated to her worship but today only one still survives. Her Temple in the city of Thebes, in Karnak (Carnac) lies in ruins as an open air museum in Egypt today. Some parts of it were believed to be originally built by the pharaoh, Queen Hatsheput. Later when it had been destroyed by invaders it was commissioned to be rebuilt again by Amenhotpe. Many Egyptian Pharaohs had a part in constructing this Temple throughout the years and part of its renowned reputation comes from the fact that it was started in the Middle Kingdom and continued to be rebuild and expanded upon through into the Ptolemaic period.

Over three millennia, whether as a concept or an actual Goddess in human form, Ma'at, the Goddess of Truth, Justice and Divine Order has reign in our lives, making herself and her laws and principles prevalent in our lives. Invoke her when you are facing anything related to the law, our judicial system or when trying to correct a wrong done unto you. Before invoking her in your workings, be sure you examine your motives and assess your own life, to make sure you are living in the most authentic, righteous and Ma'at pleasing way. She is also a powerful Goddess to connect with when you are approaching death (whether literal or figuratively). She will help you dig deep to intimately connect with you, the genuine you, and offer memories of those times when you best exemplified her attributes of truth, order and justice. She will force you to be honest with yourself and look at the many ways you can lighten your heart so that it will match the lightness of her ostrich feather. Her presence in your life will bring a greater awareness of your authenticity, righteousness, justice and a deeper contemplation on matters of the heart.

*The highly esteemed, Egyptian Goddess of Truth, Ma'at is cosmic law. She is the Divine being we expect to greet, in the golden hall of the Afterlife, where the Celestial Scales are presented before us. These sacred scales weigh our heart against Ma'at's ostrich feather, which determines our fate in the afterlife. Ma'at is an ancient, highly venerated Egyptian Deity that some believe existed before time itself. She is the personification of truth and the power of final judgment. She beckons you today to take an honest look at your whole life. It is time for some serious assessment of your soul, your heart, and the choices you are making in this lifetime. She lays down the invitation to closely inspect your heart to unearth what weights it down now and offers you the cathartic gift of an unburdened soul. She invites you to seek balance and truth in your world.

THEMIS

Themis is the Ancient Greek Goddess of Justice. She is the personification of Divine Law, Social Order, Natural Law and Truth. The scales and the tripod are her sacred emblems and therefore she is known as the Goddess of fairness, order and balance.

It is important to note that she was a daughter of Gaia and Uranus and thus, she is considered one of the Titaness. Mentioned in many of the ancient writings of the time by Homer and Ovid, she is the personification of the law and divine order.

The Greek word *"Tithemi"* means "to put," as in, to put in order or to put in place. In ancient times, Greek judges were known as servants of the Goddess, Themis, and they were given the name, *"Themistopoloi."*

Her image is sometimes depicted holding a sword, which is known as the sword of truth and also always holding the Scales. Images of the Themis as the Lady of Justice wearing a blindfold is considered a modern rendering not recognized in ancient times. As Goddess of the foreseer, she was attributed for building the Oracle of Delphi, which was given to her by Gaia and, according to one mythology, later then offered to the Goddess, Phoebe. She was also believed to have birthed, with Zeus, the Moirai; also known as the Three Fates. These two examples are indicative of how she was also connected to Foresight and Karma.

Justice was seen as quintessentially critical to moral living, religious and cosmic order, survival of traditions and even connected to proper relationship between a man and a woman. Her existence was at the core of an effective, evolving civilized society. There is no question, Themis was an important deity for the Ancient Greeks but her veneration and her indisputable significance to our world still reverberates greatly today. We see her in everything connected to our legal system as the Lady of Justice; holding up the sacred scales that champion's truth, fairness, balance, justice and the law

25

AMATERASU

AMATERASU O-MI-KAMI (Ohiru-menomuchi-no-kami)

Amaterasu, the Japanese Goddess of the Sun, whose name, in some text, is interpreted as meaning, "the *exalted deity which illuminates the Heavens*." Like Athena, she was birthed by her father, according to Japanese scriptures. Prior to the creation of the world, Japanese cosmology declares there were invisible Gods in the Heavens. The first God Izanagi, translates as, "*He who invites*"and the name of the first Goddess, Izanami, translates as, "*She who invites*." According to Japanese legend these two respective male & female deities were the first known Gods and they were called upon to create the island of Japan and its eight nearby islands. They were also called upon to populate the Earth with humans and thus, they united, resulting in the unearthing of sex and procreation. Together they created a number of deities, before Amaterasu came to be.

There are two known stories regarding these Japanese deities. One comes from the Nihongi, an eighth century collection of Japanese myths and legends and the other from the Kojiki (712 C.E.), the oldest of the two. The Nihongi makes Amaterasu first born from white copper mirrors held by her father, Izanagi alone. According to the writings in the Kojiki, when the Goddess Izanami, gave birth to the God of Fire, she was severely hurt. As can be expected, she was horribly injured during the birthing of this scorching God and consequently, it forced Amaterasu's mother to go into the underworld. Izanami descended into the land of the dead where she began to decay. Her lover, the God Izanagi, was devastated and sought to find his love in the underworld, but when he arrived there, she refused to be visited by him in her putrefying condition and she sends him away. He returned to the land of the living, surprisingly, unharmed, but as was the tradition of this time, he underwent a purification upon his return, by bathing in the streams. In this special purification bath, came forth three Gods; Tsukiyomi, Susano-o and Amaterasu.

According to Japanese Mythology, from the left eye of Izanagi was born the first Deity, the beloved Goddess of the Sun -Amaterasu. From the right eye came forth the second Deity, Tsukiyomi, the God of the Moon. From the unfavorable nose of the God Izanagi, the God Susano-o came forth and he was to rule the Ocean and later the underworld.

Tsukiyomi, is God of the Moon and this God ruled the night. The Goddess Amaterasu, was to rule over the almighty Heavens, as the Goddess of the Sun. Susano-o, as God of the Ocean, was not a pleasant deity and thus, he was not well received. His wicked, untamable, irrepressible, ego centered ways, were viewed as dangerous to a flourishing society. Some feared that the early death of his mother had affected him adversely and he was much too dysfunctional to interact in a stable, proper Japanese society. Fearing his son's unpredictable volatile ways would destroy the Earth, he was soon cast into the underworld to rule this realm and join his missed, beloved mother. Needless to say he had acquired a bad reputation. One legend reveals that he tried to endear his sister prior to going to the underworld. Somehow, he had this idea that if he aligned himself with his adoring, most popular Sister, the Goddess of the Sun, he could improve his status and make himself more appealing to the world.

One day he crawled out of his dark realm to have a word with Amaterasu. Susano-o approached his sister desperately explaining his plight and pleading his case to welcome him in the world. Always benevolent, she agreed to help him in whatever way possible and soon she found herself uniting with her brother. From this union, eight important deities were born. According to Japanese mythology, the Sun Goddess took her brother's sword, broke it into three pieces and chewed them. She then spat it out and thus three Goddesses were born from her. Susano-o, in turned, took five pieces of his sister's jewels. He chewed the jewels and like Amaterasu, he spat it out. Five Gods were born from his action. According to Japanese Lore, these Gods became direct descendants of the royal Imperial Japanese families.

It seemed all was well with Susano-o's initial honorable intentions, but quite quickly he changed his tune and was back to his old irrepressible volatile ways. As one mythology tells it, one day he entered Amaterasu's sacred temple and started haphazardly tossing excrement all over the holy sanctuary, where first fruits were often offered to the Goddess. The final act of vile disrespect took place when according to one Japanese lore; he broke into the sacred palace where all the women were weaving holy garments. The horse was considered a sacred animal to Amaterasu, yet Susano-o, in an act of unfathomable behavior, violently threw a horse unto the priestesses that were weaving. As a direct result of his wretched action one of Amaterasu's beloved priestess was killed. The myth divulges that the blow of the horse killed her, but other myths reveal that she hit her own genitalia and then killed herself after this traumatic event. The symbolic language used in this myth might be a reference to perhaps being raped or sexually assaulted by Susano-o himself and this very act thus resulted in her own suicide.

The Sun Goddess was so outraged at her brother's repulsive disregard of her sacred temple and his defilement of her worship with this vile action. Some believe that perhaps she too was a victim of Susano-o sexual assault and thus, incest, a most vile traumatic incident, would've taken place. Regardless, Amaterasu was clearly distraught beyond measure and so greatly traumatized that she could no longer shine her divine light. She took her despondency and retrieved from the world, burying herself into a cave. Amaterasu withdrew all of her glorious divine light from the world and as a result the Earth stood in darkness. Susano-o's chaos now reign on the Earth and without the Sun Goddess, discord was ever prevalent in the world. At this time, he threatened civilization and the earth's survival with his ego driven, wild untamable ways.

The pantheons of Japanese Gods were needless to say, very concern for the Earth's survival. After sometime they grew desperate and joined to collaborate on a way to disentomb Amaterasu and bring her Divine light back to the world. At first, they brought out the cocks and enticed them to crow, as this was a trusted symbol of dawn. As the sun begins to rise in the mornings, these feather creatures are usually crowing to announce the impending new day. The Gods believed this would surely bring out the Sun Goddess. Next, they hung stringed jewels, sparkling tiny reflections of her light, all around the trees by the cave she had now resigned herself to. They also decorated the trees with cloth streamers all in an effort to entice her to stay. As the mirror was one of her most prized sacred symbol, they also erected a very large, special eight sided mirror for the Goddess to catch her own reflection upon exiting the cave. The last step in their plans to bring back Amaterasu, was calling on the Goddess Ama no Uzume to come to their aid. Uzume adorned herself with plants and bamboo shoots, appearing very much like a frolicsome Spring Maiden. She was encouraged to dance by the other Gods but her dance soon became rather frenetic, lewd and an ecstatic dance where she stripped her clothes off. It caused quite a raucous of laughter and an unexpected loud commotion. From deep within the cave, Amaterasu heard this and it confused her. She had taken her divine light away from the world and, instead of silence and mourning, all she heard now, from outside her cave, was laughter and merriment. This made her very curious. Gingerly, she slid the rock, slightly opening the cave entrance, just enough to get a peak. When she saw her own brilliant reflection caught in that special eight-sided mirror she was mesmerized. Then she came out a little further and caught a glimpse at all those brightly colored jewels hanging from the nearby trees. As she stepped out even further, the Gods quickly moved the boulder to close off the entrance to the cave, forcing Amaterasu to stay out longer and return to her post as Goddess of the Sun.

From this Myth we can extrapolate many facts about this beloved Goddess and her worship. We learn about some of her symbols and appreciate their value. According to Japanese lore, some of these gifts were bestowed to her Grandson, the direct descendant of the Japanese Imperial Family, and thus they take on even greater importance to the culture.

According to Japanese scriptures, to her grandson, Ninigri, she gives him three regalias - divine gifts from the Goddess herself. Amaterasu gives Ninigri the mirror, which she instructs him to assume as the Goddess herself, reflecting truth and light. She gives him the Sword, which was originally an impressive gift from her very own brother, Susano-o. Perhaps, it was seen as a powerful weapon, but we must also remember that she broke and chewed three pieces of the sword and thus three Goddesses were born. Her brother's sword, thus, played an important part in the procreation of important Japanese deities, linking the country to its future leaders. The last gift was the Imperial Jewels. They were seen as symbols of the Goddess- gifts of fertility and agricultural procreation. We must also remember that her brother took five of her jewels, chewed them and spat out Five Gods as a result. Like the Roman Goddess, Diana sends Aradia to Earth as a messenger and Like the Christian Father God sends Jesus to Earth to be the messiah, so too here we have the Divine Mother sending her grandson Ninigri to Earth, to the Japanese people, to continue her laws of order and civilization.

It also becomes very apparent that Amaterasu's withdrawal from the Earth was reminiscent of an actual Solar Eclipse. It can also be linked to the season's natural cyclical rhythm; for the Sun's bright power seems to wane, almost dying during the Autumn/Winter months. Upon the Winter Solstice the Sun is reborn again and slowly regains its full power leading us into Spring and then Summer. The Goddess Ama no Uzume can be seen as a Spring, fertility, Maiden deity drawing the sun's powers out by dancing her licentious dance. Amaterasu thus takes on an important role as an agricultural Goddess, who lends her light to help Japanese crops multiply and prosper. Here she is reminiscent of Demeter the Greek Goddess of the grain.

She also appears like a warrior Goddess, in her intolerance of Susano-o's destructive, sabotaging behavior, which put Japanese Society in great danger, almost destroying Japan. She is therefore seen as Japan's defender and the country's divine protector. Interesting to note, Japan's early name was "Dai Nihon" which literally means "Great Sun Source," revealing Amaterasu's strong connection to her birth country.

Throughout history Amaterasu is often seen as a parental, direct ancestor of the Japanese people In school text books there are even references to Amaterasu as a universal deity directly connected to the royal Imperial family. Her divine grandson, Ninigri, married a woman from earth and they had two sons. These two sons find wives and get married as well and have children. One of these children gives birth to a son - Jimmu and He then becomes the first Japanese Emperor. Here we have that Important evidence that the Imperial family is directly related to the Great Divine and can justly assert its power over its people.

Amaterasu is one of the few Japanese Goddesses still highly venerated and worshipped today. Her existence reflects a belief in Japan as a divine land with divine people as it is believed that this Sun Goddess is ancestor to all of its people. Thus, she is the ancestral founder and protector of Japan. Shrines were created everywhere in her honor. During colonization many shrines were erected for her expanding worship. The most famous and largest shrine can be seen at The Ise Shrine. Here the sacred, eight sided mirror is reputed to be maintained. At these altars people might worship the Goddess with special ceremonies, invoking her powers of light & order and also with acts of purification. The Sun Goddess, Amaterasu, is seen as holy and pure, and as a reflection of truth, and she inspires her people to live life with the same ideals. It is for this reason why Amaterasu is an ideal deity to include in our chapter on leadership.

*The Japanese Goddess of the Sun; of truth and light, the mirror. She asks you to bring clarity and order into your life. Amidst turbulence and disruptive chaos, she calls you to breathe, regroup and reconnect to your authentic self. Look into the mirror and do not fear your own reflection staring back at you. It will reveal truths that perhaps, you have avoided seeing. She is the mirror and a personification of truth. She will awaken your own self-worth -a vital component for all magick. Do not let situations or other people dim your brilliance. Amaterasu reminds you of your own gifts and your divine light. Stop hiding and shine your light; you are a powerful being!!! Your light is needed within your community but first you are required to recognize and fully embrace your own light.

*"Every day is an opportunity to be creative-the canvas is your mind,
the brushes and colors are your thoughts and feelings,
the panorama is your story, the complete picture
is a work of art called, "my life."*

"Birth is the sudden opening of a window, through which you look out upon a stupendous prospect. For what has happened? A miracle; you have exchange nothing for the possibility of everything."
William MacNeile Dixon

"Birthing is the most profound initiation to spirituality a woman can have..."
Robin Lim

GAIA

The name of this chthonic Greek Goddess is a compound word. The first part of her name, "Ge" means land or Earth, in pre-Greek substrate, while the second half, "Aia" refers to, grandmother, and has origins in the Indo-European language.

Primordial Goddess of the Earth, Gaia is maternal archetype, who was the personification of the Earth itself. Gaia whose powers created all living creature and beings on this planet, the sea and the sky. Gaia who was from the beginning, before the existence of Time, for Time was an actual child of hers. She was born from the dark, formlessness of Chaos and wasted no time in producing numerous beings on the Earth. Ancient Greek Goddess Gaia, whose origins and worship has been absorbed by numerous cultures and probably originated from Attica. Even today, Pagans and Non-Pagans alike see the Earth, and all of its intricacies, as Gaia herself, still breathing and living today, thousands of years later.

Gaia Theory and Gaia Hypothesis were documented in 1976 by James Lovelock. Here the Earth's living; producing, self-regulating system is seen as Gaia herself, a living tangible Goddess. On April 22nd we celebrate "Her" via Earth day, which has become her modern day holiday, as we honor the Earth and concern ourselves with its survival and wellbeing.

According to Hesiod's Theogony, in the beginning was dark, formless, open, vast space known as Chaos. There was also desire, known as Eros. From the union between Chaos and Eros our beloved Gaia was born. One can view this delicate beginning described by Hesiod as very similar to the beginning of all life. The vast, dark, empty womb, mysterious and yet so full of potential, un-manifested until Desire comes into play. The joining of the two gives birth to our Primordial Mother Earth and from her all living creatures proceed.

According to the Greek myths, after Gaia manifested herself, she gave birth to her son, Uranus, who soon became her consort. With him, but also via parthenogenesis, she produced a multitude of beings, some monstrous and some Gods and Goddesses and not all anthropomorphic. She gave birth to Nymphs, the Sea, the Sun, Themis, Phoebe, the Cyclopes, One eye giants, Multi headed creatures, Memory (who would birth the Muses), Time, Cronos (who would later birth Zeus) and a multitude more. Her awe striking powers of fertility, procreation and abundance were evident in her ability and desire to populate the grand universe. Unquestionably, she is the raw power of fertility and creation- multiplying herself with and without a partner.

Uranus, as her son and lover, became very jealous, scared and angered at Gaia's obvious powers of creation- birthing and multiplying as continuously as she did. I suppose bearing witness to all those magnificent and monstrous creatures was probably quite intimidating for Uranus. Cunningly and with ulterior motives, he noted her birth canal and decided he would block her sacred passageway, with his own genitals, to prevent any more monstrous offsprings from being born. Daily, Uranus would enter Gaia, causing her much pain and blocking the birth of any further creations from being born. As can be expected, her womb, which served to procreate, grew and grew and expanded with each creation she manifested and retained, inside of her, unable to unleash them. Her fertile womb continued to grow and expand, holding in all of her multitude of creations. With her blocked passageway she keeps them inside, a painful, selfless act to protect them, but eventually she knew she had to devise a plan.

According to one myth, she crafted and constructed a sickle which was to be used specifically on Uranus himself. She called upon her first born, Cronos, and enlisted his help to end her agonizing pain by castrating his very own father. Carefully, Cronos followed his mother's detailed instructions. Upon approaching his father, he held the sickle and chopped off his father's genitals, tossing them into the Sea. From this act, his severed penis brought forth the sea foam Goddess of Love-Aphrodite. It also put an end to Gaia's labor and safely, she was able to release all of her contained children from her crowded womb. She became the grandmother of the first generation of Gods and Goddesses, and in her, we can see that we too are direct descendants of her lineage and intimately connected to this ancient deity. She is indeed our benevolent immortal, Mother Earth, who has garnered great respect and reverence through-out the ages by all.

Gaia is seen as the Goddess of creation, abundance, multiplicity and fertility. In her ability to create numerous children with and without partnership, we see her autonomy and her wholeness. We can tap into any one of her numerous Goddess gifts but also, we can call upon her as our Great grandmother to guide and protect us, as she's been known to do, for her beloved children of the Earth. She is a living, breathing relevant Goddess that was, is and ever shall be, long after we are gone.
Blessed Gaia, Hail to you Earth Mother!!!!

*Primordial fertile Earth Goddess who is the essence of fertility, proliferation and the powers of creation. Life is full of wonderment and all around us, there are examples of her fertile creative gifts. It is her very nature to proliferate and multiply her sacred creations and she invites you to do the same. It is encouraging and inspiring to know that her primordial gifts are vibrantly within us as well, for her blood courses through every single one of her creations and that includes her earth children- humanity. There is much that we can create in the spirit of the Goddesses of abundance and propagation. She comes into your life at this time and asks you, "How do you create? At this stage in our Goddess journey, the sacred wheel of the year supports our endeavor to multiply and tap into our own powers of fertility; whether they are used for creativity, prosperity, ideas or actual birthing of children. She awakens in you a desire to multiply and manifest your gifts on the earthly planes. She invites you to enjoy the birthing process and tap into the sacred energy of the fertile season and the earth.

BRIGIT

BRIGIT

Brigit is the Celtic Goddess of the Forge, The Fiery Goddess of Poetry and Inspiration. She is Goddess of the healing well waters and of the hearth. She is a Goddess of transformations, smithcraft, midwifery and the bard. This beloved agricultural Goddess was known by many names like; Brigit, Brigantia, Brighid, Brigid, Briget, Brid, Bride. Her name means *"the Exalted One"* and Breo-Aigit (another one of her many names) means *"Fiery Arrow."*

One story tells us that Brigit was the wife of the ruler of the Children of Danu, Bres. With him she conceived one son who was tragically killed in battle. She mourned for her beloved son on the battlefield and introduced the Celtic practice of Keening. Caoine or keening, as it is better known, was the act of sorrowful, very audible, weeping and wailing and Brigit is credited for inventing this practice when she herself lost her beloved son.

There is another known tale of Brigit being the wife of Tuirean and with him birthing three boys; Ircharba, Brian, Luchar. These three sons were said to have killed the God Cian, Lugh's father.

There are many myths about Brigit and her life. Some of these tales conflict with one another. For example, in a 10th century text she is described as the daughter of the Daghda, who was the God of the Tuatha de Dannan. In her role for the Catholic Church, as Saint Brighid, she was known to have been the daughter of a Druid, pagan priest, by the name of Dubthach. Some believe she was actually baptized by St. Patrick himself and some early Christian poetry of the time, claimed that she was the beloved, foster mother of Christ himself.

According to one legend, as a young maiden, she feared her father would push her into marriage. To make herself less desirable to romantic suitors, she disfigured herself by making her eyes pop out. Supporting this story is the numerous myths regarding the eyes and Brigit's sacred well waters bringing miraculous healing to people with opthalmological disorders.

This Pagan Celtic Goddess was so beloved by her people that there was great resistance when the Catholic church tried to assert its power to eradicate Paganism across the land. Her shrines and temples were converted to Abbeys and monasteries and she was thus converted to the Christianized, St. Brighid. Her Gifts of transformation were exemplified best in this very act, as her survival all these years has come about because of that transformation. From Pagan deity, she allowed herself to be transformed into the Christianized saint and thus her devotees grew and remained throughout the decades.

At Kildare, her sacred shrine was kept and sustained allegedly, by nineteen vestal virgins tending to her sacred flame in the guise of nuns. Nineteen has thus become known as a special number associated with this Goddess. These sacred Brighid flames had been tended to for over six hundred years, but the Archbishop of Dublin, Henri de Loundes, put out Brigit's divine flames when he feared and suspected these as Pagan rites. Thankfully, in 1993 her sacred Flames were re-lit again by Sister Mary Minchin. Today her undying flames are maintained by the Brigandines, an order of Sisters of Bridget.

Brigit was known to have provided many gifts to her people. She was attributed to inventing whistling as a way to call her friends, after the death of her son. She was credited for inventing Ogham, an ancient form of writing.

Beloved as a Healer, she healed with the waters from her numerous sacred wells. At Kildare there were more than 30 known wells dedicated to her. The largest well is still in use today and famous for bringing all sorts of healing, particularly healing of eye diseases. In her myths there were many known stories of miraculous cures for all sorts of ailments at her numerous sacred wells. It was a common practice to highly decorate these special wells with ribbons and flowers and leave various gift offerings to the Goddess there; like cakes, milk and honey.

Brigit was worshipped as a triple Goddess of healing, inspiration and the forge. Her symbol was the fire, like the sacred fires of creativity and the forge, but her symbol was also of the waters, with her healing sacred wells. Interesting to note how she can rule over two such opposing elements but certainly, a lesson about balance is to be learned here. In this example, she is reminiscent of the Hindu Goddess Saraswati, who also rules over two opposing sacred elements- fire and water.

Brigit was and still is well-known as the muse; inspiring the bard, the poet, the storyteller and the songsters. She was Goddess of the blacksmith, the glasswork creator, the artist, the sculptors, the weaver, the jewelry maker, needle worker and knitter. Brigit is a Goddess for those who use their hands to forge and create, for inherent in these skills, is the sacred act of transformation, which she rules.

This Celtic Goddess, whose sacred trees were the Rowan, Apple, Birch and Willow trees, was closely associated with the sabbat of Imbolc. Oimelc or Imbolc, was also known in its Christianized name as Candlemass, celebrated February the 2nd. Imbolc, means, *"in the Belly"*, a reference to the Earth's potential Spring stirrings in the womb. According to the Carmina Gadelica, the Celtic Goddess, as a snake, would emerge from her wintry hibernation. She would appear slithering from the mountains or a cave, where she had been all winter long. The tale was similar to our modern custom of the male Groundhog announcing the season's status. The snake was seen as a prediction of Spring's arrival, to inform us whether the Goddess will allow Spring to arrive early or let Winter linger on. During this Sabbat, cakes were left out for the Goddess. Loaves of bread and pitchers of milk were often left at the entrances of homes, as offerings, or they were shared with neighbors to attract Brigit's goodwill and better crops for the coming season. The cross plaiting with straws from the harvest was believed to protect the home from fires and bring good luck throughout the year and they were often hung around the home and farms.

Brigit is a Goddess of great transformation, for she takes our pain and transforms them into healing. She takes ideas and transforms them into creative works of arts, like songs, art works, sculptures, poetry, stories. She transforms us at the forge and with her flames forges our soul -as metal works are transformed into smith craft, so is our soul able to metamorphosize and undergo magical transformations with her imput, guidance and blessings.

*Brigit, the Celtic Creativity Goddess of the forge, is our divine healer, the matriarchal nurturer and the sacred "creatrix." Deep in the dark belly of the earth's womb, magick is awakening slowly, unseen by the naked eye but unquestionably forthcoming. All things are born from the hidden, in this deep dark, moist abyss, and it is embodied by the Goddess. Brigit is the Goddess who thaws and warms our winter heart with inspirations to create and express ourselves. She, who also through her bright flames, is able to transform us inside and out, is our beloved matriarch. She offers us the healing gifts found in both fire and water and beckons you to approach her at the sacred well with ribbons of supplications. Brigit enters your life now, asking what needs to burn to ashes, and like the Phoenix, be transmutated so that the power of creation and healing may come. She brings self –transformations, sacred initiations, creative awakenings, and the willingness to begin "the Journey."

SARASWATI

"An artist paints, dances, draws, writes, designs or
Acts, at the expanding edge of consciousness.
We press into the unknown rather than the known.
This makes life lovely and lively..." Julia Camaron

SARASWATI

Saraswati is the Hindu Goddess of Learning, Wisdom, Music and Cosmic Knowledge. Saraswati is considered Supreme Knowledge herself. She is Mahavidya (holder of supreme knowledge), Maha-vani (the transcendent word), Smirtishakti (the power of memory), Maha-vidya (transcendent knowledge) and Arya (the noble one). She is the Goddess of the word, education and all Art forms; music, poetry, dance, writing, crafts, science, literature and because of this, she becomes a patron Goddess to students, teachers, scientist and those in the creative arts. Saraswati is also known as Vagishvari (mistress of speech), Jnanashakti (the power of knowledge), Bharati (eloquence). In Japan she is known as the Goddess Benzaiten. Subhaga (the bountiful one who provides immortality), as she is sometimes addressed, is also the Guardian of Truth. She is the representation of Sattua Guba which is; Goodness, Grace, and Purity. Born from Brahma, Saraswati is both daughter and wife of the creator of the universe and thus becomes known as Mother of the Universe.

In Hinduism, She is part of the Feminine Divine Trinity, also known as Trimurti, along with Durga and Lakshmi and she was one of the very first Deities in Hindu mythology addressed and revered as Mother. Long ago, it was believed that Vishnu had three wives that quarreled constantly. Vishnu, enamored by Lakshmi's brilliance, kept her as his wife and gave Ganga to the God Shiva. The Goddess Saraswati was bestowed upon the God Brahma. Her husband, Brahma, was the God of creation, creator of the Universe and she is considered his counterpart. Saraswati is the feminine aspect of the creator and thus, is revered as the Creatrix -overseeing all forms of creations in the Universe. Known also as Satarupa, Savitri Gayatri and Brahmi/Brahmani (related to Brahma), Saraswati, is a Goddess also called upon for Divine protection and spiritual enlightenment.

In Sanskrit, Sara means "*Essence*" and Swa means "*self.*" Saraswati thus literally means; the "*essence of self.*" In Hindu mythology, she is at times referred to as "dhaara-pravaah", a Sanskrit word meaning "The One who flows." This is more likely a reference to her role as a River Deity.

Aryan history presents her, first as the Saraswati River, a river that purifies and nourishes. She was known as the sacred river that imparts the flow of creativity, hence Saraswati becomes known as "*the One who flows.*" Though it does not exist today, it was a mighty river that once flowed from the West-End of the Aravalli Hills into the East-End of the Rann of Kutch, flowing into the Arabian Sea. Ancient text, like the Rig-Vedic Hymns, praise Saraswati, depicting her as a great, powerful river, bursting with energy; a fertile roaring invigorator, with strong flowing movement and able to break down mountains. It is in this sacred work that we get a strong descriptive image of this beloved Hindu Goddess.

As a River deity, Saraswati was associated with fertility, prosperity and the agricultural growth and productivity of her land and thus like the Greek Grain Goddess, Demeter, she becomes very much a Mother Goddess; protective and nurturing of her people.

There are numerous beautiful detailed images of Saraswati, but immediately, in all of them, we note that she is not heavily adorned, with heavy colors and jewels, the way Lakshmi is. Unquestionably, this reveals a strong symbolism, that knowledge is valued and more prominent than earthly riches for this deity. Saraswati's skin is often depicted as luminous white or light yellow. The predominance of the color white is quite evident, as she is often shown wearing a white sari and more often than not, sitting on a white lotus. The color white represents her purity, truth and her supreme knowledge.

Sometimes she is depicted ridding a white swan as her vehicle and this is a symbol of her powers of discrimination. The Swan is a bird with the reputable gift of discrimination, known for its ability to separate milk from water, it represents one of Saraswati's powerful attributes- as she is able to discriminate between the good and the bad, falsehood and truth. In some depictions we sometimes see a beautiful peacock sitting by her side, gazing up at the Goddess, almost as if it is awaiting her gifts. Peacocks are birds associated with arrogance and pride. Traditionally known as a vain, temperamental, yet beautiful creature, the peacock becomes a symbol of the supreme beauty, possible through her powers of creations, but it also warns against vanities and the preoccupation on external beauties and appearances.

Saraswati is often portrayed with four arms and they reveal some of her most important divine gifts. They are a symbol of her omnipotence and the four human personality elements; mind, intellect, alertness and ego. Her two front arms, represent her engagement in the physical realm, and they are usually occupied playing the Vina/Lute. Her obvious connection to music and the arts is well represented in this pose. Her two back arms represent her connection to the spiritual realm, as one arm holds a book, the sacred Vedas/scriptures, also known as Pustaka. On her other arm she holds Akshamala, also known as mala or prayer beads.

Saraswati is sometimes worshipped as a purifier, an attribute directly related to her gift with fire; the fires of creativity and those found in our belly. The Navel Center region, sometimes depicted in the color gold, with 64 lotus petals or 64 sun fire flames, is often associated with the Goddess Saraswati. It was considered the center of transformation, the source of energy of creation and here we meet one of Saraswati's attributes as a blood purifier and healing Fire Goddess. In Vedic scripture, sometimes she is referred to as Shonapunya, which is a sankrit word meaning, "one who purified blood." In this case she is reminiscent of the Celtic Fire Goddess Bridgit, who was also closely associated with the elements of water and its purifying fires, both for healing and creativity.

Saraswati's home was believed to be in the state of Kashmir, among the Himalayas. In many parts of the U.S.A. and in India today, Saraswati is still very much loved and revered. There are numerous festivals all across India that honors this beloved, Creatrix, Mother Goddess. In the South, there is the Navaratri, a nine day festival honoring the feminine divine, it celebrates this Great Goddess and there is also the infamous PUJA, a three day Spring Festival in Bengal and North India, which also honors Saraswati annually.

Kalpanashakti (the power of forming ideas), Sarada (giver of essence), and Dhaneshvari (the divinity of wealth) are among some of her other numerous titles. This beloved Goddess was also known as Kamadhenu, which means, *wish fulfilling cow.* Reflected in this particular title is a deity that nurtures and provides sustenance for her people; much like the Egyptian Goddess Hathor, who was considered the Celestial Bovine for Egyptians. Interesting to note that Apples, which have always been a symbol of supreme knowledge, are her favorite food and it is customary to leave offerings of honey, water and fruits upon your devotional altars to this iconic matriarchal Hindu Goddess. All Hail and welcome Divine Mother, Goddess Saraswati!

*Venerated as one of the first matriarchal deities mentioned in the ancient sacred text of the Rig Veda, Saraswati is the beloved Hindu Goddess of Wisdom and Sound. She is the Goddess of sacred learning and embodied as the once fertile Saraswati River. She awakens in us our powers creativity, higher learning and the value of our voices. Do not think you are immune to her gifts as the swirling power of creativity has numerous guises to reveal itself. The written word, scriptures and sacred sound are her gifts to us as well and she blesses the writer, the teacher, the songstress, and the artist. When Saraswati appears in our lives we have the ability to create various works of wonder - big and small, they are all of equal value to the Divine. Saraswati asks you, "What are you creating? What artistic projects are you working on? Ask yourself, "How is my unique soul transmitting through my hands and voice? Do I have the spirit of creativity? The Hindu Goddess arrives in your life at this time to awaken artistic offerings of the self to the Great Divine.

OLWEN

OLWEN

The name Olwen is translated to mean, *"Golden Wheel."* She is the patron Welsh Goddess of the arts and creativity and a benevolent obstacle remover. She overcame numerous obstacles to find her freedom and obtain true love. She is often depicted with bright yellow tresses reminiscent of the sun's rays.

The Goddess, Olwen is also known as "Lady of the White Track," because it was rumored four white trefoils clover blossoms (White Shamrock flowers) would always spring forth wherever her footprints were left. She was also alleged to leave her rings and rays of sunlight wherever she bathed. She was purported to be the Daughter of Goleuddydd and her father was the chief giant Ysbaddaden Penkawr (also known as Giant Hawthorne Tree). He was a gruesome ogre much feared and was determined to keep his beautiful daughter unmarried because his death was imminent upon her marriage, as his fate was foretold. Olwen was breathtakingly beautiful and obviously, many suitors tried and failed, to their detriment, to gain her hand in marriage. The Mabinogion reveals much of what we know about this Welsh Goddess.

She is briefly mentioned in the Mabinogion in relation to King Arthur's cousin, Culhwch. This story is believed to be one of the oldest in the Mabinogion and, although her mention is temporal, it hints at Olwen's true ancient nature. It delves into this great love story between Culhwch and Olwen; the trials and tribulations they faced in their journey towards love. It explores their seemingly impossible union and the 39 inconceivable obstacles her father imposed on Culhwch to prevent their marriage. After much struggle, Culhwch manages to accomplish all 39 tasks by the first of May but the gruesome Ogre still refused to allow this marriage thus averting his own death. Culhwch loved Olwen and was determine to marry her, despite her father. He and the Ogre went into battle, resulting in the decapitation of Ysbaddaden and his death.

Some speculate that upon closer inspection this tale speaks about the struggle between the old and the usurping new order in the world. Olwen and her family lineage represent the old order, the ancient Gods and their rulership, much like the Titans in Greek mythology. Culhwch, King Arthur and their family lineage appear to represent the new order approaching; Christianity slowly asserting itself into the tapestry of this world.

Olwen and Culhwch finally were able to marry on May Day, cementing this day as a special holiday, and the blood of her father was shed as the sacrifice of the old order before the new is manifested. His blood drops are reminiscent of the ripe, dark, Hawthorne Berries ready for plucking and consumption in the spring.

Olwen is the Golden wheel that spins the sun's rays upon the earth. She has rulership over three realms; the earth, the heavens and the underworld. Like Persephone, she too rises from the underworld to inaugurate spring and bring her white flowers track, on May Day. She is the golden wheel that awakens both the sun and the earth to light at this sunny time of the year.

NU-KUA

NU-KUA

Nukua, also known as Nu Wa, Nugua, Nu-Gua, Nu Kwa, Nu Kua Shih, Nu Hsi, is the foremother of Humanity in Ancient Chinese mythology.

Nu-Kua is a primordial Chinese Goddess connected with the creation of Humanity and Civilization. She is a half dragon, serpent bodied Goddess, sometimes appearing almost like a melusine or a mermaid due to her half creature and half divine makeup and yet, sometimes depicted in contemporary Chinese art as a beautiful woman. She is also associated with the sky, the heavens, waters, the moon and the earth. She is often depicted as a divine woman with her lower body resembling a snake or a Dragon's tail but she was a known shape-shifter, like many primeval ancient deities. She is worshipped as a fertility Goddess and a patroness of marriages and childbirth. Nu-Kua is the beloved Goddess of Order and Creation, a benevolent matriarchal deity associated with teaching humanity about agriculture, dam building and irrigation and even introducing the art of whistling. She is attributed for inventing the *shenghuang*, a reed-pipe musical wind instrument and the vertical bamboo flute, known as *xiao*. Nu-Kua is a Goddess who helps restore order and clarity amidst chaos and disarray and as many of her Chinese myths will reveal, this matriarchal deity is also venerated as the savioress of the earth and its inhabitants.

What is most interesting to note is that in a culture that has a plethora of male deities and in its contemporary state, so often appearing to be downright patriarchal, here is an ancient female deity, in its midst, held in the highest regard, as the supreme mother of humanity. This Goddess called on me as the perfect deity to present in this chapter, although she could easily be included in a number of other chapters found throughout this book. Nu-Kua's most prominent myths greatly resonated with me in their obvious exaltation and positive depiction of our gender.

While in Christianity, and many other mainstream religions, humanities birth is attributed to a single male God and women are depicted as secondary or as a lesser form of man, in ancient Chinese writings a vastly different depiction can be, thankfully, unearthed.

Nu-Kua's name frequently appears in early records of the Hans Dynasty, most notably the ancient texts of "*Huainanzi,*" but also text from the Warring State era, like the "*Shanhaijing*" and the "*Tianwen*" in "*Chuci.*" Interesting to note, in the *Tianwen*, her actual insides are credited for nursing and birthing ten spirits that would later spread across the earth's wilderness and become humanity, of course that is only one obscured version of her myth.

According to the ancient text of the second century CE, found in "*Fengsu Tongyi*" (*Popular Customs and Traditions*) Nu-Kua is the foremother and creator of humanity. The early myths explain Chinese cosmology by introducing the belief that in the beginning of time there was simply a cosmic egg. There was chaos, nothing formed; no earth, no sky, no star, no moon, no boundaries set... nothing... just an egg. And in this cosmic egg was a microcosm of chaos and within this contained chaos, a sleeping giant named P'an Ku dwelled, in a tiny embryonic state.

The first part of his name, "P'an", means "coiled up" and "Gu" or "Ku", the second part of his name, refers to "antiquity." Thus this divine being was the old or antiquity curled up, encapsulated in this cosmic egg and it held the promise of our earth's creation, according to Chinese cosmology.

As the years went by, the giant P'an Ku grew and grew within this cosmic egg. He slept, as various myths reveals, for 18,000 years and as he slept he grew bigger and bigger. The sacred egg also grew and expanded to accommodate the growing giant. Amidst this chaos of light and darkness, jumbled and crammed inside this encapsulating egg, the Giant slept, until one day the deafening sounds of chaos woke him up. He stretched out his enormous muscular physical form and the egg, unable to support his out-stretching limbs, cracked and shattered open. Everything that, up until that point, had been held together inside this cosmic egg was now released, surrendered to the nothingness of the formless Universe. All darkness and the light that had been held pinched and strangled by it, was now released with the Giant's birth. All the fragments of light united as they levitated and rose up to create the sky and all the essence of darkness fell down, creating the earth. The giant who was, according to some scholars, around thirty thousand miles large, watched as light and darkness separated before him. He saw the fragments of the shattered egg rise up to create parts of the moon, the sun and the stars. He witnessed the Universe forming itself, as light created the sky and the darkness sunk, creating the earth. And in his fear that the sky would fall unto the earth and chaos would return if they would collapse into each other again, he decided to hold up the sky and hold down the earth to keep them separated. P'an Ku took it upon himself, as the only living being, to banish chaos and preserve order with the sky and the earth separated.

For centuries the giant, P'an Ku held up the sky with his strong muscular form but he then began to age and inevitably grew fatigued. Slowly, he began to lose his strength according to some folklorist. As he got older he started to get weaker and weaker and, exhausted, this impaired his ability to continue holding the sky upward. Eventually the giant died. Now some scholars claim he had held the sky up, long enough, probably over ten thousand years as some sources claim. And being confident that his mission to maintain the sky and earth separated had been accomplished, he then gave himself permission to release it and expire.

Regardless, P'an Ku's exhaustive mission was accomplished but he could not live forever. His death, however, brought about a number of important gifts to the earth. According to Chinese mythology, P'an Ku's body served to become the mountains, the hills and the land. His tangled long hair and beard became the trees and the bushes. His remaining teeth and pieces of his bones sunk down into the earth to become precious metals, gems and minerals. Chinese myths claim that the precious gemstone of Jade, which is highly regarded in Chinese culture, manifested from P'an Ku's decaying bone marrow. His blood flowed as streams and rivers while his veins became the arteries of the earth. His semen became pearls, his sweat and final tears became rain droplets and dew. And P'an Ku's voice became thunder while his very last breath became the winds and the puffy clouds in the sky. In this way, the giant P'anKu was indeed the traditional sacrificial entity whose death created the lush, colorful, fertile earth. This was documented in the third century CE, in "Wuyun Linianji" (A Chronicle of the Five Circles of Time,) a compiled book from the Three Kingdoms era.

We must note that P'an Ku is well-regarded and considered one of the "Three Divine Sovereigns," the earliest divine beings highly venerated in ancient Chinese mythology. He is accompanied in this honor by Nu-Kua and Shennong (the Divine Farmer) although other variations include Fu Xi. P'an Ku is first mentioned in the Three Kingdom era and his myths can be found in ancient text of the third century CE; Sanwu Liji, "Historical Records of the Three Sovereign Divinities and the Five Gods." He was described in some text as being a giant with a cat's head and his trunk, like that of a serpent. The people of the Henan Province in Central China viewed P'an Ku as divine protector of humanity and executor of the earth. They believed he had horns, as it was a common belief all primordial divine beings in ancient times had horns. He is also depicted with a Dragon's head in the Wuyun Linianji.

In some myths P'an Ku is associated with earth-quakes by the people in the Gansu Province of Northwestern China. Here there was a lore that connected him to an ox. In this myth P'an Ku would hold up the heavens but he required additional help keeping the earth below from sinking. It was then that P'an Ku crafted an ox from clay mixed with his own saliva and he breathes life into it and assigns it the duty to maintain the earth. At this time, P'an Ku also crafted a divine rooster to help keep watch over the ox's important duty. Keeping the earth from sinking proved to be too arduous a job for the ox and one day he wanted to take a break and nap. The rooster however, would not let the ox rest, as it firmly upheld P'an Ku's commands and this angered the divine ox. In his anger he shook the earth on his back three times and this explains early earthquakes in ancient Chinese lore.

P'an Ku is still venerated today in many of his temples found in Henan, Guandong, Jiangxi, Zhejiang provinces and the Guangxi Zhuand regions. Henan Province holds his most famous temple on mount P'an Ku and many from distant lands sojourn to gather on his feast day, celebrated on March 3rd of the Lunar calendar.

When P'an Ku eventually expired he left the earth as a beautiful oasis and it was perfect but no one inhabited it, according to most myths. Then from across the sky slithered the half Dragon Goddess, named Nu-Kua. Her birth or origins are unmentioned and unknown, we simply are told that she roamed the heavens and upon P'an Ku's death she descended to find his divine body spread across the earth below. She marveled at the great beauty of the earth and what P'an Ku had accomplished and yet, she felt a twinge of sadness in her isolation and inability to share this great world with anyone. Of course, later we will address another version of this myth where Nu-Kua is not alone at this pivotal time in the myth, but rather, paired with her older brother. But I digress, in her sadness at finding herself alone, Nu-Kua sat by the river banks, where she picked up the accumulating yellow clay and began to shape it into a ball and then into an image like hers, only with legs. She continued to gather the yellow clay and formed numerous human beings in her image to keep her company and banish her loneliness but they were inanimated and they simply stood there as rows upon rows of tiny human clay figurines. She longingly picked one of them up and placed her divine breath upon it. Remarkably the clay statue became animated with her vital breath of life upon it. It gave her great joy to see her statue creations come to life and she derived great pleasure in their laughter as well. She decided to animate all of her clay creations and then started crafting more beings; both male and females.

As time went on, the Goddess Nu-Kua began to get tired and overwhelmed at the thought of how many humans she would have to sculpt by her hands, with the yellow clay, in order to fully populate the earth. She looked at the arched reed near the river (although most myths state she took a cord or a rope) and she dipped it in the mud to complete the human race. Wherever a dripping of the mud fell on the ground, a new animated human being emerged. In this Chinese myth we have an explanation for the two distinct types of people on the earth. Those that are noble and rich were descendants of Nu-Kua's initial hand crafted yellow clay human being and those who were poor peasants were the descendants of the human figures she crafted afterwards with the rope's mud droplets. A rather prejudicial, harsh way of looking at things but revealing that for the Chinese, there are only two types of people; the rich and the poor, those divinely touched and sculpted by the Goddess herself and those that came later as a result of her fatigue, via the mud droplets.

Yet there are other versions to Nu-Kua's myth to consider. There is even a tale that holds an uncanny resemblance to Genesis in the Old Testament of the bible. In this Chinese tale, Nu-Kua is not just attributed for birthing humanity, but for creating all of the creatures upon the earth. The myth claims that on the first day she created chickens and on the second day, she crafted dogs. Then it goes on to state that on the third day she made sheep and then pigs on the fourth day. On day five she created cows and on the sixth day she made horses. Finally on the seventh day she created humanity from the yellow clay by the banks of the river.

The Goddess Nu-Kua resembles the Greek Goddess Gaia in her primordial matriarchal Creatrix abilities. Both are ancient deities credited for populating the earth with its inhabitants. It is also interesting to note another tale linked with Nu-Kua and the seeds of similarities it holds to many other deities from various cultures. Quite often with primordial Goddesses there is a connection between their creation, bloodline and their consorts. With Nu-Kua there is one version of her myth that alludes to her sexual connection to her brother, who becomes her husband, Fu-Xi. And there is some ambiguous concern or guilt she wrestled with concerning procreation with her brother, according to some interpretations of these Chinese old folklores, which is why she begins to impart to humanity the importance of marrying, birthing children and admonishes the practice of incest.

In the ancient Chinese text, *"Duyizhi"* (*A Treatise on Strange Beings and Things)* by Tang dynasty writer, Li Rong (ca.846-974CE) we have a different tale of the Goddess Nu-Kua connecting her to a partner. According to this Chinese folklore, Nu-Kua was initially not alone on the earth after P'an Ku's death. She was accompanied by her older brother and they lived on the mountain of Kunlun. In this myth they desired each other and wanted to procreate and fill the earth with their children but the shame and guilt of incest caused them much apprehension and distress. Together the siblings prayed to the heavens asking for direction and a clear sign that would grant them permission to unite and procreate. They began to divine by numerous interesting means, for example; the Goddess would run down the mountain and if her brother could catch her, then they were ordained to be married. Another way of divining involved threading a needle successfully from a long distance and yet another test was if the smoke from a fire would gather and unite, then that was a sign that they indeed had divine permission to marry. Although they were given clearance to unite as husband and wife, according to these various myths, the shame was too much for Nu-Kua. As a result, she gathered and weaved grass into a fan to cover her face and thus, this is the Chinese explanation why traditionally brides hold up fans during their nuptial ceremonies.

Her consort Fu-Xi resembles Nu-Kua in his half dragon, half human appearance and when they are depicted together sometimes their Dragon tails are actually intertwined to show their deep intrinsic partnership. He is seen in artistic depictions holding a square to represent the heavens, although some sources say he holds a representation of the round sun, while she often holds a compass in her hands to represent earth or the moon. Together they unify the heavens and the earth.

Fu-Xi is a Chinese God who imparts to humanity the gifts of tending to ones flock, hunting and the art of fishing with a net. He was also known to be a music teacher, inventor of musical instruments and a song composer of a melody known as "Jia Bian." He was credited for the eight tiagrams/diagrams, the Ba Gua, which helped develop the Chinese form of divination known as the, I-Ching. He taught humanity to barbecue food and is attributed for inventing the calendar, matrimony dowries and written characters for documenting life events, instead of the traditional knots on a cord. Fu-Xi also made copper coins and manufactured many tools and objects from metal. While Nu-Kua's main myths always seem to present her alone or single, it is interesting to also make note of who she was inevitably paired with in Chinese Mythology. Writings, particularly in the Hans Dynasty, refer to Nu-Kua and Fu-Xi as the parents of Humanity and the first of the San Huang people. Nu-Kua is also highly revered by the Miao people.

Some folklore reveals that Nu-Kua did not want to spend eternity tending to her clay human figures. And she did not want to continue laboriously hand crafting mud or clay beings. It was becoming much too tedious for her to craft daily and tend to the earth's population. Thus, she taught humanity the importance of joining male and female, ying and yang, to procreate, self-populate and maintain the human race upon the great earth. In this way, Nu-Kua expressed a desire to equip humanity with all the tools they needed to thrive and succeed upon the earth on their own, without her constant watchful eyes. It gave her great joy and satisfaction to empower humanity in this manner and it allowed her to simply enjoy their existence.

Nu-Kua's name itself can be looked at for further insight as some suggest the Goddess contained both male and female essence. The first part of her name "Nu" is translated as "first male" while the second part, "Kua" or "Kwa" denotes a "first female." Perhaps revealing that in this Goddess we see the "ying" and the "yang" uniting and the very first male and female embodied.

HOW SHE BECAME SAVIORESS OF THE WORLD

The earliest mention of the collapsed pillars of the heaven and Nu-Kua saving the earth is found in the early Chinese writing of the "Tianwen." She is also mentioned in the Lunheng (*Critical Essays, written by Wang Chong*, ca. 27-100CE) and "Bu Shiji Sanhuang Benji" (*Biographies of the Three Divine Sovereigns: A Supplement to the Historical records*," Tang dynasty). According to the text of this period, one day a quarrel ensued between a few of the most powerful deities in Chinese mythology, the details of what they were arguing about are lost to us but according to folklore the quarrel turned into a huge vicious battle. Included in this battle was the Water God named Gong-Gong and the God Zhuanxu (also known as, Zhurong, Di Ku or Shengnong). Some sources refer to Gong-Gong, also known as Kaghui, as a monster so we can only assume he was quite powerful and volatile in Chinese mythology. As the story elucidates Gong-Gong became angered when he feared he was losing the battle and in his volatile anger he proceeded to whack his head against one of the sustaining sacred Pillars of the sky, which was known as Mount Buzhou (meaning, "not full"). Needless to say this resulted in the imbalance and tilting of the sky towards the northwest and consequently the shifting of the earth's axis. With one pillar off course the existing pillars collapsed and the sky could no longer cover the earth. And the earth was said to be unable to hold all things. The "*Huainanzi*" text, however, states that initially all four pillars collapsed but this challenges other sources. Nevertheless, the Chinese nine sacred regions of the world were exposed and in severe jeopardy. Gong-Gong's thoughtless explosive act inaugurated much devastation upon the earth, as it set a chain reaction to numerous catastrophic events. Floods and roaring fires ensued, as well as the strange manifestations of man eating beasts spreading across the earth, threatening humanities existence. The earth was badly plagued with insurmountable chaos and devastation at this time.

The Chinese Goddess, Nu-Kua came to rescue humanity during these monumental calamitous times. Some tales claim she used her very own body, as a half dragon deity, to seal up the torn parts of the sky and this helped stop the flooding that was permeating the various realms. She was also believed to have gathered the ashes of the reeds to help stop this flooding. To this day, some parts of China worship Nu-Kua in an annual Water Splashing Festival that honors her as the one who saved ancient China from the cataclysmic floods. She is a Goddess attributed for the seasons and the rain falling where it is most needed upon the earth.

A more popular myth reveals that Nu-Kua gathered colored rocks (some sources say seven different rocks, others say five) and she melted these colored stones and used them to patch and mend the various holes in the sky that were causing the flooding. She managed to stop the flooding in this manner but the sky could not be fully fixed and remained slightly tilted. This folklore explains the earth's unusual tilted axis and why the sun, the moon and the stars move northwest, while the river in China is said to flow southeast into the Pacific Ocean.

The beloved Goddess Nu-Kua is highly venerated for rescuing humanity and restoring the balance of the earth during this catastrophic time. The earth's cardinal points fell out of alignment when the monster God, Gong-Gong, banged his head on one of the pillars of the sky.   Her myths reveal that she helped support the compromised four corners of the sky by utilizing the four cut legs of the sacred giant tortoise and replacing the pillars with these cut turtle legs. She confronted and killed the Black Dragon that was one of the creatures causing much havoc on the earth. Eventually Nu-Kua pacified the numerous hideous creatures that were devouring human being and because of this she became a Goddess recognized for introducing animal domestication. There is another myth that tells of her taming a treacherous giant named King-of-Oxen, at another time, by jamming a rope through his nose. This miraculously allowed her to tame him, as well as many other wild animals she encountered, according to Chinese legends.

When the earth was restored to her peaceful state, Nu-Kua, without seeking accolades, humbly departed to the heavens, where some believe she remains today. Some claim she rode to the heavens seated on a chariot of six winged dragons and yet other creative depictions reveal she was carried off by a thundering chariot containing two winged dragons and two green hornless dragons. A special mattress is reputed to be under her as she travels on her chariot while holding her sacred compass. White dragons are before her and a flying snake is visibly behind her and she is said to be surrounded by the most celestial gilded clouds. Clearly, references of this Goddess in ancient Chinese literature idealize her with much respect and grand adoration and she continues to be worshipped today, especially among women.

Nu-Kua's worship continues in Shexian County and Hebei Province. There is a great Temple dedicated to her, named *"The Palace of Empress Nuwa"* and from February 15th till March 18th in the Lunar Calendar, festivities take place to honor the Divine mother and great grandmother of humanity. March 15th is notated as Nu-Kua's birthday and thus, this day takes on great significance for the Chinese. She is exalted with singing and dancing on this day, in the hopes that she will bless her worshippers with fertility, good health, happiness, safety and blessing on marriages and children. *"The Temple of Human*

Ancestors," also known as *Renzu Temple* or *Tomb of Tai Hao,*" found in Huaiyang County, Henan Province, celebrates the God Fu-Xi, along with the Goddess Nu-Kua, for a month long. From February 2nd till March 3rd in the Lunar Calendar, women offer the Goddess dances like the *"danhualan"* or the *"danjungtiao."* These are ancient ritual dances for the Goddess Nu-Kua, performed solely by women. At the Renzu Temple, contemporary worshippers might burn incense, paper money, paper architectural buildings to represent ancestral dwellings and offer handmade shoes, lovingly dedicated and ritualistically burned to Nu-Kua.

Clearly Nu-Kua is a beloved Chinese deity that exemplifies women's creative powers and her innate ability to manifest peace and order out of chaos and calamitous situations. For feminist Wiccans, she is a beautiful symbol of matriarchal energy, attributed for humanities birth, and our gender unearths a great source of empowerment in this beloved highly venerated ancient Goddess.

MUSING ON NU-KUA,
CHAOS & ORDER AND THE NEED FOR POLYTHEISM

"Chaos is what we've lost touched with. This is why it is given a bad name.
It is feared by the dominant archetype of our world, which is Ego, which clenches because its
existence is defined in terms of control..." Terence McKenna

As an artist and a mother of three boys and numerous household critters, Nu-Kua is a Goddess that I can easily identify with. Even as I write this and research this highly revered Chinese Goddess I feel her energy, for as mothers we are always called upon to find order amidst chaos.

My home is often subjected to the challenge of maintaining itself organized, most days it suffers from a topsy-turvy, laundry piles waiting by the laundry machines, piles of animated shoes by the entry doorway, dirty dishes gracing our kitchen sink, various children's toys scattered about with every step one tries to take in our home and yet, I am required to thrive and somehow find order amidst this chaos, as well as facilitate my loved ones to do the same. It is in these moments that I *sense* some of Nu-Kua's important attributes and I am able to connect with this ability to confidently get organized and get things done despite the less than ideal situations and challenges.

Yes, I feel her necessary presence in my life and her great importance for my own sanity and sense of accomplishment. There are things that, as a womyn, I must do, things related to my own personal well-being that sometimes differ and conflict with the things I must do as a mother. Finding time to connect with my spirit, commune with my inner voice, write, paint, meditate and be in stillness feeds my wellbeing as a womyn but goes in complete opposition sometimes to being a mom of rambunctious little ones. Needless to say, finding a moment of serenity and quietude in our household is somewhat challenging but even amidst these obstinate obstacles, it is indeed achieved and I do manage to find those important moments to cultivate inner peace and order.

There is a beauty and order I must create for myself daily amidst chaos and disarray (whether it's physical or mental) and yet, I am also required to create it for others by providing an environment that is safe, clean and conducive to raising healthy children. There are things of beauty and expressiveness that, as an artist, I am passionately obliged to create for my own happiness and wellbeing, just as I imagine the Goddess Nu-Kua felt, as she created that first yellow clay human figure. It made her feel good to create this being in her beautiful image (the mother archetype must create). It also helped her feel less lonely and it made perfect sense to add this, almost necessary, finishing touch to a world that seemed incomplete without it.

As a matriarchal Goddess I find Nu-Kua fascinating, even more fascinating is her part in a cosmology that differs so greatly from what mainstream religion would have you believe. Her role in cosmology greatly contrast the tales found in Genesis; a tale most mainstream religions wholeheartedly accept and believe. Here in this ancient Chinese tale, explaining humanity's birth and the earth's creation, is an empowering tale for our gender, certainly much more empowering than the crippling, degrading explanation of a male god creating man and then creating a woman from the rib of that man. There is no sense of equality in that myth, dare I say, there is no sense of true Divine love in humanity's manifestation in those tales in the bible. There is an obvious perverse domination and distasteful hierarchy that serves only to disempower one gender and thus harm one half of the human race. When you compare the two tales; one deems a male god creating humanity in his image and that was Adam. Then a female was formed by taking of this man's rib. Inherent in this biblical tale is the potentiality for massive injustices, obvious discrimination and a subordinate view of women; a downright cruel view, clothed in divine reasoning of why women should be deemed as the lesser human than man.

Herein this ancient Chinese tale is an explanation of humanity's birth filled with the potentiality for gender equality. We have a loving Goddess, composed of both creature and divine essence, for she is part dragon (a sacred ancient serpent) and part human and she hails from the heavens. She embodies the sacredness of the earth and the sky and yet also the waters and fire in her savioress and creatrix abilities. And she lovingly creates humanity out of sheer love, desiring someone to share the great beauty of the earth - the earth that had been created and passionately maintained by one who was birthed and formed inside of chaos in the sacred cosmic egg, the giant P'an Ku. And after maintaining the sky above and successfully keeping the earth and the sky separated, an act that he does for fear of the destruction of something he finds so precious; our earth, he then finally grows weary and old and dies. He is the sacrifice so commonly recurring in many ancient mythologies regarding humanity and the earth's existence across numerous prominent cultures. It is not from a place of soveignty or a great self-imposed power that the giant creates and sustains the earth but from a place of love. Something beautiful is before him and P'an ku does not want to see it destroyed; he was after all, birthed from its essence. The creation of the universe and humanity is thus beautifully shared by both genders, both male and female, and by all really, for less not forget Nu-Kua is half beast and P'an Ku is a giant, sometimes also depicted as half beast as well. And thus this cosmology includes everyone as being part of the creation of this Universe, not just one male deity as we so often see in other patriarchal religions. It is not one person, nor one ruler, not one god who is attributed for creating the earth and the human race, it is a combination of many who left their divine imprint on us and because of this we are many, in respectively different sizes, colors, shapes, gender, different life paths and titles. We are not one type of people, we are many and this diversity is mirrored for us in this cosmology much more so than in the one presented to us in Christianity. It is this noted fine detail that purports polytheism vs. monotheism.

I must say that here is where the study and connection to the Chinese Goddess Nu-Kua has been the most impactful for me personally, and where I may stray from some established Pagan, Christian and Non-Christian viewpoints. There are many who discovered Paganism after years being indoctrinated into other monotheistic religions and this obstinate belief in "the One" has a way of lingering rather subtly into newly adopted religious and spiritual practices. This "one deity" concept seeps into our culture's prejudicial practices and seeps into the fibers of our so called melting pot that seems to only want to lump everyone into the same mold, whether that mold is Christianity, Paganism or Americanism etc.. It seems to feed the "oneness monster" that is so often threatened and intimidated by anything that stands out in its diversity and its eccentricities. I think the rise of monotheism has brought about a wave of unconscious and conscious prejudicial harm and I can see that issue harboring in many aspects of our lives.

The problem with our nation's intolerance for differences becomes most apparent when we see the epidemic of bullying taking place in schools now a day. From an early age children are indoctrinated into this perverse practice of tearing down and degrading anything or anyone that appears different or dares to assert itself as unique. And the evil of this world is not in our differences, the evil in this world is in our inability to embrace, respect and seek understanding of differences. No... it's much easier to bully people into submission to assimilate, abandon their culture, race, belief, sexual orientation and succumb to social pressures. It's much easier to manipulate, beat down with alienation until they question their very own self -worth and whole purpose to exist... that's the world we've become, a world that fears the unknown, the different, and does not seek to conquer its fear with knowledge but rather, feed it with hate and prejudice and false assumptions.

I think Polytheism supports diversity and honors differences and, dare I say, reveres unconventionalities and this has magnanimously more far reaching implications than we can fathom –it extends into all human and civil rights matters.

I, personally, do not like to impose a "oneness" belief tenet in my spiritual practice; advocating for Polytheism and opting for diversity and great respect and embracing of all cultures. We are indeed all human beings composed of spirit and matter and most cultural myths do unify us as being divinely manifested, but we all come from different parts of the world, with different cultural myths aligned to our ancestral genetic makeup and that's a great thing!!! It is not something to shake off or be admonished for. The Gods of our ancestors are just as indispensably important as the Gods of this new found land and neither needs to be placed on a pedestal at the expense of the other.

While some mainstream religions set out to eradicate any cultural religious allegiance people may have, with numerous violent crusades, wars, persecutions and persistent missionaries, a belief in Polytheism renders these practices unnecessary and almost tragic. We have much to learn from one another but the "oneness" concept found in monotheism purports that there is only one way, one culture, one supreme race and one being and one God and one religion, leaving little room for anything else. It is these consistently narrow definitions in our world that are at the root of all forms of prejudice.

We pride ourselves in being a melting a pot of various races and cultures but the operative word is melting pot because you are expected to melt away what makes you, you, and blend into the vanilla-ness of the "ruled over." It allows for the "one" to have full authority to declare what should and shouldn't be accepted. It is irrespective of people's various cultural, ancestral differences and it begs one to assimilate and assimilation is disregard for one's uniqueness and history. Assimilation is the one thing that has destroyed so many beautiful ancient cultures and religions and yet, assimilation, is almost required to herd the sheep, control and manipulate the masses. We've become a nation intolerant of differences, as if differences can and would destroy the very fibers of our nation and yet, difference are not what causes strife and wars, it is our intolerance and prejudice, which is rooted in ignorance, that creates wars and devastations, it is our insistence that everyone be ruled by the "one theory."

Diversity is a positive thing only when we respect and embrace our differences. I think the problem in our society is that a lot of people want to glaze over it and not respectfully acknowledge differences of race, religion, sexuality, culture and class and deceptively lump everyone under preordained stereotypes or categories and if you don't fit that societal criteria you get ostracized. This has the stench of monotheism because we are not so easily classified as the same but to someone who sees this as positive trait, this is a gloriously divine human attribute to be celebrated not a reason to persecute, dominate or destroy. These differences, while they appear like societal chaos, are in fact that sacred kaleidoscopic beauty of our very human divine nature which upon closer inspection has perfect order.

*Nu-Kua is the ancient Chinese Goddess of creation and order. She is attributed for creating the human race out of little clay figurines. It is so empowering to our gender to learn of this rather unique cosmology. Naturally, as the Goddess who created humanity, she is highly revered. Her gifts to us are similar to Gaia's, as one can surmise, and thus Nu-Kua awakens us to our own gifts of creation. Nu-Kua is a powerful sovereign Goddess that is deemed as the Mother of humanity and her presence awakens our own creative gifts. She was also known as humanities' saviouress whose ingenious quick thinking helped save the earth from a cataclysmic disaster. She represents the strength to dive into chaos and create order and peace out of Global disasters. Calamitous events do not need to destroy us but rather can give us an opportunity to display our strength, our creativity and our problem-solving skills; this is yet another one of her powerful messages to us.

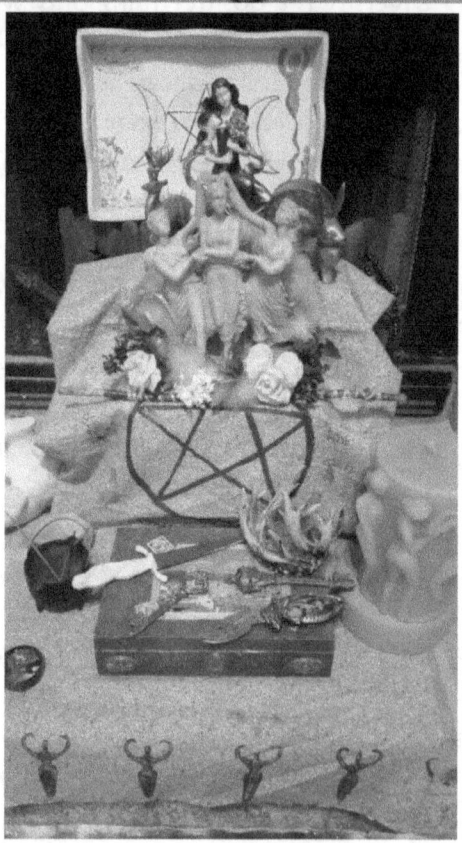

CHAPTER THREE
JOY
SHE WHO TAPS INTO THE POWER OF WHAT SHE LOVES

"Love makes your soul crawl out from its hiding place..."
Zora Neale Hurston

HATHOR

"For all acts of love and pleasure are my rituals..."
Doreen Valiente, -The Charge of the Goddess

HATHOR

Hathor is a Pre-dynastic Goddess, worshipped for over 3,000 years. She is the Egyptian Goddess of Joy, Pleasure, Beauty and Love. Yet Hathor is known by a multitude of other names and titles. As is typical of most ancient deities, Hathor appears to be an important Goddess of many names, duties and significant attributes. The name Hathor means, "House of Horus," perhaps a reference to her role as mother of Horus. Hwt-Hrw, Het-Hor, Het-Hert, Athor-Athyr are just some of the names ascribes to her in the writings of her time period.

She was most commonly known and depicted as the *"Celestial Bovine"*, nurturing all of humanity. Images of her appeared as a beautiful winged Cow with stars over her head and sometimes as a cow on a boat over water, alluding to her connection with the Nile River. This image later developed into a lady with the head of a cow, wearing the illustrious head dress of a pair of horns and a moon or solar disk in the center. Eventually she was depicted with a human head and the ears or horns of a cow, while wearing the Goddess head-dress. As a cow, she represents all of the generous attributes typical of a bovine and was believed to have given birth to the universe, according to one Egyptian cosmology.

Interesting to note, Hathor seems to embody all the elements; earth, fire, air and water. Often depicted as a Sky Goddess, existing before time and called Mistress of the Heavens, she is also the Goddess of Moisture, associated with the inundation of the Nile River. She was seen as a Solar Goddess in her connection to her consort Ra- the Sun God and also in her aspect as the Fiery Lioness, Sekhmet. She is the Goddess of the Moon and the Goddess of the underworld, protecting dead souls and guiding them to the Judgment Hall. Known as Mistress of the Necropolis, she tenderly cared for the dead souls and offered them water, with the branch of her sacred Sycamore tree, as they journey to the underworld.

In ancient times, she was considered the Goddess of Agriculture and, to Egyptians, she was called upon to assure the fertility of the land. Unquestionably, Hathor was a beloved, multifaceted, ancient Deity, greatly revered by both men and women.

Her main Cult was in Dendera, but she had many devotees and followers throughout the world. From Africa (places like modern day Ethiopia, Somalia and Libya) to Semitic West Asia she was highly venerated in ancient times. She is a patron Goddess for wommin and all Feminine aspects of life, but she was also adored and worshipped by many men as well.

Hathor was the protectress of pregnant women and all women at different stages of their lives. From birth to death, she was believed to oversee and be invested in the many stages of a womyn's life. A Goddess of perfumery, cosmetics and jewelry, she was known as Lady of the Malachite and Lady of the Turquoise. Malachite was mined in her Providence of Sinai and thus easily attainable in this region and some of these precious stones had many sacred usage, some were even grinded and used as cosmetics. As a Goddess of cosmetics and beautification, Hathor often adorned her eyes but so did both, priestesses and male priest in Egyptian temples.

The Menat, a multi strand necklace, was her beloved symbol. This was a necklace that was not used for mere adornment but rather was used during special rituals. As a Goddess of Music, the Sistrum was also another sacred symbol of Hathor that was used mainly to bless, ceremonially cleanse and purify a place of worship.

Hathor was believed to be the daughter of Nut, Sky Goddess and Mother of all Gods, and Ra, The Sun God. She was also the wife of the Sun God and given the esteemed titled of the "Eye of Ra." This daughter- wife relationship (similar to the Hindu Goddess Saraswati and the God, Brahma) appears to be a common occurrence among ancient deities of the time.

According to a famous legend, Ra feared his kingdom was coming to an end. He was angered at the Egyptian people and their apparent lack of respect and commitment to him, as their God. He sent his beloved Hathor as the bloodthirsty Sekhmet, to go out to kill off those who appeared to be going against the old ruler. Rather unexpectedly, however, Sekhmet became uncontrollably blood thirsty and was determine to massacre everyone in sight, regardless of their political allegiance.

As Sekhmet, she is an irrepressible force, determined to draw blood, feast and dance on the multitude of corpses. I can't help but see the image of the Hindu Goddess, Kali Ma in this depiction of Sekhmet, but I digress. Ra feared the worse and recognized his impulsive grave error. In a desperate attempt to end Sekhmet's killing spree, he poured red colored beer and tricked the Goddess into drinking it, believing it to be blood.

According to one myth, Sekhmet became so intoxicated after ravenously ingesting all of that beer that she completely passed out and the next day woke up in total contrast, as the sweet, benevolent Hathor once more. In this myth, we see our Egyptian Goddess as the savior of Egyptian people and we also see her association with intoxication. Interesting to note how Sekhmet becomes representative of this fierce dark aspect so often seen in most revered mother archetype, like Hathor. It reflects the double aspect most often exemplified by matriarchal deities. They are sweet, generous and nurturing, yet capable of fierce protection, and severe destruction swiftly, if the situation calls for that energy.

When later, the cult of Isis and Osiris came to Egypt; it changed Hathor's popularity and worship. Many of her aspects and functions were taken over and absorbed by the new Egyptian Goddess, Isis, whose worship spread to Rome, Africa, some parts of Asia and throughout Europe. Though on the surface they might appear the same, these are two quite distinctly different deities. In the myths of Isis, we learn of her pain, tragedy and grief but with Hathor, such emotions almost seem foreign to her character. In her myths, Hathor is the embodiment of success, happiness, joy, pleasantries and beauty —in complete contrast to her dark aspect as Sekhmet. Hathor is benevolence, pleasure and the pinnacle of Solar brightness-rarely do we hear of any hints of ugliness, nor tragedies in her tales and she has remained a beloved Egyptian Goddess, who bestows joy and pleasure to her worshippers and she continues to be a Feminine deity many wommin can easily connect with in this modern era just as in previous years past.

Hail and Welcome Bovinian Goddess Hathor!!!!!

*Hathor is the Beloved Egyptian Goddess of Pleasure and Love. She is the bringer of beauty, joy and sensual gifts. She is the highly venerated Bovinian Goddess that awakens us to our physical body and the importance of pleasure in our life. Whatever you do in life, make sure it brings you joy and gratification. When it seems as if the vibrant earth is a vision of great delight to all of our senses and we are in a state of titillation and arousal, the Celestial Bovine becomes the ideal Goddess to call upon. Her message to you is to seek joy, harmony and pleasure. She exalts the transformational magick of music, dance, sex and physical adornments. Amidst the doldrums of our obligations and the unavoidable mundane, seek to know and honor the highly cathartic power of ecstasy. She beckons you to delight in all the beauty that is surrounding you from within and from without, across the earth. Seek to know and explore the power of ecstasy!

UZUME

UZUME

Uzume is the Japanese Goddess of Dawn, revelry and joy. She quintessentially represents the cathartic power of laughter and is also depicted in Japanese Kyogen farce- as a woman who delights in her sensuality, called Okame.

Her full name is Ame –no-Uzume no Mikoto and it is quite intriguing to note that her name is sometimes interpreted as meaning *"The Terrible Female of Heaven."* In the Shinto religion, the name Uzume is linked to a "strong, brave woman." Today you might even hear the term *"osushi,"* to refer to a Japanese woman, a modern reference to one who exemplifies Uzume herself and the attributes she blesses women with.

As a deity often associated with the springtime, Uzume is considered a patron Goddess of the Rice fields. She is also very much connected with trance drumming and Shamanic practices. And, as her most popular myth will reveal, she is a Goddess of revelry and dance, more specifically ritualistic, ecstatic dancing. She is known also, as the wild chaotic abandonment sometimes found amidst the powerful surge of creative energy. Uzume is embodied Shakti energy and she is a Goddess often linked with early forms of Divination and psychic powers. Though often portrayed as the maiden, there are some texts that suggest another aspect of hers, represented as the wise crone.

There is very limited scholarly research and information on this early Japanese deity but we can extrapolate much from the ancient writings found in the Japanese sacred texts of the Kojiiki and the Nihonghi. The Kojiiki (*The Japanese Records of Ancient Matters*), C712 C.E./712 A.D. is one of the oldest existing written record of Japanese myth, legends and historical narrative related to Japan's imperial family and its assertion of Divine connection. The Nihonghi, (*Chronicle of Japan from the Earliest Times*) AD 697 AD, also sheds a great deal of insight into Japanese mythology, its origins and the worship of deities in ancient times. In these early sacred texts, the Goddess Uzume, is known as *"The Heavenly Alarming Female"* as well as *"The Great Persuader"* and she is still very much worshipped today as a prominent Shinto deity.

Shinto comes from the Chinese word, *"Shen-tao,"* meaning the way of the Gods. It is the indigenous, native religion of Japan that quite possibly has its roots in the Animist religions of Siberia. It is an ancient religion that lacks dogma yet practices the venerations of nature, spirits, ancestors and deities (referred to as Kami) and it pre-dates Buddhism. There is a strong belief in animated and unanimated objects and it is a Polytheistic religion that venerates a myriad of superior beings and spirits, known as Kami.

Interesting and most important to note, the Japanese name for Japan is Nippon, which literally means; Sun Origin and this is a direct reference to the highest venerated deity in Japan, the Sun Goddess, Amaterasu. Shintosim is a religion whose central deity is female unlike other World religions. And the Sun Goddess, Amaterasu, is of great significance because she is attributed for birthing Japan itself. Thus Shintoism is a spiritual practice intimately connected with Japan's divine origin and its people.

The Goddess Uzume is most often associated with the Japanese Sun Goddess, Amaterasu and she is attributed for playing a big part in tricking the Goddess out of her cave and self- imposed imprisonment. In the ancient myths, it was Uzume, with her ability to raise a ruckus that helped return Amaterasu back to her rightful place in the heavens, as the Sun Goddess and restore balance upon the earth.

According to Japanese lore, the Sun Goddess, Amaterasu O- Mikami, had retreated from the world when her volatile brother, the Storm God, Susano-O-no Kami, had defiled her sacred Temple. In one of his usual uncontrollable episodes he haphazardly tossed excrement and a colt (her sacred animal) unto the weavers of her holy temple. This vicious act singlehandedly caused great distress and misfortune to Amaterasu and her Priestesses. The benevolent Sun Goddess had tried many times before to reconcile with her brother, forgive him and somehow live peacefully in the world with him but this time he had gone too far. In his violently explosive behavior he had not only defiled Amaterasu's sacred temple but also injured many and killed one of her beloved priestesses. The Sun Goddess, saddened beyond measure, reached a monumental turning point and decided she could no longer shine her light for the world in his presence. Grief stricken, she retreated into the Heavenly Rock-Cave, where she removed her brilliant light from the world and stayed hidden, refusing to come out again. The earth, as a result, stood motionless and was needless to say negatively affected by the darkness that ensued. Nothing grew upon the earth without her divine light. There was famine, chaos and much calamity without the bright power of the sun. Both mortals and Gods alike were adversely affected by this indefinite Solar eclipse and they were greatly concerned about the state of the world, as the wild untamable, Susano-O- no Kami, now reigned freely. The ancient text found in the Kojiiki stated that the eight million Gods (or Kamis, as they are known in Japan) gathered to discuss a possible resolution and devise a plan to bring back the Sun Goddess. They too suffered gravely without her Divine light and the Kamis were desperate to restore balance and world order. The Japanese God, Takami-Musubi-no-Kami, called upon the council of Gods and they gathered on the Eight-sand-Bank River, in the heavens, according to Shinto lore and they began to brainstorm. The craftsman God, Ishiko-ritome-no-Kami was to build a great big mirror made out of copper, brought from the Heavenly mount Kagu and it was their hope that if Amaterasu caught a glimpse of her own Divine reflection in this sacred mirror she would enchant her own self with her brilliance and finally return to her post as the venerated Sun Goddess. The deity, Kushi-Akarutama-no-Kami was in charge of creating yet another magickal tool of enchanting distraction- sparkling jewelry. It was their hope the sparkling brilliance of these divinely crafted jewels would entice the Sun Goddess to come out further for a better look and hopefully remain in the world, out of her dark cave. Woven white cloths, made from mulberry paper, were also among the many items made and hung by the sacred trees surrounding the cave entrance all in an effort to entice the Sun Goddess. Ame-no-Mahitotsu-no-Kami crafted and offered swords, axes and tinkling bells of iron as well. The Sakaki tree from the Heavenly mount of Kagu, with its multitude of braches, was carried by the Gods. It was decorated with all the bright jewels, reflective items and finely woven cloths and streamers in an effort to lure the Goddess even further out of her cave. The God, Futotama-no-Mikoto held the sacred Sakaki tree while he began to

63

eulogize the Sun Goddess and Ame-no-Koyane-no-Mikoto recited invocations to Amaterasu... still the Goddess would not come out of her cave.

Our Goddess here, the spring maiden, Ame-no-Uzume-no-Mikoto then took center stage. Uzume wore a scarf made of club moss around her shoulders and a wreath. And while holding a tinkle belled crafted spear and bamboo grass and leaves, she lit the sacred bonfires before the Heavenly rock-cave. With all the Kamis surrounding the area, intensely waiting for a sign from the Sun Goddess, Uzume jumped on top of an overturned bath tub and began a silly, almost burlesque-like, dance. This wild dance was steeped in licentiousness and it stirred up the audience of tense Japanese deities. The laughter that ensued from Uzume's bawdy striptease created quite a commotion and it, unsuspectedly, also stirred Amaterasu's curiosity from behind the dark, blocked caved. She wondered how there could be any laughter or joy upon the earth in her absence. Hearing all the laughter and frivolity, she wondered if they had forgotten her or had somehow replaced her with another deity. These gnawing, uncomfortable doubts motivated her to investigate even further and so, she proceeded to crack open the entry of her cave, just enough to get a peek at what was going on outside. Naturally when she took her first glimpse outside of the cave she caught sight of all the brilliant sparkling jewels hanging from the trees and its beauty moved her to come out even further. Then she caught sight of her own divine reflection. Needless to say she was enamored by the golden luminescence of her own reflection. The surrounding Gods seized that very moment to quickly close off the cave entrance behind her to secure Amaterasu's staying presence in the world. She then discovered that it was Uzume's dance that had inspired such a wonderfully loud, joyful noise outside of her cave. Thus, Uzume and her bawdy, sexually liberating dance is attributed for pulling the Sun Goddess out of her grief and self-imposed exile, in the same way as the old nurse maid, Baubo, in Greek Mythology, helped awaken the Grain Goddess, Demeter, from her own despondency. Just as it was Baubo's bawdy lifting of the skirt, exposing her genitalia that snapped the Greek Grain Goddess out of her depressive hopeless state, so it was the Japanese Goddess Uzume who achieved the same feat. With her licentious, frenzied dance, lifting her kimono, she roused up not only the eight million Kamis but the dark grieving earth itself. And their collective joy and laughter over what they witnessed in Uzume, eradicated the darkness and brought forth the rebirth of the great Sun, Amaterasu. It becomes clear that Uzume is a Goddess who speaks to women on the power of laughter and the unabashed joys found when one embraces their sexuality. Yet, Uzume also speaks to us about the incredibly cathartic powers found in our physical body, Shakti energy, our body's rhythm and our personal dance.

There is another tale in the ancient Japanese text found in the Kojiiki and the Nihonghi that allows us yet an additional alternative glimpse into the beloved Goddess, Uzume.

When the Sun Goddess was ready to send to earth her beloved grandson, Ninigi, the August Child, to rule the people of Japan and proselytize her divine teachings, there was conflict. The heavens were divided, as some supported Amaterasu's decision, while other Gods were not happy to see Ninigi as first Japanese emperor to establish the first Imperial family. According to the Kojiiki, as he was about to descend upon the earth he noticed something blocking his entry way. It was a huge, monstrous looking creature that was described in great detail in the ancient Japanese text. This deity blocking the pathway for Ninigi was a frightful sight. It had a nose seven hands in length and glowing fiery eyes according to text found in the Kojiiki. This being was huge in size and was fiercely intimidating to Amaterasu's divine grandchild. Desperate, Ninigi called upon the Goddess Uzume who had acquired the powerful reputation for being the one who could always be relied upon to help the Gods.

The August Child called upon the Goddess Uzume, explaining his plight and asking for her assistance in this matter. She quickly descended to the heaven and earth threshold to confront the blocking monster. With her pushed down band across her navel and her exposed pendulum bare breast she confronted the monster and asked what business he had to be there. The monster was taken aback by her nakedness and bold candor. Bewildered by her appearance he introduced himself as Saruta-Hiko-no-Oho-Kami and then inquired about her reasons for this unconventional approach. He proceeded to tell her that upon hearing the Heavenly Grandson was about to descend to the earth he wanted to make himself available to the Future First Emperor of Japan. He was there waiting for Ninigi, not as an enemy, but to offer his assistance in whichever way served the Heavenly grandchild best. Thus, Uzume's bold confrontation births knowledge of Ninigi's true ally, unblocking the pathway to his destiny and it becomes the vehicle for the first Imperial family to be born. Ninigi was too frightened to see for himself who or what was blocking his destiny but it was Uzume's typical bold feat that resolved the paralyzing standstill and allowed the Sun Goddess's Grandchild to take his rightful place upon the earth. Again Uzume is called upon and acts as an intermediary so that the Gods are able to take their rightful place upon the heavens and the earth.

Known as the Crossroad God, Saruta Hiko or Sarutahiko-Okami as he is sometime known, was to guide the heavenly Grandson from the plains of high heaven to the wondrous peak of Takachiho in Hyuga, Tsukushi and then, thereafter, Saruta Hiko would leave to the river, Isuzu at Sanagata, in Ise. He was so impressed by the bold Goddess that he invited Uzume to join him in this journey and she did, becoming later on, his wife according to Japanese ancient text.

Saruta-Hiko-no-Oho-Kami, is venerated as the God of the Crossroads and he is paired with the Goddess Uzume as her consort. There is something to note when we consider that Uzume is joy, ecstasy, magick and trance dancing. When she is paired with her consort (a monstruous deity connected with the crossroads) it adds another dimension to our understanding of this ancient Japanese deity. It is as if she invites us to the edge; the mysterious, pivotal crossroads of magick and ecstasy.

Together, Uzume and Saruta Hiko are credited for both accompanying, the Heavenly Grandson throughout his journey to become the First Emperor of Japan and build the first Imperial family. It is this reason why Uzume and Saruta Hiko are considered the ancestors of Japan's sacred Imperial family.

Consequently, Ninigi held the Goddess, Uzume with great honor for her help in facilitating his Imperial journey. She was made the founder of the Sarume Order and the patron Goddess for the ritual dancers who perform in annual Sacred Festivals. These were mostly women and their dances take on a comical appearance which is valued as divine and necessary, in most traditional Japanese religious ceremonies. At the First Fruit Festival, Japanese perform the Saru-Mahi, a monkey dance. The word Sarume actually means "She-Monkey," thus, it is clear Uzume's sacred dance is a primal one, wildly connected to a monkey's movement. Many Shinto ceremonies incorporate other Uzume dances like the Nakatomi and the Imbe. These are the origins of the Kagura (a ritualistic dance-mime). Uzume's dance upon the overturned bathtub during the ancient myth related to the return of the Sun Goddess is still venerated and widely performed today in many Shinto ceremonies. These dances were often associated with early forms of medium possession, trance and shamanistic practice.

It is clear the Japanese Goddess Uzume played an important role in ancient women's lives and her significance for contemporary women needs to be highly considered. This is a sacred feminine, immortal Goddess whose spirit and energy is still very much venerated today in Shinto religious ceremonies just as it has been for hundreds of years. For those in the Goddess community, seeking to unearth, connect and worship the multitude of ways the Feminine Divine appears to us, Uzume is yet another wonderful expression of womanhood (wombmynhood) and thus, another sacred aspect of Goddess.

*The Japanese Goddess of merriment, Uzume, is often closely connected with the Sun Goddess, Amaterasu; much the same way as the Goddess Baubo is forever immortalized with the Greek Grain Goddess, Demeter. She is boldness and merriment all contained and reflected in the physical body and she introduces us to the powerful art form of the Burlesque. Uzume exemplifies for us the power and magick, found in our beautiful physical body and the gift of dance. She also awakens us to ecstatic trancing and the value of shamanistic practices. Uzume's silliness and buoyant laughter helped eradicate darkness on the earth and return the Sun Goddess to her rightful place in the heavens. She is thus, the cathartic power of laughter, ecstasy and the joys found in our physical body.

BAUBO

BAUBO

Baubo is the bold, Greek Goddess of laughter, joy, and liberated sexuality. According to the Greek philosopher Homer, Baubo was born out of the union of Pan and Echo. Her name is believed to mean, *"belly."* Other interpretation state that her name means, *"old crone."* We can understand this interpretation of her name because during her time, the word crone had a different meaning than it does today. The word crone, back then, was believed to be a Wise mature woman, not the old hag stereotype meaning its become today. Thus Baubo, right from the start, appears to us as the wise matron who has something to teach us regarding our belly.

In mythology, we speculate that Baubo was married to a known Swine herder, as some of the writing of the time allude to this and this was consider quite a profitable occupation. During this time in history, a Swine Herder made a rather good salary and thus it was considered to be a desired vocation for a man. Baubo was believed to have had a son from this union and his name was Eumolpos. Eumolpos literally means *"Sweet Singer"* and often, the writing of the time reveals that many aspiring singers in folklores were notorious for referring to him as their own original Singing teacher, to gain for themselves some credibility.

According to one of the popular, well known Greek lore, Baubo was employed as the nurse to the lame daughter of King Celeus, named Iambe, but the bawdy Goddess will forever be known in mythology as the one who succeeded in breaking through Demeter's sadness and lament. The Goddess Demeter, distraught by the disappearance of her daughter, Persephone, wandered the Earth aimlessly. In disguised, she came upon the King's abode and was welcomed to stay with their family. Everyone in the kingdom tried to cheer up this sorrowful old looking woman, but no one was able to reach her soul. Baubo offered her Barley and started to talk to the Grain Goddess, who at this point was disguised as an old woman. Still to no avail, Baubo was just not able to reach her and Demeter remained sad. In a moment of complete and utter silliness, Baubo lifted up her skirt to Demeter and reveal something that must have been strange and hilarious because it not only shocked Demeter, but also moved her to smile. That initial smile busted into a laughter that somehow helped her recover parts of her old forgotten Divine self. Somehow through this very act of her boisterous belly laughter, Demeter rediscovers her brilliant self, once more. Because of this occurrence, she was able to move to action and eventually return to her post as Goddess of the Grain. Consequently, she was able to return the Earth to its natural cycle, thanks to Baubo.

It is not clear what Baubo revealed under her skirt that made Demeter laugh so greatly, but some text allude to transgender genitalia, or a deformity or just an over exaggerated open vagina, like the Celtic, Shela-na-gig. Throughout history Baubo is often drawn and depicted with this exaggerated genitalia to reflect the sexual freedom she so expressed with Demeter in this tale. Sometimes she is also depicted with her face drawn or painted upon her belly, to reflect her connection to this sacred place in our body.

Unquestionably, Baubo is a Goddess that takes pleasure in bawdiness, friendship and unabashed light in her sexuality. She is the healing power of laughter and light heartedness. She is the Goddess of friendship because of her connection to Demeter and she wields the power of laughter. When she is invoked, she brings joyful mirth, fun, and helps connect us to the powerful healing nature of a good healthy laugh; the kind that emanates first from our core. Cathartic deep laughter that is found in our sacred belly.

"Close friends contribute to our personal growth.
They also contribute to our personal pleasure, making the music sound sweeter,
the wine taste richer, the laughter ring louder because they are there..." Judith Viorst

BAUBO'S GIFT TO US

As with some ancient Deities there are always bound to be conflicting stories about their origins and their myths, Baubo is no exception. However, I would like to focus on Baubo's unquestionable attributes, her importance among the assemblage of Feminine divine deities and most importantly her gifts and relevance for us, as modern day wommin.

Baubo, is known as the Goddess of sexual liberation, bawdiness, a good hearty belly laugh and the healing power of joy, friendship and laughter. These are gifts that transcend time, as laughter has always been deemed magickal and alchemical in its ability to transform severe pain, spiritual malaise and heartache, into something we don't need to collapse from, but, quite possibly, can overcome and actually trascend. It is a widely known occult knowledge that the presence of boisterous laughter can eradicate even the most obstinate negative energy.

There have been numerous scientific studies revealing the positive effects laughter and regular comedic relief has on our serotonin levels and our overall health and well-being. No one can deny the power of a good chuckle when we are feeling less than our best. It is also a well-known fact, among occultist, that laughter is the death of all maladies, awkwardness and even negativity is weakened by a joyful heart. The phenomenon of trolls, psychic vampires, dark entities and malign spirits are weakened and dissipate with the piercing sounds of jovial laughter -especially those of children, who can teach us a thing or two about surrendering to the joys of unabashed silliness and cackles. One of the best ways to raise the vibrations in a home plagued by strife, arguments and darkness, is to create multiple opportunities to laugh in that home. Thus a house warming party full of joviality has become a great customary ritual and an ideal way to bless a home and assure the grumbles will stay far away from the premises. These are just some spiritual remedies Baubo alludes to in her myths. Laughter can indeed heal, elevate and cure all temporarily weakened souls, as it did with Demeter.

The Greek Goddess of the Grain was in severe mourning and had suffered a great lost. Her sole, beloved daughter had been abducted and possibly raped by her own uncle, Hades. The tragedy of such a devastating occurrence appeared to have moved her to the brinks of her own death, as Demeter was no longer recognizable, no longer shone in her effervescence divine brilliance. And in her mourning, she willingly relinquish her duties and her authentic self. The story is very reminiscent of Amaterasu (The Japanese Sun Goddess) in that, both Divine Deities are so traumatized by the tragic occurrences in their respective lives that they surrender to great depression, retreat from their daily duties and their sadness almost seems to engulf, drown and overpower who they really are.

As the myth goes, Demeter was inconsolable and it appeared no one, nor anything, not even the multitude of decadent God offerings, could bring her back. I contemplate on how often unexpected tragedies have a way of traumatizing, shifting us into this dark realm where we too temporarily forget our inherent gifts and abilities to resurrect and regenerate ourselves. Yet as wommin, regenerating ourselves is clearly our domain and it is where we excel.

Everything about us, as wommin, points to this inherent gift and the exposure of our Yoni makes it undeniable because it's such a powerful ancient symbol of our

Womynhood and our regenerative powers. In both Uzume's and Baubo's iconic stories, the liberation and exposure of the Yoni results in a necessary, personally transformative Global change. Both Amaterasu and Demeter experience a sort of death and rebirth, an awakening, through this unveiling of the naked Yoni.

We, as wommin, are truly regenerative creatures and Baubo chooses our yoni as the sacred vehicle to remind us of this vastly awe-inspiring detail. The gift of rebirthing and regeneration is ever exemplified in our blood; its monthly cycles, in the way we produce eggs every month and release those unfertilized eggs in our monthly menses. We are example of that power of regeneration in our ability to rebirth new eggs, a month later, and again repeat this same cycle of death and rebirth. Some of us even bleed (menstruate) in conjunction with the appearance of the full or new moon in the heavens and we're able to synchronize our menses together within a group of sisters. Our ability to birth new life within us, if we wish to, is another obvious example of women's ability to regenerate herself over and over again, if she chooses to.

We are regenerative in the way our breasts (as new mothers) knows just the right amount of milk to produce to feed our infants and after breast feeding, hours later, our body is able to reproduce even more milk than before, in order to meet the expanding, nutritional demands of a growing human being. That is the gift of creation and re-creation at its finest.

Our multi orgasmic nature compared to a man's lack thereof, also exemplifies this inherent gift of regeneration. In the way that we, as wommin, can be multi-orgasmic and after pouring out our juices of ecstasy, we can come again and again and again, whilst a man will ejaculate once and lose a great deal of his vital energy and life force in that one expulsion. Hence the reason men are more likely to fall asleep after an orgasm, while a womyn experiences a resurgence of energy.

It is in our very nature to continually regenerate ourselves and unearth our strengths and rebirthing skills, over and over again. The image of our Yoni is a powerful symbol and reminder of this gift. And because of this, birth, death and rebirth are closely linked to our gender's gift.

"Baubo's sudden exposure of her genitalia reminds Demeter (of who she is) that being a woman, having a yoni, gives her the power to endlessly create new life...." *(page 61, "The Yoni...." by Rufus C. Camphausen)*

I imagine that the sight of a middle aged woman, unexpectedly exposing her genitalia would shock anyone into a fit of laughter. Some speculate that what Baubo exposed was far more than just your average Yoni. There are some that suggest Baubo was a hermaphrodite, containing within her, both male and female genitalia. Still there are others that suggest that Baubo might have just had a very unusual, exaggerated large yoni. One will never really know what exactly Baubo exposed between her legs, but whatever it was, it held the antidote and remedy for Demeter's lament. The act of such an unexpected, some might say, crude gesture, was enough to shock the Goddess OUT of her despondent state and place her back on the road to remembering her authentic self and her divine capabilities. In Baubo's rather exhibitionistic display of her Yoni, she rather beckons the Fertile Grain Goddess to remember her inherent womanly gifts of rebirth, transformation and regeneration found within her own magickal cavernous yoni.

When greatly grieved and saddened, it is dangerous to forget that within us (more specifically our womanhood, our yoni) there is a capacity to regenerate, transform and re-connect with our inner joy; our sacred sanctum and the power of unabashed, belly laughs. These are the gifts of the Goddess Baubo. She introduces us to the healing powers found in our Yoni, our gender and the cathartic magick of laughter. Baubo shows us how our belly laughs, in particular, can move mountains, even those obstinate, self-destructive state of beings, like depression, while directing our attention to one of the most ancient powerful symbol of the Goddess- our Yoni.

      *Our immortal friend is found in the cackling, supremely bawdy, ancient Goddess, Baubo. She arrives, like an old dear playmate, bubbling with jubilee and radiating with laughter and naughty jokes. Just when you started to feel the pull of sadness and stress caving in on you, she comes with warmth, jokes, encouragement and sincere friendship. She lightens your load and reminds you of your most precious weapon against feelings of defeat, sadness and depression. It is within you, your gender, your labyrinths and inner caverns, where cathartic treasures are to be found, and Baubo has no inhibitions about revealing this to you. Have you ever looked at yourself, really looked at yourself and marveled with laughter? Do you take pleasure in your existence? Have you ever heard the funny stories of an old friend echoing in your ears after a long, hard stressful day? This is Baubo's gift to you. She awakens you to the transformative powers of laughter. Take the time to laugh; lighten up & allow the cathartic power of joy & friendship an honored place in your life.

OSHUN

OSHUN

Oshun is the powerful Orisha of sensuality, attraction and the sweet waters of life. Always dressed in shimmering gold and yellows, she rules over all matters of the heart and pleasure. Hers are the gifts of sensual dances, lovemaking, romance and sensual sweet sticky foods, like honey. She is hypnotic swaying hips, shimmering lights, suggestive smiles, cascading waterfalls, verdant ripe fruits and fertile moist lands. She is benevolence and magick, for she was taught the art of Divination by Obatala, as a reward for helping him. As a result, she became the patron Goddess of the art of divination of cowrie shells and a teacher of magick.

According to African folklore, in the beginning there were a few Gods/Orishas sent down to earth to help mankind and establish civilization. In this early tale of Yoruban cosmology, Oshun was present and much needed as a Goddess that rules over waters and love. One of the orishas questioned her value upon the earth and managed to convince the other Orishas that she wasn't as vital to their work upon the earth. Well, Oshun was not one to argue with them, instead she pulled back all of her divine energy and retreated to the moon. There, she lounged without a care in the world in confidence that they would soon see and regret their disrespect of her gifts. Sure enough, when the Orishas found themselves unable to accomplish anything upon the earth without her sweet waters, and vital energy, they were forced to seek her out once more, beg for her forgiveness and bessech her return to the earth. With the intermediary of the God/Orisha Odulomare, she was petitioned to return but she only agreed if they vowed never to devalue or disrespect her again, and so they did.

Another folklore that shows the power of attraction Oshun possesses involves the Orisha, Ogun. Ogun is the God of blacksmith, war, civilization and advances in technology. According to one famous legend, Ogun grew tired and frustrated with humanity and decided he had enough with human follies. Despondently, he departs from civilization and retreats into the wild woods, far away from any human contact. The earth and its inhabitants starts to suffer as a result of his departure and the Orishas are much grieved by what begins to ensue in his absence. Oshun is implored by the Gods to help but her approached to the situation at first appears unconventional for she doesn't resort to brute force or demands. Instead, Oshun simply goes into the wild woods were Ogun is reportedly hiding and in her usual manner, she strolls and dances around the woods with her honey pot, giggling incessantly. She is clearly having some fun and emitting her golden light into the atmosphere. She then dips her curvaceous golden body in a nearby pond and starts to play with her beloved element of water. All along she is totally submersed in her joy and sensuality. Ogun catches a glimpse of her and finds himself instantaneously captivated by her beauty. Intrigued by her overflowing giggles and golden beauty he slowly draws nearer and nearer to her until he is right before her. At that pivotal moment, she is said to have dipped her finger in her honey pot and smeared it seductively upon Ogun's lips. In this very act she eradicates his despondency and any malaise and he is thus returned to humanity. It is her powers of attraction and seduction that mends all situations and this tale reveals her supreme skills of subtle persuasion.

When petitioned appropriately she will bless her devotees with great love, fertility, beauty and all the sweetness desired but cross her and you will soon meet another side to her. Her passionate nature can be expressed in numerous ways and most prefer to see that passion manifested in sweet loving ways not retaliatory or withheld.

Oshun is the beauty and love awakener! She seductively beckons you to care for yourself and invite sensual experiences into your life. She stirs your heart and ignites your inner flames so that you may awaken to passion. She opens your eyes so that you may value romance and finally embrace all the beauty and love surrounding you.

"Seduction is more powerful than coercion"
Joseph S. Nye Jr., Soft Power: The Means to Success in World Politics

APHRODITE

Aphrodite is the Greek Goddess of Love and Beauty, her Roman counterpart was Venus. Aphrodite is one of the oldest and most recognized, powerful deities of our time. Her origins can be traced to the East of Cyprus and Cytheria. She is known as the Goddess of Beauty and Gracefulness. She is cherished as Goddess of Attraction and the iconic, beloved Goddess of love, but more specifically, she is about that instant attraction and she can bring pleasure as well as pangs of love.

Aphrodite doesn't concern herself with consequences for she is the one that arouses desire and great passion, regardless of the situation. She is about physical coupling, infatuations and sexual longings. She is not about the institution or sanctity of marriage but rather that of sexual attraction, first experienced and necessary to maintain within a marriage.

She was sometimes known as the Goddess of the Prostitutes, for here again, in this profession, her powers of seduction and attraction was greatly needed and called upon. Hetairai, as they were called, were not only beautiful, but were highly skilled in music, dancing, art, eloquent speech and the art of seduction -all considered Aphrodite's domain.

Sea foam born, according to one Greek myth, she was born of the severed genitalia of her father, Uranus and this myth clearly supports her role as a Goddess of sexual pleasure - strongly emphasizing her own sexuality. Sometimes her sea foam birth reveals her coming out of a scallop seashell. This again is hinting at her role as a Goddess of Sexuality, as the sea shell highly resembles the form of a female's genitalia. The word scallop in Greek is, "Kteis." In Greek literature this word is also used to describe a woman's yoni.

Golden Aphrodite was often depicted and described as nude or half naked, or dressing, undressing, or being adorned. This called attention to her incredible physical beauty as a sexual Goddess. Often she was depicted with the Three graces: Algaia (*the bright one*), Euphrasy (*the glad one*) and Thaleia (*the abundant one*). They are reflections of Aphrodite herself and they assist her in ornamenting her curvaceous body. The Graces are often employed to help with anointing the Goddess with divine oils, bathing, dressing and adorning her according to the writings of her time. They were always seen happily dancing, acting maiden-like and again emphasizing the flowing elements of the Goddess of Love.

The laughing One, giggling with a smile that would reduce men to babbles, her skills and art in seduction were unmatched by any other being. Aphrodite was the definition of feminine warmth, sweetness and lightheartedness, rarely ever depicted as scornful, sobbing or angry but rather always light and inviting. She was portrayed as the Golden one, whose fragrance lingered long after her absence. Her presence aroused great passion and often as a result, some tricky situations. Some of her many symbols are; honey, semen, gold, sweetness and flowers; like Roses. Sweet smelling fruits like the apple and passion red pomegranate, are also her symbols.

There are two different tales about her birth according to Hesiod and Homer. Homer states that Aphrodite was born out of the union between Zeus and a Sea nymph. The most commonly accepted tale of her manifestation comes from Hesiod's literature. According to Hesiod, Gaia's consort, Uranus, was causing upheaval by not allowing Gaia to give birth to their children.   Cronos, one of their sons, sought to come to his mother's aid and took a sickle and cut off his Father's genitalia. The severed Penis was thrown into the Sea, where its semen mixed with the ocean creating foam. Aphrodite emerged from this foam as a fully grown Goddess in all of her curvaceous splendor. In the early Renaissance, the Florentine Artist, Sandro Botticelli (1444-1510), created a masterpiece artwork around 1485, called *"The Birth of Venus"*, that will forever encapsulate this moment in Greek Mythology, when newly born Aphrodite came ashore the Island of Cyprus.

She was the only Goddess allowed to choose her own consorts, unlike some of the other Greek Goddesses that were either raped, seduced, abducted or tricked. In mythology there are countless of stories of her amorous conquest and entertaining tales, involving her many dalliances.

She married Hera's son, Hephaestus, the Smith God, deity of craftsmen and the fire of the Forge. They had no children together. She also consorted with, Ares, God of War. This was a known, long term, love affair that resulted in three children. Together they had a daughter Harmonia (Harmony), and two sons, Deimos (Terror) and Phobos (Fear). The boys, according to the writings of the time, were often depicted joining their father in the bloody battlefields. Aphrodite also found a consort in, Hermes, Messenger God, God of science, magick, and trickery. With Hermes, She bore him Hermaphroditus, the Bi-sexual God, who had both sexual characteristics of his parents. Eros, who also had a very mystical birth and who has a number of conflicting tales describing his manifestation, was in later mythology considered Aphrodite's fatherless son. He was also known as "Amor," in Rome and today is depicted as the beloved, celebrated Cupid, exalted during our U.S.A. Valentine day celebrations.

Aphrodite also found lovers in mortal men. She was aroused with great desire upon seeing, Anchises, the Mountain Sid cattle grazer. With him she conceived a child that later would become the founder of Rome, Aeneas. Aphrodite was also completely smitten with Adonis, a youthful handsome hunter, who was later torn to pieces by a wild Boar. According to Greek myths, he was sent to the land of the Dead, but was permitted to return to his beloved Goddess part of the year, as a symbol of returning fertility. The Cult of Adonis performed this sacred rite -commemorating the annual return to Aphrodite in the same way Demeter and Persephone did in the Eleusinian Mysteries.

In the story of Pygmalion, the King of Cyprus creates his ideal woman by carving a large ivory sculpture. Little by little he becomes completely enrapture with his creation and falls in love with this image. During a festival honoring this great Deity he beckons Aphrodite to help him find this ideal woman in the flesh. Aphrodite in turn allows the sculpture to come to life. With one kiss from the king, his work of art comes to life, and the king finds love and marries his ideal woman.

There are also numerous tales involving women being touched and affected by Aphrodite. Throughout the story of Hera and Zeus, we learn of Aphrodite's powerful girdle and its ability to make its wearer irresistible, when Hera lays hands on it. Myrrha was made to fall madly in love with her own father and have relations with him because she neglected her Aphrosinian worship; still another probable cause was because her own mother had boasted that Myrrha was more beautiful than Aphrodite.

In yet another tale, Aphrodite caused Phaedra to have great desire for her own step-son. Uncontrollably, she finds herself in love with her step-son, Hippolytus, because Aphrodite was displeased with the son's disregard for the Goddess of Love. Hippolytus had taken vows of celibacy and devotion to the Virgin Moon Goddess, Artemis. To punish him, Aphrodite created a horrible situation in which Phaedra committed suicide and left a note falsely accusing her step-son of rape. As a result, Poseidon was summoned to kill Hippolytus.

Another interesting tale was that of Psyche. Psyche was considered so beautiful, that she was often revered as a Goddess herself and she had garnered the reputation of often being compared to the Goddess of love. Obviously, this did not sit well with the supreme Goddess of Attraction. Aphrodite created a number of challenges and road block that Psyche, eventually, was able to successfully master and as a result, she received Aphrodite's blessings in her union with her son, Eros.

Aphrodite had many important symbols like the apple and the pomegranate fruit. These fruits are commonly associated with fertility and sexuality. Sweet scents and flowers, in particular; roses and the lily, are also her sacred symbols, again suggesting sexuality and generative sexual organs. She is often depicted with dolphins - a reference to her birth at Sea and perhaps because dolphins were considered sociable, frisky and very friendly, particularly to sea travelers. Doves are associated with her because they coo and are publicly affectionate. Sparrows were said to be her charioteers and they too were her beloved symbol for their wantonness. Their eggs were often eaten as an aphrodisiac in her honor.

Anything gold and shimmering was attributed to her divine essence. Throughout the literature of her time the Goddess of love is often described with these complimentary, golden, demonstrative words. Gold is a metal that is brilliant and does not tarnish and is appropriate for this Cypriot Goddess who seem to exemplify those same qualities.

This immortal brilliant goddess is ever present in romantic and sexual unions but her engrossing spirit is easily detectable in so many other areas in our lives. In our very own creativity we can also encounter Aphrodite's gifts. For as artist, sometimes we find ourselves creating things of beauty and sensuality. When the artist is at work, there is a feeling of enrapture, drive, obsession and the type of attention and focus that most lovers experience for one another at the beginning of a romantic relationship. This is an Aphrosinian experience. In creativity there is great love, cultivations, attraction and engrossment throughout the creative process. A heighten sense of aesthetics is experienced as well as during the creative process...here too; this is Aphrodite's divine essence and gift to us.

Hail to you, captivating Aphrodite!

*Greek Goddess of love, beauty and attraction. Sweet, curvaceous watery Queen, she brings you the power of beauty and attraction and most importantly, the unwavering power of self-love. You say you want a new lover but are you the honey and light, love so often seeks to meld and attach itself with? She is the embodiment of attraction and love, in its many guises. From a gentle stirring, to an all-consuming passion, her Venusian gifts spread into so many different areas in our lives. Even in the passion we might feel towards our goal's fruition, creative projects and its unfolding sacred processes. Here she helps you cultivate your own powers of attraction, to attract whatever your heart truly desires. She invites you to acknowledge your own beauty and your powers of attraction, for these are her domain. Who or what do you ensnare in your life at this time? Where can you cultivate further, your Aphrosinian powers of love and attraction?

FLORA

*"To describe my Mother would be to write about a hurricane in its perfect power.
Or the climbing, falling colors of a rainbow..."*
Maya Angelou

FLORA

Flora is the Roman Goddess-Nymph of Flowers and springtime. She was also believed to be of Sabine origins; an old italic tribe, of Apennines pre-dating Rome. In Greece she was known as Chloris, wife of Zephyrus, the westward winds. She was given dominion over the blossoming of flowers.

Goddess of ceremonies, magick, sexuality, nature, the earth and time itself, Flora is the patron Goddess of youth and pleasure. She is a Goddess closely linked with the veneration of Flowers and Beauty. Much like the Egyptian Goddess, Hathor; dancing, sensuality and perfumed floral scents, were an important part of her worship at her temples and annual Festivals.

In ancient times her famous salacious festival was the Floralia. It was held annually, for six days (April 28th through May 3rd) during her sacred month of April. The Floralia, also known as "*Florifertum*," with games known as the "Florales Lundi," started around 238 BCE. It was reputed to be a lively debaucherous, flower festival, dedicated to her worship and held at her sacred temple. It offered numerous opportunities for fun, games, gift-giving, various dances and blessing rites for flowers and crops. It was a time for releasing inhibitions and tapping into Flora's powers of fecundity. Honey and milk offerings were common at this time and there was an air of frivolity and joy. Obviously, an abundance of colorful flowers and floral head wreaths were prevalent at this festival and animals were incorporated into many of the fertility rites. There were countless open air theater performances and pantomimes and of course, lots of brazen nudity, according to the writings of the time.

The Floralia was actually passionately embraced by prostitutes, and the courtesans of local brothels. They saw this annual festival as their very own and venerated, Flora as their patron Goddess.

Flora is also a powerful Goddess of magick; most notably the magick of flowers and floriculture & horticulture studies. According to one Roman legend, it was the Goddess Flora that presented the Roman Goddess Juno, with a most auspicious magickal flower. She provided Juno with an enchanted flower of fecundity that allowed Juno to become pregnant parthenogenesis, that is, without male contribution. Thus, Juno later gives birth to the God of War, Mars.

The Pagan holiday of Beltane still celebrated today and the incorporation of the Maypole were all attributed to her ecstatic, joyful flower festival and the worship of the Roman Goddess, Flora.

When working with the ancient Goddess Flora, she will heighten all of your senses and awaken desire for fun, pleasure and the enjoyment of life. She invites you to abandon your inhibitions and bedeck your beautiful body with her sacred flowers. With her energy, she asks you to prioritize love and sensuality and calls you to admire the beauty found in her myriad of colorful flowers and explore her numerous gifts.

CHAPTER FOUR
WEALTH
SHE WHO TAPS INTO HER OPULENCE

ERZULIE FREDA

ERZULIE FREDA

Erzulie Freda, with her penchant for lounging around, is the Haitian Voodoo loa Spirit, or (most appropriately termed) Mystere of Love and Beauty, like the Greek Goddess of love, Aphrodite. She is the watery, Feminine mystere or Goddess (as I like to use these terms interchangeably) of all things that bring you pleasure, including decadent sweets, jewelry, cosmetics, fragrances, lacy feminine textiles, soft music, and affection. She is the benevolent spirit of sensual pleasures and sweet scents like the Egyptian Goddess, Hathor. Erzulie has also been compared to the Hindu Goddess, Lakshmi, as she is also the Voodoo loa Spirit of luxury, opulence and abundance.

Maitresse Erzulie Freda can be seen as a Goddess of Romantic ideals. She is the beloved feminine supreme archetype in the Haitian Voodoo pantheon and rules over all matters concerning relationships, flirtations, sensuality as well as prosperity, and her worshippers' wellbeing. But she is also known to have another darker side. There are some conflicting stories about her depiction, as some sources claim she was often portrayed, in New Orleans, as a light skin mulatto, sometimes almost white, with long, dark straight hair, while another aspect of her, more specifically, Erzulie Dantor, was depicted as the dark skinned Loa with a scar from her husband, upon her face. The author, Milo Rigaud, in his reputable book, *"Secrets of Voodoo"*, states that Erzulie was considered a very dark skinned Ethiopian and that the notorious, Queen of Sheba, was often identified with her. Because in Voodoo, the bright Sun was the Masculine spirit, known as Damballah/Danbhalah Wedo (also known as Legba), Aida Wedo (his wife), was his opposite, the night, the Moon and the Feminine Spirit, known in Haiti as Erzulie. It would make sense that in Haiti she would be represented as the dark skinned loa while in New Orleans, with the influence of colonialism, a lighter version emerged.

Erzulie is the Mystere of eloquence, refinery, French culture, opulence and good fortune and, as can be expected, a very much beloved, powerful loa for all who practice Voodoo. She is so important to the culture, that she is considered the Heart of Voodoo.

Her catholic counterpart is the Virgin Mary, Mater Dellorosa (suffering Mother) as she is often depicted crying towards the end of Voodoo ceremonies, while in possession of her serviteur. Some believe she cries because she is never quite able to attain enough of what she wants. Others feel that she cries lamenting for those who are hurt by poverty or unrequited love and her tears symbolically take on the pain of the world so that others do not need to cry. In this compassionate role, she begins to resemble the Buddhist Goddess of Human Compassion, Kwan Yin, carrying the weight of human suffering upon her own heart.

Originally, the name Erzulie referred to a river in Benin and her worship comes from the West coast of Africa, but soon it traveled to New Orleans and Haiti and all across the Americas with the advent of slavery. There are many names given to this loa depending on the role that she is fulfilling. She is also known as Ezili and some Haitian literature claim that there are several aspects of this one Spirit such as; the older Grande Erzulie, Erzulie-Mapiangueh, Freda Dahoumin, Negresse Imanou Ladeh, Negresse Miroi-Ze, Erzulie Dantor, to name just a few. Here we will focus on Erzulie Freda as one spirit.

In Voodoo, a loa was seen as a powerful spirit, a mystere, and not as an archetype or Goddess aspects, the way we are accustomed to hearing about in Wicca and other earth based religions. A Voodoo loa, like Erzulie, was revered, honored and seen as an actual living person, who might even live near you and possess the same complex, yet tangible personality as any family member would. These spirits were not ethereal beings up in the sky, but were rather viewed as real, here on earth, and they were appeased and given flattery and various offerings.

Even the practice of Voodoo, in general, utilizes common every day household items and ceremonial rites, are not restricted to just church edifices. In this way the practice of Voodoo is appealing to all kinds of people, regardless of class or financial status.

The name for a Voodoo temple is an Oum'phors and it contains a partly enclosed area in the middle called a peristyle. In the center of the peristyle is the Poteau-mitan, which is a most significant center post that plays an integral part in almost all Voodoo rites. Among its many meanings, it acts like a cosmic axis and connects earth to sky.

Two ways that this Voodoo Loa communicates with "Her" worshippers were through dreams and possession. Possession is when the human body becomes a vessel or container for the loa to act and speak from. It is reminiscent of evocations and aspecting in traditional Wicca and, often time, it is also referred to as "ridding the loa", for indeed, the worshipper appears to be taken on a wild ride, as the mystere incarnates into its worshipper, completely taking over the body and ridding it like a horse. When Erzulie is in full possession of a serviteur (worshipper), they will often speak French, even if they have only spoken in the Creole language all of their life. For this opulent feminine spirit is all about status and class, something that the French culture and language exudes, *that is*, according to popular Haitian belief. It is quite a phenomenon to witness someone who may never even have had a proper education, as is the case for most citizens within impoverish countries, and to see them quite suddenly start speaking in French as a result of a possession. It only serves to confirm that the loa do exist. Along with crying lamentation for the world, you can expect to see her serviteurs dance with sensual movements (girating and slithering their hips) and flirt incessantly with the male gender. It goes without saying that a man possessed by Erzulie Freda is going to express very frilly, feminine mannerism and have eyes only for his gender, therefore uptight heterosexual men might want to steer clear of her, for she is a true lover of men.

Erzulie Freda can also be seen as a spirit of promiscuity. It was quite obvious that she relished and loved men. She enjoyed giving as well as being lavished with affection and was quite skilled at flirting. Her views on women were very different however. As Erzulie Dantor she was defender and very protective of women, but as Erzulie Freda, she was indifferent. Often depicted wearing three rings, which symbolize her three husbands, but interesting to note, her role with them appears to be more of a mistress than sole wife. Her Consorts were; Met Agwe (Lord of the Ocean), Ogou Ferraile (The Bold Warrior), and Damballah (The Wise White Serpent). Yet these three Voodoo loa were heavily invested in other prominent romantic relationships. For example, Agwe was said to have another wife in, La Sirene and, according to some Haitian writings, Damballah really loved Aida Wedo, (The Rainbow Spirit). Erzulie's third husband Ogou, had a strong attraction to Erzulie Dantor, who some considered Erzulie Freda's actual sister and not just an aspect of her.

This strong, iconic, Voodoo Feminine Spirit, is known to be very generous, but extremely demanding, with high expectation from her worshippers. It is not taboo to bargain with this Mystere, but be sure you remember your promise to her, for she will wreak havoc if you forget. When creating a shrine or altar for Erzulie, one is advised to use her favorite colors like baby pink and white. Never offer anything in the color black or red, as red is the color for her warrior sister, Erzulie Dantor.

An offering to Erzulie would not be complete without some kind of bouquet of flowers, like roses, champagne, and sweets; like chocolate, honey and candies. Generously court her and offer Erzulie Freda all the romantic accoutrements you would, to a new love in your life. She wouldn't expect any less from her worshippers. During

Voodoo ceremonies, mirrors (one of her sacred symbols), fine clothing and fancy jewelry was made available to the serviteurs, who would come down with this spirit. At all cost, one is discouraged from exposing her to dust, dirt or any kind of smoke for she detested these things. She loves cleanliness and order, so you would be wise to provide a clean altar for this Voodoo loa. Because she is known to be very jealous, it is also best not to share her altar with the worship of other deities or spirits. It is best not to offend her by having a shrine in her honor, in your bedroom, where intimate relations are expected to take place. Strangely, this might offend her or stir-up her powerful jealous streak. Remember that the loa are real spirits, with strong human-like personalies and that includes some sticky ones like, jealousy and spite. If these demands seem too intimidating, know that it is okay to make the occasional offerings to Erzulie without a permanent, established shrine to her. Also, according to Haitian folklore, you cannot invoke Erzulie without first getting a pass from Legba, for Legba is the door opener to the spirit realm. Connecting with Legba will allow you to worship and invoke any Voodoo loa you choose.

Another way to connect with Erzulie is through her Veve. Veves were sacred symbols drawn to invoke the Voodoo loa spirits and they were usually drawn over the floor with corn flour, spread across the ground or walls in special ceremonies. They were also drawn on doors and painted on ceilings and walls. It is quite a magickal act to re-draw one yourself, as you prepare to work with Erzulie. Redrawing a veve is quite meditative and almost becomes a sacred ritual to honor her, by its very nature. In this very simple act you will begin to feel her energy transpire. Another way to work with Erzulie and invoke her energy is through the common practice of ritual baths called *"Lave tet."* Since she is a spirit that loves fragrances, creating a ritual bath of clean rain water with basil, sugar and rose petals is a wonderful way to purify yourself before beginning a ritual for her, or as a ritual on its own. It is often suggested to bathe beforehand with a French fragranced soap and then create this sacred bath to soak in, while offering flattery to this beloved Voodoo Goddess. When you are finished, allow yourself to air dry.

Voodoo is an oral tradition but also initiatory, as some believe you cannot declare yourself a priestess of a Loa without proper initiation from a Hougan or Mambo. Finally, it is also highly recommended to study, respect and support the Haitian Culture of your chosen Voodoo Loa spirit, to receive the utmost blessings from them. Voodoo is not a textbook religion but rather a spiritual practice that can be understood and appreciated best when, experienced. To benefit and work positively with a spirit requires you to build a respectful, loving relationship, slowly, cautiously and with a sincere com-mitment. I suppose the same rules apply for any solid relationship, whether human or spiritual. All relationships require time, patience, nurturance and careful cultivation, and above all, love.

Take the time to get to know your loa and if you can, create a shrine for her. Spending time meditating and conversing with Erzulie Freda, daily, can open you up to the beauty of Voodoo and its intricate pantheon. In this way you build a personal relationship with your chosen Loa and will soon be gifted with their message(s).

Make special note, however, that there are times when a Loa spirit will just not be drawn to you. According to Hougan and author, Kenaz Filan, if you have been invoking a spirit for some time, with petitions and offerings and making special shrines while praying to a loa and nothing seems to change for you, perhaps this is not the right loa for you to work with or perhaps, just not the right time for you to connect. Remember the Loa are real, with complex personalities, and they will either genuinely like you and attach themselves to you and your cause, or show no interest... but rest assure you will know when they are at work in your life. Voodoo loa make themselves very well-known and very obviously so, and you will know, without a shadow of a doubt, when you are being blessed by them.

All Hails to you and Welcome Maitresse Erzulie Freda!

*Voodoo Loa of love, beauty, refinement and abundance, she is the embodiment of romance and those delightful luxuries of life. She, who demands nothing but the best, invites you now to hold the same standard for your own life. She awakens in you a desire to pursue prosperity, abundance and all that is juicy and good for you; including the right type of love. What are some of life's luxuries that you are willing to manifest at this time? Is your "Love" bringing you true fulfillment? Are you approaching life from a place of lack or from the rich fertile realm of abundance and appreciation? She enters your life at this time to awaken a desire for the finer things in life and calls you to treat yourself with reverence and love.

SRI LAKSHMI

SRI LAKSHMI

The name Lakshmi in the Hindu language denotes "Good luck." In Sanskrit text it comes from the word, "Laksya" which loosely means "a goal" or "an aim." In yet another text, the name Lakshmi has been interpreted to mean; a sign, an omen (good or bad). The first part of her name, "Lakh" means, a "hundred thousand," that is to say, a multitude and this supports the understanding that Lakshmi is a Goddess who bestows abundance, a multitude of blessings and prosperity.

Lakshmi or Sri Lakshmi, as she is best known in later Vedict text, is the Hindu Goddess of wealth, well-being and prosperity. Known by over one hundred eight different names, she is the radiant, golden one. She is known as Padma, Kamala in this role as the beautiful one who bestows riches, great fame and beauty. She is also the embodiment of the ideal wife in Hindu culture, as she exemplifies; chastity, truth and righteousness.

It is believed that Sri Lakshmi is actually the amalgamation of two Goddesses, for in the early Hindu sacred text we learn only of the Goddess Sri and this name, later in the Vedas, becomes appended to the name Lakshmi, evolving to Sri Lakshmi. These two respective Hindu deities hold numerous identical attributes that makes it nearly impossible to separate the two. To get a clearer insight into who we worship today as Lakshmi, it helps us to begin, by first taking a closer look and researching further this earlier version or aspect of her.

Scholars note that we don't even begin to see the name Sri Lakshmi in early Vedic text but we do find the isolated name Sri. Later, during the Upanishad period, we begin to unearth the acknowledgement and amalgamation of Sri Lakshmi as the supreme Hindu Goddess of wealth.

Sri is possibly a Pre-Vedic fertility Goddess possessing many of the same attributes as Lakshmi. A bringer of wealth, fortune, fertility, power and beauty, she was sought after by many, including those pursuing positions within royalty. According to author Carl Olson in his book, *The Book of the Goddess, Past and Present*," Sri might have been a pre-Aryan Goddess and possibly considered a Yakshinis, which were the feminine aspect of the Yakshas. Yakshas were semi-divine chthonic spirits and known to be guardians of wealth. In particular, Yakshinis, as feminine spirits, were guardians of the root of trees, as one can surmise the roots of trees and its overall good health and wellbeing, determine the potentiality for fruits, sustenance and richness upon the land and its inhabitants. It is the source for humanities nurturance and prosperity and a logical place for these beloved prosperity spirits to tend to. Yakshas were also known to be shape-shifters and they were attendants to another great, well known Hindu deity of wealth, Kubera. Interesting to note, much like Lakshmi, the Yakshinis were often linked with the waters of life.

"I invoke Sri Lakshmi who has a line of horses in her front, a series of chariots in the middle, who is being awakened by the trumpeting elephants, who is divinely resplendent. May that divine Lakshmi grace me. I hereby invoke Sri Lakshmi who is embodiment of absolute bliss; Lakshmi who is of pleasant smile on her face; whose luster is that of burnished gold; who is wet as it were, (just from the milky ocean) who is

blazing with splendor and is the embodiment of the fulfillment of all wishes; who satisfied the desire of her votaries; who is seated on the Lotus and is beautiful like the Lotus..." (a excerpt from the Hymn to Sri in the Sri Sukta)

More can be learned of Lakshmi through Sri when we look at early Hindu text. There is an appendix to the later Rig Veda text, which is the Sri-Sukuta hymn of praise to Sri. She is considered bountiful, giver of fame; abundance, gold, cattle, horses, food, prosperity and riches of all kinds. And she is said to eradicate her sister, Alakshmi, who is bringer of misfortune. Sri is described as radiant as gold, illustrious as the moon and wearer of both gold and silver necklaces. She is depicted as shinning like the sun; like fire, which is a most sacred, divine element for Hindu Spirituality. The Hymn of the Sri-Sukuta which pre-dates Buddhism, reveals her powers of fertility in the description of her scented moistness and as dwelling (as described) amidst cow dung and bringing an abundant harvest, for she was also associated with the plentitude of grains and rice. She is even attributed for having a son called, Kardama and this name translates as; mud, mire, slime. This links her closely to the rich soil of the dark, moist earth. Ancient worshippers of Sri Lakshmi are known to even anoint their foreheads with cow dung as well, during the Nilamata Purana festival. Another example of her fertile, moist attribute can be found in the Pancaratra text. There is a Lakshmi tantra in the Pancaratra, in which she is quoted saying, *"Like the fat that keeps a lamp burning, I lubricate the senses of living beings, with my own sap of consciousness (50:110)"*

In the Mahabhrarata (300 B.C.E. and 300 C.E.), Sri Lakshmi is considered the daughter of Brahma, though the God Brahma is often associated with another great Hindu Matriarch, the Goddess Saraswati. In one tale she has two brothers; Dhatr and Vidhatr and she is one of ten daughters of Daksha. In this particular myth she is given in marriage to the God, Dharma. Later, Sri Lakshmi becomes associated with the special attribute of Dharma (righteousness) as one of her many aspects and names.

In the Vaishnava texts, of the late fifth to sixth century C.E., Sri Lakshmi appears as the creative power of the God, Vishnu and she is the prakriti (life force) of the Universe itself.

In the Mahabhrarata, it is stated that she is born out of the sacred golden lotus that came forth from the brow or forehead of the God Vishnu, the preserver. And here again we have what appears to be a common tenet in Hindu mythology, that of the Goddess being both bride and daughter, much like Saraswati is considered daughter and bride to the God, Brahma. It wasn't until late 400 C.E. that we see a consistent connection to Sri Lakshmi and her steadfastness devotion and inseparability to the God Vishnu, whom she lives with in Vai Kuntha.

Some of Sri Lakshmi's symbols are the lotus, pouring water, vessels, gold, the owl, elephants and the colors; pink, dark gold, yellow, white. Sometimes she appears as golden as the sun or as yellow as the corn, which was an important food stable for Hindus. She might appear glowing white as a symbol of purity, the moon, the milky waters she is born from and her Divine righteousness. In her aspect as the dutiful loving wife she would appear in pink and rose hues. In the Mahabharata she is shown as wearing white robes and white clothing, emerging from the churning white, milky sea. When she is shown with her four hands she is holding;

1. Padma,
2. Sankha,
3. Amrtakalasa,
4. Bilva, a Fruit or a more citrusy fruit, Mahalinga.

When Sri Lakshmi is shown with eight hands it is a reference to the supreme Hindu Mother Goddess, Durga. In this aspect, she usually holds in her hands; a discus, mace, bow and arrow and the additional attributes of;

5. Dharma –righteousness,
6. Artha –wealth,
7. Kama- pleasure of flesh,
8. Moksa –beautitude.

One popular image of Sri Lakshmi is of her rising from a vessel, or also, rising from a lotus flower that is in a vessel. Like the Japanese Sun Goddess, Amatersu's association with the mirror, Lakshmi is distinctly linked with vessels. They are known for their receptacle, womblike quality, succinctly resembling the Yoni and their feminine qualities of containment, openness and universal receptivity. The Goddess of wealth is the ultimate sacred vessel and the Divine cornucopia; with its food association of nurturance and its open shape, it is a perfect example of her many gifts and relevance to women.

The Lotus is an extremely powerful ancient symbol in Hindu mythology. Often Sri Lakshmi is shown holding a lotus in each hand or sometimes holding her sacred fruit, the Bilva. The Bilva, much like the pomegranate, was a citrusy, sometimes bitter fruit associated with longevity and the removal of illusion (Maya) and misfortune. Lakshmi was known as, Mahamaya, as the Goddess who removed illusions and blessed women's womb.

According to the Brihadharma Purana, Lakshmi in her devout worship offered one thousand lotuses to the God Shiva daily. When one day she noticed she was missing one, she quickly offered, in its place, her breast and this was transformed into the sacred Bilva fruit.

Lakshmi is almost always adorned with lotus garlands and some text describes her adorned with gold and silver necklaces around her neck. Standing or sitting on a lotus, Lakshmi is often in yellow to represent her association with Gold, the sun and even the yellow nurturing corn. She was sometimes known as Gauri, linking her to these essential foods and grains in Hindu culture.

Another popular image of the Goddess Lakshmi can even be seen in the royal coinage of ancient times. One image found in the early coins of India, reveals Sri Lakshmi being showered by two elephants, one on her left and one on her right and these elephants are holding her sacred vessels, pouring or spraying her with water, as a sign of her fecundity. This popular image, known as Gaja Lakshmi, represents her fertilization gifts of wellbeing and earthly Goddess attributes.

There are eight known forms of Lakshmi and they are known as the Astamahalaksmi. Some of her most popular forms are mentioned below.

- Gaja Lakshmi -this most popular image of her found on door frames, and royal coinage, shows her seated on an eight petal lotus. She has four hands and a conch, framed by two elephants. They are shown pouring water over her.
- SamanyaLakshmi or Indra Laksmi, Here she is depicted with two hands in this role.
- Varalaksmi, holding two lotus in two hands and mudras in her other two hands she is known as Varalaksmi.

Other Sacred Names Sri Lakshmi is known by are;

1. Adi Lakshmi - here in this aspect known as Rama (bringer of happiness to humanity), and also known here as Indira (holder of lotus of purity) servant of the whole of creation via her consort. She resides with Lord Narayana/Vishnu in Vaikuntha. She is Shakti, energy and the source and power of Narayana.
2. Dhanya Lakshmi – Harvest aspect as Dhanya means grains. In this aspect she is the guarantor of good Harvest.
3. Dhairya Lakshmi – infinite Courage and strength are her gifts in this aspect. She grants patience and inner stability.
4. Gaja Lakshmi – daughter of the Ocean-a most common depiction of the Goddess being born from the churning ocean like the Greek Goddess Aphrodite. She is seated or standing from a Lotus flower, surrounded by two elephants on either side of her pouring water on her, from her sacred vessels. This most popular aspect of Lakshmi is even captured in the coinage of the time and can even be seen on entryways carvings and temples.
5. Santan Lakshmi -children and family blessings, in this aspect she blesses your family with many desirable healthy children and long life.
6. Vijay Lakshmi – Vijay is Victory and in this aspect Lakshmi presents the victory in all areas of your life.
7. Dhana Lakshmi – Dhana means wealth. In this aspect she imparts wealth in its numerous guises; love, health, intellect, prosperity, food, land etc...
8. Vidya Lakshmi - Vidya means education, thus in this aspect she imparts the numerous blessing that come from education including but not limited to sincerity, equanimity, adaptability, tenacity, generosity, purity, humility etc..

MORE OF HER SACRED SYMBOLS

Sri Lakshmi has a strong association with elephants, who are also sacred to the remover of obstacles, the God Ganesh. It makes sense that a Goddess so attached to the manifestation of prosperity would also be linked to the elephant God who removes obstacles and thus, elephants would play an important part in her own mythologies.

Long ago, it was believed that elephants had wings, and lived in the sky. Ancient Hindu mythology reveals that elephants were the clouds themselves, regulating rain showers upon the earth. The elephants lost their flying privileges and cloud connection when, according to one Hindu folklore, a Sage, one day, meditating under a tree was disrupted by the fall of one elephant. He cursed all elephants as a result, stripping them all of their wings and flying capabilities. Today, they still retain their great value to the Hindu culture, as we see them so often incorporated in marriage nuptials and other important Hindu ceremonies.

In ancient times, elephants were extremely important to Hindu Culture, as war artillery. They were considered weapons in wars, as valuable vehicles for the King to ride and as a sacred symbol of Royalty. The King always owned several of them and, as royalty, he was only fit to ride on the massive regal looking, elephants. Even the Rajasuya, a royal consecration ceremony, involved the abhisekha ritual in which the king would be blessed with the pouring waters from elephants to validate his Divine rights. This royal ritual mimicked the popular image of the Goddess herself being divinely showered by the elephant's pouring waters in the Gaja Lakshmi portrayals.

"There is a Goddess who possesses eyes like a Lotus flower (Padma, Kamala), her thighs are like the Lotus, she possesses a Lotus face and her skin is the color of the lotus. She dwells in this aquatic flower, sometimes envisioned as standing erect on the lotus and often holding the lovely flower in her hands. Once upon a time she was born from the lotus, her ears delighting to the trumpeting sounds of elephants...."

"The Book of the Goddess, Past and Present" by Carl Olsom, Chapt 10 page 125.

The Lotus is an aquatic, sacred flower born and rooted in the muddy waters, yet miraculously able to blossom and shine in its exquisite beauty, uncontaminated by the mud. It is one of the most recognized, venerated symbols of transcendence for Hindu and Buddhists, as it connotes spiritual authority. In this flower's wholeness and its ability to hold, nurture and water its own seeds, there is a divine reflection of the Universe itself and this links it to the Gods of the Hindu pantheon. We see the Lotus associated with many other deities, like Saraswati. It is also shown growing from Vishnu's navel as well as his forehead, where it is believed to have birthed the Goddess Lakshmi herself. Thus, the symbols of Divine source, purity, spiritual authority and the nectar of all creations, is represented in the Goddess Lakshmi through the Lotus flower.

Of all the creatures to be associated with the Goddess Lakshmi, it seems, at first glance, odd that the Owl would be one of them. The Owl, however, has often been associated with various deities from different pantheons; like the Greek Goddess of Wisdom, Athena, the Sumerian ancient Goddess, Lilith and the Welsh Flower-born Goddess, Blodeuwedd. The Owl is a sacred symbol of wisdom and divine insight and in Hindu mythology it is depicted as Lakshmi's vehicle. Known as an Uluka, in the Hindu language, the owl was also another name for Indra, the King of the Gods. One can only surmise that Lakshmi ridding an owl, or the King of the Gods, is a reference to her powers over anything connected with Kings and royalty. It is Sri Lakshmi who can bestow fame and fortune, fertility, longevity and success and thus, her blessings are sought after by all, especially those seeking sovereignty.

ROYALTY & COINAGE

We first see images of Sri Lakshmi appearing in coins during the Gupta Dynasty (320-540 C.E.) During the Samudragupta (ca.335-376), her image in the coinage is now seen on a throne with a lotus to hold her divine feet. And in the Chandragupta II (ca. 376-415) period we begin to see the King now portrayed on the opposite side of the coin holding a lotus in his hand, while Sri Lakshmi's image, an exact pose with the lotus, is revealed in support of the king, on the other side of the coin. By the Skandagupta period (ca. 454-467) Lakshmi is shown on the same side of the coin, standing right next to the King, who is holding a bowl. This is remarkable evidence of the King's Divine right to rule and Lakshmi's blessings on his kingdom. It was believed that only through her blessings of wealth, fame, longevity and wellbeing, could any King rule with much success and thus it is Lakshmi who blesses and ordains sovereignty. Sri was so valuable to a King that it was considered the actual cushion which the King must sit upon, for she bestowed not only prosperity and success but also physical health, longevity, beauty, and special blessings to the ruling Kingdom.

HER BIRTH

The Hindu Holy book of Srimad Bhaganata tells the story of Lakshmi's birth, known as Samudra Manthan. According to this sacred text, one day there was a battle between Demons and the Devas (minor Gods), and they both wanted the nectar of immortality, also known as Amrit. *(This story already sounds familiar, reminding me of the Norse tales of the Goddess, Idunna and the Apple of immortality for the Gods of Asgard, but I digress.....)* Desperate, the Devas consulted the God, Vishnu, who was now in the form of Kurma, the wise tortoise. Vishnu instructed them to churn the ocean floor; churn it and while they churned, the wise tortoise would endeavor to maintained and hold up the mount of Mandara on his back. Thus the Devas churned the ocean into a frothy milk and there unearthed Amrit, the Elixir of immortality, in the birth of Sri Lakshmi herself. Then as she appeared, Sri Lakshmi elected to reside in Vishnu's chest, his heart, making this her beloved dwelling place.

HER CONSORT

Most of Hindu mythology connects Sri Lakshmi to the God, Vishnu, also known as Narayana, among his numerous incarnations. She is inseparable from her consort and the sacred text of ancient times reveals that however Vishnu incarnates, Lakshmi is always there by his side; whether he appears as human or as creature; she too, almost always appears in a complimentary aspect to her consort. They have a relationship of supreme, tender love and for Hindus, an aspiring model of an ideal marriage. Lakshmi is viewed as the ideal dutiful wife, always tending to her partner's needs and comfort. She exemplifies devotion and self-surrendering to her husband and the embodiment of "Prema," an ideal love that rises above carnal desire. One common depiction of the Goddess by the feet of her reclining consort expresses their relationship best. In this image, Vishnu has one foot resting on the Divine Serpent, Sesha, and the other foot is upon his adoring dutiful wife, who appears to be massaging his foot, catering to his comfort.

Sri Lakshmi is held in high esteem as the model of a Hindu devoted wife, exemplifying chastity, beauty and controlled proper sexuality. Their marriage appears to be the personification of pure love, tenderness and profound fondness for one another, according to Hindu culture. The numerous depictions of the two together, gazing lovingly into each other's eyes, supports this conclusion, as well as the images of the two deities exchanging lower body parts, revealing their supreme unity.

Lakshmi is considered to be the energy or Shakti of Vishnu. Sometimes Vishnu is depicted with other wives like Sri and Pusti (prosperity) or Sri and Bhu (earth Goddess) but Sri Lakshmi herself always appears on his right side, denoting supremacy.

Interesting to note, when depicted with her husband, Sri Lakshmi only appears to have two arms, unlike the four arms she is typically attributed with, when depicted alone. She also sometimes appears diminutive in size compared to Vishnu and some believe this is yet another patriarchal representation of her subordination to her husband. I would like to think that perhaps with a loving strong spouse by her side the need for four hands becomes superfluous –maybe... or maybe her powers are so great that displaying them all at once on the table could threaten the patriarch, represented by the God Vishnu. Despite some of the interpretations of Hindu sacred text I've encountered, it is hard for me to view a Goddess, especially one of her great caliber, to be subordinate to anyone, let alone her mate but perhaps what we as humans interpret as lowly or subordination is really, in actuality, something effable and completely beyond our understanding in relation to ancient deities and spiritual beings.

She is known as the dispenser of grace. She grants all desires and salvation and she is the bestower of liberation. Lakshmi's worship has withstood the test of time. She is a Goddess still worshipped today much like in ancient times but it's important to note here her worship in relation to her consort, as she was widely worshipped both alone and in succinct connection to her husband. In the Maharashtra region of India, in the city of Pandharpur, there is a temple dedicated to the Divine Couple but interestingly enough, the shrine for Lakshmi is found in the Southern region of this temple, which, according to some Hindu scholars, was typically considered the region associated with dark, esoteric or demonic forces and the dead. Some might view this shrine's positioning, again, as a reflection of Lakshmi's subordination but remember, she was called upon to remove evil with her golden light, as well as to keep the dead at bay, so this placement makes perfect sense not as a place of subordination but as a critically compulsory and valuable for any temple.

As protecting powers of Vishnu, Lakshmi is known as;
- Sridevi- Goddess of wealth and fortune
- Bhudevi – earth representation
- Sridevi – again but as junior sort of consort Vishnu, symbol of sovereignty over the earth
- Saraswati- Mother of Learning
- Priti – Love personified
- Kriti and Santi – Fame and peace

- Tusti and Pusti – grants pleasure and strength
- When propitiated, she can dispel evil and bring prosperity –She eradicates Alaksmi, the opposite of Laksmi, a goddess of misfortune…

RELATING TO OTHER GODS

In some sacred text Sri Lakshmi is the wife of Dharma and her father is Daksa, the Virtuous conductor. Some other Hindu text reveals that she resided in Prahlada with the Demon God, Bali, when he succeeded in defeating the God Indra. And here we have a reflection of her attraction to the energy of Success and Victory, for she only draws near him due to his great achievement. Later on she withdraws from him when Vishnu intercedes on behalf of Indra to reclaim his power.

To the male rain God of Indra, who becomes the King of the Gods, she bestows Royal authority and powers. And there are images of the Goddess ridding Indra as an Owl. She appears and blesses the God Soma; Lord of plants, vegetation, associated with saps, when he performs a sacrifice in her honor. And as already mentioned, she is often associated with the God of Wealth, Kubera. Kubera is known as the Lord of Yakshas, the race of supernatural beings who dwell in uncivilized areas; like the wilderness and forest. They are guardians and distributors of wealth, and are linked with her early incarnation as the Goddess Sri. In Prajapati, it states that all the gods having witness Sri and her gifts of fortune, fame and prosperity, desired with all their heart to be blessed by her presence. The Gods, seeking the Elixir of Immortality, found it in her and thus, sought after her continuous blessings forever more, thereafter.

FESTIVALS

Lakshmi is a Goddess who has transcended all time as she is very much venerated today as in ages past. Her known month is October and coincidentally, her festival Dipavali (Diwali) is usually held in late autumn. Lakshmi's birth and wedding day are commemorated at this time, for three days, during Navarathri. And Friday is also a very special day for Lakshmi's celebrations. The Friday before the Full moon, of the month of Sraavan, is of great significance to her worship. Known as a festival of light, lamps are lit in her honor and there is merry making and lots of great celebratory noises to drive out any maladies or signs of her sister, Alaksmi. Merchants use this time to bless their financial documents, accounting logs and businesses plans. Sheep and goats are sacrificed and offered to the Goddess during some festival ceremonies and there is also cow dung veneration, for this is how the ancient sacred text depicts her; as the moist, fertileness of her sacred animal's dung. Her close associated with cows, due to their nurturing attributes, is very reminiscent of the Egyptian Divine Bovine, the Goddess Hathor.

Lakshmi Puja is celebrated, again, on the Full moon night of the Kojagari Purnima. At this time of the year, in late autumn, she is also called upon to keep the ghost of the dead away from the living. It is not surprising that this festival coincides with the ancient Pagan/Druid holiday of Samhain and the themes of the final harvest, surviving the darkness and the propitiating of the dead, as these are the prevalent theme at this time of year.

Kaumundi Purnima Festival -In this festival, women honor her in the mounds of seeds and grains and together they recollect the ancient tales, quite similar to the Greek Goddess Demeter, in which Lakshmi had temporarily disappeared from the Earth taking away her gifts of prosperity from the land. They pay homage to her gifts in the hopes of never experiencing her devastating withdrawal from the world.

Caitra-Gauri Festval -Held during the second month of spring. Here in this festival Lakshmi is celebrated for her vegetative attributes to the land.

Durga Puja-Here in this festival, Lakshmi is also celebrated as another aspect of the divine mother and in her agricultural association. She is supplicated to bring back the crops, make them abundant and fertile. This festival takes place at the Full-Moon following the Durga Puja.

Pujabi Festival-In this festival Lakshmi is exalted with gratitude for her fertile, womb blessings. Women celebrated her with colored cord representing each child they were able to conceive and offering these cords in gratitude to Sri Lakshmi's blessings.

There is also a festival in the **Summer** time that honors both Sri Lakshmi and Vishnu in their role as the ideal Divine couple. In this festival sometimes Vishnu is known to take on a second wife or he is believed to hibernate and fall asleep for a long period, either way, he will not be available to his beloved Lakshmi. At this time, worshippers call upon the Goddess and her gifts of steadfastness, loyalty, truthfulness, and strength within all relationships.

Gobardhan Puja - In this festival Lakshmi is celebrated as the fertile, prosperous giving mother and exalted as an incarnate Bovine.

The Goddess of abundance, beauty, royalty and prosperity is very much alive and worshipped today as she was in years past. She has transcended time and has remained a beloved immortal Hindu Goddess that speaks to our gender on the exclusively unique gifts of the Feminine Divine. She introduces yet another important aspect of the sacred feminine, one that is sought after by both men and women who seek to know success, victory, beauty and abundance.

SOME MANTRAS DEDICATED TO LAKSHMI AND MANIFESTING ABUNDANCE

1. *Om Shreem Mahalakshmiyei Namaha*
   Salutations to that heart centered and great Lakshmi....
2. Kubera Yantra, for the Banker of Heaven
Chant:
Om Brezee Namaha (108x)
27, 20, 25
22, 24, 26
23, 28, 2
3. *Om Brzee Namaha Dattatreya*
4. *Om Shreem brezee namaha*
5. *Om Shreem, Om Hreem, Shreem, Hreem,*
Kleem, Shreem, Kleem, Vitteswarei (continuous repetition of her seed mantra)

6. *Shreem, Shreem, Shreem…..*
   Reciting her seed chant 108x daily also is very effective.
7. *Om Shreem Hreem Shreem Kamale Kamalaleyi*
Praseed Praseed, om Shreem Hreem Shreem MahaLaxmiyei Namaha….
   Translation: Underlying vibration of all creation, abundance please, cherishing your lotus feet, be pleased Great Lakshmi Goddess, I bow to You. *Youtube, Lilasakura, Recording sung by Shri Anandi Ma's group and Dileepji, from CD "Mantra for Abundance." Published by Sounds True also see Youtube by Lilasakura*
8. *Om Kleem, Shreem Lakshmi (another popular mantra exalting the Goddess, Lakshmi)*
9. *Om Hrim Shri Lakshmi Bhyo Namaha*
Check out, Youtube by Sainath459
10. *Om Shreem MahaLakshmiyei Swaha*

<u>Om</u> *seed sound for the 6^{th chakra that commences most mantras} , where the masculine and the feminine meet in the brow.*

<u>Shrim</u> *second seed sound for the principle of abundance*

<u>Maha</u> *means "great all" referring to quality and quantity*

<u>Lakshmi</u> *is Sanskrit word meaning the energy of abundance*

<u>Swaha</u> *new levels of energy rise uttering this simple principle of abundance.*
For more info see, Youtube by wealthful

11. <u>*Lakshmi Gayatri:*</u>
"Om Mahalakshmyaye cha Vidmahe, Vishnu patnyai cha dhi-Mahi, Tanno Lakshmihi prachodayat.."
Translation: Om. Let us meditate on the Great Goddess Sri Lakshmi, the consort of Sri Maha Vishnu. May that effulgent Maha Lakshmi Devi, inspire and illuminate our minds with understanding.

12. *Om Hreem, Shreem, Lakshmi Bhyo Namaha…*
Translation: Om, Goddess Lakshmi, resides in me and bestow sthy abundance on all aspects of my existence…   *Source: www.freemeditationinfo.com*

   *The Hindu Goddess of Prosperity, Beauty and Love has garnered quite the reputation throughout the years and as one can surmise, she has a myriad of devout worshippers. The beautiful, Sri Lakshmi, is often depicted in gold, bejeweled from head to toe, accompanied by the elephant God, Ganesh. She represents our feminine beauty, fecundity and prosperity. She enters our realm to make us aware of our many riches and our potential to maintain and manifest even more. She is the abundant golden Harvest itself with her great beauty and palpable ripeness and she beckons you to embrace, with gratitude, the gifts of abundance, love and beauty.

BENZAITEN

BENTEN/BENZAITEN

Benten is the Japanese, Shinto Goddess of Good Fortune and Prosperity, one of the few Japanese Goddesses connected to Prosperity. She is connected to white serpents and is often depicted riding a serpent or a dragon. In Japan, Benten is also known as Queen of the Sea and many portrayals of this Goddess reveal her connection to the element of water. It is interesting to note that there is also a strong similarity to the Hindu Goddess Saraswati, as both are often portrayed playing a stringed instrument; Benten plays the "*biwa.*"

GEFJUN

Also known as; Gefyun, Gefyon, Gefn, Gefiun, Gefion, Gefjun, is an ancient agricultural Norse Goddess of Prosperity, Fertility, Magick, Wellbeing and Protection. She was beloved to the Norse-Germanic people as a Goddess of field ploughing, and connected to manifesting the Danish Island of Zealand. Known as, "The Generous one," her name is associated with the verb, "*gefa*" which means to give. It is therefore indicative of her connection to abundance and generosity.

Our knowledge of this beloved ancient deity comes from the writings of the 13th century acclaimed historian, Snorri Sturluson. He shares a story in his writings about a woman that comes before the King, Gylfi, in Sweeden asking for land. Not suspecting her gifts and unaware of her Goddess status, the charitable king offers her, "*as much land as 4 oxen can plough in one day...*" Well, Gefjun invokes her four sons, which were fathered by a giant and she turns them into these four strong oxen. With their help, she successfully ploughs the land in one day and manages to connect the terrains and forms the Danish Island of Zealand. Today this land is known as Copenhagen.

FORTUNA

Fortuna is the Roman Goddess of Good Fortune. Her name mean, *"she who brings…"* Her role is therefore that of one who brings to us prosperity and abundance. As a Goddess of the Abundance, she is often portrayed holding an overflowing cornucopia. She rules over our fates and good fortune.

TYCHE

Tyche is the ancient Greek Goddess of Good Fortune, Fate and Prosperity. She is worshipped in this aspect as the Goddess, Eutychia. Her name translates as "luck," "chance" or "fortune."

She is often depicted, just like her Roman counterpart, Fortuna, holding a cornucopia. However, in some statuary depictions she is seen wearing a crown made up of the walls of a city, to denote her connection to a city's success. Sometimes she is portrayed with a blindfold over her eyes to indicate her title as the blind Mistress of Fortune, and the unpredictable nature of blind fate, blind justice, and blind luck and the game of chance. Some mediaeval art shows her with wings, holding a ship rudder (often two) or a ball to signify the up and down unpredictability of fortune. She is illustrated with a Wheel of Fortune, indicative of her powers over our changeable fate. It's important to know she also appears on many Hellenistic coins that existed before the Christian era. These coins attest to her prominence as a Goddess of good fortune.

Tyche had many known Temples in Constantinople, Alexandria, and Maritima to name just a few. In Crete, she was highly venerated at Itanos.

She is mentioned in numerous writings of the time, including, Hesiod's works. He noted that she was the daughter of the Titans; Oceanus and Tethys. This genealogy was later disputed, connecting her with Zeus. According to other Greek mythology she is daughter of Aphrodite and Hermes, making the Goddess of Good Fortune the result of unifying love and intellect.

CHAPTER FIVE

HOME
SHE WHO VALUES HER SANCTUARY

HINA

HINA

Hina is the Hawaiian Goddess of the Moon. Her name, translates as "girl" or "woman" and sometimes even more precisely as "woman in the moon." Hina, in Polynesian and Tahitian cultures, connotes the feminine spirit. According to Hawaiian cosmology, the first Gods to step foot on the great Island of Hawaii were Ku and Hina; respectively, male and female. Ku was viewed as the rising Sun, the East and Hina his opposite, the west and the setting sun. This links her directly to the Moon. Hina embodied all the attributes of a Moon Goddess. She ruled over Fertility and intuition and she ruled over the waters; the ebb and flow of life and procreation. Hina also reigned over planting, agriculture and the fishing cycle.

As the first female Goddess of Hawaii, she ruled over the procreation and population of her people. Much like the Greek Goddess Gaia, Hina is seen as the great Mother of the Polynesian people. She created a number of impressive descendants, like the Pig God, Kamapua'a and Maui, the demigod. Hyphened and variations of her name can be found in several other Goddesses throughout Hawaiian mythology. There are also some references to Hina as a triple Goddess, much like many significant, ancient Goddesses throughout mythologies of various cultures. She was attributed for bringing numerous gifts to the Hawaiian people including the revered coconut.

According to one myth, Hina, in the heavens, was so enamored by the lush landscape of Hawaii that she decides to descend upon it and make it her temporary home. Hina came down from the cosmos and made the island of Maui her abode and there, she fell in love with a mortal. She married a man known as a great warrior. Together they lived in Ka'uiki, under the volcano called, Haleakala. As the Hawaiian lore reveals, most of her days were spent working hard, pounding the Kapa board to make fine craftsmanship textile and clothing. She was known to make magic with her extraordinary Tapa cloth and her contribution to Hawaiian Textile was significant.

Once married, she gave birth to two half-human, half-deified children. Everyday Hina worked very hard, fetching water and fresh shrimp for her family. She also worked hard on her Tapa cloths but as time went on, her husband became very lazy, expecting her to do everything because, after all, she was a Divine Goddess. Her half-blood children, also became too much to handle, as they too adopted their father's laziness and arrogance. They were known to be quite mischievous and extremely demanding of their mother.

According to a popular Hawaiian lore, one day, when Hina was out by the river working, she caught sight of the most beautiful rainbow (although in some stories they say she had the ability to manifest rainbows herself). In this story she tried to climb up the rainbow to join the brilliant light of the Sun that called, but the heat of the mid-day sun was too much for her to handle and she could not bear it. After exhaustibly trying to climb it, she fell and slipped off the rainbow. Then, over heated and weakened, she fainted and passed out. Some time passed by before she finally woke up in the early evening hours. Frantically worried for her family, she got up quickly and rushed back home. As one would suspect, when she returned home, her abusive husband, needless to say, was furious. He berated her stronger than usual. The children also added insults to their mother, angered that their precious dinner had not been prepared.

Late at night, when they had all fallen fast asleep, Hina longingly stared out at the window and there presented before her, was another brilliant light that once again captivated her heart- the light of the Full moon. She remembered the light of the sun beckoning her in the day time and yet, here was another brilliant light strongly urging her to come again. It was then that her heart stirred and she felt the strong urging to leave her misery behind and unite with the familiar divine light before her. She wasted no time and immediately packed her bag with her prized calabash and tapa cloth. Hina endeavor to take only her most cherished possessions with her. One look at the brilliant light of the moon and she was enamored by its comforting light. She knew there was peace and harmony within the moon.

Enchanted by the glow, she was determined, more than ever, to leave her painful situation on earth; to go and join this beloved light, now beaming from the moon. This light was a spark of remembrance, a familiarity she had long forgotten that was now being restored to her via, the Moon.

A rainbow appeared, as if by magic, she manifested this sacred vehicle to lead her to her Divine destination. As she began her climb, she was invigorated and felt a renewed determination to reach the moon. Alas, she was getting closer, when all of a sudden; she felt the sensation of her leg being pulled. It was him...her abusive, earthly husband. He caught sight of her trying to escape and he violently tugged and pulled on her leg. He threatened her and screamed at her, not to go...but this only made her more determined to leave. With all of her Divine strength she pushed onward, towards the Moon. But he was strong and had the strength of a warrior. He pulled and pulled and with a mighty force he yanked her foot right off. He severed Hina's foot and, simultaneously, fell down to the ground, while she managed to muster up enough strength to continue onward on her journey, until she made it safely inside the moon.

Within the moon Hina found rest, peace and eventually was able to heal, recuperate and grow a new foot. Legend says she still feels throbbing in her foot as a reminder of what she endured and left behind on earth. Hawaiians today still worship Hina and seek her reflection in the full moon. She continues to be revered as the beautiful Lady of the Rainbow-Beloved Feminine Goddess of the Moon.

Hina Musing -Creating Sanctuaries

Our beloved Polynesian Goddess of the moon and her legends can be seen as a metaphor for women in need of safety. Whether it is a safe place, in our own individual mind/soul, or an actual physical place or room. Our safe space can be found in a number of places, like rituals (whether solitary or within a group) or a special meditation that transcends and transports us there. Even a simple prayer (as one envisions Hina reciting to the light of the moon she saw from her window) can bless us with a sanctuary. In times of stress, we can utilize our imagination and simply visualize this sacred temple or we can actually create it physically. Either way, Hina and her most popular myth, teaches us the importance of this sacred space for women and encourages us to find our freedom.

When we are feeling hopeless, overwhelmed and confused in our daily living or when sadly, our own lives are compromised and threatened, a personal sanctuary becomes absolutely invaluable. It allows us a chance to regroup and rethink our personal situation. It allows us an opportunity to find healing and renew our sense of self-worth. Sometimes this sacred sanctuary, whether real or imagine, can make the difference between life and death for some women.

Having endured so much abuse on earth, Hina reaches that pivotal point when she begins to long for freedom and an exodus from the pain. Hina's escape into the divine Moon and the very act of selecting it as her new home is symbolic of this transformative phase in her life. The moon, which has always been a symbol of intuition and feminine spirituality, becomes her sanctuary and she looks upon it now, as her way out of her unhappiness –the Moon thus becomes her "savioress." Herein the Moon is Hina's safe place, to retreat from her troubles -in this case, her lazy human husband and half blood, mischievous children.

Inside the Moon, she endeavors to heal, regroup, regain her sense of self and reconnect with something that goes so deep, far deeper into her lineage and ancestry than she could possibly begin to understand intellectually. But she comprehends it intuitively, and the call is to her soul, which has no boundaries, or timelines and unquestionably, she can no longer deny the call. Hina follows her intuition and goes inside the nurturing, grandmother moon that calls unto her, leaving behind her stressors and those painful earthly trials and tribulations. She finds her liberation within the moon.

It is also quite a powerful metaphor is when we get to the part of the lore when her leg is severed. At the most pivotal point, when she was approaching her sacred place, her scoundrel of a husband grabbed her leg, pulling and violently yanking it- not letting her go, not letting her take care of herself. He pulled her so hard that her foot breaks off. Yet the Goddess perseveres, abandons her severed, bloody foot and continues on her journey towards the moon. She knows then the value of her freedom and is willing to sacrifice even her foot, to attain it. There is a powerful message here, for we learn that, sometimes, there are parts of us that must be cut off and severed, before beginning any journey of self-healing and self-discovery. As the cutting off of a foot is bloody and violently painful, it is what Hina must face and endure before reaching her sacred sanctuary within the Moon.

The husband tugging at her foot can be seen as a symbol of our obligations and our roles, making every effort to tug, break and defeat us. And sometimes this gruesome act, being fueled by selfishness, anger and volatility, is so intense, that indeed, parts of us are broken in the process of our healing. The husband, in this case, is that which keeps us in the perpetual state of hopelessness, bondage, paralysis, keeping us where we are or where we have always been.

Sometimes our obligations and responsibilities keep us stagnant and, in the only place we've probably ever known, thus blocking us from any further growth. Opportunity for change and transformation are stunted. That tugging of the leg is symbolic of being blocked from what could essentially transform us... improve us and give us wings. Her foot is tugged and ripped like the clipping of a bird's wings (or an attempt to do so) right at the critical moment it's about to take flight. In this case, Hina did not let this sabotage her flight and, with mutilated "wings" (aka leg) she continued on her journey.

Oftentimes, those you least expect, those you believe love you the most, are the ones that can impede your progress in life. Those beloved people or situations can try to stunt our own personal growth and transformation, like Hina's husband and family. It can be a brother or sister, a mother, father, relative, lover, boyfriend, girl-friend, professor, boss, even a mere acquaintance. Sometimes it's a deliberate action and sometimes it's on another unconscious level or even a dark part of our own psyche, but the intent remains the same, to keep you in your place.

In Hina's tales we learn of the importance to care for our own selves as womyn and the value in finding our own personal sanctuary, whether it's "Calgon moment" in our sudsy bathtubs, an elaborate candle light ritual or trance meditation or in severe cases, a woman's shelter or friend's home. Our sacred sanctuaries are Important to define and possess, as we go through life's numerous trials and tribulations and endeavor to grow spiritually. She is symbolic of women awakening to their need for freedom, independence, self-care, and safe sanctuaries in their lives. In Hina, we find a brilliant Goddess that, according to her lore, recognized her need for freedom from those who had tried to oppress or control her. She is beckoned by the rainbow and the divine light of the moon and instinctively recognizes the value of this peaceful sanctuary. Hina invites us to seek and embrace those journeys that will inevitably bring peace, freedom and great transformation.

*Hina is the primordial Polynesian rainbow Goddess, who makes the ancient Moon her home. She comes into your life to remind you of the sacredness and necessity of your freedom and the need to create your personal sanctuary. She arrives at this point in your life to ask you, *"Do you have a personal space that nourishes and heals you and keeps you protected?"* Where can we retreat to regain ourselves? Physical vacations are common and act as our temporary escape where we may touch upon a certain type of freedom but, what if we have available to us, a mental and spiritual place to retreat to, whenever situations require an escape? The question she now presents to you is, *"Can you find your freedom?"* *"When confronted with toxic situations or people and negative relationships, are you able to find a sacred space (within) to guard and recharge yourself? Are you able to manifest safety, serenity; a liberated peace of mind?"* She enters your life at this time and beckons you to erect your core spiritual home and unearth a place of peace. With the Goddess Hina you are invited to create Sacred Space & your personal Sanctuary.

HESTIA

HESTIA

Hestia is the keeper of the Sacred flames on Mount Olympus and was highly respected and regarded as one of the original twelve Olympian Gods/Goddesses. According to numerous ancient writings, first offerings were always offered up to Hestia and her flames were the first lit. She was revered and greatly cherished by all Gods and mortals alike.

Greek Goddess of the Hearth and Home, Hestia is the personification of Hearth Flames. Her Roman counterpart was the Goddess Vesta. She is a Fire Goddess and her name literally means *"heart."* In Latin, the word is interpreted to mean *"Focus."* The hearth, in a domicile, was indeed considered to be the focus and heart of all dwellings and thus, she is embraced throughout the ages, as the patron Goddess of Hearth and Home. Her symbol is the infinite, sacred circle and in ancient Greece, a circular Hearth Fire was a place of reverence for this beloved deity.

Not much is known about this ancient Virginal Goddess, but what we DO know, we have learned mostly through her rituals, the Homeric invocations and her worship, documented in the writings of her time. For example; the hearth, in most Greek homes, was considered the center of the home. The architecture of the time reflected its importance as most homes were built around this important entity. One common documented rite that reveals Hestia's importance was the blessing of a newborn. When a baby was first born to a family and the child was five days old, they would walk around their hearth, the center of their home, presenting the child to Hestia for her divine blessings. Afterwards they would commemorate the event by having a huge feast in gratitude for her blessings.

Another documented rite, that has still survived the ages, involves the blessings of newlyweds. It was customary for the mother of the bride to light a torch from her hearth fires and bring that light into the newlyweds' home, to reflect the undying flames of lineage, being passed down from one generation to the next. Here too, Hestia's blessings would be invoked for a happy marital home life. Today this tradition continues only more subtly, via the unity candles incorporated in many marriage ceremonies, as bride and groom light one flame from the joining of their own, two, respective candles.

Hestia was greatly adored as the oldest of the Olympian Gods. She was the first born child of the Goddess Rhea and the God Cronos and thus was the oldest sister to all the Olympian Gods and Goddesses. As a result she was also the beloved Aunt of the second generation of Olympian Gods. Hestia was one of the first Olympian Goddesses on Mount Olympus, but was later replaced, in Greek mythology, with the God of Wine, Dionysus. Sadly, some believe this is reflective of a society that was already starting to undervalue the importance of wisdom, traditions and spiritual enlightenment -attributes Hestia represented and defended.

As Vesta, in Rome, her fires were attended to by the Vestal virgins, who took vows of celibacy as part of their initiations and service to her. They were supposed to be human, living embodiments of Vesta/Hestia herself, who was often depicted as pure and bright, a living flame, and thus the Vestal virgins had strict rules to live by. They were severely punished if they dared deviate from their role as celibate priestesses. Young girls, no older than six, were recruited to Hestia's service and their hair and clothing were unified to create anonymity within the priestess-hood community.

The Goddess Hestia was rarely depicted in female flesh form, but rather as a flame, a spirit, a feeling of warmth and comfort. All of her attributes are deemed helpful for those in leadership roles. Her immortal spirit continues to live on today as she transcends all time and space. As a Virgin Goddess, she was an advocate for wommin's spirituality and was sometimes compared to Sophia, the Gnostic Goddess of Wisdom.

Hestia is synonymous with purity, sincerity, and spiritual devotion. As the oldest of the Virgin Goddesses, Hestia was one of three Deities unaffected by Aphrodite's charms and love enchantments. However, Aphrodite did manage to arouse great love for the beautiful Hestia, in both the God of the Sea, Poseidon and in the Sun God, Apollo. The chaste Goddess refused both of their advances, choosing to dedicate herself to her role as Goddess of the Hearth and vowing to remain pure and unfettered by romantic love liaisons.

She espoused celibacy and valued Spirituality above sensuality and derived great pleasure and satisfaction simply being herself, honored in the home, and being of service to humanity and her Divine family. Many of the myths of the time, are all in an agreement that Zeus was quite supportive and respectful of his older sister, thus he willingly (according to patriarchal writings) gave her the honored place of the hearth in the center of the home, as the ultimate expression of reverence to this Goddess. At Mount Olympus, hers were the first sacred flames lit, always in her honor first and she was given dominion over the entire maintenance of this Divine home. Unlike other virginal deities, she really does appear fully whole unto herself, content with simply being and serving her Olympian family and the whole of humanity with her sacred flames. She was disinterested in the power, drama and notoriety her siblings were incessantly engaged in.

When I think of Hestia I think of calm, tranquility and the embodiment of a deep spiritual love and peace. I think of profound devotion to high ideals and service to our family traditions, our tribe, and our community and home. With Hestia, I reflect on those things that bring about stability and serenity, as she was never documented being involved in any of the numerous quarrels or disputes between the Gods. Hestia is the comfort and safety of our hearth fire, our core, our heart, our spirit and thus, both our internal and external homes.

Goddess of the Hearth and home, today she is still venerated and tended to with great honor. Hestia still lives on in the flames we tend to - the flames of our hearth found in the core of our homes and the flames we tend to in the core of our spirits and souls. Hestia is the flame that sparks our inner desire to be of service to humanity.

Greek Goddess of the Hearth and one of the beloved twelve Olympians, Hestia is the immortal Maiden Goddess. She is the embodiment of our hearth fires, the flames of our spirit and the core of our very being. Hestia comes to remind you to honor that part of yourself that is in tuned with the Feminine Divine and the archetypal leader. It is Hestia that invites you to tend to your inner flames, for they light the way for others. She arrives with the gifts of old, venerated traditions and honored communal customs that extend our families & home. With Hestia, it is time to honor your journey and give thanks to all those who have added the invaluable, loving, diverse, golden threads of your strong communal tapestry. She invites you to begin to create traditions, structures in your home life and communities that will stand the test of time. She is longevity and traditions, afterall. Hestia, in ancient Greece, was the oldest among her Olympian sibbllings. They looked to her for wise counsel and prudent leadership. Let her surviving ancient hearth fires stir and inspire your heart to serve your home, as she served on Mount Olympus.

IXCHEL

IX CHEL

The Goddess Ix Chel [Pronounced: *ee shEll*] is the ancient Mayan Goddess of the Moon. Also known as "Lady Rainbow," due to her association with moisture and rain, she rules over the various phases of the moon and thus, a woman life. Ix Chel is a Goddess that rules; fertility, creativity, sexuality, intuition, and childbirth. Known also as a patron Goddess of expectant mothers and the healing and medicinal arts, she is the Goddess of artisans and weavers. Textiles, decorative cloths and weaving were sacred women's handicraft, considered very important in many cultures, including Central and South America. Ix Chel was called upon to bless young girls with this vital and prosperous skill.

As Goddess of the Moon, which rules over the ebb and flow of the ocean waters, it is not surprising, all waters are her domain. She is the patron Goddess of intuition which also falls under the Moon's realm. This Lunar Deity was in charge of regulating the waters that can bestow fertility onto the land or great destruction, with her uncontrollable floods. In this respect, she is seen as a Goddess of abundance and fruitfulness, in the same way that Demeter and Gaia (Earth Goddesses) are seen as bringer of abundance and fruitfulness to their native land.

According to some mythologies it is believed that the well documented (Haiyococab) flooding of the Earth, many years ago, was attributed to Ix Chel who unleashed her sacred waters from a giant earthen vessel. As the legends describe it in this part of Mayan cosmology, she poured out her waters upon the earth to cleanse it and revitalize new growth. In this depiction we see her great powers as a water deity providing nurturance and quenching the earth's thirst. But here, we also see her potentially destructive nature if she inundates us, pouring forth an inordinate amount of water with the potential to destroy.

As a water deity she was also regarded as a Goddess of medicine and healing. In ancient times, it was believed she would approach and tend to the sick. If proper supplications and offerings are made, some claim to see her shadow, as a crone, by the foot of the bedridden and it was believed she could heal, as well as make the transition smoother for those who would need to cross over into the realm of the dead. The rising smoke from a smudge of Copal and tobacco would draw her near, as well as other offerings like; guava tips, sap of a rubber tree, turkey broth, haaz papaya and pulverized crab powder. Here was a Goddess who unquestionably ruled over the realms of life and death for Mayan people.

Ix Chel also has been seen as Goddess of creativity and commerce in her ability to inspire and teach wommin to provide for themselves by way of their handicrafts and creative arts. A Goddess of wommin who need autonomy and financially independence, She thus became a patron Goddess of weaving and textile because these were the skills and trade accessible for wommin to excel in. One myth tells of her intense concentration upon a spider weaving her web and from this act, she was able to pass on this critical knowledge and imperative skill (which would prove to be profitable) to wommin on earth. Textile knowledge, like how to work with looms, spinning cotton, and how to dye cotton in various colors, were examples of her Divine gifts to wommin. Most importantly she championed wommin's use of their sacred hands in various hand-crafts, artistry and numerous creative and profitable outlets.

She was sometimes depicted holding a sacred urn (vase) upside down, which was a symbol of her watery wombs being released upon the earth. Water lilies were also sacred to her. This Mayan Goddess of the Moon was most beloved by wommin because of her well documented ability to impart fertility and ease in child birthing. It was a custom, in ancient times, for all pregnant wommin or those wanting to conceive, to make the journey to her famous Shrines in Cozumel or "Isla de Mujeres," for it was believed that in these sacred waters, fertility and her blessings were guaranteed.

As a Moon Goddess, she unquestionably rules over all the waters; including the waters of our womanhood, our blood, our urine, our moisture, sexuality, amniotic fluids and childbirth. Her Shrines can still be found today on the island of Cozumel, near the Yucatan Peninsula… just to the northeastern coast of the Peninsula. A quick Google search on the internet will provide a list of numerous tour companies eager to share Ix Chel's Temples, waters, caves and ruins, still accessible today.

As an ancient deity, Ix Chel was known as a triple Goddess that could take the form of a beautiful young maiden, brushing her long hair upon the moon, or as a nurturing mother helping her people or as a crone; a hag with a skirt of bones. Other popular images show her with a crown of snakes upon her head, pouring water from an earthen vessel. Still other depictions show her as a voluptuous, naked, sensual enchantress alongside her totem animals; the hare, the snake or the jaguar. Sometimes she is depicted with eagle feathers and was known also as "Eagle Woman" because the eagle was known as a messenger of the Moon. For the people of Guatemala, Campeche and the Yucatan region she was considered the First woman of the world, and thus, a mother deity who gave birth to all succeeding women and Goddesses.

THE STORY OF IX CHEL and THE SUN

According to Mayan cosmology, the earth began with two very bright, luminous beings in the sky; the Sun and the Moon. The Moon, Ix Chel, was known to be the most beautiful enchantress, but she had a notoriously jealous grandfather who guarded her carefully and as her numerous tales reveal, her life was plagued by this theme of jealous, oppressive beings, trying to control her. The Sun God, was in love with Ix Chel and he infatuatedly watched her daily, although in some tales it is Ix Chel who is greatly enamored by the Sun God, Kinich Ahau. While she was actively pursued by numerous deities, she only had eyes for the great Sun God and she tries to attract his attention, despite her vicious, jealous grandfather's threats.

One Mayan Tale, reveals that Kinich Ahau, the Sun, endeavoring to endear Ix Chel and get closer to her, disguised himself as a Hummingbird. In his Hummingbird form he flew to her home and as a bird he was quite welcomed by the Goddess. She offered him honey from the tobacco flower and as they were sharing a quiet moment, the hummingbird fell down, wounded by a fierce clay pellet that had been shot and aimed at him by her jealous grandfather. With great empathy, she quickly safeguarded the helpless bird and nursed him to health in the privacy of her room. According to folklore, this very act awakened and stirred in her, deep, unknown affections for him. When he recovered and flew robust and full of life again, he revealed his true identity and convinced her to leave her home and her monstrously, oppressive grandfather and so... they fled together.

When Ix Chel's grandfather caught sight of the two luminous divine lights escaping, he became greatly infuriated and in his raged he called upon the assistance of Chac, the one who controlled lightning and the storms. According to this tale Chac hurled lightning bolts to both the Sun and the Moon deity as instructed by her grandfather. Although they appeared to be able to retreat momentarily into the water, Ix Chel as a crab and the Sun as a turtle, the Moon Goddess was not able to escape. She was eventually killed by the lightning bolt. In another tale, it is Ix Chel's grandfather himself that aims and shoots the lightning directly at Ix Chel, killing her instantaneously.

The next part of this ancient tale is retold differently by various accounts, but they all reveal a great deal about Ix Chel's sacred symbols and her connection to dragon flies, the number thirteen, death and resurrection and snakes. Some tales tell that while she lay lifeless, thirteen dragonflies sung to her and brought her back to life. Another story tells of how her lifeless body was nursed for thirteen days by a multitude of celestial dragonflies, that sang to revive her. And in this particular story we learn of how the dragonflies created thirteen hollow logs and on the thirteenth night, twelve logs broke open to reveal twelve divine snakes -while the thirteenth log, broke open to reveal the Goddess Ix Chel, alive, resurrected and brilliant, once more. The Sun God, who had been mourning her death up to that moment, rejoiced to see her come back to life, bright and whole. He immediately proposed marriage to his beloved and she agreed. Together they set up their home in the heavens, side by side, they were also believed to have given birth to the four Jaguars Gods, who became the guardians of the four corners of the world. But alas, married life soon proved to be very difficult and more challenging than anticipated for the Moon Goddess.

The Sun's brother, the morning Star, Chac Noh Eck, was known to visit their marital abode much too often and apparently he appeared to be quite fond of the Moon too, lingering closer to her than to the Sun himself. This made the already hot tempered, volatile Sun, extremely jealous. He accused the brilliant Ix Chel of unthinkable infidelities with his brother, Chac Noh Eck. Lashing out cruel words and false accusations, he refused to hear her defense, and the Sun God, violently expelled her from the heavens.

Banished from the heaven, she landed near a volcano, not far from Lake of Atilan and there she contemplated this horrible turn of events. She was angered at the unjust accusations made by her husband and was of course saddened by his abuse. A vulture appeared nearby and having sympathy, offered her a ride to his home, way up high in the mountains. Here she met the King of Vultures and together they took residence in the mountains, where they also became lovers.

When the remorseful Sun God learned of this amicable union, it did not sit well with him and he soon struggled to devise a scheme to entreat his wife once more to forgive his brute ways and return to the heavens. One story tells that he hid himself in the hide of a dead deer and waited for the predictable vultures to approach the carcass. Unsuspectingly, he jumped on the vultures back and was flown to Ix Chel's new abode. When he arrived, he managed to corner Ix Chel and pleaded with her to give him another chance and to recall all the wonderful moments they had shared as young lovers. Tugging at her heartstring, she allowed his words to move her and… sadly prepared to leave the home she and her Vulture lover had so successfully created. She returned to her throne in the heavens, but the story does not end here.

No sooner had she returned to the heavens, when the jealousy and volatile accusations of her husband started up again. According to some tales there was incessant verbal abuse but also physical abuse, as the Sun God tried to destroy her beauty and disfigure her with scars, to lessen her enchanting nature. They say this is why the moon has visible carved craters on its surface.

One night, the Moon Goddess had endured enough and with all of her willpower and strength, she left into the night. Some say she shapeshifted into a Jaguar, vowing to stay away from the Sun for eternity. She is known to hide in the day when he is awake and wanders through the dark of the night. And although her beauty made many lovers propose marriage to her, she opted to embrace her freedom, belonging to no one, but herself. Ix Chel was known to truly relish her freedom after the torment she endured with the Sun God and she vowed never to dim her light or become owned by anyone else again. It was believed that she retreated to her Island in Cozumel, where she could enjoy her freedom and delight in assisting women in child labor and all aspects of feminine activities.

In this myth we see her as a champion for the oppressed and a Goddess of bold action, who teaches us as women not to become victims of abuse. She teaches us to assert ourselves and not allow ourselves to be emotionally, nor physically victimized. Anything that negatively affects our soul and wellbeing must be eradicated in order for our inner light to shine. Much like many other Lunar Goddesses from various cultures and throughout the ages, she exemplifies the independent spirit of a woman with no ties to any man. Some believe she was touched by the cries of myriads of struggling women everywhere on earth, but especially those making offerings, prayers and supplications at her shrines on the island of Cozumel. She proudly devotes herself to women, their struggles, answering prayers and being an advocate for women's freedom, strength and creativity.

*Ancient Mayan Lunar Goddess, Ix Chel, rules over the waters, our intuitive gifts, the moon and our gender's emotions. With Ix Chel we begin to open ourselves up to the gifts of our gender; reflected in her watery realm and the sacred Moon. This Mayan Goddess has a story to tell and it echoes the story of so many women throughout

"Herstory." She empowers us to forge our own paths and like many lunar deities, she encourages our independence and autonomy. Ix Chel is the inspirer of our creative gifts and the profitable handcrafted skills needed to assure our autonomy and financial success. She is the awakeners of our internal unique voices and advocates shinning our own light brightly, despite those who would prefer us hidden and unnoticed. She imbues us with the courage to follow our path, and embrace our ancestral, matriarchal lineage. As divine Creatress, she reminds you of your own fertile, luminescent gifts. No matter, if you are a spicy-wild maiden, nurturing mother or a wise old crone, all of these archetypes reside within you and all are sacred reflections of Creatrix Lunar Goddess, Ix Chel.

ERESHKIGAL

ERESHKIGAL

Ereshkigal is the Mesopotamian Goddess of the Underworld. She is reminiscent of the Greek God, Hades and even shares some connection to the ancient Goddess, Hecate/Hekate. She has full dominion over the land of the dead, known as Kur, and she is the omnipotent law and judgement in this dark realm. What makes her even more fascinating to us, as we study early Sumerian writings mentioning Ereshkigal, is that she appears to be the sole ruler of this realm. The underworld oftentimes, in later myths, was relegated to male deities, thus it's a powerful message to see a Goddess as the sole ruler of this very significant realm. Later, we see the introduction of her consort, sharing rulership with her, in the underworld, also known as Irkalla.

Her name literally translates as, "Queen of the vast Earth," more specifically, "Queen of the under earth." She is embraced as the Goddess of the Great Below.

As the older sister and aunt to the Queen of Heaven, the Goddess, Inanna, their brother was Utu, a Solar Deity. Their parents were Nanna, the Moon God and Ningal, the Moon Goddess. Ereshkigal had several consorts. Her First husband was Gugalanna, *the Bull of Heaven*, and with him she birthed Ninazu, who became another deity of the underworld. With the God of Air, Enlil, she birthed Namtar (meaning Fate /Destiny). Coincidentally, Enlil would be considered her grandfather, as he fathered the God, Nanna. She was later associated to the God of war, pestilence and plagues, known as Nergal, and together they had the Goddess, Nungal. Nungal was also known as Manungal and she too became a deity of the underworld like her mother. Later known as "Queen of the Ekur," she married the God, Birdu. Interesting to note, Nungal's role became the Judgement of the wicked in the underworld.

Ereshkigal's main temple was located in, Kutha, but she also had temples in Azzur and Umma, according to discovered tablet inscriptions and writings of the time. It is clear her worship was not limited to Mesopotamia as she was known in other lands. She was said to live in Ganzir, which was the entryway to her realm, the netherworld. Her worship and petitions by her devotees was meant to secure a comforting afterlife for she was the guardian of the dead and many feared they would be utterly lost in the underworld. The underworld in ancient times was seen as a dark, painful, muddy realm where the dead would suffer hunger and thirst, if neglected and forgotten by their loved ones remaining on earth. ...Hence the great emphasis on frequent food offerings, prayers, ritual and proper burials, regarding the dead. Ereshkigal, however, was not what you would consider the stereotypical evil view of a deity ruling the dead. Instead, in many of the remaining, early Sumerian writings you can easily empathize with her character and the many situations she found herself in. Yes, Ereshkigal is a strong, powerful deity and was prone to, anger easily and express quite a temper, but like most of us, she is multifaceted. As Goddess of the netherworld, it is believed her role was more significantly, the protection of the earth, and humanity, by creating a boundary and maintaining a final resting place for the dead. She was a patron Goddess for those inexplicably experiencing spiritual possession and thus, it was clear her role was to make sure the dead remained in her realm, behind the seven gates of Irkalla.

There is much reference to Ereshkigal's temper and jealousy of her younger sister, Inanna, and it is easy to understand why there would be such turmoil between the two. No matter what era we are in, it is not uncommon for siblings to struggle with such powerful emotions as jealousy and anger. Given how Inanna was deemed the Queen of Heaven and a beloved deity, gifted with great beauty and the realm of love; it is easy to empathize with Ereshkigal's plight. She was given the dark gloomy realm of the underworld and some have even suggested that Ereshkigal was actually tricked into being the Goddess of this realm. In the Sumerian poem, **"Gilgamesh Enkidu and the Netherworld,"** the Goddess Ereshkigal had been abducted in the same way Persephone, in Greek mythology, had been abducted by Hades. In this poem, Ereshkigal gets abducted and dragged into the underworld by a dragon named, Kur and she is forced to remain there in the netherworld and rule over this gloomy terrain.

In yet another interesting, ancient Sumerian myth, there is an example of her legitimate reaction when she feels disrespected. According to the legend, all the Gods had planned this great lavish banquet on earth and Ereshkigal, as a noteworthy Goddess, was of course invited. But, as a Deity of the underworld she could not depart her realm and the Gods could not bring the banquet to the Goddess because law stipulated that no one could leave the underworld once they arrived. Saddened to hear of the dilemma, the Gods encouraged her to send someone in her place to stop by, gather some of the feast, and return it to the Goddess for her enjoyment. Ereshkigal decided to send her trusted servant and son, Namtar. When he arrived to the Banquet as her representative, all the Gods stood in respect and honor of the Goddess, except for one...The God of Pestilence, Nergal. He showed great disrespect by not standing up and it was immediately noted. Namtar quickly wanted to defend his mom's honor by taking care of Nergal himself, but instead, he was convinced to share the details with Ereshkigal and let her deem the final, proper punishment.

There are many variations to this legend and how it ends, but essentially the God, Nergal is sent to the underworld to explain himself to the Goddess and receive his punishment. With the protection of fourteen beings (or demons) he ventures into the netherworld with the intention of breaking the rule and eventually getting out. He gets through all the gates and by the time he approaches the seventh gate he instructs two beings to leave the gate open behind him so that he may escape. Long story made short here, the God of war and pestilences is forced to stay in the underworld as her consort. There are other versions and interpretations of this legend. Some speculate that the Goddess managed to seduce him while in her realm and that together, they feasted and made wild, passionate love. Whether he was kept in the underworld as punishment for his disrespect or simly as her lover, his presence becomes evident. Nergal becomes the only other deity that is required to stay with the Goddess and co-partner with her as ruler of the underworld. In this way, a male deity is introduced as a co-ruler of the netherworld, sharing power with a female deity in this critical realm. His contractual presence in the underworld is reminiscent to Persephone's with Hades, as he, the God of war, is only required to stay with Ereshkigal for half of the year; returning to the earth the other half. It is demonstrative of the primeval idea that war (God of war, Nergal) could only be endured on earth for a part of the year.

Remnant of Sumerian and Akkadian writings found on tablets throughout the years by archeologist has fascinated many of us. They confirm an unquestionable truth, that the Sacred Feminine, in her numerous guises, was at the center of ancient civilization. When pieced together they reveal some of the most beautiful poems, stories and prayers (Hymns) to the numerous deities venerated long ago. They are also yet another reminder of how relevant the Goddess was then, as she still remains today.

By far one of the most impactful, beloved legends found among the early Sumerian writings was, **"The Descent of Inanna."** In this work we not only journey with Inanna into the underworld but also encounter her powerful sister, Ereshkigal.

Inanna makes her way to the entryway of the underworld. Her sister's husband, Gugalanna, *The Bull of Heaven*, has died and she wishes to pay her proper respects by attending his funeral rites. However, it's important to note that his death is partly due to her carelessness. In a previous story, it was Gilgamesh and Enkidu that slaughtered Gugalanna in a type of retaliatory act towards Inanna herself. The reality was that Inanna, shared blame for his death and her appearance at the gate of the netherworld was partly due to her own guilt.

Inanna prepares herself for the visit and the confrontation with her sister and dresses in her finest Royal adornments. She reaches the entryway and cries out to the gatekeeper, Neti, to let her inside. Neti quickly alerts Ereshkigal of this shocking visitor to her queendom and the news stirs all sorts of emotions and worries. Ereshkigal already has a tenuous relationship with her sister, the beloved Queen of Heaven, and she suspects that Inanna has come to try to lay claim to the underworld as her own, in order to expand her powers. She carefully contemplates the situation and then instructs Neti to *"bolt the seven gates of the underworld."* She tells Neti that in order for Inanna to be granted passage through each of the gates, she must surrender one of her Royal adornments and garments. These Royal adornments were closely linked with Inanna's Divine power. They were intimately connected to her supremacy as a Goddess.

Inanna humbly arrives at each of the gates of the underworld and she complies with each demand; sacrificing one of her adornments or clothing article at the entryway of each gate. By the time she arrives at the seventh gate, Inanna finds herself completely naked, stripped of all of her power as a Goddess, and weakened. Ereshkigal rises from her throne and faces her sister. Full of much intense bottled up emotions, Ereshkigal declares aloud all the offenses against Inanna and presents it to the, Annuna, the judges of the Underworld. She accuses the Goddess, Inanna, of trying to usurp her Queendom and of being directly responsible for the death of her husband, . The Annuna passes judgement against Inanna and she is given to Ereshkigal to put to death. The Goddess of the Underworld takes the naked body of Inanna and hangs her to die. Like a piece of rotting meat, for 3days and 3nights, the naked Inanna hung from a hook.

Now three days and three nights have passed and Inanna's servant, Ninshubur, is frantically worried. She goes to implore all the different Gods for their help but no one would dare. Finally she goes to the God of Wisdom, Enki, and after hearing the story he agrees to help. He fashions two genderless creatures from the dirt under his fingernails. He names them; *Kurgarra* and *Galatur*. He instructs them to fly into the underworld and rescue Inanna by giving her the food and drink of life. He warns them of Ereshkigal and the painful moaning she would emit and he instructs them on how to get the Queen of the Underworld to surrender Inanna's corpse.

The two creatures reach the throne of Ereshkigal and they find her moaning in agony. They begin to imitate her sounds and empathize with the pain she was feeling. Somehow it brought the Goddess so much comfort that she grants them a wish. Naturally they ask for the corpse of Inanna and Ereshkigal complies. They find Inanna lifeless and immediately offer her the bread and drink of life. Revitalized, they attempt to get Inanna out of there but as they were ascending out of this dark realm, the Annuna stopped them; reminding them of the law in the Netherworld. The only way Inanna could be escorted out of the Underworld is if she had someone to take her place. A multitude of demons from the underworld, called the Galla, attached themselves to Inanna. They harassed the Goddess, Inanna and would not leave her alone until she found her replacement for the underworld. They traveled upon the earth with her, as she was now resurrected from the dead. When Inanna returns to the Earth she finds that her death, while it was being mourned by so many, her beloved consort, Dumuzi, did not express a single sign of remorse for her death. He was found enjoying himself, dressed in his finest royal garment; unmoved by her absence. She confronts Dumuzi and seeing how he had not one shred of grief for her death, she offers him up to the Galla, in anger and disgust. He protested but the decision had been made. The Demons of the underworld gladly took him as a replacement for the Goddess, Inanna. In some text it is stated, his sister volunteered to accompany and console her brother to the underworld.

Ereshkigal is yet another powerful image of the Sacred Feminine and the value of our Queendom; Our Home. We meet in this Sumerian Goddess an image of great strength and autonomy. She is a reminder to honor the core of our emotions and the place we call home. She serves as a message to stand our ground, assert our voices and thus, our power to build our inner & outer edifices. There is a strong aspect regarding her domain and her domicile in the underworld. She encourages you to embrace and defend your own Queedom. Ereshkigal is the awakener of the voice necessary to defend ourselves from anyone that is disrespecting or disregard us and our home. Her voice is ultimate authority, what she states is a decree, and throughout the ancient texts, it's clear she is both feared and highly regarded. The autonomy of this Goddess becomes evident in every tale she is mentioned in and it serves to inspire our own personal journey.

CHAPTER SIX
COMPASSION
SHE WHO SACRIFICES FOR THE GREATER GOOD

*"The Heart of a Mother is a deep abyss
at the bottom of which you will always find, forgiveness..."* Honore de Balzac

SELU

SELU/CORN MOTHER

Corn, or Maize as it is known by most Native Americans, was first developed in Central Mexico over 7,000 years ago. It was not something that grew naturally on its own in the wild but rather needed to be cultivated. According to historians it was started from the wild grass known as teosinte and in the beginning it looked very different from our modern day corn husk. As the Native American Indians migrated, corn began to be introduced to Peruvian culture, further south, as well as further up North, in the Southwest region of the Americas. Eventually its consumption became wildly popular throughout the Americas and when Christopher Columbus returned to Europe, after his expedition, he introduced the comestible to Europeans.

Corn became an imperative source of food for Native Americans, but also a significant part of their daily lives and culture. Various part of the corn was utilized to make sleeping mats, moccasins, ceremonial masks and games and baskets, which helped transporting many different vital items. The ability to feed a whole nation with the grains of corn made it one of the most important staples in aboriginal's diet. Today Corn is no less important than it was 7,000 years ago. Reflect, if you will now, on what our lives would be like without corn.

Today our dependence on corn goes beyond the obvious; bread, cake, tortilla chips, popcorn, corn-muffins, sweet corn on the cob, etc., etc. It might surprise you to know that corn is employed in our aspirins, glue, cosmetics, shoe polish, and in our books as corn starch, as well as our clothing. It is utilized as corn syrup in our soft drinks and often used to feed farm Chickens that provide for our eggs. Corn can be found in the ink that graces our books and newspapers and it's a key ingredient to Ethanol, which is found in automobile fuel. So it becomes clear that Corn is incredibly valuable to the sustenance of a nation today, as it was with its inception.

It is therefore not surprising that corn would receive such veneration from aboriginals. To indigenous cultures that practice animism and saw spirit in all things, one could easily see how something so crucial and important, like corn, can become deified. Studies into these native cultures reveal that it was customary to craft a puppet made of stalks of maize from the first corn husk in a harvest and great care was taken to preserve this puppet or corn dolly (as it was sometimes referred to) in order to guarantee a continuous fertile crop for the year. It was ceremonially dressed in woman's attire and it was well regarded, for the duration of the year, until it was ceremonially burned and replaced with the first corn of the next harvest.

Corn woman appears in numerous indigenous tribes by various names and with a multitude of myths and folklore traditions, intertwined into Native's culture. And because they have been passed down, throughout generations, via oral tradition (through song and dance) we are blessed to have many surviving tales.

Mayan believed humans were actually fashioned out of corn and Penobscot Indians believed Corn mother to be the first mother of her people. The Lakota plains Indians correlated the existence of Corn mother with White Buffalo woman and for the Seneca Indians of the Northeast, they believed in a beautiful Woman who lived high above the mountains as their divine Maize Goddess. The Creeks, in Southeast Americas, viewed Corn Mother as a highly revered Old Woman, while the Zuni people of the Southwestern United States of America had a myth about eight corn maidens. To the Aztec and Mexico, Corn Mother was known as Chicomecoatl, the Goddess of Maize but to the Cherokee nation, she was known as Selu. She was also known as yellow woman and Iyatiku to the Keresan people of Southwest Americas.

Giving birth and being born brings us into the essence of creation,
where the human spirit is courageous and bold,
and the body, a miracle of wisdom..." Harriette Hartigan

In researching and becoming acquainted with many of Corn Mother's various myths, there is a similar thread running through all of them. Inherent in the corn, and the myths related to Selu, are the themes of sacrifice, forgiveness and the cycles of birth, growth, life, death and rebirth. I have elected to elucidate here and share one of the Cherokee tales of Corn Mother, also known as Selu.

Some claim Corn woman was a spirit that was sent down to earth once a year to help the crop grow tall and strong, others tell a different story. Cherokee folklore reveals she was sent down to earth to live and feed the people. In this tale Selu, living on the earth, gave birth to two sons, who apparently were always hungry. Every time they complained of hunger and asked for food, she would instruct them to sit and wait patiently, while she would quickly disappear into a nearby hut and magickally always come back with a basket full of corn. This happened quite often and the boys (while dutifully relishing their meals and plumping up on corn) started to wonder where and how their mother was getting food. One night curiosity got the best of them and they defied their mother's instructions to wait patiently. Instead, on this night, they decide to follow; creep and spy on their mother, as she entered the small hut. What they saw was far beyond compre-hensible for the minds of two small boys and needless to say quite traumatic. Inside the hut, they saw their mother squatting above the basket, producing a multitude of corn from her very own body; filling the basket with their next meal. There are some lore that state Corn Mother produced corn from scabs on her body and some say from her feces. In either case she is essentially producing corn from her very own body and, the boys, in their ignorance and immaturity were completely baffled and disgusted. That night at dinner time, the boys would not eat, they confronted their mother with what they had seen and here again, some myths vary, claiming that the boys, horrified, threaten to tell the entire village. In this Cherokee lore, Corn Mother realizes that her children and her people are now in jeopardy of not being able to provide for themselves and sadly she realizes the sacrifice required of her. She tells her boys that now that they know the truth, they must kill her and drag her body through the fields to ensure that corn will continue to grow and sustain her people. Wherever droplets of her blood spilled, there, corn will grow and now the children will need to feed themselves from this point onward. Some other myths tell another version of this story, claiming that Corn Mother's body had to be cut up into tiny pieces and scattered around the various corners of the world to ensure the survival of corn for the Native American people.

In this popular folklore of Selu, we meet the universal archetype of the fertile mother and her message of procreation, nourishment, death, rebirth and sacrifice. In her sacrifice, she willingly sheds her body and blood, to save and secure a nation of people and the future generations of Native Americans to come. With her sacrifice, she ensures her children will thrive and not starve to death.

As a powerful Matrirachal archetype there are many obvious aspects we can explore with Selu. She invites us to explore what it means to be a mother, more specifically what it means to sacrifice as a mother. We are asked to contemplate the legacies we hope to leave behind to our grandchildren and future generations and recognize our part in the tapestry of our great-grandmothers. Deep within Corn Mother we may find yet another gem to consider while working with her. Yes, she is a mother archetype and inherent in this title is the theme of nurturance; whether it is self-nurturance or extended to our creations, but there is also a lesson about balance. Working with Corn Mother might unearth a lesson on cultivating balance in our lives and improving our personal relationships to foods we chose to nurture ourselves with.

I find that tapping into the energy and lessons of Corn Mother makes perfect sense to me as we work through the theme offered in this chapter but like many other Goddesses with multiple powerful attributes, she can easily be incorporated into various other chapters found in this book. Corn Mother/Selu is also a wonderful deity to work with at Mabon, the second harvest. For most Pagans, honoring Selu at this time of the year seems most appropriate, although I have also called upon her during the first harvest, at Lammas. I find that the holiday of the Autumnal Equinox, presents the theme of equilibrium in our lives, as we stand, in perfect symmetry, between both night and day. It is therefore a good time to reflect on what requires perfect balance in our own lives. Selu also touches upon the issue of food and nourishment, and I can't help but consider how food and our relationship to it, is not always in perfect balance.

Our society struggles greatly with issues related to food. Just perusing through a contemporary woman's magazine I can't help but notice the predominance of malnourished looking, skinny models and then walking outside my door and seeing the unusual amount of unhealthy, obese people. Clearly as a society, we struggle with finding a balance or right relationship with food. We either abuse it (consume too much of it, without regards to its sacred vital role) or we disrespect it and call it the enemy, avoiding it, to fulfill an unreal body image. In either case, food is not being respected, nor approached with the reverence it deserves. Yet, if like indigenous people and our ancestors, we too saw Corn as Goddess, wouldn't our approach to food be vastly different? Wouldn't our relationship to food be immeasurably different than what it appears to be today for millions of people?

As I endeavor to present Corn Woman and her numerous cathartic lessons in this chapter, I also reflect on the lessons she has taught me, as a Goddess womyn, about nourishment, balance and proper alignment with food.

*Selu/Corn Mother is the nurturing sacrificial iconic Corn Goddess, embraced by the myriads of indigenous tribes, across the Americas and abroad. Corn Mother shed her blood so that her people would strive onward and not extinct. She, who willingly sacrificed her very own truncated body so that her people would never hunger again, is the supreme being of compassion. Despite the unappreciative nature of her greedy children and her community, she understood her role and obligation in the larger scheme of life and thus, she awakens the sacrificial Mother within every one of us. She calls to mind your core, your heart-chakra and asks you, *How do you nurture yourself?* Step back, if you will, and consider for a moment what sacrifices are required of you? What is in your heart now, that requires sacrifice for the greater good? What symbolizes your sacred blood and where is it being required to pour forth and serve a greater good in your family or even within your community?

DEMETER

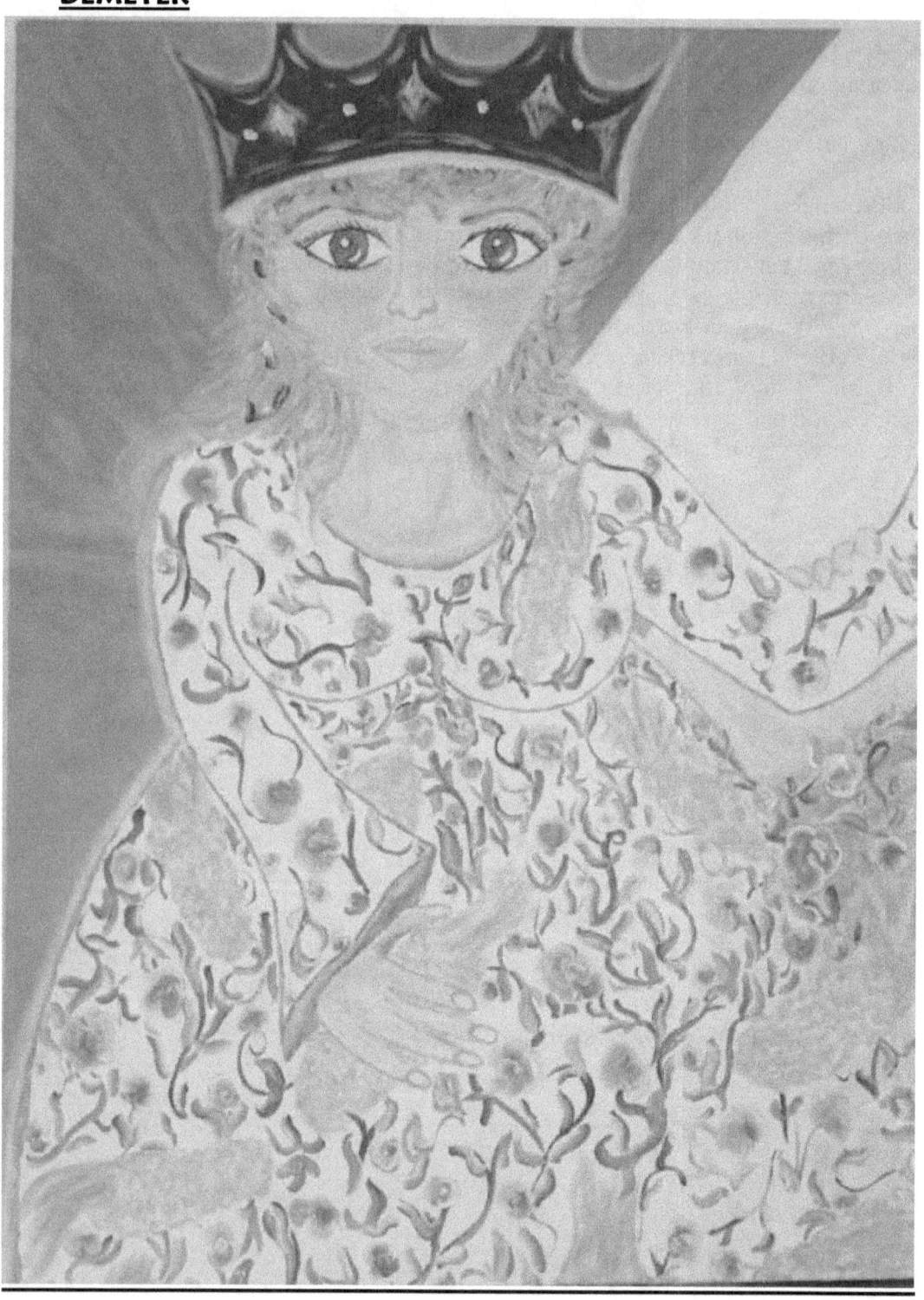

DEMETER

Demeter is the Greek Goddess of the Grain, also known as Deo and Chloe. Her Roman counterpart was Ceres. She was the most generous of the Greek Goddesses, representing the bounty of the fertile Earth. She was depicted as warm, altruistic and beautiful, with long luscious golden hair. Wearing a blue robe, wherever she was present, there was divine light and growing crops sprouting abundantly by her feet. Often seen as very matronly in a seated position, her presence brought celestial lights and a most wonderful fragrance, according to the writings of her time. She was responsible for the fruitfulness of nature and the fertility of the Earth. Her gifts to humanity were the harvest and agriculture. Interesting to note, the last part of her name, "meter", translates as Mother, revealing her other significant role as a Maternal Deity. She was a mother Goddess, with a most emblematic role as Persephone's mother.

Demeter was the granddaughter of Uranus and the primordial Earth Goddess - Gaia. She was the second daughter of the Goddess Rhea and the God Cronos. Rhea was mother of the first generation of Olympians and thus she was also mother to Hades (God of the Underworld and Maiden abductor) and Zeus (Husband and Father to Persephone). According to mythology, Demeter's father swallowed up his children and as the second child to her mother, she too was swallowed, then later released and saved by her sibbling.

According to Greek mythology, Demeter married her brother, Zeus, and became his fourth wife before Hera, who was ultimately wife number seven, and the last of Zeus' wives. Her union with Zeus produced their only child, the beautiful maiden, Persephone, also known as Kore.

According to the well-known Eleusian myth so often linked with Demeter, one day Persephone and her maiden friends were out picking flowers. Attracted by a beautiful Narcissus flower, the young girl reached out her arms to pick it and it was then that Hades, God of the underworld, abducted the beautiful Maiden. According to one legend, he opened up the Earth and snatched her up and only two Deities heard her cry; Hekate and Helios. As the myth reveals, for nine days and nine nights, the once brilliant, benevolent Goddess Demeter, now roamed the Earth, sadly searching endlessly for her daughter. It was on the tenth day that Hekate, Goddess of the Crossroads, finally came to Demeter and told her she had indeed heard Persephone's cries. The sympathetic Crone, Hekate, now endeavored to help and console the despondent Goddess.

Upon hearing that the Lord of the Underworld, Hades, had abducted her daughter to become his unwilling bride and that Zeus, could've probably sanctioned this horrid act without her authority, enraged her beyond belief. To add insult to injury, Demeter (who at times, appeared to exist solely for her daughter) was made to feel as if she had no power over this situation and she was suppose to simply accept the abduction and disappearance of her beloved child. Demeter was beyond grief and anger and would not accept this fate. Betrayed and full of grief, she withdrew her divine gifts from the Earth and left Mount Olympus. Inconsolable and terribly distraught, she wandered the Earth, in a stuporous haze of sadness and misery, as If her very soul had been stripped and her inner divine light snuffed completely. Disguised as a very old lady, in dark veils, concealing any hint of her previous Divine golden essence, she traveled throughout the cities and countryside and then came upon the city of Eleusis.

According to the Homeric Hymn, the despondently dark, unrecognizable Demeter found herself sitting by a well, on the outskirts of the city, when four bright maidens, endeavoring to draw water from the well, approached her. Callidice, Cleisidice, Demo, Callithoe were the daughters of Celeus, King of Eleusis and these four maidens approached the old lady, before them, with much intrigue and curiosity. After introducing themselves, they asked Demeter where whe came from and tried to understand why a woman of her suspecting age, was alone, outside of the city center and not already employed as a nurse by a household. Demeter introduced herself as a woman from Crete, by the name of "Doso" and claimed to have escaped the capture of pirates, who were going to sell her off. She weaved a convincingly good, yet, sad tale that captured the sympathy of the King's children. The maiden, Callidice, who was described as the "godliest" in the Homeric Hymn, suggested that the old lady follow them home. She convinced Demeter that their father, the King, would surely welcome her services in their household and that their younger brother would benefit from a nurse of her caliber.

Upon meeting the disguised Demeter, the King Celeus, and his wife, sensed that indeed she would be a welcomed addition to their Kingdom and a fine nurse for their young son Demophoon, although in some text he was also known as Triptolemus. There is also some conflicting stories about Iambe as yet another daughter of the Queen or perhaps another name for the bawdy, jovial Baubo herself, who was the nursemaid that ultimately helped end Demeter's lament.

And thus Demeter, still in disguise, was employed by the Queen, Metaeira, to become nursemaid to the baby boy. She raised this baby as if he was her very own. Time spent with the boy employed her inherent divine matriarchal gifts and also became a diversion from the worries over her ubducted daughter. As time went on, she indeed grew quite fond of this child. In Demeter's care, Demophoon was raised like a God and her love for him, oneday inspired her to bless him with the fires of immortality.

The child was about to become immortal by her own making, as Demeter had the special fire rite of immortality prepared for Demophoon. His mother, the Queen, came upon them as it was about to take place and intercepted the frightful looking, fire ritual. Imagine her surprise to discover the old nursemaid they had hired, was actually the Goddess of the Grain, Demeter. Immediately, Demeter's divine luminescence manifested, upon being caught by the Queen in the midst of this rite. And, Metaneira was no sooner, harshly berated by the Fertile Grain Goddess for her interference in the will of the Gods. In her anger, the Goddess demanded that a temple be built in her honor there in the city of Eleusis, immediately.

Once the temple was built, the Goddess Demeter planted herself there until the return of her daughter. She vowed she would not step foot on Mount Olympus, or allow anything to grow or be born on the Earth, until her daughter was returned to her. And this was a most tragic state for the earth and humanity's wellbeing. Zeus tried to implore her to return to her post. Other Gods and Goddesses also came to her, bearing gifts and supplications. The people of the land also left numerous offerings to the Goddess to entreat her to return. Demeter was unmoved and refused to give into their demands. In one myth, Zeus finally sends the messenger God, Hermes, to retrieve Persephone from the underworld and bring her back to her mother. In another more accepted version, it is the Crone, Hekate that finally helps unite, Mother and daughter.

Their overdue reunion was full of intense heartwarming emotions but in the end, bittersweet. Demeter learns then that Persephone had eaten the fruit of the dead, pomegranate seeds, while in the underworld and must now come to accept that her daughter will only be with her part of the year and return to her husband, Hades, in the underworld, for the remainder of the year.

The Homeric Hymn to Demeter focused on Demeter's response to Persephone being abducted by Hades and this was the basis of the Eleusinian Mysteries - the most powerful religious and sacred rites of ancient Greece. Held in secret for over two thousand years, these sacred rites ended with the destruction of the Eleusis Temples by the Goths around fifth century A.D. More recently there has been a resurgeance and interest in ancient mythology, anthropology, Paganism and Goddess spirituality. Research into these archaic, longstanding Greek rites, reveal a great deal about our ancestors and their spiritual practices - knowledge that can enrich our own present day beliefs and religious practices.

In the Greek Goddess, Demeter we see another aspect of the Mother Archetype. We are introduced to a Mother deity that is passionately and wholly submersed in her role as Mother. She appears solely defined by her role as Persephone's mother. It is not only the land and the harvest that she is commited to but to her daughter, Kore. Demeter exemplifies for us what it means to be a fierce defender and protectress of our children and our creations. In Demeter we see a mother exercise her convictions and negotiating skills. She knows the power she has as a Mother and she wields this power for her child. Her great strength and determination to secure her daughter's wellbeing is evident in the myths and, with her energy, we traverse into the matriarchal realm where we find sacrificial love so deep that we realize there is nothing we wouldn't do to protect and bless what we love.

*Greek Goddess of the grain, she is the benevolent Harvest Mother who sacrifices, supports, protects and nourishes. She comes into your life at this time to inaugurate the Mother within. She awakens in you a connection to all things that need nurturance and protection, including yourself. Like the immortal Goddess, who would not let the grain grow until her daughter's return, where are you being asked to take some form of action and establish what you are, and are not, willing to do for your desired outcome? Where are you being called to consider the bigger picture and yet, not compromise your dignity? Where will you utilize your own bargaining power and where will you need to make some initial sacrifice to attain the end goal? It is a time of assessments and preparedness. Demeter invites us to consider our role as committed, nurturing mothers to our creative pursuits and take this brief pause in our journey to reflect, assess, and consider the bigger picture that may require our Divine matriarchal nurturance.

As a Goddess connected to the Fertile Grain and the feeding of humanity, Demeter, like Selu, becomes an irrefutable deity to acquaint ourselves with. In her myths we see again the presence of a Goddess who has the power to feed or starve; not only humanity, but the Gods themselves. It is Demeter who is petitioned & venerated to end the famine across the earth, but she initially sacrifices her inherent gifts of fertility, in order to negotiate for her daughter's return. The sacrificial mother archetype is present in Demeter, as it is in many matriarchal deities. In this chapter, we can explore the strength of our own negotiating skills in order to manifest an outcome that would have global ramification for all. We can consider the power and choice we have within us to willingly sacrifice in order to attain a higher goal that would universally impact many.

YEMAYA

YEMAYA

Yemaya is also known as Yemonja, Yemoja, Yemanja, Yemaja, Iamanje, Imanje, Ymoja, and many other variations of this name. Yemaya is the Yoruban Orisha and Goddess of the great Ocean. She is a powerful matriarchal Goddess who is attributed to birthing many of the sacred Orishas in the Yoruban pantheon, including birthing the sun and the moon. She is widely embraced as the divine mother that hears the cries of her children. Her compassionate and nurturing attributes cannot be underestimated and her devotees know they are heard, supported, loved and well protected by this great Goddess. Hers are the gift of fertility, sexuality, love, feminine beauty, healing and mothering. She is very sympathetic to her devotees and is not known to anger quick, though, like most deities, she can express another aspect, if crossed.

Her worship can be traced back to West Africa and regions like Ghana, Benin and Nigeria, yet this beloved Orisha appears to be known worldwide. From Brazil, to Cuba, to Puerto Rico, and parts of the United States, to so many other countries, her worship has clearly grown and expanded throughout the years.

She is the Queen of the ocean, a matriarchal Goddess, a powerful Orisha in Lucumi, Umbanda, Macumba, Santeria and the Brazilian Candomble religion. As a mother archetype she is called upon for numerous healing rites and love workings. Annually by the sea, Yemaya is worshipped and honored in special rites in Brazil, and all across the globe, to commemorate her day on New Year's Eve (December 31st).

While Oshun is the Orisha or Goddess of rivers, Yemaya rules over all of the waters upon the Earth; saltwater, freshwaters (rivers, lakes, and oceans). Her name translates as mother of a multitude of fishes. It derives from the Yoruban word, "Yeye Omo eya," which translates as, mother of fishes or mother whose children are the Fish.

Often depicted in her shimmering blue and white colors, she has overflowing large breast to denote her powers of fecundity. You will often see images of her as a beautiful woman, crowned with long flowing dark hair, resembling a mermaid, with her mermaid's tail upon the foaming ocean waves. Statues of her resemble the Catholic Virgin Mary, donning a blue and white robe. In Cuba, they connect Yemaya with Our Lady of Regla.

As a great matriarchal deity she is attributed for birthing many of the Orishas (gods/goddesses) and because of her great matriarchal gifts, it is said she would often even take care of Oshun's children. Her strong maternal gifts, also links her with adoptions. According to folklore, she adopted Chango/Shango, the God of Thunder. His greatness as a leader and Lord of Thunder is mostly attributed to her nurturance and special guidance. They share a profound love and much, much later on, it is said, he becomes one of her great lovers. As can be expected with a beautiful water deity, she had numerous lovers. Her known accepted consorts were Olokun and Ogun. Ogun is the warrior God, the blacksmith and patron of civilization and human technological advancement. Olokun is the Orisha or God of the depth of the Ocean and consequently the depth of our unconscious; together they are a force to be reckoned with.

As a Goddess so intrinsically linked with women and the ocean, Yemaya is also very much connected with the moon. It is believed her mother is the Orisha, Oddua; the dark womb mother of all.

Yemaya's sacred number is 7 and altar offerings to her can include seashells and anything sweet: like chocolate, candy, coconut balls, syrup, honey, melons, watermelons, cakes and cookies. Even fried green plantains, hens and fried pork can be offered to her on her altars but never offer her fish, as she is the mother of fishes and will take great offense to this. There are some, however, that say you can offer her shrimp dishes, just not fish. Obviously any Altar to Yemaya would be incomplete without some type of chalice, bowl or vessel containing water. Altar candles to Yemaya can be blue, green, white and even better, seashell shaped candles, if you can find them.

Sometimes on her altar she is worshiped with her sister, Oshun, as both of these Goddesses were connected with the sacred element of water. Oshun is a love Goddess that shares many attributes with Yemaya. Oshun rules the rivers, while Yemaya rule's the oceans and essentially all waters upon the earth. Yemaya rules over all fluids; our tears, our amniotic fluids, our saliva, our womanly juices, waterfalls, showers, all expansive waters are her domain. When she rides or possesses her *servituer* in religious rites and ceremonies they often dance a sultry rhythmic dance that mimics the swaying ocean waves.

Yemaya is a beautiful, highly recognized Orisha that personifies the great expansive, sacred element of water. She is the compassionate mother that illustrates for us the gifts of nurturance, healing and love. Invoke her energy to explore self-love and acceptance, and to further learn ways to Mother your inner self best.

*"You have to find a Mother inside yourself. We all do.
Even if we already have a mother, we still have to find this part of ourselves
inside..."*
Sue Monk Kidd, The Secret Life of Bees

KUAN-YIN

KUAN –YIN/Quan Yin/ Guanyin/Kuanyin

Kuan-Yin is the Chinese Buddhist and Taoist Deity of Compassion and Mercy. Her full name is Kuan-shih-yin and it translates as, *"She Who Listens to the World's Sounds."* More specifically, it refers to, *"She, who hears the cries of humanity."* Kuan-Yin is by far one of the most recognized and embraced ancient deities across China. Her worship can be traced as far back as the first century and she continues to be a Goddess highly venerated today.

In ancient Sanskrit she is known as *Padma Pani*, which translates as, *"Born of the Lotus."* Early Sanskrit Buddhist scriptures speak of Kuan-Yin and the *Lotus-Sutra*, which was later translated into Chinese, delves into her worship and her illustrative myths. The section of the *Lotus –Sutra* that highlighted Kuan Yin's worship, was later re-titled and redistributed as, *Kuan-Yin-Sutra* by the Chinese. These scriptures along with many other writings helped to spread the worship of Kuan-Yin even further.

It is important, however, to recognize certain paramount observations about Kuan-Yin. She is renowned as the Chinese female Buddhist, Bodhisattva Avalokitesvara. In early Sanskrit Buddhism the Avalokitesvara is male but by the 11th century it is clear through many of the early writings of the time that this female deity was becoming more prevalent. Avalokitesvara incarnates in many forms but the distinct presence of Kuan-Yin as a Goddess reveals itself more definitively between the 10th and 11th century.

By the 11th century, Kuan-Yin becomes fully embraced as a female deity and a revered manifestation of Avalokitesvara. She is closely connected to the Tibetan White Tara. Tara is a Tibetan Buddhist Goddess who was believed to have been born from the tear shed for humanity's suffering, by the Buddha. She is the female Tibetan Buddha and Kuan-Yin shares many similar attributes to Tara. Both are recognized as female manifestations of the Avalokitesvara.

Kuan Yin is a Buddhist-Chinese deity. She is embraced as the archetypal Goddess of Mercy and Compassion. She is the Celestial one who hears the cries of humanity. As a beloved Matriarchal deity she is connected to the Sheng Mu, the Holy Mother, the Goddess of pregnancy and bringer of children. In this aspect she becomes a very personal deity that is welcomed and venerated by her devotee in their homes and businesses. Her connection to Buddhism is not as magnified in this aspect but her role as a Goddess of fertility, protector of women, mothers, and bringer of children is strongly highlighted.

Kuan-Yin is also association with the Goddess Matsu. Her connection to Matsu links her worship as that of a Goddess that protects fisherman and all who are connected to the sea. Hence her worship grew near coastal towns where she became a protector and patron Goddess for all who traveled by sea. There are numerous shrines and temples dedicated to Kuan-Yin. The island of P'u t'o loka was the place of her erected first temple, which became one of many shrines and temples created for her. Here, her worship exponentially propagated and eventually spread to nearby regions. It is clear her worship spread not only across China but eventually spread to the west. The plethora of images, sculptures, shrines, temples and personal home altars to Kuan-Yin only support and illustrates how widely embraced she has been throughout the years as a Goddess much revered.

DEPICTIONS

The myriad of diverse images of the Goddess, Kuan –Yin, makes her and her worship more accessible to us and helps us better understand this extraordinary, matriarchal deity. When we look closer at some of her depictions throughout the centuries we get a better glimpse into Chinese culture and this much revered ancient deity.

Often she is depicted dressed in a flowing white robe, to symbolize her unquestionable purity. She has a strong association with water and thus, she is often seen holding a slim vase/jug filled with her sacred restorative waters. It's interesting how water is typically seen as connected to the realm of emotions and so she is very much linked with this sacred component. She is the one who cries for humanity and feels deeply the struggles and pain of the human race. Her blessed waters are described as always offering transformation, rebirth and vitality. She is also seen holding a Willow tree branch which she uses to wet and sprinkle those she chooses to bless with healing. The Willow tree is known as the first tree to bloom in the spring and the last tree to give up its leaves in autumn and thus, its powerful symbolism is connected to Kuan Yin. This Goddess has also been illustrated holding a peach. The peach is a symbol connected to longevity and youthfulness. In one of her famous legends the peach was given to her so that she would not hunger or thirst during her long journey to P'u-t'o-Shan/ P'u t'o loka (a special island off the coast of Southeast China, this would become the site of her first sacred temple in 847AD). Kuan Yin has also been depicted on a white Lotus and ridding dragons and Tigers. In one of her myths she is transformed into a Tiger and rescued from harm.

Often Kuan –Yin is seen with two attendants by her side; a young male to her right and a young female to her left. Devotional piety is exemplified by her young male attendant, *Shen-ts'ai*; his name means Golden Youth. According to one legend, one day, he approached the Goddess vowing complete devotion. In an effort to test his devotion she staged her death; falling from a high cliff. He immediately and selflessly chased after her to try to rescue her but found his own demise instead. The Goddess was so moved by his bravery and devotion that she brought him back to life and made him her attendant.

The female figure to her left represents steadfast piety. Known as, Lung-nu, her name translates as *Jade Maiden*. She was the grand-daughter of the Naga King who was sent to deliver a special repayment gift to the Goddess at P'u -t'o- Shan. Kuan Yin had rescued the King's son and he wanted to show his gratitude by offering the Goddess a "luminous pearl." The young maiden presented the Goddess with this magickal pearl which facilitated her ability to read the scriptures in darkness, at night, and had many other magickal usages. Upon meeting the Goddess the young maiden felt so captivated and inspired that she begged to be accepted as a student of Buddhism. Kuan Yin placed her as one of her attendants, after she succeeded proving her devotion.

HER MYTH

As an ancient Chinese deity one can expect many stories and legends connected to this Goddess. One myth in particular, written in the 11th century, speaks of how she came to be and it is the story of a noble princess that lived in 700 B.C.

King Miao Chuang had three daughters. His youngest was named Miao Shan. They say that when she was born, they knew she was special because there were indications on her actual body that she was of noble blood and possibly the incarnation of a holy person. As she grew older she exemplified unusual traits not commonly regarded in a royal princess. She dressed in plain clothes and carried herself in a way that would prove she indeed was not your average young lady.

Her two older sisters married, as was the custom, but when it was time for Miao's wedding to be arranged, she protested. She wanted to renounce the world, much like the Buddha himself. She told her father that she did not wish to marry, instead she wanted to become a Buddhist nun but this did not sit well with her regal father, who had great expectations of her imperial wedding. His daughter appeared very rebellious in her protest, something eschewed in Chinese culture but after much resistance the King finally gives in. He sends her away to a special monastery. However, he arranges for his daughter's stay at this monastery to be nightmarish, in the hopes his daughter would give up the idea of becoming a Buddhist nun. He asks the attendants at the monastery to be extra harsh on Miao and overwhelm her with numerous tasks and harsh labor that she was not accustomed to doing. Miao Shan, however, took on all her responsibilities apparently with great joy. She was in her element being of service at the monastery. It appeared she was able to magickally accomplish all of the tasks she was given, even those that seem nearly impossible to do. Some say she had celestial aid intervening on her behalf to help her because it was the only way to explain how she was able to complete some of these arduous tasks. It seemed there was no way of discouraging Miao Shan from her devotion to her compassionate vocation. Upon hearing of his daughter's progress at the monastery her father became enraged. It is said he became so infuriated that he lashed out and killed his daughter or, according to one version of the story, had her executed. He was so enraged that he destroyed and burned down the monastery. As with most ancient myths there are varied versions to the ending of this tale. Some claim Miao manages to escape her father's execution, another version tells she is rescued by a spirit and turned into a tiger. And yet another version she is killed and actually descends to the land of the dead where she becomes much like the Greek Goddess Persephone; a compassionate attendant to the dead. In the realm of the dead, Miao devotes herself to caring for the sorrowful dead; nurturing them compassionately, serving them food, quenching their thirst and changing the entire energy of this darkened realm. Her light and compassion nearly eradicates the land of the dead. She eventually gets removed from this realm and gets sent back to earth to reenter her body and become the Goddess Kuan-Yin.

Meanwhile, the murderous king is not free from his atrocious crimes against his pious daughter. He finds himself battling with a deadly disease that is resistant to any medicinal cure. A monk finally exams him and prescribes an unusual cure that apparently can only be performed by the severed arms and eyes of a living person that is free of anger. The king resigns himself to never being cured because he doesn't believe such a person exists in the world but the monk assures him there is one person who can help. The king sends word out that he is in dire need of help. His daughter Miao Shan, hears of her father's terminal condition and in her usual compassionate nature, she willingly sacrifices her arms and eyes to help heal her father. As the tale continues, the king becomes healed and later learns that it was his daughter who helped him. They reunite and Miao Shan then is transformed into the thousand armed and thousand eyes, Beloved Chinese Deity of Mercy and Compassion. This becomes yet another popular image she is often depicted as; the multi-armed, multi-eyed Goddess.

In this story we can also see her important connection to the dead and the afterlife. She becomes known as a savioress, not just to the living, but to those suffering, lost souls, in this dark realm. She becomes like a mediator between the living and the dead, helping the deceased transition into the land of the dead. Chinese believed the living had an obligation to their deceased ancestors. Those living were supposed to perform rites and prayers to assure that their deceased ancestors would not suffer too much in the realm of the dead. The Goddess Kuan-Yin is called upon to help in theses distinct sacred rites and assure the nurturance of the beloved deceased ancestors.

The Buddha, initially in ancient Tibetan and Buddhist scriptures, was presented as a male figure and that was pretty consistent until about the middle of the 10th century, possibly even earlier. Little by little the presence of a female Buddha started to reveal itself in these early writings and by the 11th century it was clear there was a noteworthy change and an important addition to the pantheon of Chinese Gods. The female Buddha, Kuan-Yin, was now manifested as a highly revered matriarchal Goddess of Compassion. Her veneration was so great; it was believed that simply reciting her name, numerous times like in a mantra, would result in incredible miracles.

There are a plethora of personal accounts, documentations of devotees and their personal prayers answered by this great Goddess. Ancient Buddhist and Chinese scriptures reveal just how beloved and impactful this female deity became over time for the Chinese.

Part of her appeal for us as contemporary women, especially in the story about Miao Shan as Kuan-Yin, is her strong message about our own choice in the role we agree to play in society. For the Chinese, she is not only exemplary of a proper Buddhist in their culture; self-sacrificing, compassionate, renunciation of worldly possessions and merciful, but she exemplifies for us as women an admirable strength. In Miao Shan/Kuan -Yin, we see modeled for us great fortitude in standing our ground and a real examination of women's role in society. We see in Kuan-Yin not just a merciful, compassionate figure but also a rebellious, tenacious spirit that exercises her choice, which in ancient times women often didn't appear to have many choices. In Chinese culture, upon penalty of death, you were expected to obey your parents and then you were expected to obey your husband and it appeared you didn't have much of a choice in your role or the direction of your life, for all was decided for you. In the ancient scriptures, Kuan -Yin as Miao Shan, stood her ground and crafted for herself her divine choice. She saw, perhaps, a freedom from the oppressive role as a wife and mother and instead saw her inherent womanly gifts of nurturance and compassion as best, serving humanity. For Miao Shan, becoming a Buddhist nun was a more suited choice in alignment with who she was and what she strongly believed was her life purpose and this is incredibly empowering for women to witness. There is great power in recognizing our choice and exercising that power.

The legend of Miao Shan and Kuan-Yin's presence is also a powerful teacher about Justice, Karmic balance, temperance and forgiveness; which ultimately leads to our own inner liberation and enlightenment.

For a matriarchal, female Chinese deity to command such monumental veneration; beloved increasingly throughout the centuries, by not only the Chinese but across foreign lands as well, it's profoundly noteworthy. Her shrines and temples (both personal and public) were numerous in ancient times and they continue to flourish even now, centuries later. As in ancient times, Kuan-Yin is unquestionably a powerful deity for us to connect with as women and she awakens our own gifts of fortitude, compassion, nurturance and empowerment.

MAIA

MAIA

Maia, is the Greek Goddess of Springtime. She who is bright joy, love, frivolity, fecundity, and blossoming flowers. She who is beautiful and maternal, nurturing and makes the flowers grow, in the spring. Maia is the patron Goddess of nursing mothers and a deity deeply connected to theme of mothering. In this chapter, Maia takes her rightful place among the many matriarchal deities we are exploring together as part of our journey.

She was the eldest daughter of the strong Titan, sky holder, Atlas, and the Oceanid, Pleione. She is one of the seven Pleiades sisters. They were known as Taygete, Elektra, Alcyone, Asterope, Kelaiono, Merope and Maia.

Her name is often linked with the word mother but for the ancient Greeks, her name meant, *"She who is great."* Maia was also connected with several other deities like Bona Dea and Magna Mater.

Upon deeper inspection of the name Maia, we can see evidence of her chthonic origins. Within her name we see "aia," a reference to the Earth; more specifically underneath the ancient Earth.

According to Greek mythology, Maia became one of many of Zeus' secret lovers. Together they birthed Hermes, the cunning God of travelers, boundaries, languages, eloquence, commerce and magick. Hermes was also known as Mercury, the emissary and messenger of the Gods. He had a reputation for being a trickster and was even known to be a God of thieves. Because he was attributed for discovering magick, Maia has often been given the title, Grandmother of magick.

Maia was known as a Mountain Nymph (nature spirit) and found herself living most of her life in Mount Cyllene in Arcadia. She gave birth in this region and remained there to protect herself, and her son, from Hera's jealous wrath. Maia's maternal nature is evident throughout the Greek myths. She was reported to have raised Arcas, the child Callisto had with Zeus, when her mother was turned into a Bear by the jealous Hera.

In Latin, Maius, was the month of May. As one can surmise by looking at her name, the month of May was sacred to her. The celebrations most Pagans revel in as part of their Beltane celebrations are connected to the Greek Goddess of May, Maia. Annually, a May Queen would be crowned at this lively ecstatic holiday. We also cannot dismiss how all Mothers are venerated in the U.S.A. on Mother's day in the month of May.

As you connect with the Goddess Maia, it is a perfect time to reflect on all the mothers you are blessed to know; Your mother, your grandmothers, and your Great-grandmothers, as well as your aunts and elder aunts. It is a good time to create an honoring rite to your matriarchal lineage by gathering photos of all the women in your family herstory and lighting a votive candle for each woman or offering a potted plant or flower to each. Contemplate on aspects of their lives and the impact its had on your own. You may be inspired to quietly gaze at the photos to receive spiritual messages from your maternal ancestors.

Take this moment to pause and reflect on your own personal journey towards Motherhood (whether you are a mother now or hope to be one someday). You can make a special pledge to yourself to nurture, love and mother yourself in the healthiest manner or you can send out Universal love to all mothers. As part of our journey in this chapter you are invited to explore compassion and honor the Archetype of the Mother.

SIF

SIF

The beloved Norse Goddess with the long sun-kissed colored hair is known as Sif. Her long golden hair was reminiscent of the wheat, the yellow corn, the harvest she exemplifies. In Old Norse text she was also known as the Swan Maiden because she could easily shape-shift into this form. She is Goddess of abundance, prosperity, self-sacrifice and peace. Consummate wife and mother, she is a symbol of community, family, the clan and the protection of the whole, as oppose to the individual. Sif and her long Golden hair, is often considered the Harvest and the Earth itself. She represents the sacrificing of the individual for the greater good of all and as the guardian of the family she represents the importance of strengthening lineage, family bonds and community.

Sif is worshipped as a fertility deity, connected to the archetype of the Mother and very much like the Greek, Grain Goddess Demeter. She is worshipped as the Earth itself which is reminiscent of Gaia and most Earth fertility deities. But her numerous tales in Norse mythology reveal to me that she is indeed very reminiscent to the Aboriginal

Goddesses of the Americas; Selu, Iyatiku and Corn Mother. This will be revealed when we delve further into the numerous examples that depict her role as a sacrificial Harvest Goddess who concerns herself with the wellbeing of her family and maintaining peace and harmony for all.

SIF'S ETYMOLOGY

Perhaps it's best to start with the etymology of her name. The word, *"Sippe,"* in the German language means *"kin"*, *"kindred"* and or *"kith"* and the word *"sibling"* comes from the word *"sib"* which is very closely linked to this Norse Goddess. Scholar, Andy Orchard, believes her name means *"relation,"* while scholar, John Lindow, notes the meaning of Sif to be, *"in-law-relationship."* It becomes clear from numerous sources that her name is intimately linked with the idea of kinsmen, family, relationships and or related via a marriage. And these definitions are corroborated by her well known myths in Norse mythology. More precisely, her name is believed to be the singular form of the plural word "Sifjar," which is an Old Norse word, related to siblings, relations and again…connection via marriage. Some sources define the word "Sifjar" to mean, "to marry" and thus, the name Sif connotes a relationship via marriage and it aptly describes Sif, as she does become a highly venerated Norse Goddess exclusively via her union to the supreme God of Lightning, Thor.

SIF'S ATTRIBUTES

Sif's ancestry is a mystery and sadly not much is known about her origins. We don't know who her mother and father are, nor if she had any brothers or sisters in her mythologies. We don't know where she exactly stemmed from but we can make some inference based on what little has been written about her and those she interacted with in her myths. She was believed to be part of the Elder race of Gods, possibly a part of the Vanir, a second clan of Gods that existed before the Aesir. Vanir concerned themselves with cultivation, fertility, wisdom and prophecy. Sif was viewed as an Asa-Goddess that was later assimilated into the Aesir (newer clan of Gods that concerned themselves with power and wars) due to her marriage to Thor. Hence she is embraced as part of the modern race of Gods. Surprisingly not much is noted in the ancient text of the Viking period about this Goddess, thus what we do know about her comes from a few surviving poems, some fragmentary references to her and the few excerpts that have survived in the Elder Edda, the Prose Edda.

We do know that Sif is worshipped as Thor's wife and this very fact bestows on her a great position of importance among the Aesir Norse Gods, for Thor was highly revered as the beloved son of the King of the Gods, Odin. Thor's mother is the primordial earth mother Goddess, Jord, considered the last evidence of an earth deity who's position was later taken over by Frigga and Freyja, though some would argue that Sif herself was often mixed and amalgamated with these deities and might actually be the best representation of one generation or elder race, bequeathing her divine attributes to the next.

Sif garnered for herself a great position of power as the wife of the Great God of lightning and protection, Thor. He was liken to the Roman God, Jupiter and the Greek

God, Zeus. And because marital unions in those days had less to do with romance or great love affairs and more to do with contractual business arrangements in an effort to preserve and strengthen the clan, we can only conjecture the dynamics of their marriage. She is actually his second wife and he is her second husband, as she was previously married to the Giant Orvandil. Interesting to note, this association with Orvandil also connects her even more to the Elder race of Norse Gods, the Vanir.

Sif comes into the union with her Divine second husband already with a child- a son named Ull or Ullr, the God of Snow & Archery. Ullr is associated with Winter, skiing and all things related to snow. His name means "the Magnificent." Known as a God of Archery, he later becomes the perfect consort for the Jotunheim Giantess, Snow Goddess, Skadi. The father of Sif's son is unknown or at least not mentioned in the text of this time period but we do know he is not considered Thor's child. He is not listed as one of Thor's children but Modi (which means Anger or the Brave one) and Magni (which means Might) are indeed listed as Thor's offspring and consequently, Sif's step children. They were conceived with his mistress and enemy of Sif, the giantess, Jarnsaxa, which means, "Iron Sword." Together, the Goddess Sif and her Aesir consort do give birth to one child; their daughter, Thrud (which means "Might"). Thrud becomes the Goddess of Storms and Clouds and one of the Valkyrie.

Our knowledge about the Golden haired Goddess comes from a compilation of the writings in Norse mythology. Deciphering, researching, compiling and putting all the little pieces together helps us get a better look at who Sif is and still remains to be, in the sacred realm of Asgard. It is through the writings found in The Prose Edda, written in the 13th century by Snorri Sturluson (c.1179-1241) and also the Poetic Edda, which is the oldest of the two and is considered a compilation of earlier traditional writings, that we are privileged to get a closer look at Norse deities. Sif is mentioned in both, though not with great frequency. Astonishingly enough, her name is not listed by Snorri Sturluson (c.1179-1241) in the Gylfaginning among the numerous other Norse Gods but her name does appear in numerous other tales. There are a combination of probably four different stories I will mention here that will help us learn, in greater detail about Sif, her lineage, her character, her important gifts and attributes and her vital role within the Norse pantheon. We will look at her presence in the Lokesenna, the book of Gylfaginning, the Skaldskaparmal and the story of the Giant Hrungnir.

SKALDSKAPARMAL

By far the most notable myth revealing a significant amount of information about this Norse Goddess is in the Skaldskaparmal tale in the Prose Edda.

One night while Thor was probably away, his stepbrother, the trickster god, Loki, also known as Loki Laufeyarson, decided to sneak into Sif's bedchamber. While the Goddess slept he crept, ever so sneakily and in his usual manner, and he cut off the beautiful golden hair of the Goddess while she slumbered. Now her beautiful golden long tresses had greater value than one would initially expect. Her hair was symbolic of her fertile powers and succinctly represented her as Goddess of the Harvest. A woman's hair in ancient times represented her powers of fecundity and often measured her beauty.

Most ancient text, when describing a Goddess, do not frequently refer to physical bodies but will commonly make reference to the length of her hair, as a measure of her great beauty and fertile powers. And thus Loki, cutting off Sif's golden long hair was considered to be severely offensive; an act of monumental significance and detrimental to the Goddess herself. It was a symbol of her great sovereignty. When Thor returned home and discovered what his stepbrother had done and the pain and heartache it caused his wife, he became outraged. And when he got a hold of Loki, he proceeded to break every single bone of the scoundrel's body. In desperation, Loki begged Thor to spare him and promised he would make amends and rectify the situation.

When released from Thor's deadly grip, Loki then hurriedly arrives at the land of the Svartalheim, one of the nine sacred realms of Norse cosmology and here he connects with the Black dwarves to explain his plight and acquire their help. Some interpretation of the Norse text reveals he connected with dwarves or craftsmen-elves but a more common interpretation states that Loki connected with the sons of Ivaldi in this realm.

The dwarves came to the rescue and handcrafted a magickal wig that would grow hair made out of purely spun gold when placed upon the head of the Goddess, Sif. They truly outdid themselves with this magickal creation but they went even further by also crafting more gifts for the Aesir Gods. The sons of Ivaldi crafted powerful tools of magick for Odin and for Frey. Both Odin's Spear, known as the Gungnir and Frey's magic boat, known as the Skidbladnir, were manifested as an indirect result of Loki's mischievousness deed. Upon their completion, Loki was needless to say very pleased and relieved but... as was his nature he could not leave well enough alone...

On his way back to Thor and the Gods of Asgard, he ran into two more dwarves from the Elf-smith clan of Sidri; Brokk and Eitri. And he started to boast heavily about what had happened and the great successful craftsmanship by the sons of Ivaldi. He showed off their impressive works and questioned the two dwarves before him and their own ability to do better. As was his mischievous nature, he presented an irresistible challenged to the two dwarves. Loki placed a wager with Brokk and Eitri that they could not surpass the artistry, skill and craftsmanship of the sons of Ivaldi. He challenged them with a bet that if they crafted something grandeur and far superior than the sons of Ivaldi had, he would offer them his own head on a platter. Well, this wager excited the Dwarves as they did not care much for Loki and they delighted in the possible conquest. Together they began crafting three additional tools that would prove to be most powerful for the Norse Gods. Loki watched in amazement and in his fear of losing to them, he shape-shifted into a horsefly to pester them while they diligently worked on the divine tools but it didn't stop the clever Dwarves from completing their grand masterpieces. Eventually, they won the competition by crafting; Frey's golden Boar, Gullinbursti, Odin's multiplying ring, Draupnir and Thor's revered Hammer, Mjollnin.

When proudly they presented their work to Loki, he refused to admit defeat and he would not surrender his head to the dwarves as promised, claiming that it was attached to his neck and he never promised his neck along with his head in the wager. The Norse Gods were called upon to decipher who indeed was the winner and when they gave their stamp of approval to Brokk and Eitri, it was Loki who had to eventually pay up. The Gods allowed the Dwarves to sew and shut up Loki's mouth for his chaotic shenanigans and mischievous dealings and while the Dwarves took great pleasure in being declared the winners and finally punishing Loki by sewing up his mouth, it was the Norse Gods who were the ultimate winners, benefitting most by the exquisite magickal creations of the Dwarves.

PROLOGUE OF THE PROSE EDDA -REFERENCE AS A SYBIL

One thing is clear, the cutting off of Sif's locks by Loki resulted in the growth, extension and advancement of the Norse Gods, for her hair being chopped off, acted as a sacrificial rite that resulted in the manifestation of five of the most important Divine gifts and powerful tools of the Gods.

In the Prologue of the Prose Edda by Snori Sturluson, Sif is actually called a seer, a prophetess. She is described as a Sybil and thus someone with the gift of prophecy, powers of Divination and great psychic abilities. And in this prologue we learn of how she and Thor meet for the first time in the realm of Thrace or Thrudheim and then they later marry. Interesting to note, Thrace is the place that some scholars have claim Hekate, the Greek Goddess of the Underworld and Patroness of Witches and Seers, originates from. It is certainly thought-provoking to consider that Sif, with her gifts of prophecy, might have known and orchestrated this important, sacrificial rite in order for the Gods to grow in their powers. Of course, some would argue that many of the Norse Goddesses, like Freyja for example, had these inherent psychic abilities in varying degrees automatically as part of their numerous attributes, but it's interesting to note this ability in the Goddess Sif, paired with her role as a sacrificial harvest deity, who ultimately just seeks to create harmony and family unity.

Some would argue that perhaps the Goddess Sif, being attributed with psychic abilities, knew or had some psychic knowledge and premonition that this would need to occur for the advancement of the Gods. After all, this is her very nature, sacrificing for the greater good of all. These are parts of her known attributes and represented in her long flowing golden hair is the resemblance of the corn harvest. Upon closer inspection it would seem quite obvious that Sif and the cutting off of her long golden hair represents the first harvest pruning so often required in order to facilitate and help proliferate the subsequent harvest. As is her nature, she sacrifices for the harmony and greater good of all and thus her hair, which is so intrinsically a part of her, is shorn, surrendered into the hands of the trickster God Loki, in order that the Norse Gods grow in power and strength. The end result is that the five powerful gifts to the Norse Gods; Frey's golden Boar- Gullinbursti, Odin's ring – Draupnir, Odin's Spear – Gungnir, Frey's magic boat – Skidbladnir and Thor's revered Hammer –Mjollnin, would never had manifested, had it not been for her golden tresses being cut off by Loki's mischievous deed.

LOKASENNA- CHALICE & PEACE MAKER

We get an even better glimpse into the Goddess, Sif, when we look at yet another powerful tale in the Prose Edda, which confirms and supports her established role as a peacemaker. In the Lokasenna, (Stanza 53-54), we meet Loki once again, only this time he arrives at the sacred banquet hall of the Gods to manifest yet another stage of cacophony and mayhem.

Prior to this moment, Loki had been banished by the Gods from the banquet hall for killing a host servant but he now returns with much to say. He stands in the middle of the sacred hall and with much malice and disgust, he begins to accuse the male Gods of being cowards and a fearful bunch. This is Loki's attempt to hit below the belt, so to speak. Then he proceeds to speak of the women present, the Goddesses; referring to them as flirts and "trampish." He even goes as far as making inappropriate claims about the Norse Virgin Chaste Goddess, Gefjion. Clearly in that moment, Loki is being very cantankerous, unstable and quite vulgar to the Norse Gods and in his usual manner, he's creating quite a scene, as he angers the Gods of Asgard. Yet, in the middle of this disruptive mayhem, it is the Goddess Sif who bravely steps forward to confront Loki and attempt to rectify the situation. Holding her sacred crystal chalice in hand, she approaches Loki and offers him the antique mead linked to the powers of her husband, Thor. In her efforts to calm his belligerent heart and bring peace and harmony to the banquet hall, she says to Loki, that as she is being cordial to him he should do likewise with her, but Loki has other plans. She mentions that she is blameless and his insults to the Goddesses do not reflect her own true character, but Loki appears to have some insightful knowledge that he elects to maliciously divulge before all the Gods, as if to try to embarrass her.

> ***"Hail to thee, Loki, and take thou here,***
> ***The Crystal Cup of Old Mead;***
> ***For me at least, alone of the Gods,***
> ***Blameless thou knowest to be..."***

Loki drinks down the Antique Mead given to him and afterwards begins to direct all his insults towards Sif, amongst the tribe; insinuating that she has not been as chaste, nor as pure and faithful as she claims. He goes on to reveal that the wife of the great Norse God, Thor, is not so innocent and has actually had intimate relations with him. Loki in his volatile, mischievous state actually makes the claim of infidelity with almost all the Goddesses throughout Norse mythology, so it is not clear how much truth there is in his statement. However, what is important to note in this poem is that Sif, again, has placed herself willingly in the middle of a very disruptive, uncomfortable and potentially dangerous situation, in her effort to manifest peace and harmony for the greater good of all and to protect the Gods from Loki's insults. Loki was being obnoxious and riling up the Gods in that banquet hall and it is Sif who decides to approach him to calm him down. Yet in the end, she again acts as the sacrificial one, for Loki diverts his attention now unto her and instead of continuing to insult all the Gods present, he turns to deliver his most venomous accusation and insults towards her. She makes herself available to circumvent a potential war and redirects his insults to spare her Divine community.

There is also an important connection between the chalice (cup, goblet and cauldron) regarding Sif, for she is considered the vessel or cornucopia that holds the essence of life. She is the Chalice, the feminine, the Yoni, the receptor and her consort,

Thor as the masculine; is the mead, the fertilizer, the semen. In the Lokasenna she is thus, the cup bearer who is essentially offering herself when she offers the Crystal Chalice to Loki, filled with old mead. In this very significant act, she is also standing in her power as true representative of her husband's authority in his absence, which reflects her great sovereignty.

In the Lokasenna, we see a perfect example of her role as a peacemaker, as a Goddess who is looking out for the greater good of her community and as the one who steps forward to offer herself as the chalice; the sacrifice, to help diffuse the already volatile environment that Loki has created. In her efforts to make peace in that banquet hall among her family of deities, she is the one who ends up being trampled on because Loki begins to attack her, making inappropriate claims about her true nature and their past carnal history. It certainly leaves one more intrigued and wondering if there is any truth to Loki's claim, especially when we remember how he entered her bedchamber and cut off her hair in the Skaldskaparmal tale in the Prose Edda but none of this matters more than her consistent role as the one who self – sacrifices for the wellbeing of all.

This tale is yet again another example of how, Sif, in her effort to manifest peace puts herself in the mist of the chaos for the greater good of the Clan. But it's interesting because it turns your attention to yet another possible aspect of hers. And we don't know if there is any truth to Loki's claim but certainly there are other writings in the Prose Edda that alludes to this beautiful Goddess as having many intimate relations apart from her husband, Thor.

GYLFAGINNING

In the Gylfaginning, it is Thor's father, the God Odin, who also makes a claim that Sif is entertaining lovers. In this tale, stanza 48, Odin, in disguise, meets his son and the two begin this sort of bantering, throwing jabs and insults at one another. One of the claims Odin makes, is that Thor's wife is back at home being unfaithful to him. Thor is not moved by this comment and neither does he appear angered or combative. He simply replies by accusing the masked Odin of lying.

We don't know all of the validity of these accusations or even if it merits further investigation. It makes me wonder if this was just a common way to teasingly insult and degrade a Goddess, especially one who was known for her great beauty and discriminatory gifts of inciting desire. But perhaps what becomes most obvious is that not much has been written about the Goddess Sif and this creates a kind of tugging at all hints of her nature, subjecting any mention of her in writings, through rigorous investigation, gravely analyzing every mention of her in ancient text; whether it was small or large, truth or fictional. Consequently, there is not enough written about her and thus every little bit of information we can discern from fragmentary comments, poems and excerpts, becomes weighted with great importance for those seeking to know her best.

It is important to note that marriages were contractual agreements that afforded greater power to tribes for the Norse and it becomes clear that infidelities were probably not such a big issue or concern among the Aesir.

GIANT HRUNGNIR

To say that she is a beautiful Goddess is an understatement, for almost every mentioned of Sif in the writings of the Viking and pre-Viking period reveals her as being exceptionally beautiful.

In the Hymir Poem we see how much she is valued and desired by one of the strongest Jotnar Giants. When the Giant Hrungir, in a drunken stupor, begins to berate the Gods and makes outlandish threats that he is going to destroy the Aesir Gods, he reveals his desires for the two most beautiful deities in all of Norse mythology. In this poem, Hrungir shares aloud his plans to destroy the Gods and take for himself the two most beautiful female deities; Freyja and Sif. This is very indicative of how important these two deities were. Eventually Thor kills off the Giant but it's interesting to note that these two Goddesses, lumped together, were the only two the Jotnar Giant wished to save for himself, as if they were the most valuable prize in all of Asgard. This becomes more intriguing because some scholars have even attempted to claim that both of these Goddesses are really one and the same, due to their many similarities. It is more likely however, that Sif, being from the Elder race of Gods, came before Freyja and while both share in similar attributes, especially their gift of prophecy and their reputed magnanimous great beauty, they are more than likely two different Goddesses that came to us from different periods and tribes, and are now equally embraced as two separate, powerful deities in modern Norse mythology.

SOME ADDITIONAL OBSERVATIONS

Sif is the fertile land; the yellow corn, the wheat, the Harvest. She is the Chalice that holds the essence of life and the mother archetype that protects and unifies the clan. Sif is a prophetess, beautiful beloved wife of Thor and a sacrificial fertility Goddess intrinsically linked with the prosperity and sustenance of her tribe. Like Selu, the indigenous Corn Mother deity of the Americas, there is a striking resemblance in their attributes and roles as Sacrificial Harvest deities, for both were considered representative of the land itself and both... willingly sacrificed themselves in an effort to save or sustain something bigger than the individual. Selu, whose very own body produced the harvest corn, allows her body to be cut up and scattered across the land so that when she is gone her children will survive, thrive and not be extinct from hunger. Sif, in a similar manner, allows her hair, which is the harvest corn itself, to be cut up, shorn, and as a result, the Gods are strengthen and their powers expanded upon, via the new tools they acquired from her sacrificed tresses.

It is through this sacrifice that she must surrender a part of herself, a valuable part of herself for the benefit of the greater good and the clan-which she and Thor are responsible for protecting. Her hair is what helps manifest the Divine gifts; Frey gets the golden Boar (Gullinbursti), the magic boat (Skidbladnir) and Odin gets his Spear (Gungnir), the ring (Draupnir), and Thor gets his Hammer (Mjollnin). Just as it is through the willing offering of Selu's spilt blood across the field, that the land then becomes fertilize to forever feed and sustain her people, in much the same way, Sif, as a prophetess, knows her role is to sacrifice, to strengthen the Norse Gods, facilitate their longevity, for she is their chalice and the fertile land.

Another example of her role as family protector, peace keeper and sacrificial Goddess is the way she takes on the two children (Modi and Magni) of her Husband and his mistress. Under most normal human circumstances, a wife would be conflicted to learn that her husband's mistress was birthing to life two children but Sif is a Goddess whose sole role is to create harmony and wellbeing for the clan and thus, the children of her enemy, Jarnsaxa, are embraced as her own. All are taken in by Sif and gathered, unified as one, to sit amidst the family dinner table. And any antagonistic emotions that would surface as a result of learning about this affair are relinquished for peace and the greater good of the whole family.

I find it titillating that she enters her union with Thor already possessing a child (paternal lineage undocumented) and both, She and Thor, come from starter marriages. Together they have a child, Thrud, but along with the two previously mention step-children; it appears Sif's familial situation is very similar to our Modern day, 21th century blended, nucleus family. In this day and age of unconventional unions, where divorce rates are at record high number and multiple marriages (unions) carry with them the potential for numerous step-children; combining households seems to be the norm. This ancient Norse Goddess is reflecting a modern condition affecting our growing society as a whole today. The grace in which she handles this sacrifice of herself, despite any pain or heartache she may deeply feel, for the benefit of the whole Divine Clan, is exemplary of a Goddess and one we can fully identify with in our modern day era.

*The beautiful Norse Goddess, Sif, is the embodiment of the Harvest. Sif is the sacrificial one, who chooses to act considering the bigger picture and her community. She is less concern with the individual and chooses to align herself with the overall good of the clan. Sif is the one who seeks to formulate peace and harmony among her tribe and will often offer herself up in sacrifice for the peace and greater good of all. This is precisely what makes her an exemplary leader for us to explore in our chapter of leadership. The Goddess Sif willing surrenders parts of herself for the protection and sustenance of her tribe. With her, we are made aware of our leadership role within our community and the sacrifices sometimes required of us for peace, harmony and prosperity. Her beautiful blonde tresses, which resemble the wheat in a Harvest, is cut, pruned, and sacrificed, and this very act blesses the clan with a number of additional, invaluable gifts. Sif is the golden Harvest that must be sacrificed and pruned in order for greater prosperity to eventually ensue and bless the community at large.

CHAPTER SEVEN
SOVEREIGNTY
SHE WHO CHARGES FORWARD IN LEADERSHIP ROLES

DURGA

"We are what we repeatedly do,
Excellence, then, is not an act, but a habit..." Aristotle

DURGA

Durga is one of the most beloved and widely embraced Hindu Goddesses. She is often considered the supreme Goddess (Mahadevi) and a Universal Mother credited for protecting the world from demons in Hindu religion and Mythology. She is the warrior Goddess who combats anything that threatens the stability of the cosmos and is devoted to fighting the evil and negativity afflicting the world. Her numerous aspects and incarnations makes her one of the most multi-dimensional deities and by far one of the most intriguing.

Most of what we know today about Durga and her worship can be extrapolated from the puranas, the agamas (ancient Hindu texts) and the ancient Vedic text of around 4th century A.D. The Yajur Veda, Vajasaneyi Samhita, Taittareya and the Devi-Mahatmya all reveal a great deal about this well esteemed Goddess. We know that, although her worship can be traced to the 4th century B.C.E. and during the Harappan period, her worship became more prevalent after the 6th century. There are several puranas (sacred text) ranging from the third and fifteenth century, that mention her and several are even dedicated exclusively to her. The Devibhagavatan is one such purana, as well as the very similar, Durgasaptasti, better known as the Devi-Mahatmya. This seventh century text dedicated to Durga can be found in the Markandeyapurana also known as Chandi Mahatmya. It is one of the most highly recognized and venerated text to Durga and it is even often used as a mantra dedicated to the Goddess. There are also many Hymns like the Narayanistuti, which describes Durga as the mother of all creations and the physical embodiment of the earth. The Aparajitstotra Hymn praises Durga for her unconquerable abilities to defeat the demons; Sumbha and Nisumbha. Further research into this Goddess reveals there is no other deity among the vast impressive Hindu pantheon that comes close to exemplifying all that Durga does.

Her name is often translated as *"a Fort"* or *"One who is unreachable"* or *"difficult to know."* Sanskrit interprets her name as *"invincible"* and already, these combined translations of her name begin to paint a perfect picture of this ancient deity. Some scholars believe the name Durga is actually an abbreviation for Durgatinashini, which translates as, *"the one who eliminates suffering"* and this definition probably describes this Goddess best. It is interesting to note that **"Du"** represents, in Hinduism, the four devils; poverty, suffering, famine, evil habits, while the **"r"** represents diseases and the **"ga"** in her name represents, destroyer of sins, injustices, cruelty, laziness. *(Source from kalikraft.com)*

Durga protects mankind from misery and evil by destroying the demons known to man as selfishness, jealousy, prejudice, hatred, anger, and most of all, ego. Some of her incarnations are known as Kali, Bhagvati, Ambika, Lalita, Gauri, Kandalini, Kaushiki, Chamunda, Parvati, Java, Rajeswari, to name a few. Sometimes she is referred to as "Triyambake" meaning, Three eyes. Her left eye is representative of "desire," connected to the Moon. Her right eye is "action," connected to the Sun and the middle or center eye is "knowledge," linked with Fire. (www.Hinduism .Com, KOAUSA .org/ gods/goddess Durga)

Durga has numerous Feminine cosmic powers and aspects and I will mention a few of her most known aspects here. She is known as Kali (power of eternity and infinite night) and as Tara (void and night of anger). She is Chinnamasta (sacrifice and night of courage) and Kamalatmika (perfect happiness, night of paradise). Durga is also known as Dhumavati (deprivation and night of frustration) and as Tripura Bhairavi (death and the night of destiny) as well as Matangi (domination and night of illusion).

As her numerous myths, found in the sacred Hindu text, will reveal, Durga is the defender and protector of the Universe. She is slayer of numerous demons like; Sumbha, Nisumbha, Raktabija and Mahisura and she is the one who eradicates all the demons that plague humanity, represented in ego, lust, hatred, jealousy and greed.

The Goddess Durga is the embodied strength of the Gods. The Hindu Scriptures note she was born from the assemblage of all the angered and infuriated male deities who had gathered on one fated night to express their collective rage. Long ago there was a demon who was threatening to destroy the world and because this demon appeared to be succeeding in his venomous endeavor, it angered the Hindu pantheon. The story begins with the sly, demon Mahisa (Mahishasura). He was born to a Goddess who bestowed on him great powers. One day his mother approached the creator God, Brahma, and asked him to make her son immortal but the God refused, believing every man that is born must eventually meet his own death. Mahisa, trying to outsmart Brahma, asked, *"Then, let me meet my death in the sole hands of a woman."* He secretly thought, surely this would render him immortal, for what woman could possibly defeat this powerful demon to death? Women in India at this point in time, just didn't engage in wars and battles. Unsuspecting Brahma agreed to the wish and granted Mahisa his desire, never considering the consequences of his action. Soon thereafter Mahisa, believing he would live forever, gathered an army of demons and marched to the capital of heaven, the home of the Gods, known as Amarapur, to make his demands and claim the heavens for himself as Lord of all the worlds. On the turf of the Gods a horrific battle thus began between the King of Heaven, Indra, his league of Gods and the army of demons, led by Mahisa. This terrible battle would last for hundreds of years, according to Hindu writings.

Eventually, the Hindu pantheon of Gods was defeated. Angered and hopeless, they were removed from their home by the demon Mahisa. They did not know how to reclaim their sacred realm and overthrow Mahisa and his Demon army and they felt disheartened. Desperate, the Gods consulted Brahma but when he realized his part in this disaster, since it was he who granted the demon his wish, he suggested they all consult Lord Shiva. Then utterly frustrated and hopeless after speaking with Lord Shiva, together they traveled to Lord Vishnu to see what he might have to say about the situation. The three fuming Gods; Vishnu, Shiva and Brahma were beside themselves in complete rage that they would lose their sacred abode to the deceitful demon, Mahisa. The more they talked about it, the more their anger grew and grew. Their collective rage grew until it literally created a piercing bright light that first emanated from their mouths and grew brighter, until the form of a women's body, brighter than a million suns, appeared before them. As they expressed their anger it spilled forth, creating a powerful energy and this energy transformed itself into the great Goddess, Durga.

According to Hindu scriptures, Durga's body was formed by these male Gods. They also equipped her with copies of their own powerful weapons. Hindu scriptures state her face was fashioned by the light of the God Shiva. Durga's ten arms were formed by the light of Lord Vishnu, while her feet were formed by Lord Brahma. Her beautiful long hair came from the light of Yama, the God of Death; although some text claims it was Brahma who created her hair. From the King of Gods, Indra, her waist was formed. Her breasts were created by the Moon God, Somanath, while her toes were created by the light of the Sun God, Surya. Varun, God of the Oceans, gifted her with her legs and thighs and her swaying hips came from the light of the God of the earth, Bhoodev. It was the light of Prajapati, the Lord of creatures, that created her teeth and the light of the Fire God, Agni, is credited for manifesting her three eyes. Her ears were fashioned by the light of Vayu, the God of the Winds and the two Sandhyas, known as sunrise and sunset, created her eyebrows. (source; www.dollsforindia.com) It is clear Durga embodies the sacred Hindu Gods with every fiber of her being and she is their great anger and fury personified. This indeed makes her a powerful force to be reckoned with and evidently, she could've been included in our chapter exploring rage or a number of other chapter themes in this Goddess empowerment book. All of the Goddessess presented throughout this book have a plethora of attributes that can be explored in various chapters.

Upon her magnificent birth, Durga was gifted with the most treasured weapon possessions and many other powerful tools from these Gods, all in an effort to equip her with the necessary tools for victory in battle. Lord Shiva surrendered a Trident to her and Lord Vishnu presented her with a discus. Her spear was given to her by the God Agni and Vayu gave her the arrows. The Thunderbolt was given to her by the King of the Gods, Indra, as well as his white skinned elephant. The God Varuna gave her the sacred conch and a noose she would later use on Mahisa. Yama surrendered his sword and shield to the Goddess. From Vishwakarma, Durga received the axe and armor, while the God of the mountains, Himavat, gave to her, jewels and the magnificent Lion/Tiger as her sacred vehicle. Many other Gods bedecked her with numerous other gifts and weapons to arm her for full battle with the demon, Mahisa. (Source;www.dollsforindia.com) There are also many variations to this tale as can be expected with ancient deities and myths. Some, for example, claim it was Brahmna who bestowed to her the bow and arrow.

Although she was created by the Hindu male deities, the Goddess Durga is known to be fully autonomous, never requiring their direct aid in battle and never producing male helpers, instead opting to manifest female, bloodthirsty, helpers in battles, like Kali. Her ravenous female helpers are known as "Matrikas," which interestingly enough means, mother. Durga does indeed fight for her male creators when invoked and she defends them without their assistance, one of the only deities in Hindu mythology who can boast this attribute. She also does not lend her (Sakti/Shakti) powers to the Gods, unlike many other Hindu Goddesses but she is known to seize their powers and their fires for battles. And their inner strength is quite often surrendered to her freely. Vishnu for example is made to sleep and is rendered powerless and helpless in her presence. She causes him to be unconscious and he is thus, disempowered in her presence. In this aspect she is

Mahamaya, the supreme creator of illusion and the one who puts powerful spells that even Gods, like Vishnu, cannot escape. She bestows the Yoganidra (meditation and deep sleep) the power of sleep, cosmic slumber unto Vishnu at the inception of the Universe according to some text.

This brings us to her connection with the God Vishnu. Durga is personified Maya, also recognized as the mysteries power of Lord Vishnu. Some texts refer to her as the female version of Lord Vishnu, because of her recognized ability to create, sustain and destroy the world and yet, repeat the sacred cycle numerous times. She intervenes on a grand cosmic scale, to rid the world of anything that threatens its balance and equilibrium. She becomes not only a sheroe/saviouress of the Universe but also a personal saviouress for her children and devotees. Durga is known to come to the aid of her worshippers during times of great calamity. She is personified power and strength and when invoked by her devotees, she proves to be most helpful in battling both inner and outer demons. Forest fires, imprisonment, robberies, attacks, executions and even threats from wild animals also fall under her protective domain.

The Great Mother Goddess, Durga, personifies Maya, that which deludes individuals into thinking they are the center of the universe. Maya is ego, individualism, personal identity and a delusion according to Hindu tenet. Yet creation and delusion fall under this domain and are under her jurisdiction. She is known by many names and each name describes an attribute or prominent role she plays. As Raktadanta, she is the one with red teeth. As Sataksi she is the one with one hundred eyes. As Bhima, she is the terrible one and as Simhavahini, she is the rider of Lions. One of Durga's epitet is "Mardini" the slayer of the demon Mahisa (Mahishasura).

As Durga's famous legend continues on, upon her birth she was immediately dressed in the weapons of the Gods and sent to the Vindhya Mountains where she would meet and confront the demon, Mahisa. She is known in this aspect as Mahisasura-mardini. The demon, upon hearing of this brilliant beautiful mysterious woman arriving at the sacred mountain was smitten and he sent a personal message to the Goddess, that he had every intention to claim her as his bride, since he was now the Lord of the Worlds, but Durga had other intentions. "I can only marry a man who can defeat me in battle," she said to him and he took this as an invitation for battle. He brought his army of demons with him to claim her and what ensued was a gruesome, catastrophic battle that is forever memorialized in the sacred Hindu text.

Upon meeting the beautiful Battle Queen, the demon was greeted with a proper introduction to his destined killer but he didn't believe it to be so. Durga reminded him of the wish Brahma had granted to him and with great confident, she engaged him in battle. Mahisa was a known shape shifter and when he saw how great Durga's strength was, he changed himself into his true form, a black buffalo. He charged at her but he was of no threat to the great multi-armed Goddess who was riding her fierce lion and wielding her multitude of arms with commanding weapons. She is destined to be victorious in all battles. Durga relishes in the bloody battle as if it was a game for her (Lila aspect). The gruesome harsh battle continued with no end in sight and Mahisa was astounded at

Durga's great strength. Many demons died by her hands and despite Mahisa's numerous animal shape shiftings, he could not defeat the Great Durga. In one version of the story, Durga pins him down with her trident and kills him but in another version of the story Mahisa, desperate to be the victor, cast a spell to make every droplet of his blood spilled on the ground, manifest into new fiercer demons. In this way, his army would only multiply and grow in power with every drop of his spilt blood on the earth. The Goddess Durga, for a temporary moment, found herself overwhelmed by the sheer multitude of demons springing to life and in her rage and supreme powers she manifested the Blue/Black bloodthirsty Goddess, Kali from her brow. She would then become the embodied manifestation of Durga's wrath and great fury. Kali thus, sprang forth from Durga's furrowed brow and with her long darting, magnificent tongue; she immediately began lapping up every droplet of blood preventing it from spilling onto the ground, lessening the volume of demons on the battlefield. With Kali, Mahisa and his army of demons were finally defeated by the Goddess.

This aspect of Durga, ferociously helped defeat the demon Mahisa and restored harmony and dharma upon the earth once more but it was not the only time Durga battled demons with her fierce bloodthirsty helper, Kali. There is another tale of Durga fighting the Demon brothers; Sumbha and Nisumbha and their generals; Canda, Munda and Raktabija. These demon brothers drove the Gods out of heaven and again, Durga comes to their aid, in her form as Mahatmaya (mother Goddess). The Devi-Mahatmya text reveals it was the demon, Raktabija, whose spilt blood on the earth continued to birth even more demons and it was Kali who emerged from an aspect of Durga as Kaushiki, to lick up this blood, again, preventing any more blood to fall on the earth. Ultimately Kali swallows Raktabija whole and the battle against the myriads of demons is won once again.

Durga is described as exceptionally beautiful but her beauty lacks its normal function according to Hindu text, for it is an exquisite beauty that is not meant to attract a spouse but rather to lure her victims into fierce battles. And while it was most common to depict women in relation to men, as daughters, sisters, mothers, wives, lovers, Durga's appearance breaks with these conventionalities. She is depicted autonomously and without significant reference to a consort. She simply is and stands on her own in the bloody battlefield fighting without the aid of male Gods. There is no man coming to her rescue but on the contrary, it is Durga who is invoked to come to man's rescue. It is interesting that while she is worshipped as a Matriarchal Goddess who cares and protects the world and her children, Durga's image in these early writings is quite the contrary. She quintessentially appears as a maiden, unwilling to marry any of her numerous embattled suitors and she appears to take great pleasure in her freedom and her ability to defeat any man who thinks he might be worthy of her hand in marriage.

"In many respects Durga violates the model of the Hindu woman.
She is not submissive; she is not subordinate to a male deity,
she does not fulfill household duties and she excels at what is
traditionally a male function, fighting in battle.
As an independent warrior who can hold her own

against any male on the battlefield,
she reverses the normal role for females
and therefore stands outside of normal society…"

Page 97 -Hindu Goddesses, Visions of the Divine Feminine in the Hindu Religious Tradition, by David R. Kinsley, University of California Press, Berkeley and Los Angeles California, 1988

In one of her festivals, held during the Autumnal Harvest, she is worshipped as the returning daughter, which contradicts her role as a matriarchal deity. And here we start to see a resemblance to that other highly venerated daughter archetypal energy, the Greek Maiden, the Goddess Persephone.

A closer look at this fierce, multi-armed, Goddess and how she is portrayed both in Hindu art and ancient writings reveals a wild ferociousness unlike any other Hindu deity ever seen. She is a warrior Goddess who delights in the flesh and blood of the battlefield, as well as on her altar offerings. It was customary to petition the Goddess Durga with offerings of flesh meat, alcohol and blood sacrifices in ancient times. There are still hidden, far away parts of this world that continue to worship her in this manner. It becomes clear that she is a power that stands outside of what we deem as societally acceptable and civilized. One look at Kali, Durga's most well-known aspect, will convince you of this, as this aspect of hers appears, wild, primal, dark, untamable, violently bloodthirsty, gruesome and strong beyond belief but this is just proof of Durga's very well known, liminal nature.

Durga was known as Vindhyavasini (she who dwells in the mountains) and Tribal people on the outskirts of civilization, like the Sabaras, venerated her and held her up to high esteem, offering flesh and blood sacrifices. It is for this reason why one may conclude that her worship originates with non-Aryan or pre-Aryan people, for the Aryan would have considered this type of worship unthinkable as they viewed wine, flesh meat and blood as pollutants to religious rites. In the Devi-Mahatmya her devotees are even encouraged to offer their own flesh and blood as offering to the Goddess Durga.

When we consider the harsh terrains of the Himalayas and the Vyndhya mountains and its geographical location, outside and far away from civilization and city centers, we begin to understand Durga in a different context. Also keep in mind the frightening, hostile appearance of tribal people and how they would've been viewed by Aryan society, yet this is where Durga's worship manifested and flourished most. She has a liminal nature that almost requires her worship to take place outside of understood civilized edifices and confinements. This is what makes Durga's presence only found when we step outside of orthodoxies. She can only be understood in this way.

HER DEPICTIONS

Durga is often depicted dressed in the color red, which symbolizes both death and birth, our blood, action, war and the victor in battle. She appears standing next to or ridding a tiger/lion to denote her supreme powers, although it may also denote her ability to control and have power over others. She is also sometimes depicted riding a Buffalo, representing her defeat of the Buffalo-demon, Mahisa. The Goddess is often depicted with a multitude of arms; sometimes, four, eight, ten, eighteen, or even twenty arms. Each hand from her arm always holds a significant weapon, the various tools necessary to combat the numerous kinds of evil that plague humanity. Displayed in her many hands are the Trident, Bow and Arrow, sword, discuss, mace, spear, rosary (mala beads), bell, conch and wine-cup, to name just a few of her most common Divine tools.

The conch shell she carries is used as a musical instrument to make the primordial sound of creation, "aum." The bow and arrow represents the energy of the thunderbolt. The lotus, also known as Pankaja (and born of mud) is a symbol of steadfastness amidst the obstinate obstacles of the world. The sword represents knowledge and the discus instrument, which she spins on her finger, represents the unfailing weapon that destroys evil. The Trident or trishul, a gift from Shiva (Siva) represents three qualities; Satwa (inactivity), Rajas (activities), and Tamas (non-activity). As fighter of evil, negativity and injustices, she stands in "Abhay Mudra" to guarantee freedom of fear.

In a rarer, domesticated role, there is an aspect of Durga as the wife of Shiva, she is known as Parvati. In the "Skana Purana" she is the demon that threatens the world, Lord Shiva calls on the Goddess Parvati, who then becomes Durga herself, fighting this demon also named Durga. Seems rather confusing but it is important to note that when Parvati endeavors to fight this demon she sheds her outer sheath and it is thus the great warrior Goddess Durga that arises.

Durga was also connected to Lord Shiva in yet another aspect, as the Goddess Sati. As Sati, she was the first born daughter of King Daksha. From an early age Sati showed exemplary devotion to the God Shiva and thus, upon learning of her great devotion to him, Lord Shiva sought to have her as his bride. The King however, did not approve of such a match for his daughter but despite his disapproval the two got married. Later the story reveals the eventual demise of Shiva's beloved bride. After the union, the King arranged for his daughter, a Yagna, which is a kind of penance ceremony in which offerings were made to a fire deity. Lord Shiva was not invited to this event but he attended it anyway and was subjected to a multitude of grave insults and humiliation by the King. His daughter was so distraught by the entire incident that she sacrificed herself within the sacrificial altar fires. The grief-stricken, enraged Shiva picked up the body of his deceased beloved and there commenced his violent dance of destruction upon the earth, known as the Tandava. The witnessing Gods were frightened as the earth shook terribly in response to his powerful dance. The only thing that finally pacified Shiva was Vishnu's successful attempt to cut up Sati's body, while being held up by Shiva, into little pieces that were scattered about the earth. When the last piece of Sati's fragmented body fell, Lord Shiva was placated and now it is believed the land known as Shaktipeeth holds her scattered sacrificial body parts. This was one know aspect of the Goddess Durga as wife to Lord Shiva.

There are also three important elements Durga illustrates; Sakti, Moksa and Prakrti.

Sakti/Shakti: It is the creative, powerful force of the Divine. It is the underlying power or source of the Gods. Sakti is different from the term **Tejas,** which is understood as the energy or fire of the Gods; the power and source of the Divine.

Moksa: In this element, she is protectress of the cosmos and destroyer of demons. Created by the male gods, she acts on their behalf and defends them, as well as transcends them. She restores harmony in the cosmos. She births, destroys and rebirths again in continuous sacred cycles.

Prakrti: In this element she is the actual physical world. Durga is the embodiment of the earth, and the rhythm of the Universe. Durga sustains and protects the world and its inhabitants. As **"Sakambhari"** she provides the world with food and sustenance from her very own body and this is very reminiscent of the indigenous Goddess of the Americas; Selu/Corn Mother but also resembles the Greek Goddess Demeter and the primordial Goddess, Gaia, as an actual embodiment of the earth.

Durga is the personification of knowledge, memory and wisdom in this aspect she is Aparavidya (knowledge of secular Sciences). As Paravidya, she is linked with higher knowledge concerning spiritual matters. She is Tamasi (darkness) and she is the great delusion as Mahamoha. She descends from time to time to defend the earth. She helps the Gods and humanity, and restores the earth's harmony; in this way she resembles the Chinese Goddess, Nu Kua, who was also a creatress and saviouress of ancient China.

FESTIVALS

There are numerous Festivals associated with the Goddess Durga and her worship but there are two that are universally, well known; the Navaratra (Durga Puja) and the Dasara. It is also important to note that her worship in the North of India varies from the South.

Durga Puja is her annual festival held for nine days near the Autumnal harvest, it is also known as Navaratra. This festival is held during the lunar month of Asvin and it is a splendor to behold. During the Durga Puja she is often depicted with four other deities considered her children; Sarsawati, Lakshmi, Ganesa, Karttikeya. Other texts, however, reveal she is the mother of Jyoti as well. The altars for Durga during the Navaratra festival are often elaborate with numerous offerings and larger than life images of the multi-armed Goddess, made out of Clay but also made of many other interesting materials like; fibers and food. Durga's many appellations are commemorated for each of the nine days of Durga Puja, they are listed below.

DURGA PUJA AND HER NINE APPELLATIONS, mentioned in the Devi Kavacha of the Chadipatha scriptures...

DAY 1.Shailaputri, This word means daughter (Putri); daughter of the mountains (Shaila). She is worshipped on the first day of the festival and she embodies Brahma, Vishnu and Shiva. She rides a bowl and carries a trident and a Lotus in her two hands. Also known as Parvati, Sati, Hemavati, daughter of the Hemava/Himalayan.

DAY 2.Brahmacharini, (meaning unmarried) In her second form as mother goddess she is worshipped on the second day of the Navaratra festival. Her name means one who practices devout austerity. This was Parvati during her period of great devotion waiting for Lord Shiva to recognize her as his destined bride. She holds a rosary on her right hand and water utensil or a Kumbha, which is a water pot, in her left hand. She is blissfully happy and peaceful and is the way to emancipation. She bestows prosperity and grace upon all her devotees who worship her. This aspect of Durga is the holder of knowledge and wisdom. Divine grace is gifted to us in her presence.

DAY 3.Chandraghanta, The third form of the Goddess and worshipped on the third day of the festival, she brings peace, tranquility and prosperity in the life of those who invoke her. She has a Chandra or half Moon on her forehead in the shape of a bell. This form of Durga is depicted with ten hands, each holding a powerful weapon and three eyes. She is a disciple of bravery and possesses great strength to fight in the battle against demons. She is giver of knowledge and bliss.

DAY 4.Kusumanda, (Kushumanda) The fourth form of the Goddess, worshipped on the fourth day. "Ku" means a little, "ushma" means warmth, and means the cosmic egg. In this form she is considered the creator of the universe and she holds weapons in her eight hands and a rosary while she rides the lion/tiger.

DAY 5.Skondamata, (Skanda mata) Her name means the mother of Skanda. Notice similarity to the Norse Giantess named Skadi. In Hindu mythology, Skanda was the son of Lord Shiva and Parvati, He was a commander in chief of the Gods, to fight the demon. In this appellation, she is worshipped on the fifth day, accompanied by Lord Skanda, in his infant form. She has a bright complexion and she sits on a Lotus. She is depicted with four arms and three eyes while holding a Lotus in her hands.

DAY 6.Katyayani, The sixth form, worshipped on the six day of the festival. She is an avatar of Durga. There was once a sage named Kata or Katyayan, who had a son named Katya and according to one legend, Kata, prayed for a daughter like a Goddess and his wish was granted when Katyayani was born as an avatar of Durga.

DAY 7.Kaalratri, Her name represents the enemy of darkness and ignorance. She is the seventh form of Durga, worshipped on the seventh day of the Navaratra festival. She is dark skinned, disheveled hair, in a fearless posture and wearing a necklace, flashing around her neck. She has three eyes, flames from her breath and her vehicle is a donkey. On her upper left hand she holds a thorn like weapon, made of iron. She is also known as, Shubhamkari, the one who does good. She resembles Kali in her midnight hue and she holds a sparkling sword in her right hand, ready for battle.

DAY 8.Maha Gauri, her name means "Fair." She is exalted and worshipped on the eighth day of the Navaratra festival. The sins of the pass, present and future get washed away and purified in her presence. She is intelligent, peaceful and calm. She wears white clothes and displays four arms while riding a bull. Her right lower hand holds a trident. Her left upper hand holds a damaru. She expresses unfailing and fruitful attributes for her devotees.

DAY 9.Siddhidatri, The name means the giver of siddhis (magical or spiritual powers to control the self and others and the forces of nature) This is Durga in her ninth form and the most powerful form. She is worshipped on the ninth day of the Navaratra Harvest festival where she exemplifies supernatural healing powers. She has four arms, holding a club, a lotus and a conch shell. She is always happy. She rides on a lion/tiger as her sacred vehicle, displaying great powers and she blesses the entire Universe.

DASARA

Durga's second festival, held after the Navaratra, is the Dasara. The Dasara festival is much more connected to military feats and the impactful influence of the powerful Goddess, Durga and her ability to bless military weapons and grant victory in the battlefield to her worshippers. She is exalted as Abita, Ambika or Aparajita, as the one who blesses the military and its soldiers, but she is also directly connected with the fruitfulness of the Harvest as we will see in her other Festival.

Returning to Durga Puja, it is celebrated during the lunar month of Asvin, which coincides with the Autumnal Harvest in North India. During this festival, Durga is the power inherent in all vegetation. Nine different plants are bundled together, they create a Navapattrika, which is a bundle of different plants worshipped and venerated as the Goddess herself. Durga is associated with the successful growing, fertile crops. She is the sacred crops and frequently, as an offering, worshippers will bring to her altars, sugar cane juice and sesame seed oil. Durga in this aspect is unquestionably connected to the fecundity of crops. There is also another ritual during this festival in which a priest takes five grains, scattered firmly on the dough, rice wheat and barley, the burghii, also known as "mas." The sesame is placed on the dough as the priest says the invocation that alludes to the Goddess actually being these grains.

Durga is the power of life which the Gods utilize to achieve immortality. She is the one who appeases the hunger of the world and protects her worshippers from the numerous demons plaguing society. At these Festivals, blood sacrifices are common and an intrinsic part of the ceremonies to reenact her ancient myths, connected to the buffalo demon and the blood that was shed. Goats and sheep are also sacrificed and sometimes, to quench Durga's thirst for blood, worshippers would even sacrifice their own blood as offerings to her. This was done to replenish her powers, to invigorate the Goddess and give her back life force, now contained in the form of blood and animal sacrifices. Blood was seen as a recharger and re-awakener needed to refuel the strength of the mighty protectress Goddess.

"Om, you are the rice, Om, you are the life,
you are the life of the Gods, you are our life, you are our internal life,
you are long life, you give life, Om, the Sun with his rays
gives you the milk of life and Varuna nourishes you with water..."

pg 111-112 Hindu Goddesses, Visions of the Divine Feminine in the Hindu Religious Tradition, by David R. Kinsley, University of California Press, Berkeley and Los Angeles California, 1988

The interdependence of human sexuality with fertility and the success of harvest crops are evident in the worship and rituals of many different cultures and this extends to

India as well. Particularly, when such a wild, primal powerful deity, like the one who lives outside of the boundaries of civilizations, is propitiated, one can expect an intense experience. It is to be expected, that Durga's worship might take on a boisterous, wild, rambunctiously liberating and even pleasurable undertone. It would not be unlikely to see couples, copulate in the field of India, just like in many other cultures during this time of the year, believing that their copulation and the spilt secretion of their lovemaking would result in a more prosperous harvest. This is a form of giving back vitality and energy to the spirit underlining the crops. Semen and sexual fluids were believed to have great fertilizing powers, powers that were necessary to fertilize the field and manifest a prosperous harvest.

NORTH INDIA -DURGA PUJA

However, in North India, we are privy to an alternate approach to her worship. It was almost compulsory for girls to be married at an early age, and as was expected they would leave their family to join their husband's clan. This was not a transition most found easy, on the contrary, young brides would suffer much separation anxiety during those early honeymoon years of marriage. In Bengal however, daughters were allowed to happily return to their home villages once a year during Durga Puja and this was often a highly emotionally charged event for young brides, who were probably deeply missing their home and family of origins. This returning home theme is why Durga herself is sometimes perceived as the returning daughter, during this Harvest festival. Many chants sung during the Durga Puja Festival support this belief. Songs with the theme of welcoming back, farewells and the difficult life of a daughter, when she is in her husband's home (in contrast to her loving parent's home) are a prevalent theme. In these documented songs Durga is identify with the Goddess Parvati, wife of Shiva, daughter of Himalaya and his wife Mena and she is the perpetual sacred daughter returning home before having to sadly depart once more.

Many worshippers during this festival view Durga as the beloved daughter returning home and it's a very intimate experience, as worshippers' commune and connect with their beloved Goddess. A clay image of the multi-armed Goddess is often found on her altar and it is worshipped as the Goddess herself. Worshippers caress affectionately and highly venerate the image of their beloved Goddess as if she indeed is an intimate family member. She is depicted triumphing over a powerful demon but many worshippers in this part of the world simply see her as – sacred Daughter, returning home for her annual Autumnal visit. It is also a time when worshipper will consider the returning daughter, Durga, as an actual family member and lavish onto her all the love, attention and adoration to her image. It seems almost as if their Goddess becomes Persephone, returning home to help the crops grow and to share her powers of fecundity upon the land. The devotees then appear to take on the role of the Mother, like Demeter welcoming back Kore. *"We become the mothers that are welcoming back the daughter, the Persephone, during this festival..."* When this festival comes to a close, everyone prepares to bid her adieu at the waters; Durga, as the daughter, is bid adieu. This returning daughter archetype in this Autumnal Harvest festival will often find women gathering around the representative images of Durga; weeping, mourning, crying as an expression of the melancholy they feel over the daughter preparing to leave and her inevitable departure during the Dark season.

SOUTHERN INDIA - DURGA PUJA

In the South there is a vastly contrasting approach to the worship of this great Goddess in the Navaratra Festival. There is a wild, untamable, almost sexual tension that is highlighted between Durga and the buffalo demon, Mahisa. A Buffalo is sometimes sacrificed on the altar to Durga and blood is significantly featured during ceremonial rites to represent the blood many shed in battle with the Goddess. This demon is viewed as her suitor who she ultimately engages in battle, defeats and refuses to submit to. Her untamable sexual energy is indisputably dangerous and almost deadly to any man who dares to approach her. There is an implication that one must submit to Durga before engaging in any safe sexual encounter with her. Mahisa loses the battle and is unable to do so, but other myths reveal that Lord Shiva becomes her consort, yet, this is only as the aspect of Parvati and Sati. Durga is a fatal threat to those who try to conquer her or approach her sexually. In the South, Durga Puja festival gives more credence to Durga's role as a determined, fierce independent and untamable Goddess, whose origins are found among tribal people, in the far off distant mountains. Her worship in these southern regions are considerably more wild, free and more ecstatic than in the North.

In conclusion, it is important to note the slight difference in her worship, for in Northern Indian traditions, Durga is viewed more prominently as the returning daughter (or young bride) in need of family tenderness and adoration. She is viewed as the returning daughter, suggesting a shift in season, while in the South; she is seen as wild, untamable, strong independent, and an unmarried Goddess; delighting in her liminal aspect.

*Multi-armed, Hindu Goddess, Durga, is the ferocious tiger. She is the fierce warrior maiden but also the protectress guardian Mother of humanity. She is compassionate towards her devotees, and she's called upon for help, like the Goddess Kwan Yin and many other Mother Archetypes, but she is a fighter. In the Hindu Goddess Durga we find a warrior who will fiercely fight to protect humanity from all kinds of maladies in the world. Durga is anger manifested and employed into action. She was born from the collective emotion of anger that stemmed from the Gods. This anger is not held within to self-destruct, no, she uses that anger as a vehicle of action for her victory, while defeating those who are trying to destroy her. She is the embodiment of sovereign autonomy and awakens us to our own potential for victory.

Durga is the Goddess, embodying supreme strength and power. When presented with demons and threats to her world, she fights and she delights in that combat. She takes great pleasure in the act of this battle and she is always guaranteed victory. With her numerous arms there is nothing she cannot tackle and her wielding arms are so reminiscent and symbolic of our gender's numerous roles and obligations. It is her Divine energy that helps us connect to our ambition and powers of manifestations. Multi-armed to denote her supreme powers and capabilities, she is a Goddess that juggles numerous tasks with great ease and success. Her ability to achieve her heart's desire is evident and an inspiration for us to emulate. She is the charioterer able to tap into her powers of concentration, to drive and get much accomplished. Durga is the embodiment of sovereign autonomy and she awakens us to our great strength when pursuing our dreams or facing adversity.

"Om Dum Durgayei, Namaha..."

Om and Salutations to that Feminine energy which protects from all manner of negative influence and for which dum, is the seed.

"...Once women are free to bestow their favours and affections where they will, the whole structure of patriarchal society starts to crumble..."

The Cult of the Black Virgin," by Ean Begg, Page 137, Chiron Publications, Wilmette, Illinois 2006

158

MACHA

MACHA

Macha is an Irish and Scotland Goddess of War, Protection, Victory and Sovereignty. She is particularly connected with land and the province of Ulster, in ancient Ireland. She is also connected to fertility, strength and childbirth. Often depicted wearing the color red, with distinctly red long tresses, she is connected to horses and fire.

The Celtic Goddess, Macha, is also considered an aspect of the Triple Warrior and Death Goddess, Morrighan. There are many varied opinions on this subject because there

159

were many different Machas mentioned in various Celtic and Scottish folklores yet her veneration cannot be underestimated. As part of the trinity connected to the triple Goddess Morrighan, there was; "Badb" (Scald Crow), "Nemain" (Battle Fury) and "Macha" (the Raven One).

According to one of many folklores connected to Macha, there was a story about a grieving farmer in the land of Ulster who was alone in his remote distant home, his name was Cruinniuc. He had recently lost his wife and in his grief his entire household was falling apart without the loving touch of a wife and mother for his son. One day, out of the blue, a lady is seen approaching his castle. She enters his home and quite inexplicably, begins to fix things and brings order into the neglected home. She is said to lie in bed with him that night, thus inferring her acceptance as his new bride. In her presence all things that were chaotic, uncared for and neglected became organized and well-tended to. She was his savioress. For Cruinniuc, there was nothing she couldn't do as she brought so much love, healing and order into his life. Together they built their home and family, and life was good.

One day, Cruinniuc decides he want to attend the annual fair held by the prideful king of Ulster. The lady of the house was now pregnant and much too far advance in her pregnancy to accompany her husband to the fair. She gives her blessings for him to go alone and enjoy himself at the fair but only if her promises not to speak of her existence to anyone. Well, Cruinniuc agrees and when he arrives at the fair, he begins to enjoy himself a bit too much and partakes of many libations. He then breaks his promise to his wife and begins to boast to everyone about his wife's many gifts.

After watching the chariot races, he brags to the king's men that his wife is so powerful that she can even outrun the kings' horses. Well, upon hearing his assertion this did not sit well with the prideful king and he angrily detained Cruinniuc until his men could fetch the wife and personally attest to the claim. When they met her they explained the situation and warned her that her husband's life was in jeopardy if she did not come with them to prove the claim that her husband drunkenly made. She was obviously very pregnant and tried to implore for their compassion but they refused to reason with her. She assured them that she could partake in the race with the horses if they would simply allow her to give birth first but the King would not hear of it. To save her husband's life, the very pregnant Macha was forced to partake in the grueling race against the king's Horses.

As the legend goes, it is said she painfully gave birth to her twins in that Chariot Race, in the midst of childbirth. Her great strength unmatched, she not only gave birth to twins but she won the race against the King's horses and proved her husband right. The story however did not end there. Upon her victory she cursed all the men of Ulster, for the next nine generations that they too shall know the great pains and suffering that she was, unsympathetically, forced to endure. The cursed of pain and agony would last for 5 days and nights annually for descendants of Ulster. Consequently, the place where she was victorious and where she gave birth to her twins was then known as "Emain Macha" meaning, Macha's Twins.

ODUDUWA

ODUDUWA

Oduduwa is one of the most mysterious Orishas in Yoruban religion, she is also known also as Odua, Oddua, Odduduwa. This mystery connected to her, especially regarding her gender, is partly due to a number of conflicting folklores and sets of beliefs that require deeper contemplation.

Oduduwa is one of the oldest Orishas in the Yoruba pantheon. She is essentially primordial and like most primeval deities can express itself in ways we as human beings have difficulty comprehending. But, we can start the process of attempting to understand this Orisha by first simply examining her name, as names throughout history have often provided a great deal of information.

In the Yoruba Language "O," which is at the start of many Orisha names, relates to ownership. The middle of her name "*dudu*" means Black. Oduduwa is often translated as, "owner of the black womb" or simply as Black woman. Her name is directly linked with the color black and if there was one physical attribute we can associate with her, it would have to be her beautiful dark ebony skin color. The dark ebony skin tone found among some people of African descent is deemed extraordinary and divinely blessed exclusively by her.

Oduduwa was also known by the name, *Iya Ogbe* and this translates in Yoruba as, "Mother who receives." Aside from the color black, she is deeply connected to all matters related to the womb, unity, love, mothering, fertility, creation, leadership, devotion and community.

As a Primordial being we have to first accept that they do not walk upon the earth like you and I. They tend to be powerful energy forces that we as humans try to reimagine, often in images that make more sense to us. However, the fact is, most primordial energy/Gods can challenge some of our most accepted view of divinity. And thus, the confusion regarding Oduduwa's true gender can be understood but when you examine this Orisha's name, it becomes obvious. It is also well supported by the surviving oracular folklores, from various regions in Africa, that she was indeed the Female Principle, and in direct contrast to her consort, Obatala, who is considered the Male principle.

In Yoruba Mythology, it is believed that both, this male and female; Obatala and Oduduwa, were well contained in the sacred Calabash. Inside this crammed Calabash, Obatala was positioned on top, representing the obvious, the Consciousness and Oduduwa was positioned on the bottom, representing the hidden, the Subconsciousness. She is darkness, receptivity, earth/water, female, while he is light, expansiveness, sky/air, male. Together they behold the mysteries of life and death. They would eventually mate and create evolution; the joining of opposing forces. She is the Black womb and he is the King of the White Cloth. Later on, Oduduwa then gives birth to Aganju (the Land) and she gives birth to Yemoja/Yemaya (the water).

According to Yoruban Cosmology, in the beginning was The Supreme Being, Olodumare, and he decided he wanted to populate and create a universe. He instructed his emissary, Obatala, also known as Orisha-nla, to go down upon the earth and create humanity. Along the way to fulfill his mission, the Orisha Obatala becomes very thirsty. There are some versions of this tale that state he had a pebble placed in his stomach by Eshu to make him unusually thirsty, but in any event, Obatala found himself very parched. He decided to quench his thirst by drinking lots of Palm Wine. He drank so much Palm wine that he became inebriated and eventually passed out in the middle of his mission. When Olodumare noticed he had failed to report back, he sent down the Orisha, Oduduwa, to check up on him. Oduduwa descended and much to her surprise she finds Obatala in a drunken stupor, passed out. With Olodumare's permission she took on Obatala's failed mission and went on to successfully complete the human race. She is attributed for creating mankind.

As a primordial Orisha we know she is linked with the womb and the color black. She was also believed to be blind or possibly only beholding one eye. There is a common folklore that speaks of Obatala ripping her eyes out while they were inside the sacred Calabash during a heated disagreement. It is believed Oduduwa is instructed on Ifa (a system of Divination and an African spiritual tradition or path) by the Orisha, Orunmila. He becomes her chief consultant.

For the people of Yoruba, Oduduwa is ancient. She's primordial; existing at the beginning of time but it is Orunmila, who in his great wisdom, creates Ifa and further develops the Yoruba religion. He becomes Oduduwa's chief counselor and passes down this wealth of esoteric knowledge to her. Therefore, she unquestionably becomes highly instrumental in the expansion of the Yoruban culture and religion. She is the one who takes all of Orunmila's wisdom, and highly developed spiritual systems, and shares it with others; serving her community and birthing a new emperor.

Like the Goddesses Amaterasu and Athena, there appears to be a Divine direct connection between the first Emperor of a region and their patron deity. One can speculate this has happened here for the people of Yoruba because the first Emperor of Yoruba becomes King Oduduwa. This is perhaps another reason why many people confuse this Orisha's gender.

Part of the confusion regarding Oduduwa's gender might be connected to another prominent individual in Yoruba folklore sharing the same name. In the 12th century CE there was a prince who eventually became the First King of Ifa, his name was Oduduwa. There is much confusion about his birth origin but he became the beloved Emperor of Yoruba and it is through his existence that Ifa (spreading) becomes expanded upon.

Because she's primordial, like the Chinese Goddess Nu-Kua or the Greek Goddess, Gaia, she could have easily been included in the chapter exploring the theme of creation. Some would say she's the mother of humanity, after all, she is the one attributed for creating humanity. As the mother of Yemaya/Yemonja, her matriarchal attributes cannot be overstated. She is clearly a pinnacle Mother deity/Orisha and could have also been included in the chapter about Nurturance and Mothers. Like many of the other deities presented throughout this book, there are a multitude of attributes Oduduwa offers us to explore. In this chapter we're looking at her leadership attributes and how they can inspire our own growth. As part of your evolution, you are invited to work with her potent energy to unearth your own inner wisdom, honor your powers of creation, develop your leadership gifts and expand on your community building skills.

ODUDUWA MUSING

I am excited to present the Orisha, Oduduwa, in this book as I felt a very strong calling by her to be included in this chapter. All week long my eyes have been strangely, itchy, watery and giving me some concerns regarding my vision. And yesterday, I woke up to a red bump, on my right eye lid which swelled up. I can't help but wonder if this is connected to my work with Oduduwa. The dreams I've been having may also be connected to her and I share them here, as personal as they may be, because it sheds light on the subtle way Orishas/Deities and Spirit begin to affect our own personal journeys.

Two nights in a row, I've had very telling dreams. Last night, in this dream, I found myself in an outdoor market, where lots of beautiful, ethnic and African wares were being sold. There were also lots of large religious statuaries and I noted the Yemayas and Virgin Marys in the dream. A proprietor singled me out among the crowd, took me by the hand and walked me to the back area where a curtain was parted so that I may see. It was an old railroad station but it was turned into a river and there was water everywhere. You could even see the old tracks of the railroad under the flowing river water in the dream. They had covered up this old significant railroad station with a man-made lake, lots of water covered the area, and for some reason it was a secret that was being revealed to me. I looked at it, and then left to continue perusing the large religious statuaries throughout the market.

Today, I woke up from another strange detailed dream. I was seated among some people at a very long banquet table. The table was fully set, covered with plates of food offerings. It was literally adorned with lots of different types of rich foods fit for a King. Nearby, I noticed there were lots of very diverse looking people. I happened to notice that nearby, to my right, were a plethora of children, beautiful black skinned children. Lots of joyful, African children, laughing together, preparing their dances. They were rehearsing some dance moves and it was clear there was about to be some type of spiritual rite or Voodoo ceremony taking place soon.

At the banquet table, I was seated before a man and what appeared to be his family. He was speaking to me very passionately, almost fighting his tears, as he talked with me. I can't recall all the details of what we were speaking about (was it unrequited love or some other dramatic situation?) but I do remember very clearly the word; LUCUMI. This word came out of his mouth as clear as can be Lucumi.... and he was fighting the tears as he was making some type of compassionate plead. Our intense interaction was interrupted by what appeared to be a Caucasian man approaching the table...probably my husband. It propelled me to get up from the table and go to the back of the other side of the room, where the candles were set. I searched for my candles and lit one at the altar (it was like a unique waterfall altar). Then I picked up my other candle and started to walk with it, when I noticed, oddly enough, it had a double wick.... I think I eventually lit this candle as well before waking up from this strange dream.

"A Woman is the Full Circle, within her is the power
to create, nurture and transform..." Diane Mariechild

ASHERA

ASHERAH

We first learn about Asherah through the Ugaritic documented mythologies of the 14th century BCE but evidence of her existence can be traced three centuries before this time. Asherah is a Pre-biblical; Canaanite Goddess whose worshipped was tenaciously found throughout various tribes in ancient times as far back as 1750 BCE. The Creatress, known as the consort of the Canaanite Chief God of the heaven's, El, and later, controversially, coalesced and addressed as the wife of Yahweh, upon Christianity's inception, her worship was unquestionably cemented in the inhabitants of this land in the far and Middle East.

Some suspect that her numerous names in various regions were; Elath (meaning Goddess and the feminine aspect of the God, El), also Athirat, Atharat, Astarte, Ashtorah, Ashratum, Ashrurah. And there still exist confusion regarding her titles and attributes in various regions, as they are used interchangeably in the writings of the time. The bible also seems to indistinguishably address her as both Asherah and Ashtarte, Astarte. It is clear from archeological findings and writings of this period that Isaraelite, Perizzites,

Hittites, Hivites, Jebusites, Amorites, shared in the Canaanite's love and veneration of this great mother Goddess and the cult of her son Ba'al.

In Southern Arabia she was known Atharath, in Egypt as Qudsu (meaning Holy One) and in Sumeria and Akkadia she was known as wife to the supreme chief God, Anu. There, she was more commonly known as, Ashratum, a specific name found on excavated 14th century BCE artifacts, supporting her importance in this region.

She was known as a fertility deity called upon by "cursed" barren women, as well as for agricultural blessings. She was creatress, mistress of sexual rejoicing and she who facilitated childbirth. As Qudsu, she was the revered Holy one. Asherah was considered Mother of all the Gods, princes and Kings, and as the one who suckled and nurtured both mortals and gods alike. In particular she was mother of the seventy deities in the Ugaritic pantheon, which included; Ba'al, her son, and Anath, her daughter.

As the supreme mother Deity and one of the first Goddesses worshipped and embraced by the Hebrews, who shared the land with the Canaanites, in the area of Palestine now, her worship was incised in the root of this region. At this time, numerous intermingling of marriages and religious practices was common, thus it was assumed that in marriage one naturally took on the gods of their marital partners.

In Judah, Rehoboam, the son of Naamah (an Ammonite and wife of King Solomon) marries Maacah, who helps spread the worship of Asherah in this region, as she was a known priestess of the Goddess. Another example of how the intermingling of marriages between different people of different tribes promulgated Asherah's worship is in the story of Jezebel and King Ahab. In Samaria, when the King Ahab, married Jezebel, yet another Sidonian Princess, the worship of Asherah again took center stage in this region. Jezebel ordered a more elaborate carved wood image of the Goddess (which it appears had been destroyed at an earlier date) and she had this sacred Goddess and her image placed in the center of Samaria- contributing even further to the growing popularity of this revered maternal Goddess. Another perfect example of the contribution of intermingling of tribes is found in the tales of King Solomon and his extraordinary First Temple of Jerusalem in the mid 1oth century BCE, documented in the bible and the writings of the time. This temple was dedicated to the monotheistic Israelite God, Yahweh, during King Judah's reign. Although the bible states Solomon loved Yahweh, it also claims that Solomon, was easily led astray by his old age and his many wives (700 wives and 300 concubines to be exact), in his controversial idolatry and polytheistic religious practices. King Solomon married numerous wives from various nations in his effort to gain power, wealth and allegiances. Naturally every one of his wives brought to their union, and consequently, their home in the temple, the worship of their respective gods. The Temple of Solomon had multiple sanctuaries and became known as the sacred place of worship, there were numerous deities from different pantheons who were being worshipped here, as this was Solomon's way of accommodating his numerous wives. In particular, he is credited for introducing the worship of Asherah to the people of Jerusalem, as his first wife (at the start of the building of the Temple) was a Sidonian princess, daughter of the Pharoah and a beloved priestess of Asherah. Clearly we see reflected here, the new religion of Yahweh being practiced among the existing and well established polytheistic religions of neighboring regions.

Solomon's father, King David, was attributed for unifying Israel and was to formulate the first house of Jerusalem for Yahweh but he was not able to complete this task and it was left up to his son to fully accomplish this ambitious feat. Most significantly, the Temple of Solomon was meant to house the treasured "Ark of the

Covenant" and Mose's Ten Commandments, received on Mt. Sinai. It was Jerusalem's First temple reputed to exalt Yahweh, the tenets of this new monotheistic religion and unite Israel but this is in direct contrast to the numerous finding and writings about King Solomon's temple true function.

The temple itself shared many similarities to Pagan temples of old, in particular, its three section structure with; a Vestibule, Nave, Inner sanctuary was identical to a ninth century Pagan temple in Canaanite and Syria. King Solomon also used a Tyrian craftsman called Hiram Abif (tribe of Naphtali) to help build it, including the two distinguished Pillars made of brass, a common metal often incorporated in Pagan Temples, like the one in Hazor. It becomes quite evident that King Solomon's Grand Temple in Jerusalem, though initially built by Yahweh's command and counsel, was heavily inspired, influenced and created with Pagan polytheistic ideals.

Interesting to note, it was also documented that a King, in the land of Amorite (yet another region known for Asherah worship) was known as Abdu-Ashirta, which translates as "slave of Asherah" proof of his personal devotion to the great Goddess and an indication of her reverence and popularity in this region as well. In some of the writings, we also learn about Asherah's servant who was called, Qadesh wa-Amrur, which translates as, *Fisherman of the Lady Asherah of the Sea.*" This reveals a distinct connection this Goddess had with the Sea.

Some documents translate the name Asherah as meaning; "*She who walks on the Sea.*" Her worship in the independent seaport towns of Tyre and Sidon, which were near the Mediterranean coastline, made the water's ocean a vital part of the people's wellbeing and garnered her the name, "Lady of the Sea." There are also many other indications of her strong prevalence at this time. There were towns and seaports with her name like, Elath (which is one of her many titles, the female aspect to her Consort El) it was in the south gulf of Aqaba and titles like, Elath of Sidon and Asherah of Tyre that also reflect the importance of this Goddess.

DEPICTIONS OF ASHERAH

There are some conflicting mysterious stories regarding Asherah's actual appearance. In the Hebrew Bible and the writings of the time, she was depicted as an actual wood pole, set up, planted in the ground near the altars to her son, Ba'al and she was often closely linked to his popular cult following. Yet, the altars to her son did not have the same weight or meaning as the actual planted sacred pole known as the Asherah herself. She was often depicted as a tree and or groves - sometimes addressed as singular and sometimes in the plural form. Most often she is described as a sacred carved elaborate wood pole, planted firm in the earth. Some say an obelisk represented her, as well as the Pagan, modern day phallic, Maypole.

Though the harsh rainy climate of Palestine was not conducive to preserving much archeological evidence of Asherah's sacred wood pole artifacts, we do find plenty of evidence in the writings of the time on clay tablets and even within the Hebrew bible. Numerous archeological evidence of Asherah's dominance in the polytheistic worship of ancient Israel and the whole of the far and Middle East Is found in the survival of a multitude of naked female figurine statues made of clay. These were small figurines with large pronounced breast, protruding bellies and the hands upholding, cupping, the breasts in a sign of nurturance. And the most fascinating discovery was that these clay figure religious artifacts were found in archeological sites near and within residential homes, proof that Asherah was not only a Goddess revered in public, communal town rituals, but her worship extended privately and more intimately in the homes of ancient women. This was clearly indicative of a Goddess who was so revered and loved that she was worshipped in formal public rites, as well as in domestic religious practices of women at the time.

BIBLICAL EVIDENCE

Asherah is mentioned at least forty different times in the Hebrew's Bible. Several times in the Old Testament she is documented as the "Queen of heaven;" Jeremiah 44:17-21 and Jeremiah 7:17-18

*"The Children gathered wood, the fathers kindled fire
and the women knead the dough to make cakes to the Queen of heaven
and to pour out drink offerings unto gods..."*

An invocation to Asherah found on a 7th century BCE artifact tablet, invokes the Goddess for help with fertility and childbirth and it is believed that in the very early chapters of the Hebrew bible, (Genesis 30:10-13) we encounter Leah who actually names Zilpah's son, Asher. This is an obvious reference and namesake to the Goddess Asherah who was clearly invoked for childbirth blessings and highly venerated during this period. It also hints at the likelihood that the worship of Asherah was occurring simultaneously with other deities, including Yahweh.

The book of Judge (Judges 6:25-32) reveals yet again the worship of Asherah and the poor attempt to eradicate it by the son of the town Chieftain and devoted Priest of the Goddess -Joash the Abiezrite. In the town of Ofra, in the 12th century BCE, his son Gideo ends up destroying the town's beloved Asherah and altar to Ba'al and manages to escapes the town's persecution due to his father's prestigious position as the Priest of Asherah.

Another interesting set of passages in the Hebrew bible indicative of obstinate Pagan worship alongside Yahwenism is found in *Ezekiel 8*. The chapter begins with...

*"...and it came to pass in the sixth year,
in the sixth month in the fifth day of the month...."*

Perhaps this is the month of August, as August in Latin translates as Sextilis, the sixth month, and was considered the sixth month during Augustus Caesar's reign. This coincides with the Harvest and a time when the sun's strength was viewed as dying and waning. One can only surmise that for people who depended on the fertility of their land, this was a time when they were more intimately invested in the nature deities that would assure their land's sustainable wellbeing and thus their own livelihood.

*Ezekiel 8:14- "Then he brought me to the door of the gate
of the Lord's house, which was towards the North;
and behold, there sat women weeping for Tammuz..."*

This passage reveals that the women worshipped **inside** the temple and clearly they were not worshipping Yahweh, but rather a highly venerated Pagan Sun God, Tammuz. They were described as loudly crying, mourning, wailing for Tammuz and this was viewed as normal. It was a common practice and not viewed as strange, as it was customary, at the time, to perform agricultural rites to manifest much needed rain for the land and they were doing this in the "house of Yahweh in Jerusalem." Women in their power, in ancient times, were the ones who **could** do this. Women, so closely linked to the Mother Goddess Asherah, were the ones that magickally bled once a month, connecting to the Divine Moon and evidently produced new life and gave birth. Women's power was clearly visible for ancient indigenous cultures and it is only later that it becomes perverse by patriarchy and monotheism; with lies, degradations, oppression and manipulations. And thus, at this time, women inside the holy temples actively involved in performing rituals to manifest rain, to help the crop of the land, by wailing and shedding their own tears (performing a type of sympathetic magick rite) for the Sun God Tammuz, is quite indicative of women's power at this time. It is in total contrast to what their role would develop years later at the hands of oppressive monotheistic religions. At the very least, this short passage reflects the acknowledgment, respect and power that women held as active participants in priestessing and worshipping the Gods of ancient times in Jerusalem.

Ezekiel 8:16- "And he brought me into the inner court of the Lord's house,
and behold, between the porch and the altar,
were about 5 and 20 men, with their backs towards the Temple of the Lord,
and their faces towards the East; and they worshipped the Sun towards the East..."

Again, this is reflecting the important worship of the Sun God/ the son of the Goddess, in the Temple. The Hebrew bible also reveals that women often weaved cloths for the Goddess Asherah **inside** the temple and they worked in the Holy Temples in numerous capacities, although they would essentially be described in the Hebrew bible as being temple prostitutes; a terminology also used very loosely for men employed in the temples as well. This was a debasing way to discredit women and the worship of the Goddess during a time when monotheism was trying to assert itself upon the people.

The most fascinating, controversial finding, relating the Goddess Asherah to the monotheistic God, Yahweh is discussed in *"The Biblical Archeology Review," Vol. 5, No.2 (March/April 1979), pp24ff.* It shares a more recent discovery, an inscription dated from the 8-9th century BCE, found at Kuntillet Ajrud, in the North East Sinai Peninsula, South of Israeli and Egyptian border and it reveals a most telling inscription on large storage jars (*pithoi*) artifacts.

"May you be blessed by Yahweh and his Asherah."

This is a most illuminating inscription and some speculate that it reveals a special relationship between the new God, Yahweh and the established ancient Pagan mother Goddess, Asherah. There was another discovery on a tomb at Khirbet -El-Qom which was noted for having a similar inscription. These discovered inscriptions and blessings like; *"Yahweh of Samaria and his Asherah"* and *"Yahweh of Tenan and his Asherah...."* and *"May Uriyahu* (a governor at the time) *be blessed by Yahweh, my guardian and by his Asherah, save him Uriyahu.."* an inscription dated from the 750-700BC *(Biblical Archeology Review, Vol. 10, No. 6 (Nov./Dec. 1984)pg. 42.)* indicates a possible connection between these two deities. And clearly the proselytized monotheistic initial views of Judaism and Christianity are highly challenged when we find these numerous findings connecting Asherah (a Pagan Goddess) to Yahweh (the new God claiming monotheism as the **only** way). Two Gods are clearly being venerated in these inscriptions and the presence of Asherah's name becomes quite intriguing, especially when we know her importance across numerous tribes in the far and Middle East.

These blessing inscriptions reveal the Goddess as Yahweh' right hand, worshipped simultaneously with the new, Hebrew God, contradicting the monotheistic claim of early Yahwenism. It is rather convoluted how Asherah is represented in the old testament of the bible. Sometimes she appears as a wood pole, sometimes as a place. In some other documents she is *"his Asherah,"* and then sometimes she is simply a sacred attribute. Some believe, this confusion was purposely created to diminish her importance and trivialize her great power and hold on the people. As one can surmise, the Bible, written exclusively by men in support of the new monotheistic, patriarchal religion, obviously fulfilled their agenda in maintaining the worship of the Feminine Divine veiled and behind the new God, named Yahweh. It helped implement and establish the supremacy of men over women. Anything that did not support their new patriarchal ideologies was omitted, altered or disregarded and purposely obscured. Yet, the great Goddess Asherah is actually mentioned forty times in the Hebrew bible, which reveals how powerful and prevalent her presence had to have been at this time in the ancient far and Middle East.

The people cleaved to Asherah, and her worship, for centuries even after the introduction of Yahweh and it wasn't until threats, violent manipulations and coercions and the risk of persecution did her worship begin to slowly wane, for as always, those with physically mightier armies and political influence, sadly have the power to oppress and eradicate a mass of people as we have seen throughout history.

HER CONECTION TO TREES

In researching, unearthing, learning and connecting to this great ancient Mother Goddess, I couldn't help but notice how often she was associated with trees, groves, high mountain tops and carved wood poles. Writings of the time actually reveal that the wooden pole was more than just a symbol of the Goddess; it was revered as the Goddess herself. As a result, it had more weight and value than the very altars created for her son, Ba'al, which lay beside her. The altars were a place of offering but the carved wooden pole was viewed as the Goddess herself. And ironically enough, while the altars to Pagan gods like Ba'al were quick to be destroyed by overzealous Yahwenist, the large Asherah poles that stood next to them and Asherah's strong worship was not so quick to be pulverized nor obliterated. Her worship, as is evident from excavated artifacts and the writings of the time, lingered, permeating several regions, long after the introduction of monotheism and it appeared her tenacious worship was coalesced with that of the new Yahweh.

Throughout the Hebrew bible there are numerous references and warnings about idolatry via the tree aka Asherah. And we must also remember in Genesis, the introduction of the tale of the forbidden fruit in the esteemed Tree of Knowledge, of which Adam and Eve were reputed to have eaten from before being cast out of the Garden of Eden. All this talk about trees made me wonder why the big taboo concerning trees and what could possibly be so threatening; within the tree, nature, the moon, the sun and stars and Asherah's worship, to this new monotheistic deity coming into the foreground.

Then I began to muse on trees and how numerous cultures have important folklores related to trees. I started to take a closer look at women and how intimately similar our attributes can appear to that of actual trees but I suppose the same can be said for so much in nature divinely reflects woman; from the moon, the ocean, the yoni shaped flowers and sea shells, to the erupting cavernous volcanoes, thunder and rainstorms.

Trees give forth life, sustain life and yet, in them, we see its cycles of life, death and rebirth; as it appears fruitless, leafless in the winter and then returns to its fullness, fruitfulness and splendor in the Spring and Summer. It nurtures and sustains humanity with oxygen and its fruits and thus, since the beginning of time, humanity has relied on its existence. Sacred regenerative principles are easily palpable in trees, the same regenerative qualities in "wombmyn"/woman's biological make up. I suppose this can be quite threatening to the rise of patriarchy.

The veneration of trees has existed in numerous ancient cultures and religions since the beginning of time. In Scandinavian Norse Mythology there is the Ygdrasil tree, that connects the various nine worlds; from the underworld, axis, middle, halls of the gods, heavens etc... It is a pivotal vehicle for spiritual journeying. In Genesis, as already stated, the Tree of Knowledge had fruits that were forbidden due to its inherent ability to awaken truths and spiritual knowledge, but through the offer from Lilith (as the serpent) it brought about major shifts and an awakening to both Eve and Adam, that according to biblical scriptures changed the course of humanity forever. In Egypt there is reference to the Sycamore tree being utilized by the Goddess to feed the dead souls as they journey to the underworld. For Buddhist, it was the Bhodi tree that passed enlightenment and wisdom to the Buddha. In Jewish Mysticism, known as the practice of Kabbalah, the most hallowed tree was the Ash Tree, which connected the sacred realms. It is depicted as an upside down, inverted tree, in which the roots originate in the heavens and the branches reach down through the ethers, to the earth. The Goddess Shekhinah is believed to imbue this tree with her divine energy and light according to Cabbalistic lore. The special branches of this sacred tree are known as "emanations" or sephiroth, and there are believed to be ten, which humanity is behooved to journey and work through. Interesting to note this number ten, as the day of Ashurah (*Aashrurah, Ashurah, Aashoorah*) for Muslims it is considered the 10th day of Muharram and the word *Ashrurah* is interpreted in Arabic as "ten." According to Islamic lore, the beloved grandson of Muhammad, Husayn Bin Ali, was killed by Umayyard, at the battle of Karbala (Iraq) and this day commemorates the tragedy of this event with mourning. The name Ashurah is clearly connected to the name of our venerated ancient Tree Goddess, Asherah. There are some scholars that link the ancient worship of Asherah to one of the most venerated symbols for modern day Jewish people - the menorah. The menorah resembles her sacred tree with its branches as the seven, sometimes ten, candlestick arms, holding the sacred lights so powerfully symbolic for Jews.

Women and trees share a similar embodiment of fertility and the divine, with its sacred cycle of; birth, life, death and rebirth in the outwardly appearance of fruition in the summer and spring and then the barrenness so apparent in the winter season. It is quite fascinating to consider that one of the most beloved ancient mother Goddesses, Asherah, still lives on today, right before our very eyes as a living breathing Goddess, still exemplified in the tall, sky reaching trees that surround us today. In this sense, Asherah reminds me of the primordial Greek Goddess Gaia, which seems to transcend all cultures and time and space and yet in her role as a Sea Mother Goddess, I can't help but think upon the Orisha, Yemaya. Asherah, and her tenacious worship, was deeply loved in ancient pre-biblical times, so much so that perhaps we can still see glimmers of her strong veneration being transferred and carried through in the discovery of many other nurturing mother deities. The supreme Mother Goddess archetype continues to prove itself to be an important force for all women to connect with regardless of time and place and I believe Asherah to be a most powerful immortal Goddess for modern women to invoke in their respective lives.

Hail to you Asherah!

*Asherah is the embodiment of the mother archetype and reflects our beauty, fertility, sovereignty and staying power as women. She is the grounded energy of the fertile earth and reflects the beauty found in nature. She is the Canaanite Goddess of the Tree and will ask you to embrace the distinct sacred aspect of Trees, as admirable reflections of your womanhood.

The first responsibility of a leader is to define reality.
The last is to say, Thank you. In between, the leader is a servant..."
Max DePree

OYA

OYA-YANSAN, IANSA

Her name means, "Mother of Nine"and in the Yoruban language it means: "She Tore". In Brazil they salute this Goddess with **"EPI, EPA HEYI"**, while her Afro -Cuban salute is: **"HEKUA HEY YANSA"**, thus, we begin our journey to Oya with this salute...
"EPI, EPA HEYI Oya-Yansa!!!! HEKUA HEY YANSA"

Respectively known as Oya-Yansa, Iansan, Iansa and Yansa, Oya is an Elemental African Goddess, attributed with the gift of bringing sudden drastic change. She is called upon for dramatic transformations and is considered among one of the most powerful Orishas (meaning African Deities) in the Yoruban pantheon.

Oya-Yansa is a Goddess associated with the Niger River, where it is believed she originates from, but one of the most amazing fact about this Goddess is how she permeates numerous cultures and traditions. From African and Yoruban practices, to Brazilian and Candomble, her worship stretches into the Americas and Cuba, touching upon Catholicism, Voodoo and the practice of Santeria. In the Catholic religion, she is associated with Joan of Arc and Lady Candelaria. In Santeria, she is sometimes known as Santa Barbara. In New Orleans, some see her manifested as Maman Brigitte. It becomes quite evident that she is revered and embraced by numerous cultures and various religions and this substantiate her supremacy among the African pantheon.

Often portrayed holding her sword, (her Machete) for she cuts through illusions, she is notoriously known for her abilities to cut through deceit, dishonesty and injustices. She is a force of change and anywhere she is invoked, Oya clears the way for new growth. Like cutting out that which is no longer needed, she amputates that which serves no purpose and extracts the tumor growth to make wave for healing. These are just some of Oya's powerful gifts.

Oya is known to have many attributes, but she is best known as an Elemental Goddess because of her connections to strong winds, earthquakes, roaring fires, omnipotent rainstorms, thunder-filled lightning and the drastic changes that natural disasters impart. As a matter of fact, all the elements (Air, Fire, Water and Earth) seem to be embodied by this all powerful African Goddess. In the howl of a strong wind, you can hear her name... Oya... She stirs and brings the winds of external and internal changes. It is perhaps why she is so easily embodied in the Tarot, Tower card, for she brings about structural changes. Tornadoes, cyclones, earthquakes, hurricane, lightning, rainstorms, thunder, fires etc... all of these Earth/natural disasters fall under her domain and naturally make her one of the most powerful Goddesses and a force to be reckoned with.

This highly revered Orisha was known to have two husbands. Her first husband, Oggun, also known as Oba and Ochun, was later replaced by the warrior God, Chango, who was more suited to her fiery personality. It is often stated in the Orisha lores that she joined him in battles and together they fiercely fought side by side. While Chango is considered the lightning in the midst of heavy rainstorm, it is Oya who is the torrential rain that brings flooding and the thunder and deathly electric bolts that catapults and destroys anything in her sight.

Oya is known to be very protective of her initiates and she is a beloved, patron Goddess for women. In particular, she is very protective of those women in leadership roles. Known as a Goddess of movement, her initiates would often dance, swirling in their long wide sweeping skirts, as they do a dance that can either invite the dead to join in or, with the simple sweep of their hands, keep them at bay. As can be expected from a Fire Goddess, she is known to be very passionate and independent and like most fire

Goddesses, angers easily with a fierce temper much like the Volcanic Hawaiian Goddess, Pele. It is therefore of no surprise that she has garnered the reputation for being a warrior Goddess. Yoruban folklore claims she is a Warrior Goddess, who can sometimes even grow a beard, alluding to her great powers and strong, masculine energy. It is said "...*She puts on the pants to go into battle...*" Again, in this very patriarchal statement, there is a reference to Oya's great powers matching that of a man's' and therefore equal in brute strength.

Oya is also known as Lady of the Cemeteries and in New Orleans, she may sometimes take on the name of Maman Brigitte, as both Goddesses are considered guardians of the dead, cemeteries, skeletons and skulls. These Spirits/Goddesses were to guide the souls of the dead and bring them to the underworld. Like the ancient Goddess Hekate, this aspect of Oya-Yansa is known as a Goddess of Sorcery, Magick, intuition and the psychic arts. Thus, she is also patron Goddess of Witches and beholder of ancient occult knowledge and the Magickal arts. Some of her other numerous titles are Lady of the Masks, as they were sacred to her and Lady of the Market, for she will always find you a good deal when shopping. Her energy is often described as swirling prevalently in the market place; in the midst of haggling, fast talking pitches, fast- paced sale transactions. In the act of procuring the best deal for your money, Oya is ever present. She is also titled as, Lady of the mind, because of her great intellect and shrewd business sense. It is said she can impart genius and great memory or toil with you with the curse of insanity.

According to Yoruban cosmology, she is considered to be one of Yemaja's daughters, although it is best to never invoked them together in rituals, as they have quite a volatile history and some animosity towards each other. Some of this has to do with her philandering husband, Chango, but there are numerous other tales. According to Yoruban Lore, long ago Oya, first ruled over the Ocean and through trickery, the Mother of all the Gods and the sea, Yemaja, managed to trick Oya into relinquishing her Ocean Realm, in exchange for the Cemetery, she now rules over. Thus, this aspect of her as ruler of the cemetery is probably not one fully embraced by Oya, but there are varying opinions on this matter.

Oya is indeed a powerful Goddess and there are many ways to begin working with her energy. Perhaps begin by calling her, on her special day -Wednesdays and incorporate her favorite number -nine. To honor this Goddess, offer her special ritual masks, sharp machetes and swords, and anything made of copper, like pennies and copper cooking pots. Her favorite colors of maroon, purples and reds can also adorn an altar or shrine for her and she will always appreciate jamming, drumming session with lots of frenetic, ecstatic dancing. Beware though, Oya detest smoke, palm kernel oil, ram and pork, but eggplants, grape, wine, gin, rum, kola nuts, roosters, hen, porridge, fruits, fish, anything spicy are all sacred to her and a most appropriate offerings for this powerful Yoruban Goddess.

The Yoruban Orisha, Oya, is the fierce Goddess of storms, thunder, winds and soul-transformations. In her presence, drastic change is inevitable and life will never look the same. She is the fierce flagellation of a whipping tornado, the rumbling desolation of an earthquake, the electric omnipotent thunderstorm and the power to unexpectedly crumble your neatly existing structures. She is the Goddess of Drastic Change. She invites you to take up your role as a leader to boldly stand with all of your gifts and offer them to your community. She may come like the intense windstorms and tornadoes, to sweep that which does not serve you well anymore; maybe she is inspiring you to facilitate global changes. It is only in this severing of the old and outworn, that we get to allow a new life force to take root, grow and manifest -healthier and stronger than before. She comes to sweep away, with her long rainbow colored skirt, its various colors representing nations of all diversity, held together by her power. She awakens in you the courage and strength to welcome your role as a leader.

OYA-YANSA- IANSA- NOTES

- Yoruba African Goddess. Oya means "She tore" in the Yoruba language.
- Goddess of the Niger River
- Worshipped in Africa, Brazil, Cuba, Haiti, New Orleans etc...
- Her name also means "Mother of Nine".... (She had Egungun and four sets of twins...)
- She is Winds of Change, Structural change, Known as a Weather Goddess
- She destroys Outworn structures, sweeps away debris making room for new growth.
- Goddess of Transformation
- Unpredictable,
- She can be as a gently breeze upon your skin or as destructive as the winds of a hurricane
- Lightning, Torrential rain storms with her tears
- Cyclones, Tornadoes, hurricanes, earthquakes her domain,
- Strong Storms , Fast paced movement,
- Fast paced energy of the marketplace,
- Patron of Woman leadership
- Wild Woman, Amazon,
- Protector of Women
- She is the power of Feminine leadership
- Mistress of Masquerades
- Fiercely independent
- Shrewd Business Woman
- Queen of the Marketplace
- Goddess who Can impart Great intellect /genius or Insanity
- Library/ Den in your house should be dedicated to her
- Speech is her domain
- Her Symbol is the Machete or Sword and she Cuts thru illusions, to get the truth
- She is Justice Seeker
- Fierce Warrior Goddess, fights with Chango her 2nd Husband, 1st husband was Ogun.
- She is known as the one who grows a beard and puts the pants on to go to war.
- As a Goddess of Movement, Loves to Dance and those who she possess do a special dance.
- Like Celtic Goddess Brigit with her association with Fire and water thru her Niger River and thunder and lightning rain.
- Like Athena, She is armed and helmeted to fight injustices and is associated with Wars, Air, intellect, swords.
- Like Hecate affinity to the dead and Sorcery and the magical arts
- Like Maat with her dedication to injustices, exposing deceits and dishonesty
- Like Voodoo Loa, Maman Brigitte, Guardian and Keeper of the Cemetery and the

newly dead.

- She is Lady of the Cemetery... She led the spirit of the dead. She can call forth the spirit of the Dead or hold it back.
- Grim Reaper association.
- She was known as the Buffalo before she came to have human form.
- Associated with the Dark Moon and the planet Uranus
- Her day is Wednesday
- Her number is Nine
- Copper is her metal
- Burgundy, Reds, Browns, purples, Burnt orange are her colors
- Eggplants, Plums, chocolates, red wine, roosters, hens, goats, bean fritters, fish, kola nuts,
- Shea Coco Butter, Buffalo Horns, fruits or anything spicy are appropriate offerings,
- Taboos: Smoke, palm kernel oil, ram and Pork.
- Saints associated with her are; Santa Barbara, Catherine, Theresa Dymphna, Joan of Arc, our Lady of Candelaria (whose feast day is like Brigit's -Feb2nd)
- Oya is therefore honored on Feb 2nd but also on her Feast day-December 4th.
- She is said to be the daughter of Yemaja- Yemaja being the mother of all --But you cannot invoke both goddesses together because of a love rivalry. Chango her husband, was like Zeus with infidelity issues and at some point he was a lover of Yemaya and her Sister Oshun, according to some of the oral Yoruban myths.

HEKUA OYA, EPI HEY YANSA!!!

176

MAUVE

MAUVE

Mauve is a Celtic Goddess intrinsically connected with the land of Ireland. Like most ancient Goddesses there are numerous early writings and tales, as early as the first century AD, that reveal various elements connected to the Sacred Feminine and her worship.

In early times she was known as Medb/Mebhdb and these names are connected to "Mead," a beloved beverage for the Irish. Her name, Mauve, is known to translate as "intoxication" and this might reveal her importance as a Goddess who offers libation and, in so doing divinely elects the proper King to rule the land. This was considered a very sacred rite, only through this Goddess chalice offering could the next King be chosen. May Day, a well-known Pagan Holiday celebrated with much libations and merry making, was oftentimes the season when new rulers were selected. It is precisely why Mauve is associated with Beltane and May Day Rites.

Mauve is a beautiful, passionate, Celtic Goddess of Sovereignty and the Irish land. She is a fierce warrior and a Sovereign Queen. Daughter of the King, *Eochalb Feidlech*, she was gifted the land of Connaught. Her most famous Celtic story, "*Tain Bo Cuailing*" or "Cattle Raid Cooley," is a rather interesting one, and reflective of this Goddess and her notable attributes.

Long ago Queen Mauve, who was known to have many lovers, was married to King Ailill mac Mata, in the land of Connaught. The King and Queen one day were cuddled up in bed, as lovers sometimes do, reminiscing and chatting. Well, King Ailill mac Mata, feeling prideful and good about himself begins to boast about how lucky Mauve should feel to be married to someone as rich and powerful as he is. He claims that she should be grateful to have such a rich accomplished, fine specimen. Well, she hears him and does not share in his sentiment. Actually, Mauve becomes very offended.

Her immediate response to him was to begin listing all of her own numerous accolades, riches and great attributes. She painstakingly reminds him of how many battles she had fought and won by his side and how she has proven that she is just as strong and just as rich. It is the King that should be counting his blessings with her as his bride. The two begin to banter back and forth about who's better, who's richer who's luckier...

It's important to note that in Ireland at this point, women were viewed very differently than they have been viewed in previous times in history. Women were often viewed as possessors of magick, connected to the Goddess, responsible for the fecundity of the Irish land and some were indeed considered sovereign and land owners. Irish women as Goddesses were seen as powerful and just as strong in combat as men; even depicted in the grueling bloody Battlefields. But what is most interesting to note is that there was a strong belief that your wealth and the amount of abundance you owned determine the amount of power you could wield. The richer you were whether you were a man or woman, the more power you held. Therefore this argument between the King and the Queen was a valid one. The King was trying to assert his dominion over the Queen by touting all of his riches and fine attributes but the Queen, not only disagreed with him but felt that she was the one who had more resources and therefore, more power.

As the story continues they both become so enraged and determined to prove their case that they summoned their respective servants to gather and reveal all of their personal resources. Each of their servants gathered up all of the animals they owned, all the gold and all of the proof of their abundance. As it turned out they did have equal amounts in everything. The King then brings up his prized possession, his magick bull. He claims it is the finest and the strongest and the only one owned by him alone in all the land of Connaught. He declares that ownership of this bull basically makes him the richest and therefore, more powerful. Well, it is at this moment that Queen Mauve becomes even more infuriated because she reminds him that the bull was once, owned solely by her but because the bull did not want to be owned by a woman it was given to the king. He knew she was correct and seeing how the argument had now dangerously escalated, he agreed they were thus equal. He conceded that they were equal, claiming that indeed the Bull belonged to both of them. At this point King Ailill mac Mata, just wanted to call it a truce, however, that response was not good enough for the Queen. This did not sit well with Mauve and she was determined to acquire her own bull to prove her superiority over the King.

The story then gets lengthy and more complicated with diverse versions of it, but essentially the Queen implements a plan to retrieve a famous Red Bull named, Donn Cuailnge. This bull was in Ulster, owned by Daire mac Fiochna. After numerous unsuccessful offers to acquire the Bull, she decides to take matters into her own hands and kidnap it. She rallies her numerous supporters in Connaught and gathers an army to go to Ulster to retrieve this massive, prized Bull. At Ulster, the army was led by the young, Cuchulainn, son of the God Lugh. Cuchulainn had garnered a reputation as being a fiercely, unstoppable warrior and leader of the army at Ulster. However, the men at the time were spellbound and rendered weak by the Goddess Morrigan, due to an offense towards the warrior Goddess at the hands of Cuchulainn. When faced with Mauve and her army he made a deal with them that he would fight them one by one since his army was inaccessible. Cuchulainn put up a good fight and was almost successful but eventually, succumbed by his injuries, was defeated. Had it not been for the healing restorative gifts of his father, Lugh, he would have perished entirely.

As the great legend continues, Mauve and her army were able to fight and claim the prized Bull, Donn Cuailnge. In this version, they manage to bring the bull back to Connaught to prove to the King that she was indeed superior. It was undoubtedly a long, arduous trip back and the bull suffered for it but they made it back. When the bull arrived before the King Ailill, it was immediately greeted and challenged by the King's existing bull. According to the literature of the time, the two Bulls confronted each other and engaged in a fierce battle. They eventually tore each other up and some tales state they fought each other to their deaths. Other versions speak of Mauve's Bull defeating the king's bull but later on collapsing to his own death due to the enormous strain and injuries.

Mauve is an important Goddess for us to connect with and her story almost reminds me of the Sumerian Goddess, Lilith, because here again we have a Goddess needing to defend herself and prove why she is, not only equal to man, but moreover, superior. In the case of the Sumerian Goddess, Lilith, she refused to lie underneath Adam during sex. As supreme Deities, both she and Mauve are not only demanding equality but demanding that their superiority and their sovereignty be acknowledged and honored. This is extremely important for modern women today. We are so often overly concerned about the subject of equality that we fail to see beyond it and consider that maybe, in some circumstances, it is not equality we should strive for but the recognition of our supremacy and authority.

Celtic mythology often reveals an understanding and an acceptance that women were intrinsically linked with the sacred feminine and that they were indeed equal and more often than not, superior to men. The Goddess Mauve is in this chapter about ambition and focus because this Sovereign Queen reminds us that sometimes we too have to make an argument for our own supremacy and authority. We too have to acknowledge our own gifts, gather our own resources & attributes, and let our light shine even if it blinds others. In this Irish Goddess we are also reminded to set our sights on what we want and commit to doing whatever it takes to accomplish it. A Goddess so connected to sovereignty is a beautiful reminder and an example of what we can aspire to be.

NIKE

NIKE

Nike is the immortal spirit of triumph, the Greek Goddess of victory and success. In Rome she was better known as Victoria. Often depicted standing on a globe with wings, and holding palm and Laurel wreath, she was described as quite beautiful by most of the ancient literature of her time. It appeared she was desired by everyone, for, of course, victory is that prized attribute longed for by, men and women, mortal and immortal alike. That perpetual spirit of victory is present in all wars, competitions, award ceremonies and athletic events today, as it was in ancient times and thus, her immortal presence can still be felt today.

Perhaps this is why the very successful American athletic shoe company (which began in Oregon, in 1962) adopted its name, Nike. In doing so it honors one of the most beloved Champion Goddesses in Greek mythology. Today, it is one of the most prosperous conglomerate corporations in the world; doing its part to campaign for this highly cherished Greek Goddess, sustaining her name alive in our vernacular.

In Greek mythology she is the winged daughter of the dark River Styx and the Giant Titan Pallas. Her siblings, interestingly enough, were "Cratos," which means Strength, "Bia," which means Force and "Zelus," which mean Rivalry, an indication that all three attributes were ever present, when Victory was invoked.

In Rome, as Victoria, she was worshipped quite early on and was considered the divine protector of the senate. There isn't a whole lot of detailed information on the Greek Goddess, Nike. Most of what we do know about her is extracted and derived from mere mentions, every now and then, in various ancient Greek writings. There are no long epic myths associated with her, nor any indication that she had conflict with anyone in particular. And although she was desired and welcomed by all, there is no indication of any romantic liaisons with Gods, nor with any humans.

Although, in Greece, she had no known cult following, nor any special festivals or temples, as many of the other Greek Goddesses did, she was often associated with both Zeus and Athena. Most art and sculptures of her time depicted her as a small figure held in the hands of Athena, the Greek Goddess of War and Wisdom. There is even some literature that alleged, Nike was simply another aspect of the beloved Athenian Goddess. However, more evidence reveals that indeed they were two separate deities, with many impressive similar attributes, which would explain the conflicting tales. Athena, being a Goddess of Wisdom, debates and war, would certainly want near her, the continuous blessings from the Goddess of Victory. They were considered as having a close alliance and there is even some contention in the Greek myths that directly connects Athena with the death of Nike's father, but she apparently, suffered no grave punishment due to their close relationship.

Nike's worship would have been compulsory on the battlefield, pageantries, athletic events and numerous other competitive situations for both mortals and immortals alike; with libations, offerings and sacrifices. The patriarchal Olympian head God, Zeus, cherished Nike immensely due to her help in attaining victory in the battle of the Titans. It is perhaps this reason why Zeus appointed Nike as his official charioteer and employed her family as attendants; allowing them, the rare privilege, to reside with him in the royal palace among the divine Gods.

Her most famous depiction is found in *"Nike of Samothrace"* a sculpture by Paeonius (c.424 B.C.) which was discovered on Samothrace in 1863. Presently this illustrious creation is contained at the Louvre Museum in Paris, France.

Wherever victory and success is, Nike is there too, immortal, ever present as the spirit of Victory, a pure ambitious drive, ready to award you with success. She is forever the Maiden archetype and a wonderful Goddess for modern wommin to connect with, when we are ready to tap into our fierce competitive spirit. As the Divine Charioteer, she is also an excellent Goddess to call upon for, not only Victory, but also in driving and travel rites. Invoke her when you wish to succeed in a personal endeavor or anything requiring ambition and drive. She is the energy of the marathon runner, reaching the finish line, hands outstretched towards the heavens, in pure elation and accomplishment..... This is Nike... the Goddess of Victory!

Times are indeed changing but previous studies have shown that as women, we tend to be inclusive and less competitive than our male counterparts. Oftentimes, even in our youth, as young girls, we may have been discouraged from being, *"too aggressive"* or *"too competitive"* or *"too bossy,"* etc... Admitedly, even as adult women in various different communities (work, collegiate, religious) I notice we are often still made to feel self-conscious about how aggressive or competitive we are coming across to others. If we appear too ambitious or too competitive we are easily labeled *"the bitch"* or *"the one who has an attitude"* or *"the ugly one,"* because apparently there are some blind people in this world that cannot see the beauty of every diverse Goddess roaming this earth, but I digress.

Now, I know times are changing and we are indeed in the midst of human evolution here. I strongly believed that times have changed much and it is my hope that today, we are raisng our daughters to shine their own unique light, without any preconceived prejudices on what is proper male or female behavior. Yes, inclusivity, compassion, nurturance and all the numerous gifts we possess as women should be embraced and encouraged in ourselves and the next generation. But the notion of telling another human being that they cannot aspire for greatness (their definition of greatness) is preposterous, no matter what your gender may be.

Nike is the Goddess of greatness, of supreme successs... every girl (and for that matter, every boy) should indeed be allowed and encouraged to pursue their own well defined level of greatness. Let the Goddess of Victory inspire us to unleash our inner competitive maiden, to thrive in this world with the best of them, uninfluenced by preconceived ideas of what is proper, or not, within our gender. Let Nike be our armour of inspiration and defense against those who would try to snuff out our unique, divine flames. And may we be sparked by her immortal essence to thrive and fearlessly pursue our heart's desire regardless of the naysayers and dream killers.

*Nike is the Greek Goddess of Victory. The laurel wreathed maiden Goddess of Triumph, rewards generously for works accomplished, this is her sweet domain. She anxiously awaits your success and stirs within you a healthy dose of competition and ambition. Our laurel wreath is awaiting and she stirs in you a desire for her presence –a desire for success. *Do we enter it victoriously; projecting a sense of ordained achievement? Or have we already failed before we have even begun?*

The Goddess Nike invites you to celebrate the small and large accomplishments in your life, knowing that this acknowledgement will positively influence future ones. With Nike, we celebrate our great drive and ambition and we take bold steps towards monumental victories; carving out our own unique path to successs.

FREYJA

FREYJA (FREYA,FREIJA, FREYIA, FREJA)

Freyja is the Norse Goddess of beauty, love, sexuality, fertility freedom and independence. She is also known as the Goddess of war, death, travel, gold, and sorcery. It is clear, like with many ancient Goddesses, Freyja is an all-encompassing Goddess that was and still remains today an important representation of the Sacred Feminine.

Her name translates as, "*Lady*" or "*Mistress*" and she was part of the Vanir Tribe. The Vanir were much older and came before the Aesir. They were focused on nature, animals, the wild, and even the unseen realm. It is only after the war between these two tribes, when the Aesir also came to claim Freyja as one of their own.

Freyja is believed to be very much a shaman Goddess and even had the ability to shapeshift. As a Goddess of Magick and Divination, she was attributed for introducing the Gods and Humanity with a special type of Norse magick, known as Seidr. She also had the special proclivity to connect worshippers to their Female ancestors and divine the future with their help. She could travel through all nine realms and is connected to the Valkyries; known to travel at night with them as their leader.

Her name appears numerous times in ancient writings and her image can also be found in various sources. Often depicted as the Fair one, with blue eyes and long flowing or braided blonde hair, she was known to ride a chariot led by two black cats. Theses cats were gifted to her by Thor but she was also connected with a Boar, named Hildisvini. When she wasn't using her cat led chariot she would ride this Battle Boar, who was secretly known as her human lover. Freyja also had a connection with raven and falcon. Her magickal cloak was made of Falcon feathers and with it she could fly to great heights. Many other deities borrowed her magickal cloak whenever they needed the gift of flight.

Her father is Njoror and his sister, the Earth Goddess, Nerthus, is her mother. She is a twin to her brother, Freyr. The question of her husband stirs some variations in stories. Early writings reveal she is married to Odr but this name eventually disappear in the writings and it leaves many to speculate that it is an older version of the name Odin. Either way Odin which is a derivative of Odr means ecstasy, furor, frenzy, inspiration. Most of the early writings of the time reveal that Freyja had two beautiful daughters with Odr. They were known as Hnoss and Gersemi.

Freyja, as the Norse Goddess of Love and Beauty, commands great powers of attraction. Her beauty was unmatched and it was a known fact that no man could resist her advances. Despite being married she had numerous lovers and lived her life quite independently. She is known to pursue her desires regardless of consequences or other's opinions, as is evident in many of her myths. Her connection to beautiful objects like jewelry, gemstones and gold becomes apparent when you learn through her myths that her very own tears would become amber when they fell upon water and gold, when they fell upon stones. And of course, there is the famous story about how she acquired her legendary, magickal gold necklace, *Brisingamen*, meaning fire.

One day Freyja passed by four busy dwarves, that were working on an exquisite golden necklace. She caught a glimpse of this brilliant work of art and admired aloud its beauty. The dwarves replied with an admiration of her Divine beauty but no matter, because she had already set her sights on possessing this necklace. She offered to buy it from them. She negotiated with them, proposing all sorts of gold and silver but the dwarves were not interested in these things. They felt they already had enough gold and silver in the lives but they lacked something that they knew only the Goddess of Love could offer them. They each wanted to lay with the Divine Goddess. They agreed to surrender the exquisite necklace to her only if she agreed to have sex with each of them. Her expression of love and sexual gifts were more precious to these dwarves and thus, she used her sexuality as currency to get what she wanted most, at that very moment. It would not be the first nor the last time this type of negotiation is made by this Divine Goddess.

As a Goddess of War, she and Odin shared the brave lost souls that died in the battlefield. She had the honors of gathering first, before Odin, and she delivers her half of these brave beings to Folkvangr, the heavenly field, where they are to find their final resting place. Immortal Freyja lives among the Norse Gods in Asgard and her own house is known as *Sessrumnir*, located near Folkvangr, where her first choice slain warriors enjoy the afterlife.

CHAPTER EIGHT
RAGE WARRIORESS
SHE WHO TAPS INTO THE POWER OF HER VOICE

PELE

"Strength does not come from physical capacity,
it comes from an indomitable will..." Mahatma Gandhi

PELE

The Polynesian Volcanic Goddess, Pele, is a Fire Goddess known for her passionate, unpredictable, lava spewing insatiable ways. To the people of Hawaii, she is beloved "Tutu Pele" (Grandmother Pele), a demonstrative name revealing much respect and adoration. She is also known as Pele-honua-mea (Pele of the sacred land) and also as, Pele-ai-honua (Pele the devourer of land). This Hawaiian Goddess of beauty, anger and sexual liberation among her many other titles was also known as Ka-ula-o-ke-ahi, a reference to the redness of her fires.

According to Polynesian cosmology, in the beginning was pure darkness. There was formlessness, the infinite. Similar to the cosmology of numerous cultures, in this darkness we find the Earth's womb; the feminine, the Goddess- Papa. Then light was born and this light was the masculine, known as the Sky God –Wakea. When this union between light and darkness joined, the Universe was thus formed and first born. From this union of opposites, mother darkness and father light, emerged all the Gods and all of creation. The creator God, Kane came to be and numerous other important deities followed like Lono, the agricultural God and Kanaloa and Ku, to name a few. Pele is the daughter of the Earth Goddess, Haumea and holds the spirit of the Female Goddess, Hina; as all female deities were considered her direct descendants. In some legends her father was Kuwahailo, a sky God and brother to Hina.

There are many legends about Pele and her vast extended family. We know for example that she had numerous brothers and sisters, as can be expected from her fertile Mother, the Goddess of the Earth. Most notably, her sisters were the patron Goddesses of Hula dancing; Laka and Hiiaka. Laka was a fertility goddess but she was also known as Kapo, in another incarnation, the shape shifter Goddess of dark powers and sorcery. Pele's youngest sister, Hiiaka, was especially dear to her. Hiiaka was born in the shape of an egg and Pele assumed big sister duties by being in charge of caring for that beloved egg. In Hawaiian folklore, we learn of how Hiiaka was held by her sister, as an egg, close to her armpit during the journey to the island of Hawaii, until the egg one day changed into a beautiful little girl. Some of her other important siblings were; Komohoalii, a Shark God. He was her eldest brother and guarded the fiery Goddess often. In some legends he was the Sea God who provided the canoe for her journey to Hawaii. Kane-hekili was also her brother, the God of Thunder and Kauila-nui was yet another brother, the God of lightning. Namaka was her rivaling sister, the Goddess of the Sea, and they had numerous intense battles according to Polynesian folklore. The most famous of these had to do with Pele seducing her husband and Namaka chasing her sister, away from the rest of the family.

In ancient times, Pele was considered part of the Aumakua, family of lesser Gods, and thus her worship did not require the elaborate, formal structured rituals of the major Hawaiian Gods. Perhaps this is one reason why her myths and her worship have survived all this time among the Hawaiian people. Her worship and the practice of her rituals were very informal and individualize, allowing the average laymen the ability to connect with this Divine deity and call on her, in their own personal way. Pele remains one of four most powerful Hawaiian Goddesses still revered and worshipped by natives and non-natives alike on the island. A visit to modern day Hawaii will confirm her as one of the most well-known, venerated deities still commanding our attention today.

Often, Pele was described as beautiful, but easily angered, very volatile, impulsive and jealous. Depicted with long brown hair and sometimes just as an erupting volcano, her priestesses were not allowed to cut their hair, unless it was done so as an offering to the Goddess. Frequently, her priestesses, and those seeking to connect with the Goddess, would cut their long locks as an offering and place it at the edge of the volcanic craters, where many forms of rituals and gifts were offered to her. Gin bottles would be left at Halema'uma'u crater within Kilauea caldera, as well as baked pork, coffee, flowers, fruits and vegetables.

Pele's known home was in Mount Kilauea, Hawaii, but all volcanoes were sacred to her and thus viewed as her ruling domain. Not surprisingly, lava rocks are sacred to her, as well as natural glass. The gemstone Peridot was also linked to Pele. Her colors are the colors of fire; red, orange, yellow and black. The red Lehua flower, from the Ohi'a tree was also sacred to her. During childbirth it was a common practice to call on the midwife aspect of Pele. Polynesian women would invoke her strength and the esteemed Lehua flower was used to entreat her help and ease the pain in childbirth.

Legend tells of how often she would disguise herself as an old lady to test the loyalty of her people. As a crone, she would ask for a plate of food and bless those that complied. Conversely, she would curse with fire, those that were less than generous, as is evident in many of her known tales. Similar to the Greek Goddess Hekate, Pele was seen as a Triple goddess because sometimes she would appear as an old Crone woman, or sometimes as a child. And still at other times, she would appear as a beautiful, insatiable, passionate young maiden. There are myths that tell of Pele truly being an old Hag that reveals her true self, only in dreams.

The Goddess Pele garnered herself a reputation for being, strong tempered, passionate, lustful, wanton and free. As the Goddess of liberation she was a pleasure seeker, a sexual Goddess and what we might term as a minx. Living solely in the moment without thought to consequences, she pursued her passions. Whatever and whomever she wanted, she targeted, pursued and often achieved at attaining. She is a beautiful enchantress, few could resist her and, needless to say, she had many lovers. However, her volatile persona caused much problems within her family and all around the island of Hawaii. Her myths reveal she had many problems with her siblings and was known to have slept with her sisters' husbands. Pele had a rival in the Goddess of the snow-capped mountains-Poloahu. This rivalry is not surprising, due to the fact that Fire never gets along with ice or water.

Pele was known to have had a tumultuous relationship with the Demi Pig- God of agriculture, Kamapua'a. Together they were believed to have had one child who later becomes the ancestor of Polynesian chieftains, intimately connecting the people to their Gods. Kamapua'a appeared to the Fiery Goddess as a handsome chief, who could shapeshift into numerous images from a huge, eight eye boar, to plants and fishes. He was known to have had quite the sexual appetite which meant he pursued numerous dalliances. The first sight of Pele excited him greatly and although she had no interest in him, he pursued her relentlessly; causing the Hawaiian landscape some distress. When she finally surrendered to their union it was riddled with many battles for they were polar opposites. Even their home land had to be divided, as Pele required drier land for her lava to flow and Kamapua'a required verdant, moist and fertile land and thus the two could not live together. Yet interesting to note that although, Pele makes the land from her spewing Lava seemingly separated from her mate, evidence of his bountiful gifts are seen when seeds somehow take root upon the lava, eventually becoming fertile soil. According to author, Herb Kawainui Kane, in his book, "Pele, Goddess of Hawaii's Volcanoes" (pg 31), "...Pele may build the island with her lava, but it is the incessant attentions of Kamapua'a that makes it fertile."

There are numerous tales of Pele and her volatility causing much conflict and drama on the island of Hawaii. One tale in particular reveals much about this Goddess.

Pele was madly in love with her new lover, a mortal hula dancer named Lohiau, whom she had a passionate love affair with, when she visited the Earth. They were separated after she had decided to return to her realm in her moment of restlessness. But soon after leaving the earth, she began to long for him. She asked her little sister, Hiiaka, to retrieve him and brings him back to her. Her sister agreed, but only if Pele would tend to her beloved garden during the time she was away. Pele agreed. Hiiaka ran into some trouble however, in this endeavor, and could not bring Pele's lover back to her quickly enough. Lohiau had died from a broken heart during the journey and Hiiaka had to revive him.

Their journey back to Pele was full of challenges. Much time lapsed and Pele, being a jealous Goddess, assumed her sister had betrayed her by taking her lover for her own self. Pele angry, and in a fit of uncontrollable jealousy, destroyed her sister's garden in retaliation. When Hiiaka finally returned and saw what her sister had done to her garden, she in turn retaliated by giving in to her own suppressed desires for the mortal, Lohiau. Throughout their journey, the two had fallen in love with one another, but resisted temptation. Lohiau had confessed, at this time, to loving Hiiaka more but the fear of Pele's retribution helped him resist his desirous impulses. The couple did not give in to their passions due to their vow to Pele but upon discovering Pele's betrayal, Hiiaka took Pele's lover to the sacred crater of the Volcano, where the Goddess could bear witness to what would unfold.

Hiiaka took Lohiau and there proceeded to make love to him. As you can surmised, this act angered Pele, the great Goddess of violence . She wasted no time in killing the mortal, sending him quickly to the land of the dead and making Hiiaka terribly distraught and heartbroken. The end of this tale reveals Pele's fickleness with lovers, as she later resurrects Lohiau from the land of the dead. She willingly gives him up to her sister in exchange for a new love found in the Hula dancer's best friend. Clearly, honesty was crucial to Pele and she did not hesitate to punish those that failed her. She was known to hurl Lava at her lovers when they would not meet her expectations.

Despite the introduction of Christianity by the missionaries in the 1700- 1800's Pele is one of the most well-known, venerated Polynesian deities today. As a Volcanic Goddess, Pele symbolized the internal fires found in the core of the Earth but also within womyn. She is the unbridled power of anger that moves us and becomes a catalyst for great change.

This Polynesian Goddess is a symbol of passion and perseverance and raw power. Pele is about asserting will and the expression of anger. She teaches us to honor our feelings and allow them to move us into courage and action. Pele teaches us to honor and embrace our deep rooted passions and allow them to surface, so that we can effectively pursue and attain our heart's desire. She teaches us how anger can be a catalyst for great change in our lives. She knows what she wants, is self-assured and may sometimes appear brat-like in her relentless pursuit of her desire, yet, this is a Goddess who will not allow you to become a victim or self -martyrdom, she has no patience for the weak. Like her, she expects you to be strong and passionate... And in Pele, we find the qualities of strong will, purposeful action, passion, strength and women's empowerment.

*Pele is one of the most well-known Goddesses in our modern times. She is the ancient Polynesian Volcanic Goddess, still very much venerated today in Hawaii. Her energy is palpable to us as women, when we are deeply connected to our emotions like, anger and our deep passions. The volcanic, uncontrollable, erupting, passionate Goddess awakens us to great strength, willpower, desires and insatiable energy. She awakens passion deep within and a relentlessness to pursue that which your heart desires. She inaugurates a type of boiling fire energy sweltering from deep within that needs to be approached with great awareness and reverence. She beckons you to give credence to your feelings, validate them, and give them strength. Pele demands that we give volume to our voice. *"Speak out, roar it out,"* she says. Like the rumbling of her volcanoes, she awakens in you the ability to acknowledge the sacred cathartic emotion of passion but also anger. Pele invites you at this time to banish complacency and get real with your true voice. Then let it be heard! Like the rumbling of her Volcanoes and the spewing of her scorching lavas, don't hold your true emotions inside, let them out... let it all out and let your passionate voice be heard. Pele's energy encourages you to speak your mind, value your passion and emotions, express them openly and be like the volcano; let your voice be heard.

AINE

AINE

The Lady of the Lake, Aine is also known as Aine Marina, Aine Cliach, Cnoc Aine, Aine of Knockaine. She is a much beloved Celtic Goddess whose name appears throughout several regions in Ireland where she is most revered to this day. The Knock Aine of Ireland, Dun Aine and Aines Hills in the province of Munster are most reflective of the worship of this Goddess. Three miles South West of Lough Gur is the region of Cnoc Aine or KnockAiny and this is the reputed Hill of Aine. She is also most celebrated and revered in Dunany point, which is lovingly referred to as Dun Aine, in honor of the Goddess.

The etymology of her name reveals a lot about the character of this Goddess. Her name means; *delight, pleasure, agility and melody*. In Gaelic, Aine means "*radiance*" and this would be a fitting name for a Goddess believed to be both a Solar and a Lunar deity. The Celtic Goddess, Aine was also often known as the Irish Red Mare that no one could outrun, because this was her chosen form to shape shift. Like most ancient, Celtic Goddesses, there are a number of various attributes linked to her myths.

At some point she was solely revered as a Sun Goddess and held to high esteems during the holy day of Midsummer, Litha (or Summer Solstice, as is better known to some). Burnt offerings of straw and flowers were made to this Solar Goddess in order to insure favorable blessings on love, crops and homes. There are some documented prose and rituals that support this belief and reveal her significant worship at this time of the year, with torch-lit processions through-out the fields to insure a prosperous, fertile crop. Lughnasadh (August 1st) is also a holy day traditionally associated with this Solar Goddess and most notably sacred to her are the three days (Friday, Saturday, Sunday) following Lughnasadh.

Yet, the Goddess Aine, is also very much known as a legendary enchantress; a Moon Goddess and a Goddess of Love. She was known to have numerous divine, royal and human lovers, with a preference for the latter. In ancient times, she was a goddess called upon for fertility magick, whether it was fertility for a woman's womb or the Celtic land itself. She became a patron Goddess for women, agricultural magick and the proliferation of animals and crops. Most notably she is identified as the Faery Queen of Munster and she is an appropriate Goddess to call upon when working with Faery magick.

Aine is believed to be the Daughter of King Egobagal, one of the Tuatha de Danann and there is even some confusion regarding her possible assimilation with other Goddesses like Grainne and the Morrighan. There are some that sometimes view Aine as simply an aspect of Grainne, as both Solar Goddesses, respectively, reflected the waxing and waning Solar year. Still there are other myths that depict her as a Goddess and daughter, even possibly a wife, of the Sea God, Manannan. Thus here, we see a connection to the element of water; hence the South-West cardinal points are sacred to her, as they are to two other well-known Goddesses; Saraswati and Brigit.

There are some of the opinion that Aine was an absolutely beautiful, human woman, from the Leanan Sidhe, meaning, "*Sweetheart of the Sidhe*" and a direct connection to those people with the surname O'Corra. It was believed, she possessed a magickal ring that could unearth faeries and some alleged she became enchanted by the Fae, and taken in by this magickal realm. Subsequently, she became the Faery Queen of Munster and was forever connected, lovingly, with faeries. As a Faery Queen, she was very fond of mortal men, consorting and mating with numerous lovers. She is often attributed for creating a magickal Faery race, called the Dinnshenchas [Din- sheen-k'has]. These were believed to be, more specifically, shape shifting, fire dwarf faeries that came to strengthen and assist wommin in danger of being harmed by men and they undoubtedly served their Queen, Goddess Aine.

Many of the beloved Celtic myths that survive today reveal a great deal about Aine's character and her attributes. According to one Celtic story of the time, she once made a quirky, strange vow not to sleep with a gray-haired man and this tale exemplifies her serious commitment to promises and magickal vows. When Aine's lover, Fionnis, was sadly enchanted by her jealous sister-Miluchrach, and his hair turned gray, Aine kept her vow. In yet another infamous tale we see glimmers of the strong character of this beloved Irish Goddess as she is credited for killing The King of Munster, Aillil Olom, after he had attempted to rape her. In yet another revealing Irish tale of Aine we learn of a stone, known as Cathair Aine. It clearly was an enchanted stone that belonged to the Goddess and it was believed that anyone who sat on it was susceptible to losing their wits. If anyone dared sit on her rock for more than three times they were doomed to loose themselves forever. In this tale, we again see Aine's character as a Goddess not to offend, for her fiery, red wrath throughout various myths has proven to be severe. There are, however, also tales that reflect her generous powers of creativity bestowed upon bards and writer, yet if they failed to meet her high demands and expectations she would not hesitate to severely punish them.

Most of the myths agree that Aine became the wife of Gerald, The Earl of Desmond, although it is not clear how that union came about. There are numerous conflicting tales of how they first met and fell in love. According to some legends, The Earl of Desmond came across the enchanting beauty, while she bathed in a river and he was instantly smitten. He spied upon her magick cloak, the one that was so often used by Aine to enchant men into lovers, and he saw her scattered clothes set upon a nearby boulder. Essentially, he blackmailed her into matrimony, refusing to give back her prized possessions until she agreed to the union. Another version of this story, tells of how he saw her combing her hair by the river and upon discovering her unsupervised clothes, he stole her legendary magickal cloak. Wearing the enchanted cloak himself, he used her very own magick powers against her, to ensnare and enchant her into love and marriage. Still another version tells of how she herself, having a reputation for being a beautiful enchantress and acquiring numerous lovers, wore the magick cloak and ensnared The Earl of Desmond into marriage.

Married to the Earl of Desmond, together they had one known son; Geroid Iarla, Earl Fitzgerald; although here too there might be conflicting mysterious stories. In some of the writings of the time he is addressed as "The Magician." Some believed he is indeed Merlin or an archetype of Lancelot in Arthurian mythology. According to one famous tale, upon the birth of their son, Aine warned her husband not to ever be surprised at what their son could do. It was a type of taboo The Earl of Desmond needed to agree and adhere to. One day however, he witnessed his beloved flesh and blood, jump in and out of a tiny bottle, a very non-human act and the poor man could not contain his utter shock. This very act resulted in Geroid turning himself into a wild Goose and Aine fleeing her marriage and the husband who failed to keep his critical vow.

Some believe their son, the Magician, still lives today under the Lake, inside Lough Fur, in county Limerick and one myth claims that he will one day return to remove all foreigners from his beloved Ireland. The immortal Goddess Aine is still very much revered today by the Irish and the name itself is quite common in certain regions of Ireland. There is great pride in this beloved Goddess, some even feeling an ancestral connection to her. There are some that believe she still lives on today in Knock Aine, in a Faery Castle.

Call upon the Goddess Aine for Faery magick; solar and lunar spells, fertility and prosperity rituals, love magick, creativity workings - especially for writing. When making oaths and vows, it is Aine who can be beseeched on your behalf. She can also be called upon when needing to flee an unsuitable mate. When endeavoring to give birth to a wizard; magickal offspring or a creation, she is the Goddess to call upon. The Meadowsweet is associated with Aine but also the Yew tree, which reflects her connection to life and death. She will be very sympathetic and prove to be helpful when doing rites to punish rapist as well. The Red Mare (Lair Derg) as she was sometimes titled was often called upon when blessing cattles and herds. Rabbits and Swans are also her sacred animals, and she is still often invoked and honored during her feast day, on Midsummer's day.

*Irish Red Mare, Solar and Lunar Goddess, Aine, is the fiery enchantress who inspires the writer and the songstress. She is a Fierce Protectress of Women, especially those who have been mistreated, abused, lied to, molested or raped by men. An oath and vow guardian, she awakens in you a call to action, where action is needed. Defend yourself and unearth the confidence to utilize your own gifts of enchantments, when needed. Aine connects us with the energy of Fire, in her Solar aspect, although she was later similarly connected to the moon. With the Goddess, Aine, we hone in on the various wonderful gifts of the element of fire and how to best utilize it in our lives, channeling it into the manifestation of cherished goals. With Aine's fiery solar energy, we are blessed.

Kali

KALI

The name, Kali comes from the word, *Kala*, which means, *time*. We quickly can see her divine connection to the element of time, space and the cosmos when viewing some of her myths. She is known both as a fierce Goddess in her own right and an aspect of the Hindu Matriarchal Goddess, Durga. Ancient text reveals that she was born from the powerful brow (third eye) of the Goddess Durga, in the midst of a gruesome war, fighting off an infinite number of the demons in the Universe. Durga's rage was so strong that she called forth the birth of Kali, to fight off demons and drink of their blood. According to the myth, each blood spilled by a slaughtered demon produced the birth of even more demons and thus, Kali's long red tongue was employed to prevent this vicious cycle and save the world.

Kali's depiction is one that not only raises eyebrows but is meant to evoke great fear in the uninitiated spectator. She is often depicted naked, with garlands of skulls and aprons of dead severed limbs on her black (or dark blue) colored flesh. She is as black as the infinite sky and her gruesome image is full of powerful symbolism. Four arms, sometimes even eight, are seen protruding from her dancing body. She holds swords, scythes, sharp cutting apparatuses and severed bloody skulls from these arms. How can this sight not induce fear? Her image is one that evokes nightmares for some yet not for others. She is clearly not a Deity for the faint of heart. Her very distinct, jaw dropping image reveals, she is Goddess of destruction, death courage, strength, transformation and rebirth.

Kali Ma, represents Energy, also known as Shakti, and many ancient texts speak of her well-known *Dance of Destruction*. Her disheveled black long tresses, in many of her depictions, reflect her untamable freedom and unstoppable energy. She was often seen dancing upon the body of her consort, Lord Shiva. According to the Hindu text, Lord Shiva placed his body under Kali's feet to get her to stop her feverish *Dance of Destruction*; a dance that was destined to bring about the end of humanity. She was in such a state of ecstasy through her wild, frenetic dance, while helping Durga destroy demons, that she got carried away and danced upon his corpse. It was only upon seeing his presence under her feet that she then realized what she was actually doing. It made her pause, snap out of her bloodthirsty trance, and this act put an end to the destruction of the world.

Kali can then be seen as the personification of anger and expressed rage, but she is so much more. You will find a plethora of books dedicated solely to her and her intriguing, ancient worship. She is Goddess of tantric practices and of deep states of divine ecstasy. She is patron Goddess of the purge, of clearing out what no longer serves our highest purpose and like the skulls on her garland, Goddess of severing and pruning. She is immeasurable strength and courage. She is Goddess of the fires and incinerators; connected to the crematory of India and therefore death and life. Many of the images we have of Kali serve to reveal her great strength and inspire our own courage.

Her frightful dark imagery is probably one of the most well-known across India and her numerous cults today are even more prevalent than in ancient times. Her devotees see her not as this frightful, calamitous, bloodthirsty Deity, but rather come to her, humbly, with great reverence and respect. For many, she is this extraordinary, unmatchable ancient deity that fiercely protects her devotees. In this way she is wholeheartedly embraced as a beloved Mother, defender, and protectress; and, one who inspires us to meet life with great strength and courage.

SEKHMET

SEKHMET

By far, Sekhmet and her highly recognized image is one of the most widely venerated deities of ancient time. Sekhmet is the Egyptian Lion headed Goddess of Vengeance, Retribution, Anger and Destruction. She was viewed as both a destroyer and protector. She is often depicted sitting or standing, holding the ankh and sometimes a scepter, made of papyrus reed. On her head is a solar disk, reflecting her connection to the sun and she is sometimes seen with a serpent headdress as her crown. She is the woman with a fierce looking Lionhead, donning a red dress to denote her connection to blood, life and death.

To begin to understand this important Egyptian Solar Deity, let's first look at her name. The Egyptian word *"Sekhem"* translates as *"power,"* *"might,"* or *"the powerful one,"* or *"she who is powerful."* As the ancient writings reveal, she was known then as "Mistress of Dread," *"Bringer of Plagues,"* *"Lady of Slaughter,"* *"The Red Lady,"* and *"The Lady of Pestilence,"* to name just a few of her known epithet. We know much of her because she was mentioned so often in many of the surviving text of the time and the myriad of statues representing and venerating her back then still remain today.

Her main Temple was found in Memphis and she was also worshipped with her consort at the temple of Leontopolis, at the Taremu.

Sekhmet is viewed as the personification of the destructive force in the universe. It is quite interesting because she is both worshipped as the "Lady of Life" but also "The Lady of Destruction and Terror." Ancient Egyptians believed it was her breath that formed the Egyptian desert and she was the Eye of Ra, the Egyptian God of the Sun. She was the protector of the Pharaohs and she was connected to the art of Medicine and Physicians. She could bring destruction, yes, but she could also help avert it and bring healing.

Although she may physically resemble the Egyptian Cat Goddess well known as Bast, there is no Familial relation between these two deities. Bast was viewed as a Goddess of the lower Egypt, while Sekhmet was viewed as a Deity of the upper region.

Sekhmet was an aspect of the benevolent Goddess of Joy, Pleasure, Sexuality, and Music, Hathor. Their father thus was the Sun God, Ra and Mut was considered Sekhmet's mother; although it is believed later on, Mut would absorb many of Sekhmet's attributes. There are many surviving myths connected to this Goddess and most will reveal different aspects and a deeper understanding of this astounding Goddess. For example, there is a well-known story that exemplifies best the ferocity of Sekhmet.

According to one legend, the Egyptian Sun God, Ra was growing old and weak and he believed his followers were beginning to lose faith in him. He started to feel like humanity was plotting against him; to dethrone him. This paranoia led him to make a journey into the desert and while there, he drew forth from his brow an aspect of his beloved daughter Hathor, as Sekhmet. He sent the Lion Goddess to humanity to devour and destroy all those who had betrayed him or showed no allegiance to him. As the ferocious Goddess started to slaughter and feed off the betrayers, the blood carnage grew bigger and bigger. Something strange started to happen with Sekhmet as she fell into this killing trance and delighted in the blood. The more blood was spilled the more bloodthirsty it seemed she became and she was consumed with blind rage. She fell deeper into this massacre rampage, devouring and delighting in the blood spillage. Her savagery escalated exponentially, and it appeared she would destroy ALL of humanity.

According to this famous myth, when the Sun God, Ra, beheld the sight of his Lioness daughter in the midst of this atrocious bloodbath he feared this would be the end of humanity and he panicked. Witnessing Sekhmet's bloodthirsty dance, he quickly got the idea of mixing pomegranates and beer to replicate the look of the blood that the Goddess appeared to be feeding off of in her rage. He poured the colored beer and

Sekhmet continued to lap up what she believed to be blood, only to eventually find herself terribly intoxicated, by the beer. Inebriated, she stopped the carnage and found herself passed out, asleep. Upon awakening, it is said she returned to her Hathor aspect. In another version of the story, the Goddess Sekhmet passes out inebriated from the beer but when she awakes, her eyes set first upon, Ptah, the Creator and she falls in love. Thus, combining, Ptah (creation) and Sekhmet (destruction) results in her son, healing, Nefertum.

Sekhmet is a powerful Goddess to work with. Evidence of her existence is unquestionable due to the numerous statuary remnants that have been found throughout archeological excavations. Rituals and offerings would be made to petition the Goddess to avert calamities and bring protection to Egyptians. To appease this Goddess, it was well known that her priestesses performed rituals each day to a different sacred image of hers and thus, many statues were made of Sekhmet.

Recently there was an amazing discovery of numerous Temple statuaries of the lion headed warrior goddess. 66 well preserved statues were found in Luxor by archeologist, in what was the ancient city of Thebes. It is believed that there might have been as many as 700 statues of Sekhmet at this pharaoh's temple. Here at this newly excavated site, they discovered the burial temple of the ninth Pharaoh in the 18th dynasty, Amenhotep III, he ruled during a prosperous time in Egypt and was clearly devoted to the Goddess Sekhmet.

SKADI

SKADI

Skadi is the Norse Goddess of Winter, mountains and wilderness. She is a Viking Goddess known by several other names like; Snowshoe Goddess, Ski Goddess, Skade, Skadhi, Skathi and Shinning Bride of the Gods. Interesting to note, her name bares a similar resemblance to the Hindu Goddess of Feminine energy, Shakti. Skadi is a Giantess and the beloved daughter of the Giant Thiassi/Thjazi and she became a Goddess through her union and marriage with the Gods of Aesir. She was described as a Jotunn and a fair maiden, in the Heimskringla book, Ynglinga saga. It is also widely believed that the country of Scandinavia received its name from this beloved Goddess and apparently her name, or derivations of her name, can be found throughout Scandinavia. She was also known as Ondurgodth, which means, "Ski God," and Ondurtis, which means "Ski Lady," both words come from the Old Norse language.

There are numerous conflicting stories about Skadi's etymology, but her name in Old High German is linked with the word, "Scato", which mean *Shadow*. This may reflect an older, initial depiction of the Goddess as a bringer of death or a deity of the underworld. Along with the word shadow, her name has also been translated as meaning; "scathe", "damaged," or "harm".

In Norse mythology there were three known clans of Deities; the Aesir gods, who lived in Asgard and the Vanir gods, who lived in Anaheim. Eventually these two respective clans resolved their differences to join together and recognize Asgard as the hall and home of all the gods. The third clan of Norse deities was known as the Jotun, the wise, but malefic race of Giants and this is where we find Skadi's lineage. More specifically, she was believed to be part of the Frost Giant clan.

According to Norse cosmology, the sun was the first to exist in the world and from the sun came two beings; the great cow, Audhumla, and Ymir, a great giant. From the sweat of Ymir, during his sleep, his offspring were born and thus partheno-genetically, he gave birth to the race of giants. Creation of the earth and its inhabitant can be attributed to Ymir, who appears to be very much like Gaia in his role of populating the earth, as Norse cosmology reveals.

Ymir had a reputation for being extremely cruel and one day he met his fate by being killed by Odin and his brothers. The earth and its inhabitants were thus formed from pieces of his torn body. Subsequently, all giant descendants died with his blood being shed upon the earth, all except for two. Two giants, Bergelmir (mountain old) and his wife survived, by hiding in the great World-Mill. From these two giants the race of Jotnar was born and thus, here we have Skadi's Great grandparents and her ancestral lineage traced.

In Norse mythology there are the Aesir, warrior deities and agricultural gods known as Vanir, The Jotnar/Jotun or Giants were viewed as primal, primitive, existing since the beginning of time and they seemed to be losing popularity next to the cultured more sophisticated Asa-gods (combination of Aesir & Vanir gods). It is reminiscent of the Greek battle between the old primordial Titans and their new descendant, the Olympians -the old gods vs the new ruling class.

As a giantess, Skadi makes her homes in Jotunheim [JO-tune-haym] meaning a cold cliff. The threshold to this realm was the wilderness, also known as Utgard [oot-guard] and this was Skadi's beloved realm. Not much is stated about Skadi's mother, but we know of her father and how close she was to him. He was the giant known as Thiazi/Thjatsi/Thiassi. Like most Giants in Norse mythology, he had the ability to shape shift and he would often manifest himself into an eagle. In chapter 56 of the Prose Edda book "Skaldskarparmal, Bragi tells Aegir the tale of how the giant Thjazi was killed.

The story begins with Odin (father of the Gods), Hoenir (a warrior, Asa-god, who lacked wit) and Loki, (the trickster God/giant, son of the giant Farbauti -Cruel Smiter). These three Gods were traveling through the realm of the giants. They stopped at Utgard and they failed to leave the expected traditional offering of respect as they passed into the Giant's realm. Skadi's father, Thjazi was watching the offenders very closely in his popular shape as an eagle. As the three Gods, later that day, hungrily tried to roast their dinner, Thjazi would not allow them to cook it. In the form of an eagle he kept grabbing their food and in frustration Loki tried to stop him, but ended up getting snatched up, along with the food, by the infuriated eagle. He was nearly killed but was spared upon agreeing to Thjazi's one demand.

Loki agreed and was then obligated to bring the beloved Goddess of youth, Idunna and the sacred golden apple, to the realm of the Giants. He fulfilled his promised to Thjazi but as a result, the gods of Vanir soon began to lose their strength, beauty and immortality, for it was Idunna who was solely responsible for keeping the gods youthfulness alive. And the longer the Goddess Idunna stayed in Jotunheim, the more desperate the gods became. Angered, they relentlessly molested Loki and demanded that he retrieve Idunna for the sake of all the gods in Asgard. Together the Gods desperately devised a plan and it started with the Goddess Freyja, lending Loki the Falcon shape form, so that he could remake the journey to Utgard and finally retrieve Idunna. When Loki arrived however, the Giant was nowhere to be found, so Loki turned Idunna into a small nut and quickly commenced his journey, with her, back to Asgard. Unbeknownst to Loki, Thjazi was flying about as an eagle and when he saw what had transpired he quickly gave chase to stop the abduction and reclaim Idunna. The gods of Asgard however, had prepared a large fire in anticipation of this and because Thjazi was flying so recklessly fast, he flew right into the blaze of fire and was tragically burnt to death.

This would seem like the end of the story but it doesn't end here. From across the snow covered, crystallized landscape comes a larger than life figure, donning a warrior's helmet, suit and armor and approaching Asgard, with much purpose and speed. It was Thjazi's orphaned daughter, Skadi. Enraged, fearlessly seeking to avenge her father's death without concern for her own safety, she arrived. She wanted justice and rightfully deserved it, as Norse tradition often provide great familial compensation when a Kinship had been unjustly killed and this was the case before them when she arrived to Asgard. She enters the hall of the Gods with much anger and conviction - determined to avenge her father's death with blood. She carries with her; sword, spears, arrows and war weapons prepared for retribution. Because she is primal, she is quite capable of taking on any of the gods and perhaps this is yet another reason why the Gods at Asgard avoided a confrontation with the Giantess and quickly conceded to her rightful demands. In some of the text, there is a reference to her breathtaking beauty which might have also contributing to their compliance of her demands.

At first, the father of all gods, Odin, tries to placate Skadi by offering her mounds of gold, but she is already full of riches, according to Norse mythology, due to all the pillaging of her clan and thus she is not interested in currency. Instead she proposes laughter (since, in her mourning, she has been grief stricken, unable to laugh and doubts anyone could make this happen) and since her kinship has been killed, she demands a spouse. Odin agrees with the stipulation that she must elect her spouse, blindfolded, looking solely at the feet of the gods to make her decision. She agrees, and the gods are lined up and covered, so that only their feet are exposed. Now, Skadi had hoped she could distinguish the feet of Baldur among the other gods, for she had secretly desired the god of Beauty and Light. When she spotted a pair of beautiful, clean white feet she automatically assumed they belonged to Baldur, but instead they belonged to the Vana God of the Sea, Njord. He was known to walk barefoot upon the sea quite often, making his feet appear supple and aesthetic pleasing. Imagine her disillusionment to learn that she would be partner with an older, wealthy, mediocre looking god. Still, oaths were sacred to her and she had agreed to the marital arrangement.

The next part of the agreement involved laughter and the trickster god, Loki, was only too eager to entertain. According to one story, Loki tied a string to his testicles and the other string to the beard of a goat (although some text state it was the horns of a live goat). The goat and Loki begin to engage in a weird dance, a tug and pull of buffoonery that ends with Loki clumsily falling backwards unto Skadi's lap. The entire hall of the gods was vibrating in their laughter, including Skadi and thus the second part of the agreed compensation had been fulfilled- they succeeded in making her laugh. Gratified, she had attained her compensation and a spouse in Njord.

Her marriage to Njord proved to be unfulfilling however and short lived, as neither could agree on a single place to live, simultaneously as husband and wife. Njord's beloved home was the seaside hall of Noatun, but after nine days of trying to adjust to this new abode, Skadi found the seaside home and the various sounds of this realm, aggravating. Together they tried Skadi's beloved home of Thrymheim, up in the snowy peak mountains of her father's old domicile. For nine nights Njord also tried to adjust to the new dwelling, but he complained of the wolf howlings and the sounds of the harsh winds. After eighteen nights they realized it was a hopeless, dreadful situation because Njord hated the mountain and the howlings and Skadi could not sleep with the sea birds screeching. They decided it was best to separate. Their separation, however seemed amicable and there appears to be no indication of an actual divorce but rather an understanding of their unconventional living arrangement.

It appears however, that Skadi was the model of an independent female, retaining her autonomy even in the midst of several relationships. One story tells that after Njord, she returned to her home in Thrymheim and found love with her soul mate, the God of Winter, archery and skis, Ulle. Together they appeared to share many characteristics and enjoyed their life amidst the snowy mountainous landscape- skiing and hunting. Other tales reveal that she actually married Odin, King of the Gods. Both Odin and Skadi share similar attributes, in their love of wolves and their love of fierce battles and thus, their union would seem quite natural. Although she never had any children with Njord, the myth of her time tell that she did bear Odin many sons, most notably, Saeminger, the King of Norway and the first in the line of Jarls of Hladhir (this was a clan of fierce protectors of the Norse Ancient Religion).

We can learn a great deal about Skadi's character through some of her myths. Her role as one who seeks justice is reinforced when we learn of how she punished Loki for the wrongful death of two of her beloved kinsman. As with many of the multi dimensional Goddesses mentioned in this book, their numerous attributes can easily fit into themes found in other chapters of this book. Skadi is no different, and her energy can also be explored in the chapter of Justice, but I disgress. Loki, the trickster god of Aesir, who was also a giant and blood brother of Odin, was always causing mishap. In this tale, a mistletoe dart was thrown by the blind God, Hod, but guided by the trickster God Loki, it ends up wrongfully killing the young, beautiful son of Odin and Frigga - Baldur. Now Skadi was quite fond of Baldur, if you can recall the earlier tale, in the Prose Edda, when she secretly had hoped it was his feet she had chosen as a life mate. For Skadi, this was the second man she loved, killed by Loki, and his shenanigans. Naturally, it was she who was called upon to exercise retribution for the wrongful death of Baldur. According to the tale, she bounded him and placed a venomous snake above his face, and it remained there to burn him drop by drop, making him writhe so much so, that the earth trembled, as a result we have an explanation for earthquakes. We also learn of Skadi's kind nature in Norse mythology. For example we know that despite her failed marriage to Njord, she was an extremely caring guardian and step-mother to Njord's children; Freyr and Freyja and she took great interest in their lives.

Skadi is the Norse Goddess of snow, ice, mountains, hunting, archery, justice and fairness. She is a patron Goddess to independent women and those serving the military. She invites you to reclaim the wild maiden and live your life by your own rules, in your own unique, most beneficial way. It becomes clear from the Norse writing of the time that Skadi is a strong, confident Goddess that always seems to act from a place of truth, justice and righteousness. In this aspect she is reminiscent of the Goddess Themis in her pursuit for what is right and yet her love of the wilderness, archery, wolves and her uncompromising freedom, reminds me greatly of the Greek maiden Goddess, Artemis.

Skadi is described often as a beautiful giantess, with long flowing hair, courageous and clearly following her emotions and instincts. As a snowshoe, skiing Wintry Goddess, exploring the wilderness and delighting in the mountains, she is unquestionably a very physical Goddess who will expect you to also engage your physical body in your communion with her. She challenges you to confront fear and insecurities and is a good guide when you are ready to see how far you can go. She will test your strengths and boundaries. Don't be surprised if she, manifest herself in your body, inspiring you to take up extreme sports and a more adventuresome approach to life.

*Skadi is the Norse Giantess Goddess, who fiercely defends what she believes to be right. She is part of the ancient early tribe of Norse Gods. As the Snowshoe Maiden Goddess she is an archer, connected to the wilderness and the snowcapped mountaintops and she is known for her strength and her physicality. She awakens the Amazon woman within you and offers the gift of physical wellbeing, strength and perspective. How vastly different our challenges appear when we see them through the eyes of the Giantess, up high on the mountaintops? How vastly altered you would feel, to walk and act in the armored body of a Giantess, like the Norse Goddess, Skadi. Skadi's energy is proud and strong reminiscent of the Greek Maiden Goddess, Artemis. When she enters your realm you will feel her inviting you to honor your body. She calls you to tap into your inner & outer strengths. Unearth your convictions & righteousness. You can manifest powerful changes now for Skadi, the Giantess Amazon, lives in every woman.

CHAPTER NINE
HEALING
SHE WHO DELVES DEEP INTO HER TRANSFORMATION

PERSEPHONE

PERSEPHONE

Persephone or Proserpine (in Latin) is the Greek Maiden Goddess of Spring and Queen of the Underworld. Persephone has been immortalized as the beloved daughter of the Goddess of the Grain-Demeter. The ancient myths associated with her and her mother, place her as an important integral part of the renowned, Great Eleusinian mysteries.

The name Persephone has been anglicized but to begin our study of this Goddess it's best to first begin etymologically. As a young girl and daughter to her mother, she was first known, most popularly as "Kore", (variations of this name include Koura, Cora, Koure) which translates as *"the Maiden, young girl."* This became almost a sort of nick name when referring to her in Eleusis. Some scholars also claimed that another connotation to this name alludes to *"young bride."* This would mean that right from the start, her name reflects the role and path she would inevitably take.

Many discovered ancient vases and art work of the time, show depictions of her and her name noted as *"Pherophata,"* *"Phersephata",* and *"Pherephassa."* This would appear to be her accurate, more formal name, as her actual Temple at Eleusis was called, *"Pherephation".*

The first part of the name Persephone, erroneously is linked with light and if we look at the second part of her anglicized name, *"phone."* It *is* derivative of *"phonos,"* *"phoneme,"* it roughly means *"to slaughter or sacrifice."* Therefore, upon a closer look at her name, Persephone is normally translated as *"destroyer of the light,"* a rather unusual title for the Spring maiden Goddess but perhaps not so unsual for the Queen of the Underworld.

Upon closer inspection of her more authentic name, *"Pherophata,"* we get a different meaning and a more revealing insight into this ancient deity. Her name takes on a different hue if we consider the meaning of the first half of her ancient name, *"pheros",* this word roughly means *"to bear, offer, carry, to bring."* Yet the second part of her original name *"phattas"*derived from *"phatos"* means *"the unspeakable, unutterable, incommunicable."* After much research, it would appear then that the name of this Goddess means, *"She who brings or conveys the unspeakable."* Thus, as Queen of the Underworld, the Greeks believed her to be a bringer of the indescribable, of that experience that goes beyond words. She is the "Maiden of the ineffable" and a vastly crucial component of the Eleusinian Rites, which were responsible for teaching initiates, the secrets of life and death.

The Eleusinian mysteries and the Greek myths tightly associated with this epic have forever immortalized, Persephone as the Maiden Goddess of Spring and the Underworld. The ancient writings of the time like; Hesiod's Theogony (c700BCE), Homer's Iliad (written c 750-725BCE) The Odyssey (written c743-713BCE) and the Homeric hymn to Demeter, set in Eleusis,(written around 650-550-BCE) by an unknown author, all have contributed greatly to our knowledge of this Goddess.

As a child, Kore was extremely close to her mother, one of the twelve original Olympian Deities - Goddess of the Grain, Demeter. Her birth came about as a result of typical trickery played by the Gods. In one tale, Zeus turned himself into a Bull and with his sister, fathered Persephone. There is another more obscure myth that comes from Greek scholar, Appolodorus (180-120BCE) it places Persephone as daughter of Zeus and the underworld Goddess River Styx, born already in the realm of Hades, but this version is rarely mentioned and used typically to explain how Persephone becomes the Queen of the Underworld.

Demeter and Persephone had a very close intimately relationship and some speculate that perhaps the Gods, like Aphrodite and Zeus himself, did not completely understand nor approve. In one tale it is Aphrodite who is credited for arousing in Hades desire for his niece.

One day the beloved Kore was out in the flower fields near Enna, with her young virginal cousins, like Artemis, Pallas and numerous other maidens friends like; Galaxyria, Acaste, Calypso etc... She was not alone, as some artistic depictions might lead you to believe. She was actually in great company, plucking an array of beautiful fragrant flowers and engaging in the typical games that young girls play. When behold, the most beautiful flower she had ever seen, captivated her. Some described it as a three-petalled, blue fleur-de-lys, but the Homeric hymn described it as the one hundred bloom, white, sweet Narcissus flower. Enamored by its celestial beauty, the impetuous girl stretched out her arm and reached to pull it out and upon doing so, the earth split open from below her feet, and, abruptly a chariot of black stallions came forth with Hades snatching the young maiden; disappearing from the scene. She let out one yell, but it all happened so fast, no one could claim that they saw or heard anything...no one, except for the all-seeing Sun God, Helios and the Wise Crone- Hekate.

For nine days and nine nights, distraught Demeter searched everywhere for her beloved daughter, but could not find her anywhere. On the tenth day, Hekate comes to her aid, shares what she knows and then takes her to Helios, for further information on the matter. To Demeter's astonishment and devastation, she learns of her daughter's abduction and horrid fate, as Bride of Hades. And to make matters worse, she learns that this arrangement was made and approved, behind her back, by Zeus himself. According to the popularized Greek myth, the despondent and enraged Demeter abandoned her post on Mount Olympus immediately and refused to let anything grow upon the earth until her daughter was returned to her. If humans now lacked the crop to nurture themselves due to Demeter's retaliatory actions, they would surely lack the ability to feed the Gods with proper offerings; and this was a monumental reality for the Olympians to consider. Demeter spent her sad days traveling the earth, in disguised as an old woman and pledged the earth would witness a horrid famine that would destroy both mortals and immortals alike, until she was reunited with her beloved Kore.

Meanwhile, Kore was in the underworld now, as Persephone, Wife to her uncle, Aidoneus Hades. Imagine her confusion and her own lamentation- youthful flowering bright maiden, finding herself in the abysmal dark caverns of the underworld, greeted by the stench of death and the overwhelming sadness of loss souls. On the earth, she was brightness, frivolity, fecundity, growing the flowers and the corn. As a girl she knew love only via her devoted mother. Here, so abruptly, she finds herself in this new realm, alone, in a foreign new role, as wife. The myth tells she would not eat nor drink anything in the underworld, during this time. Yet time went by and upon receiving word from the messenger God, Lord Hermes, that she would be allowed to leave the underworld and return to her mother, she partook of the food of the dead- seeds of the Pomegranate. Some conflicting stories state that she was offered 4-6 pomegranate seeds, by Hades himself and some state that someone else tricked her into taking them, in any case, upon consuming them she was now obligated to this realm. Her heartwarming reunion with her mother was bittersweet, as Demeter learned she would have to sacrifice her daughter to Hades and his underworld, one third of the year, due to the pomegranate seeds the maiden had ingested. During this time, the earth would be barren and cold and Demeter committed herself to forbidding anything to grow upon the earth while she mourned the absence of her daughter. This myth, on the surface, would serve to explain the winter season and the agricultural sacred cycles so important to the

Greeks and most civilizations at this time.

Persephone was sometimes depicted holding a torch flame or a sheath of Corn. She is often described as youthful, beautiful, trimmed ankle, bright minded, the one who makes the corn grow, and the one who has sympathy over the dead. One myth even tells of how she was not abducted but rather willingly sacrificed herself to the underworld upon learning of the sadness and confusion plaguing lost souls. She wanted to be their hope and guide. In this case she would be very reminiscent of many sacrificial Deities like Selu, the Native American Corn Goddess. As the Queen of the underworld she mothers and consoles the dead and it is through the entry of her bright aura, that THEIR hope is renewed. She appears supportive and much needed and yet, as can be expected, there are some conflicting tales of Persephone in her role as Queen of the Underworld. Some of the writing of the time makes her almost just as fearsome and mistrustful as her husband, Hades, and this is quite logical when we view unions between Gods in other cultures and other time periods. Consider how typically divine couples begin to share similar attributes. But in her, we see a consistent duality and it is this duality that intrigues me the most about Persephone.

Here is a Goddess who is required to live in two vastly contrasting worlds. Half of the year she is among the living, under the bright sun, amidst the fertile and all that grows. The other half of the year she is in the abysmal darkness among the dead, the hopeless, and the stagnant, hidden away from the brightness of the sun. Yet, when she goes from one realm to another, it is as if she never knew the other... It seems like no trace of darkness follows her when she returns to her mother's arms and her warm, carefree, maiden brilliance seems tempered in the underworld. It appears as if she surrenders herself to whatever realm she is in and locks the door, and perhaps the memories, of the realm she just came from.

Thus, she appears to me to be a patron Goddess for those who walk in two worlds. Witches, psychics, priestesses and seers also intimately know Persephone, as they too are somehow required to live in the mundane world while simultaneously, having extrasensory, spiritual experiences. I reflect on the mother who is answering her toddlers question about the spilt milk, while concurrently seeing the ghost of her deceased father hovering nearby- she is present and answering the call of two opposing realms. In my own life I think of how often I have been active in an intense community ritual, in a trance, floating, priestessing for the Divine and clearly in a completely different space, then at the end of it all, having to ground, pack up my stuff, catch the local bus or subway and travel through a vastly different realm to get back home, after communing, so deeply with the Divine.

Goddess of the twofolds indeed, we all touch upon Persephone at some point in our lives. Initially, I think about those who suffer with schizophrenia, Bi- polar disorder, depression, but perhaps less obvious are those among us who are forced to live in two realms in the exact way Persephone must. I reflect on the multitude of coal miners in our world and how they are required to live and work an inordinate amount of time under the earth, in deep caves, separated from their families and friends and then, when mining season is over, they return to the upper part of the earth's surface, rejoin their families and routines, until they are called back to mine again. I reflect deeply on our Military and how they too touch upon Persephone's journey. Countless of men and women are called to duty and get deployed to places that probably make Hade's realm look like "Candy land." The things that these men and women of service are exposed to when they are deployed in war zone, places like Iraq and Afghanistan, is horribly astounding. Death and its gruesome stench is ever prevalent for the military and while they are in service, they are subject to a world vastly different than the ones they originated from. When their tour of duty is over, somehow they are required to put all those gruesome, bloody war memories behind them and come back to their families and loved ones, assimilate into their respective community and resign themselves to civilian living again....or at least, until they are called back again. This is Persephone's experience. She teaches us how to reconcile living in two opposing realms and as wommin, in particular, with so many roles we are obligated to take on, she is an ideal Goddess to work with.

Persephone, the Maiden, is often seen as part of the well revered Greek trinity, with Demeter as Mother, Hekate as Crone, but upon closer inspection, she is not only a part of the trinity, Persephone herself IS the trinity. For me, Persephone comes across as really embodying the three most important feminine archetypes; Maiden, Mother, Crone. Some might say, she exemplifies four archetypes, the last one being the Queen. When she is Kore, her Mother's daughter, she is the Maiden and when she is in the realm of the dead, she is touching upon the Crone archetype, but also the Mother, as she is compelled to mother the loss souls. As Hade's wife she is called Queen, which is a newly adopted archetype in the 20th century. Upon her return to the fields, she again seems to touch upon the attributes of the Mother archetype in her ability to do exactly as **her** very own mother does, make the Grain grow. She is Kore and while her mother, Demeter, was closely linked with Barley, the Corn, was made to sprout from the earth and grow because of her. As Kore (whose name resembles the word corn)she had the ability to make things grow from above and below the earth.

I believe Persephone also has much to teach us regarding our relationships with our mother and consequently all wommin. As the first womyn in our lives, our relationship with our mother can have a positive or negative effect on how we relate to all other, future wommin. The Maiden Goddess had a uniquely strong relationship with her mother, but so strong was her mother's love for her that Persephone's whole identity was mostly that of "daughter" and only after Hades enters the picture does she take on another, new role. Yet she vacillated between these two very strong roles as wife and daughter (belonging to her mother then belonging to her husband) and yet, even as daughter she now exemplified the same gifts as her mother. Becoming wife bestowed upon her a Goddesss crown that had only been reserved for her own mother. I think for many of us, who do have trouble with our mothers, it stems from a lot of sources, but certainly not recognizing the thread that runs through both, mother and daughter, can contribute to some strife. When we can't acknowledge or embrace the attributes (good or bad) of our mothers' we fail to see those same attributes inherent in our own selves. And its not just our mother, dare I say, it also includes other wommin as well. When we try to separate ourselves from something or someone that we don't like, it's occasionally because, before us, they are reflecting back, something in us we are unwilling to face. Working with Persephone might help us unearth better ways to interact with our mothers and consequently all wommin and this is yet another reason why she is a wonderful Goddess for our gender to connect with. She would've been another excellent deity to include and explore in various other themes found in this book like the chapter on mothering.

*The Greek Maiden Goddess, Persephone, is the daughter of Demeter. She is the mystical one who directs the flowers and the corn fields to blossom but also gives light to a most auspiciously dark realm. Her energy is one immersed in the mysteries of life and death. Persephone is she who is Queen, Wife, Daughter, and Mother. She embodies all of these archetypes at once and she is every woman on the face of this earth. Our gender is constantly required to wear a multitude of hats and roles, sometimes even conflicting ones. Yet, we never falter in our ability to comply and execute them flawlessly.

As someone who is seeking to develop psychic gifts you might find yourself in the beginning straddle between two worlds; learning how to walk the two paths simultaneously. Persephone enters your life to offer you balance and compassion for your own self and the multitude of offices you hold. Persephone's story exemplifies this best, as she was forced to move into contrasting realms and not abandon fully her main characteristics. Walking in multiple worlds and in a multitude of different roles, while we pursue our most cherished wish is quite the challenge but the Goddess Persephone reflects an example we can anchor our faith in. She comes into your life to inaugurate your intuitive gifts and an awareness of the necessity of balance, as we walk in various roles, pursing our life's mission.

RHIANNON

RHIANNON

Rhiannon is the Beautiful Lunar Goddess in Welsh mythology, who later becomes known as a Fairy Queen. Her name literally translates as, *"Divine Queen"* and she was known to have a beautiful singing voice. She is most popularly known as the Welsh Mare Goddess, sometimes depicted as a beautiful long haired woman, dressed in gold, ridding her white mare sidesaddle and sometimes, she is depicted as the horse itself. She is closely linked with fertility, freedom, creativity and maternal concerns, typical attributes of a Lunar deity, but she was also protector of horses, animals and the stable.

As the horse was a very important, sacred animal to ancient cultures and held a great deal of esteem and veneration, there are a number of Goddesses all closely associated with horses, like Rhiannon. In Celtic mythology there is the Goddess Epona, who had a great cult following there and when she was brought over to Rome, they named her Rigantona or Rig Antonia which translates as, "*Great Queen.*" For the Irish she was sometimes known as Macha and for the Gaulic, Edain.

According to one of her folklores, Rhiannon was being pressured to follow her family vows and marry an older God who was more suited to their Divine family lineage, but she refused. Instead she sought after a mortal prince by the name of Pwyll (also known in English as Paul).

In Welsh mythology there was often an enchanted small mound in various distinct sacred areas on the land, known as a "tor." This tor was believed to be a portal for the Divine to interact and sometimes even enchant mortals. One day, the handsome mortal prince, Pwyll, found himself standing on one of these very sacred mounds. His accompanying entourage saw him and fearing the legendary tales warned him not to stay but quite unexpectedly, while standing there, he witnessed a beautiful white mare, galloping quickly right passed him. A woman with long tresses, dressed in gold, rode on this white horse and he instinctively was captivated. The next day he decided to try his luck again and see if, perchance, he can actually catch up with this beautiful maiden.

The next day, he approached the same "tor" and waited well prepared. Within minutes she appeared again, only this time she galloped even faster and his attempt to catch up with her failed miserably. On the third day, he was more determined than ever to catch up with this fast paced white mare but when, defeated and out of breath, he failed again, he finally just called out to her in desperation to please wait and stop. To his surprise, she did, and when they met, eye to eye, they were immediately enamored with one another. He asked her what she was doing there and her answer was simply that she was there to acquire his love. From the very first day he saw her, he admitted, she indeed had acquired his devotion. Rhiannon then tells him to return to the same sacred mound, a year and a day later, and promises him that if he does, they will be married on that day. And so a year and a day later, the mortal prince returns to the same "tor" to claim his beautiful Lunar Goddess as his bride and future Queen.

As promised by the Goddess, their beautiful marriage ceremony took place that very day, in the enchanted forest, with all of nature supporting their union, all except for one very angry ex-suitor. The old, resentful man she had been promised to in marriage made unwarranted scandalous advances to the new bride and in her effort not to draw too much attention to the situation and ruin their special wedding ceremony; she converted the harasser into a badger. She then placed the badger into a sack and tossed it into the ocean, but the bag became undone and he managed to sneak himself back into the Prince's entourage as they were heading back home. Later on in this tale, this would prove to be a most dreadful calculating occurrence, as he vowed to have his revenge for being rejected by the Goddess.

The wedding took place but soon thereafter, the mortal prince and his new bride returned to his kingdom, where she was greeted as a stranger with much suspicion surrounding her qualifications as a Queen, for she was not like them. She was a Lunar

Goddess, of divine lineage and now she was among humans.   They did not easily embrace her and she quickly became the subject of many rumors, gossips and distant mistreatment.   Finding fault with her at every bend, they wondered why after a few years of marriage she had not provided a proper heir, with a baby. By the third year of marriage, however, Rhiannon finally did give birth. She gave birth to a beautiful baby boy and the entire kingdom seemed overjoyed with their celebrations.

As was the custom back then, the Queen had several attendants especially with a newborn. The attendants were all required to help in keeping a close watch over the baby while the new mother would catch up with her sleep and recuperate from the strenuous birthing experience. On one particular night, as Rhiannon slept, in confident that the baby was well cared for, all six maid attendant inexplicably fell asleep simultaneously and it was then that her beloved newborn tragically disappeared. Much chaos ensued but it appeared the baby was kidnapped. When all her maid attendants woke up and, to their mortified surprise, could not locate the royal baby, they feared their own fate and knew they would be executed for child neglect. In their desperation to save their own lives they immediately sought to blamed the Queen, Rhiannon, who was already subject to much suspicion and prejudice. Frantically, they located and killed a nearby puppy, smeared its blood and bones across the slumbering Queen and prepared to plot and accuse Rhiannon of the unthinkable. They accused her of eating her own child in a moment of insanity. All in the kingdom already disliked Rhiannon for her unusual Divine blood lineage and so it was not a particularly demanding task to convince everyone that indeed the Goddess/Queen had gone mad and done this horrific, unthinkable act.

Traumatized by this horrific crime, both she and her husband reacted in the way that most people would react to traumatic news regarding their own child. Rhiannon started to question herself; guilt-ridden and traumatized she blamed herself. Her husband didn't know who to believe. He too was distraught and could not defend his wife but he neither wanted to divorce her nor have his wife executed. He beseeched the courts to spare her life and rule for clemency. He implored the courts to have mercy and find another form of punishment besides the death sentence she was expected to receive for such a heinous crime.

In the end, they allowed her to live and stipulated her punishment would be to forever greet all visitors to the kingdom with the sad, horrific tale of the death of her son. She would then be required to offer them her back, as a mare, and carry them all the way into the castle. Most people who heard her story did not take advantage of her offer to ride on her back but many came from far and wide to hear her tell this very ghastly, tragic personal story.

The years went by and Rhiannon, in her numbed state, accepted her fate. One day, a couple with a young child arrived at the entryway and as Rhiannon had done for the last seven years, she resigned herself to tell the sad tale once more and then offer her back to carry them into the castle. When she finished telling her story, she looked into the young boy's eyes and noted a familiarity within his gaze; it stunned her to the bones.

He was the spitting image of her husband, the King Pwyll and it was in that very moment that the old couple admitted they had found the baby seven years ago, abandoned in a field, and since they had no children of their own, they raised him as if he was their very own. They now believed him to be the King and Queen's royal son. Immediately the news spread of the young boy's return and when pressed, the maid attendants from that horrid fateful night finally confessed to what they had done. Later, it was revealed that the badger, Rhiannon's resentful old suitor, had kidnapped the child that night, seven years ago while everyone slept.

When the story spread quickly of this injustice and Rhiannon's innocence, they quickly restored her to her throne and re-embraced her as their Queen. She was more loved and respected than ever before because she had endured so much unjust pain and suffering in this entire cruel misunderstanding and yet, she exemplified such strength and dignity in the way she handled herself and the way she accepted her wrongful punishment for the last seven years.

Despite the horrific accusations and the loss of her child for seven years, she remained steadfast in her truth, believing one day the real story would be revealed and justice would prevail. The Goddess impressed the people of her land even further when she expressed great compassion and forgiveness to those who had placed her in such a dreadful position with their false accusations. She understood full well why her maid attendants did what they did and, despite the great loss and pain it caused her, she extended boundless compassion, understanding and forgiveness to her accusers in the end. This is the gift of this Welsh Lunar Goddess, for she teaches us to remain steadfast in the face of great chaos and crisis and above all, she exemplifies the healing gift of forgiveness and compassion.

RHIANNON MUSING

Rhiannon is a Goddess of truth and integrity and the strong belief that justice will prevail no matter what. There seems to be hints of the Justice deity, Themis, in this Goddess but more than anything, while working with this deity, I was most struck by her similarities to Goddesses like Kwan Yin, the Virgin Mary and Corn Mother, Selu, in her ability to withstand so much sadness and heartache and yet, be able to trust that in the end, everything would work itself out. There is an aspect of Rhiannon that wholly exemplifies the cathartic gift of compassion and the power of forgiveness, for despite everything that she was put though, she was able to look into the heart of the situation, face the truth and move on. In her ability to endure the loss of her newborn and then survive with dignity, the cruel accusations that she had eaten and killed her very own son is demonstrative of a Goddess who knows great inner strength. She exemplifies the art of holding onto one's truth in the mist of horrific chaos and calamities.

Throughout her myths she appears misunderstood and always going against the grain by exclusively following her heart. From the moment she refused to marry her family's first choice for a husband, rejecting the old man's advances, to her unwelcomed arrival in her mate's mortal realm and kingdom, she follows her heart. Despite surrounding pressures and great discomfort in her life, she is true to her heart. Yet, she displays great conviction and steadfasness that all will work itself out. In this case she appears to consistently refuse to play the role of victim and is continually illustrating for us inner strength and faithfulness.

These attributes; strength and steadfastness, are closely linked to her totem animal, the mare; for indeed horses are powerful, strong, grounded animals that exemplify stamina, loyalty, devotion and an uncanny ability to overcome obstacles. The Horse is also a warrior spirit; safeguarding its master. A lover of freedom and travel, the horse is, most interestingly, faithful to its master at all cost. And these are transferable qualities palpable in the Goddess Rhiannon. It is these very significant attributes that we see revealed to us in her myths.

I think for those of us who have been wronged in our lives or erroneously accused of things that go so against our very nature. Rhiannon can offer us solace and is quite a powerful message to help us sojourn to inner healing. This is Goddess work! She invites you to step back into your own power and not necessarily fight fire with fire, nor gets entangled in "he said, she said" games but rather moves beyond the drama and trust that the truth will eventually prevail. Now this is easier said than done, and it takes a great deal of patience, maturity and divine wisdom to be able to rise above certain situations and release negative events in our lives, like she so illustrated for us in her myths. In meditating on Rhiannon, I contemplate on those who are victims of gossip and lies; whether it's in a scholastic environment, religious, labor or residential community, it is an excruciating thing to have to deal with and our natural inclination might be to fight back with our own set of nasty lies and rumors or worse... but Rhiannon opens the door to yet another way of handling the situation, one where you will not lose your heart and soul in the battlefield.

With her, I also contemplate on those who at this very moment are incarcerated and are wrongly accused of crimes they could not have possibly committed but... because of gender or race or social status or any of the other ridiculous prejudicial reasons, except for the facts, must endure our flawed judicial system. Rhiannon is not very well received by her husband's kingdom, they hold prejudice views against her, right from the start and it's clear no matter what she does or doesn't do, she will not have a chance to have a fair trial. And sadly this tragedy happens too often on so many different levels in our own lives. The unfairness of judgment exercised, simply based on something other than the facts is routine in our modern day society and it is wrong... Yet, on every level from job applications, politics, to popularity contest in schools and Universities, to actual crime investigations, people are subject to unproven accusations that can negatively, destroy lives.

Rhiannon does not allow herself to be destroyed by the horrific loss of her son nor by the damaging, erroneous accusations that she was entangled in, instead she anchors herself in the truth. She accepts her punishment and remains strong, knowing that the Universe will always return to balance after periods of chaos... and truth, no matter how long it may take, will always prevail.

"Only what is true will remain because
what is true doesn't need anybody to believe it..." Don Miguel Ruiz

There is great wisdom, maturity and trust that we so often fail to have naturally within us, but with Rhiannon as our guide, we can begin to consciously practice these attributes and tap into those helpful traits, applying them to our own personal lives. She gives us the strength when strength is needed... and she helps us to stand in our truth amidst chaos and insurmountable crisis.

*The Welsh Mare Goddess, Rhiannon, is a symbol of steadfastness and forgiveness. Her story is one that classically depicts the struggles of woman as maiden, as bride and then as sacrificial mother, who mysteriously loses her child and a part of herself in the process. She teaches us the importance of balance and the cathartic powers, of releasing the painful suffocating chains of the past and allowing forgiveness to heal our hearts when tragedy has ensued. She exemplifies for us how to persevere despite tragedies and represents the strength and unwavering faith in the face of adversity, prejudices and injustices. When we feel unsupported and marginalized by our situation or a community or when we are being accused of some horrific act, we can find comfort in the messages the Mare Goddess presents to us. Karma is real and the Universe has a way of rewarding our temperance and understanding, during some of the most challenging situations in our lives.

SEDNA

SEDNA

Sedna is the Inuit Goddess of the Deep Sea and all the sea creatures inhabiting this realm. She was also known as Nuliayuk or Taluliyuk; a half woman, half fish deity of the waters. Inuit are the indigenous people of the Alaskan region and their ancient shamanistic beliefs are deeply intertwined in their way of life and very evident in their surviving folklore. Eskimos or Inuit believe in Animism, where all things are deemed to have vital life force and valued as spiritual beings. Humans, animals, all of nature, and all objects are animated with spirit and vital life force, according to their ancient shamanistic religion. Sedna's tale on the surface reveals how whales, seals, polar bears, fishes and sea creatures came to be but as a Goddess folklore, she has much more to reveal to us.

The story begins by a sea port, where a young beautiful maiden is admiring her reflection upon the frozen water. She is enamored by her own beauty and it is said, she spends most of her days submersed in her vanity, admiring her reflection upon the icy waters. Her father just lost his wife and he's a widower, struggling to financially support himself and his young daughter. Because of her great beauty there were a plethora of suitors that came offering marriage to Sedna, but she did not find any of them appealing enough to pull her away from her own beautiful reflection on the water. Some time passes and her father becomes increasingly frustrated with his daughter. Unable to financially support them any longer, he forces his daughter to marry the next suitor that approaches their home. Sedna reluctantly agrees and when a dark, mysterious cloaked man approaches them, proposing marriage, and promising Sedna a better life, she is forced to accept.

Now, as with all ancient folklores, there are often many different versions or alterations to the story. Some tales speak of the cloaked man giving her a sleeping potion to disorient her; others say she was blindfolded on their journey to their new home. In any event, when Sedna arrives at her new marital abode, she finds herself in a nightmarish predicament. Her husband is not who he claimed to be and she soon learns all of his promises were meant to deceive her into this marriage.

She discovers underneath his dark cloak, he is really a nasty vile Raven. He traps her high up on the mountains; isolated, totally dependent on him for her survival. She is forced to sleep in cold, frigid temperatures, on a filthy floor, with no tent of her own. She is fed the raw, putrid carcasses he gathers from his vile beak. Daily he mistreats her and her hope and beauty slowly begin to fade in that miserable existence. Sedna finds herself in a dark place, alone and brokenhearted. Nightly she manages to send a desperate call out to the winds, in the hopes that her father could hear her and come to her rescue.

Eventually, her father does rescue her, and together, they set out to run towards the waters, to escape in a kayak. They begin to feel hopeful in their escape plan but all of a sudden the Black Raven and his family of wild birds are spotted nearby. The monsoon of black birds targeted their kayak, rocking it back and forth, and they start to stir the waters wildly to create a much frightening turbulence. The old man panics, fearing for his life. He cries out, repentantly to the Raven, to let him live and take back his daughter as a bride. Fearing he would not survive, he selfishly tosses Sedna out, into the stormy waters. Sedna is utterly devastated and hurt by her father's betrayal but she is also determined to fight for her survival. She manages to rise from the waters and reaching for the Kayak, her fingers claw the edge of it. Holding on to it for dear life, she starts to believe she can quite possibly survive this. But... her much frazzled, selfish father takes an ax and, to her shock and horror, he chops off her fingers. In this one appalling cowardice act he destroys any chance of her survival.

Those severed fingers, gruesome symbolism of the devastating betrayal she endured, sunk into the deep waters. They become seals, whales, fishes, and the sea creatures that bless the ocean, according to Inuit folklore. Sedna drops to the bottom of the sea and there her sacrificial blood; the betrayal and tragedy she suffered, transforms her into the much revere Goddess of the Sea and its sea-life creatures. Today Sedna is a highly revered Goddess of the waters and its sea life. She is reverently petitioned by all those who depend on the waters and sea life for their sustenance and survival. Fishermen and all those who work or travel by water, make earnest offerings to appease her. She remains a very important deity for many.

SEDNA MUSING

For a few weeks I was reflecting on the Goddess Olwen, the Goddess Hina, and the Goddess Sedna, and how they reveal the thread of a common theme. Their stories reveal what happens when we find ourselves in oppressive situations or relationships, where our light or our "mere" existence literally is a threat to the oppressor and forces them to either control or want to get rid of us entirely.

In the case of Olwen, her father knows that if she finds love and happiness and goes off to marry her husband, it will result in his very own death. In the case of Hina, she is about to traverse into the moon. She has awakened by the light and finally endeavors to follow her heart; she knows that it belongs in that celestial light. She knows she must follow her bliss and that she no longer belongs to the pain and the heartache of her earthly family situation. Her husband immediately recognizes this (her Divine awakening) as a threat and goes after her; he ends up violently severing her leg in his effort to stop her from leaving.

Hina's pursuit of her divine light is a threat to him, much like Olwen's love becomes a threat to her father and in the case of Sedna (a very tragic story) we see a similar theme. Her husband ends up being yet another unveiled oppressor, trying to destroy Sedna's core being but it's her father who actually delivers the final shocking blow.

In the beginning, her widowed father is trying to get rid of her because she's a financial burden, so he forces her to find a husband. Towards the end of the story, her very existence becomes a threat to his own. In the stormy, turbulent waters, she holds on to the kayak, trying to survive. And yet, in his panic...confronted by his own mortality, he betrays her to free himself from death, by cutting off her fingers. The question that I keep hearing in my head is; how many of us have had Sedna's experience? How many countless women, have had their fingers chopped off; metaphorically chopped off, by the one person we never in a million years thought could betray us in such a vile, gruesome way....? The one person who we thought would protect us, love us, prioritize us, ends up literally killing us with their betrayal...

The question becomes do we allow them to fully kill us or do we take power into our own hands and allow ourselves to be forever transformed.... dare I say, deified by such tragedies... And by deified, I mean; reclaiming our inherent powers as Goddess women and transforming our tragedies into our strength. And lastly, allowing the death of our old selves to compost into our inner Goddess. We come out of our chrysalis to finally, fly freely, in our majestic beauty and strength - changed forever. This is the collective message of Sedna, and many of the Goddesses presented in my books.

MUSING ON DEATH

Connecting to the image of the chrysalis and how it becomes a butterfly, I realized, even the Egyptians understood this concept of death. They, like many ancient cultures, understood that death was never seen as finality but rather a process of transformation and preparation for the next stage in our soul's journey. Egyptians mummified the dead, taking great care in this delicate process of wrapping the body, much like a chrysalis. They understood that once the chrysalis was ready, it would awaken in a new realm; transformed, as a beautiful majestic, colorful, liberated butterfly. From chrysalis to a new life; wrapped & mummified, in preparation for the realm, the afterlife with Ma'at. Sedna does not die in the ocean but is transformed into the Great Goddess she becomes for the Inuit.

MUSING ON HER WATERS

At the beginning of Sedna's story, you may note the young maiden is in the realm of the water's surface; admiring her beauty reflected on the surface of the water. She is in this "superficial" realm, on the surface of this frozen water, admiring herself, yet by the end of her story, she finds herself transformed. By the end of the tale she is submersed in the deepest part of the sea; at the bottom of the water. We're talking about the most profound part of the ocean, the deep subconscious waters. These are clearly not Aphrosinian top layered, foamy, surfaced waters. This is not the bubbly, effervescent, romantic, sensual, giggling realm we so often associate with, when it comes to other Ocean deities; like Yemaya and Aphrodite. The Goddess Sedna ends up at the very bottom of the waters; at the darkest base of the ocean realm of our subconscious. The realm of intense emotions and mysterious; great powers are anchored here. According to some legends, Sedna is purported to be given dominion over the deep hallowed waters; connected to where the souls go after their death on earth. The realization that she rules over life and death through the sacred element of water makes her that much more important. Especially as we endeavor to delve deeper into our own sacred transformations.

SURVIVAL

Sedna has every right to be angry as some have speculated she was and still is. When there are powerful storms, sea life tragedies or deadly water turbulence, it is considered an expression of Sedna. Often Inuit shamans (better known as Angakoks) perform rituals to appease her. Within some of her folklore it is evident she was terribly abused and betrayed at various times on different levels before becoming a Goddess. First, she loses her mother at a young age and is left with her widower father. Then she begins to sort of lose her father as he makes it clear he is not able to care for her alone any longer. He tries to pass her up to her potential new husband. It appears he is eager to surrender his paternal duties over to her spouse. When she finds herself in the horrible predicament of an abusive marriage, she calls out to; the only one a child can call out to, her sole parent. Her father eventually does come and rescues her but only if it does not involve sacrificing his own life.

There is an uncomfortable aspect I felt channeled through as I worked with Sedna; a painful message about child abuse and neglect. Sedna speaks to me about parental betrayal, deep horrific parental betrayal and one that I could partly channel due to my own childhood experiences.

The loss of her mother at such an early age can be viewed as one betrayal, for mothers are supposed to live a long time to love, guide, teach, protect and be there for their children…but she dies. As a result Sedna is left alone, motherless, and with a neglectful father.

The next betrayal comes when her widowed father was no longer willing to prioritize his daughter. He pushes her to become someone else's responsibility. Again we have a parental betrayal. As a father, he is supposed to love, support, and protect his daughter but he's unwilling to do that any longer; it is reminiscent of parents who do not prioritize their children or those who deliberately or inadvertently abandon them.

He pushes her out the door to find a husband and it leads her into a most horrific situation where she is at the hands of an abuser, yet another betrayal. When she calls out for help, to the only one she feels she can call on, her father, he does come. He witnesses her situation and attempts to rescue her but here is the ultimate betrayal.....because he's only willing to rescue her, as long as it does not inconvenience him or require his own life..... And this is the pinnacle of parental neglect and abuse. Placing conditions on your love, protection and overall parental responsibility for your children is just wrong. As her sole parent, he is the one that is supposed to protect her, prioritize her, support, love and sacrifice for her, but he doesn't. He only meets his parental obligation as long as it doesn't inconvenience him or require his own life and this is the route of child negligence & abuse.

As a parent, when we don't prioritize our children…when we don't protect them… and look out for their wellbeing first and foremost… when we surrender them consciously to negative situations, we tread on dangerous ground. The cycle of child abuse and neglect is a horrible, devastating pestilence and it plagues our society in more ways than we realize, and on so many various levels.

Sedna's story speaks to me about this delicate subject. It is not just the obvious betrayal and victimization that so many women have been subjected to in their most intimate relationships but also the taboo topic of child abuse and neglect. Her story speaks to me about the tenacious survival amidst abuse, abandonment, isolation, and the effects on our emotional terrain; the deep waters of our subconscious. Yet, her story touches me on so many levels. It speaks to me about our great strength as women and our determination in the face of trauma, and, consequently, illustrates the potential birth of our inner Goddess through it all.

BLODEUWEDD

Blodeuwedd, pronounced [blow-dai-weth] is the maiden, Welsh, flower Goddess who was magickally created by two very powerful wizards. Her name is translated as "Born of Flowers" or "Flower face." Often labeled as the Goddess of Betrayal, and one who reflects both dark and light aspects, she is known by many other titles. She is recognized as the maiden Goddess of love and beauty, a Goddess of secret lovers and the archetype of women awakening to her desires. She is sometimes viewed as the maiden part of the trinity of Welsh Goddesses, with Arianrhod, considered the Mother and Cerridwen, the Crone. Although, I have also seen her classified as the Lover archetype, while Arianrhod was deemed the virgin.

Although we learn about Blodeuwedd in Robert Graves' "The White Goddess" We first encounter Blodeuwedd and her myths in an ancient text called "The Mabinogion," of the 13th century. Some Welsh scholars, however, believe this text was in existence long before the time of Christ and throughout long standing Pagan traditions.

According to "The Mabinogion," the Moon Goddess Arianrhod's second son, Llew Llaw Gyffes (or Llew as he is sometimes referred to)was cursed by his own mother due to a humiliating incident regarding his uncles and her chastity and reputation. As Arianrhod's curse stipulated, Llew was to never bear a sword or arms, he would never have a name and would never be allowed to marry a woman of this earth and this itself would preclude him of ever holding any rank or kingdom. This was a most dreadful way to assure her son's failure, for at this time in Welsh history these were the prerequisite and the only means by which a man could acquire power.The boy's crafty uncles, Gwydion & Math ap Mathonwy, however, had a plan to circumvent this powerful, wretched curse.

Map and Gwydion, who had become almost like beloved foster fathers to Llew, were two of the most powerful wizards in the land and they decided that since their nephew could not marry a real woman of the earth, they would then craft one magickally from flower blossoms. Some text state that Blodeuwedd manifested from simply three powerful blossoms but a more commonly accepted tale, confirms Graves', writings in, "The White Goddess." This breathtaking, beautiful woman, meant solely for Llew's pleasure, was created by layering together nine enchanted blossoms; oak, broom, meadowsweet, cockle, bean, nettle, chestnut, primrose and hawthorn. And thus, this non-human, magickal Flower woman manifested and was properly named, Flower-face, Blodeuwedd. With her as his bride, Llew (or Lugh as he was sometimes called) was able to rise to power and assert his basic privileges and civil rights as a Welsh deity. And as Blodeuwedd was created by these powerful men, one can only surmise she was breathtakingly beautiful, sexual and born fully as a grown woman. Yet it's important to note that some believed she lacked the faculties of an adult, for she was made solely to give pleasure to her husband and expected to think, act, and feel as she was dictated; never once having to unearth her own thoughts, emotions or opinions on anything. Some might say although she was unquestionably a woman, her mind and her life experiences, up to that point, were reminiscent of a child but this did not grieve anyone for many years.

Llew and his new bride lived happily for many years in their castle at, Tomen Y Mur. Blodeuwedd, who always had a pleasant disposition, had many maid attendants but very little contact with the outside world and not many opportunities to meet others. As was his custom, one day Llew left his bride alone in their castle, while visiting with his beloved Uncles in the far off distance.

During this trip away, Blodeuwedd, as always, endeavored to remain in her castle with her attendants and one day she heard the raucous sounds of people nearby the royal grounds. She looked out the window and spied several hunting hounds and a group of Hunters coming towards her direction. To her surprise this greatly excited her and the prospect of meeting new people enthralled her in ways she had not anticipated. She watched them for many hours and learned that Gronw Pebr, Lord of Penllyn, was in charge of the hunting excursion. As it was getting later into the evening, she sent one of her attendants to extend a hospitable invitation to the group for a late night dinner in her lonely abode and they gladly accepted. There are some conflicting tales that state, Lord of Penllyn actually left with his group when they were done but he later return to the castle alone to take her up on her offer for a late meal. Whichever version you accept, it is clear the two came together on this fated night and unbeknownst to both, they would be swept up in a tumultuous passionate love affair that would alter their lives forever.

According to the Welsh mythology, they talked for hours on this night and had a real soul connection. That night (and many others that followed) they gave into their strong desires for one another and surrendered to their carnal lust. They made passionate love and remained inseparable....that is until her husband's return. It grieved them terribly to think they could never be together again for they knew they belonged together. And as Blodeuwedd had a rather childlike mind and had never experienced such overwhelming emotions like desire, love and passion, she was probably beside herself. After a few days of torrid love making they decided they could not be apart and together they devised a plan to bring that to fruition by killing Llew. However, as the Sun God, he was not human and not so easy to destroy. There was a list of configurations and prerequisites before her husband could be successfully killed and Blodeuwedd had no idea what they were. She promised she would let Gronw know, as soon as she was privy to this information and the two lovers sadly prepared to say goodbye before Llew's arrival.

When Blodeuwedd's husband arrived, he noticed immediately something different about his flowered bride. She blamed it on her great love and concern for him and a gnawing worry for his life. He explained she had nothing to worry about but Blodeu-wedd having ulterior motives insisted she needed to be reassured with great details. So unsuspecting Llew explained to his wife the impossible coincidences that had to be in place in order for his death to occur and gosh... were there many.

According to Welsh mythology, Lugh's death could only happen with a spear (prepared a year and a day in advance) and this would be needed to execute the final blow. Lugh continued to explain to his seemingly worried wife that there should be a thatched roof, built over a cauldron and he would need to be in a bath, by the side of the river Cynvael and somehow have one foot on the back of a deer and the other foot on the edge of the Cauldron in order for him to be successfully killed. Blodeuwedd made special note of all the preposterous, overwhelming details and sent word to her lover.

Over a year passed and just as the two lovers had planned, they managed to have all the right circumstances before Gronw attacked and pierced her husband, the Sun God, to his death. However, he managed to shape-shift into an eagle and although quite injured, still managed to fly away. For Blodeuwedd and Gronw this was enough to allow them to fulfill their dream and together they took residence in the castle for quite some time as lovers.

After Llew flew away as an eagle, the Goddess and her new love felt safe enough to set up their love nest and fulfill their heart's desires. And since the Sun King had abandoned his post as the ruler of Dinodia, Gronw was now the successor and ruler to both Penllyn and Dinodia.

However, the injured Llew did not perish entirely. He remained high above a tree slowly dying in his eagle form. His beloved uncles started to worry, for they had not heard from their nephew in a long time and they suspected something was wrong. It was Gwydion who one day spied an injured, sickly looking eagle, high on a tree top and after several enchanting melodies, he managed to coaxed the bird to descend for a closer look. With a swish of his wand, Gwydion unearthed his nephew in the eagle, who at this point was seriously expiring. His uncle rescues him and takes him to the best physicians in Caer Dathyl to help him fully mend and it is then that the men devise a plan for revenge and retribution.

Perhaps word quickly spread of Llews recovery for when the magician Gwydion returned to Mur-y-castle, he discovered Blodeuwedd, already trying to escape off into the mountains with her maidens. But while crossing the river Cynvael all her attendants inexplicably drowned. Blodeuwedd, alone, in the middle of the river, was then cursed by the great magician to never see the light of day and she was converted into an Owl. The myth ends when we also learn that her lover suffered a greater fate when caught by Llew Llaw Gyffes and his magician, uncles. Although Gronw, in desperation for his life, offered a number of things including his own kingdom, Llew was not impressed and wasted no time in striking his rival dead. Thus ends the tragic Welsh tale in "*The Mabinogion*" and where our initial inquisition of this great Goddess begins.

BLODEUWEDD MUSING

The Welsh Goddess Blodeuwedd had been lingering in my psyche for a few years, actually two years to be exact. I kept seeing images of her and hearing her name mentioned every now and then, even though I had no idea who this Goddess was at the time. And so I started doing some preliminary research on her, first out of curiosity and then... I just stopped and turned my attention to other things in my life. The ebb and flow of my life was such that every once in a while I would have an experience or a vision that would bring her surging back into my life with intense relevance and necessity, but then, distraction would veer its ugly head. Finally, I found myself at a crossing point in my life and lo and behold found her there. She was there at this threshold, smirking at me, kind of saying, *"What took you so damn long?"* It was and is a question I still can't fully answer.

Blodeuwedd is a powerful Goddess for wommin to connect with. She is richer and so much more complex than what you might initially believe. The thought of her just being a Goddess of Betrayal does not sit well with me as there is more to this Goddess than meets the eye.

The first thing that jumps out at me in her myths is how she came to be through the element of earth via the transient, impermanence of flowers. Born of nine powerful, enchanted blossoms, she was magickally manifested by two gifted wizards. She is born and created by these men (the patriarchs in the family) solely for the purpose and pleasure of the Sun God, Llew Llaw Gyffes. She is made to be breathtakingly beautiful and sexually gratifying for Llew. She comes into being as a fully grown woman and comes into the world with no life experiences, no history, no lineage, no family, no thoughts nor emotions of her very own. Everything she is to feel, do or think, is provided for her by these men, her creators...and this for me, appears reminiscent of the modern day Stepford wives.

She appears to be created to have no desire of her own, except to please her husband and she has no existence before her manifestation; no interest or purpose besides being her husband's adored wife. And yet, because this is all she knows, she gladly accepts this way of life without any question. But lo, how one day everything changed. For in an instance, she opens up the flood gates of repressed emotions and discovers an almost undetectable buried voice of her own and it made itself known in one night...a voice she did not even know existed.... And it clamored for love and desire and engulfed her in a passion she had never known was possible. A passion so consuming and so rapturous, shockingly presented itself and quickly altered her self-image and life's purpose. Prior to the arrival of Gronw, she did know what lurked in the dark corners of her heart, yet, once this shadow and desire made itself known in her life, through this masculine catalyst, her life would never be the same.

It reminds me a little of the Abrahamic scriptural tales of Adam and Eve found in the old testament, for once Eve had tasted of the forbidden fruit offered to her by the serpent, her eyes were awakened to truths beyond what she could comprehend prior to that moment in time. Life is never the same when we are offered knowledge and experience an inner awakening. I muse and think on an extreme level, about women who find themselves in oppressive marriages. Many wives, especially prior to the 1970s, had their own voices stiffled and some perhaps even abused so continuously, that they lose the power of their own voice, that is, until one day when something happens to awaken them to reclaim their own power. Upon unearthing that repressed inner voice, life is never the same. I think of a woman who might never have climaxed, a non-orgasmic woman, who after finally experiencing the first orgasm, is awakened to her sexual nature and her life from that point on takes on a different hue. I think of a heterosexual woman who has been comfortable in her traditional role as wife and mother and quite shockingly discovers a tiny voice from within that unearths a sexual desire for her same gender. I think of women who have committed themselves, all of their lives, to being "*good girls*," following rules and expectations placed on them since birth and somehow, despite the loud external voices from society they have this one experience that allows them to finally break free and hear their long repressed inner desires and emotions. The common thread here is that in each one of these examples there is a discovery of a shocking, repressed emotion, an awakening to something we never suspected of housing within us. This is Blodeuwedd's realm. This is her potency and great relevance to us as wommin… We quit being the pretty flower (who really has no shelf life when you think about it). The flower who lives solely for adoration, causing no conflict with patriarchy and we then awaken to our deep, inner authentic desires. And it is this desire that shifts and reshapes the landscape of the remainder of our lives.

And so, with Blodeuwedd, she is an imperative Goddess for modern day wommin to connect with, for she is more than the Flower Goddess of Betrayal, she is the Goddess of Awakenings. She is the archetype that introduces us to long repressed or unknown emotions, longings and our authentic voice. She is the Goddess who awakens us to those emotions that might have seemed foreign to us or maybe even slightly taboo. And it is not just any old awakening; it is usually a dark, deep awakening because it is something that she would never have suspected of harboring within. The discovery of such strong dark emotions, like passionate desire, can catapult us causing great upheaval in our world and can take us to a very dark place in our psyche. Just look at how this great passion and love for Gronw makes her deceitfully scheme a most horrific crime to kill her husband. Prior to unearthing these emotions she was a flower Goddess; simply pretty and bright, purely happy just being adored, and now, this was no longer satisfying. It reminds me of those in our modern world still suffering in the same scenarios, overtaken by lust and desire, engaging in extramarital affairs or addictions (drugs, alcohol, food or sexual in nature) and how these dark longing lead to dramatic, sometimes deadly, life altering experiences.

It's very interesting that in the end, Blodeuwedd was not killed but instead was converted into a nocturnal animal, the owl. A winged creature that holds so much controversy because in some indigenous cultures the owl was seen as a harbinger of death, while in others, the owl was seen as wise, all-seeing, mysterious, coolheaded, reserved, cunning and highly cerebral.

For the Greeks, the Goddess of Wisdom, Athena, was often represented by an Owl and the Sumerian Goddess, Lilith also has deep connections with this night creature. It's interesting that the beautiful, earth ruled, flower Goddess would then be given dominion over the element of air and night, as an Owl. As patriarchal punishment for her earthly sins or moral crimes of the flesh, she is sent to the realm of this controversial bird, where perhaps her mind and intellect take precedence over her flesh. She's punished by removing the earthly daylight passions, first experienced and discovered through the flesh, and it is replaced now with the cool calm, intellectual qualities of the night owl. We come to realized that Blodeuwedd is the Goddess of really two opposing realms, for as a flower Goddess she delights in the brightness of the Sunlight, yet later, as an Owl, she delight in the solitude of night.

This too reminds me of the Greek maiden Goddess Persephone, because she is a bright flower Goddess. As the Sun god's wife, and a flower bride she is in her element in the light of day but once she enters the realm of desire and all-consuming passion for her lover, she begins to descend and journey into a darker realm. And I say journey because it was a year and a day of her planning and scheming with her lover to kill her husband and I'm sure during that time an array of emotions were experienced. So this Welsh Goddess begins her journey and her descent, as a result of this initial awakening. When towards the end, she is converted into an owl; she is no longer in the light of day but rather in the nocturnal dark world. As an Owl, she is now a part of night and it reminds me of Persephone because she too ruled over two opposing realms. She also has this experience of transitioning from a fertile daylight Goddess, as Kore, belonging to her mother, then to a night Goddess and Queen of the underworld; challenged and perchance conflicted in her new role in this darker realm. She too has this familiar journey, one we can surely identify with as wommin. She too has an awakening to emotions that a maiden would never suspect from within. And she too has this experience of going from one element; daytime, sunshine, brightness, happiness even ignorance, to this other side; around this dark realm of questionable shadows. It is the confrontation of night and day, ignorance and wisdom, slumber and an awakening and both maiden deities; Persephone and Blodeuwedd exemplify these traits for us as women.

I know many immediately relegate this Welsh deity simply as a Goddess of deception and lies or a deity of love and beauty and it's very easy to just pick one aspect of this deity and run with it but I personally feel this particular Goddess has a number of layers for us to study and really connect with as wommin. Blodeuwedd can be any one of us, whether in the 21st century or the first century. The inaugurated gifts, wisdom and insight that this Goddess presents to us women are timeless and invaluable for our gender.

*Blodeuwedd is the awakener of our dark shadowy places, our taboos and subconsciousness. She stirs the deep suppressed longings that society has forbidden. She is the awakener of your own personal truths. Blodeuwedd is the Welsh Flower Goddess of exceptional beauty and allure. She knows all too well the two realms of night and day; of shadow and wakefulness. She is the encased beautiful flower who becomes the free flying, night owl. She is the one who reflect the dichotomy our gender so often is subjected to; that of living in two realms. She reveals the sins of patriarchy and our gender's need to be awake and alert as the owl, in a world that would rather contain us as simply beautiful, voiceless flowers. She is both the shadow or secrets and the awakener to our inner power.

CHAPTER TEN
WISDOM
SHE WHO SEEKS KNOWLEDGE FROM WITHIN

"Wisdom outweighs any wealth"
Hippocrates

ARADIA

ARADIA

Etruscan Goddess of the oppressed; the poor and enslaved and those that lived on the margins and outskirts of society.... those who would later be called witches. Aradia is the Goddess of the Strega, or Stregheria (an Old Italian tradition of witchcraft). Her manifestation is ornately rich with interesting folklore and conflicting stories and yet, she is one of the most important deities for Pagans and modern day Goddess women.

She was known as the daughter of the Roman Moon Goddess Diana. According to Janet and Stewart Farrar's book, *"The Witches' Goddess, the Feminine Principle of Divinity"*, 1987, Phoenix Publishing Inc., Aradia was born out of the tempestuous union between sister and brother, the sun and the moon. Because she attained both of her parent's light bearing attributes, she can be seen as the Maiden who brings enlightenment and magick to her people. In the *"Vangelo, the Gospel of the Witches"*, which is attributed to being conceived by a Florentine hereditary witch named, Maddalena and later published by Charles Godfrey Leland, Diana was the first Goddess in the universe. This Tuscan Stregheria cosmology proselytizes that in the beginning was darkness and this darkness was the Goddess Diana and from her, she divided herself between light and darkness. The light, that was a part of her and that she eventually birthed, was the Sun, known as god of light, Lucifer. He became both brother and son as he was a part of her divided self and a manifestation, born of her.

In this Etruscan folklore, Lucifer was excruciatingly handsome and as the Sun God, he was divinely beautiful. In the Moon Goddess Diana he stirred within her a passion that was a taboo and an overwhelming desire for him. Being her brother and son, this deity of sunlight wanted nothing to do with what she offered and thus, the Sun fled her sight, whenever she was present. This only made her long for him even more. According to one tale, Lucifer owned a very special, beautiful cat, which he loved dearly and kept by his side. It was a known fact that he frequently slept with this cat, as cat owners so often do. One night Diana overtaken by her desire for him, shape-shifted, taking on the form of this cat and it was then, in the night that she was able to seduce her brother, the light, and with him conceived their daughter, Aradia. Aradia is she who beholds the divine heavenly attributes of both her radiant parents. It is from the sun and the moon that magick is born and thus, Aradia is the Goddess of Magick.

As recounted by Janet and Stewart Farrar in their book, *"The Witches' Goddess, the Feminine Principle of Divinity."* The Sun God was enraged to discover this grave deception, but Diana, skilled in the art of enchantment, hummed him a melody that made him succumb to her love. This humming melody was described as reminiscent of the buzzing of bees, an incessant buzzing reverberation that was symbolic of the spinning wheel of life. This spinning would ultimately weave and spin in man's life. From her all beings came to be and she ultimately controlled their destiny.

The myth goes on to tell of how one day the Goddess Diana decided to live upon the earth with mortals and quickly she garnered a great reputation, as people learned of her numerous remarkable abilities. Her powers could no longer be concealed from the world and thus they made her into their Queen. She eventually revealed her true identity and returned to the heavens, to continue chasing after the light, Lucifer, but before leaving the earth she promised to continue to educate humanity on the art of magick and sorcery. Diana looked to her daughter, Aradia, to continue upon the earth, the work that she had started – educating the oppressed and spreading her teachings on witchcraft.

It's important to note that the earth, at this particular time in these folklores, had become a nightmarish, dreadful place for those who were poor, uneducated or of the "wrong class," culture, gender and religion. The climate in Europe, in particular, in Italy at this time, catered to the church and the wealthy. They were brutal and tyrannical against the poor. It was class warfare as the rich brazenly abused and degraded the uneducated and those that lived outside of the city, in the countryside. The powers that be were enforcing all kinds of new laws meant to destroy their existence. It was a tense time in our history as the church and the rich were uniting, asserting more power, de-manding higher taxation, oppressing more people to enslave and rule over them, while demanding that they give up their Gods and replace them with new church saints.

Back in the 1300's, poor peasants were seen as the oppressed class and they were victimized by the wealthy feudal land owners. Sadly they were often desperate, highly impoverished people and when they would finally escape their abusive masters, they often found themselves living like outlaws in the woods, ostracized vagabonds, living like scavengers. These marginalized people thus, became known as the first witches of the Stregheria tradition in Italy.

It should go without saying but if you (like most of our ancestors) lived close to the land, entrenched in your familial tradition, you would certainly have great reverence for the earth and nature, not the papacy. Praying to the spirits of the earth so that your small garden would produce food, or to the rain gods, so that your thirst could be quenched or to the fire sprits to keep your makeshift hearth and home ablaze with warmth, would seem logical. But this very act extracted power away from the growing church and state. Many people were imprisoned, their lands overtaken when they failed to follow new societal rules or pay taxes, and they were treated horribly. A Goddess like Aradia then becomes necessary, almost compulsory as their personal saviouress. And, her gifts of educating people on magick and the craft of the old ways, and thus, how to thrive and rule over oppressors becomes the factor that gives rise to her popularity; given the social conditions of the time period.

As instructed by her mother, the Moon Goddess Diana, Aradia was to teach the oppressed class how to free themselves from enslavement, how to poison and how to enchant. She taught them how to utilize the gift of magick found amidst nature and how to manipulate weather patterns to work and conjure rain, lightning and thunderstorms. Aradia taught how to bind and eradicate enemies and escape their persecution.

For many of us, who follow the traditional threefold and tenfold Wiccan law, we cringe at the thought of exercising or advocating such severe hexing measures but it is very important for us to understand the validity for a Goddess like Aradia, and her teachings, when we consider the social climate of the time.

The discovery of Aradia and this prominent beloved archetype in the pantheon of Goddess Spirituality must be credited to nineteenth century author, Charles Godfrey Leland (1824-1903). He was an American journalist, anthropologist, folklorist, linguist, collector of myths and practices, and even a veteran of three wars. He was educated in Princeton University, continued his studies in Heidelberg, in Munich and then the Sorbonne in Paris. Mr. Leland spent a great deal of time in Europe researching Gypsy lore, magick, mythology and witchcraft. In particular, he spent a vast amount of time in Tuscany researching Italian Folklore. Through his research he came across a woman he named, Maddalena. Maddalena, whose real name might have been Margharita Taluti, was a type of rare witch informant for Mr. Leland, who became close friends with him during this time. Also important to note, he was initiated into *"La Vecchia Religione"* (the Old Religion), which is another term for Italian witchcraft, in 1888, after becoming the first president of the Gypsy-Lore Society. According to Leland, his friend, Maddalena, claimed to be a real hereditary witch and part of an old dying tradition of witchcraft called Stregheria, in Tuscany. He met her in 1886 and according to the legend, it took her nearly eleven years to handwrite and finally submit her documentation of her familial witchcraft practices and folklores, to the author. In this manuscript we learn a great deal about Aradia and the ancient Cult of the Moon Goddess, Diana, as recounted by the hereditary witch.

Mr. Leland, who was by this time already in America, took her manuscript and tried to translate the Italian and decipher her fragmented handwriting as best as he could. It took him two years to finally get this work published but in 1899, his book, *"Aradia-Gospel of the Witches"* was finally published by David Nutt. It remained fairly unknown, until around the 1950's when other writers and practicing occultist unearthed it, recognizing its scholarly importance, at a time when there was an obvious resurgence of interest in witchcraft in the U.S.A. and abroad.

Today some of the beautiful invocations in this little book have become a sort of liturgy for all Wiccans. *"The Charge of the Goddess"* first found in Maddalena's handwriting, appeared in the Gardnerian witch, Raymond Buckland's book, in 1968. Doreen Valiente (1922-1999), another well-known witch during this enlightening revolutionary time period, later adopted it into her own writings. Both, Starhawk and Z. Budapest have also rendered their own versions of this beloved adopted invocation. Today it continues to be a beautiful expressive prose, often recited and adopted by most Pagans as a part of traditional Wiccan liturgy.

The Goddess Aradia, though initially she was not viewed as a Goddess but rather as an avatar, appears to be very much like the Christian Messiah. Aradia was her mother's messenger. She was imparting magickal wisdom that was to be shared while on Earth, to spread the word and teachings of her mother, the Moon Goddess. In this case she fulfilled the role of a teacher and messenger about Witchcraft to those who were sorely oppressed by the Catholic Church. She becomes, in essence, their heroiness and savioress. In Aradia we see the spirit of the Priestess, the teacher, the messiah and the spirit of the daughter (like Persephone with Demeter) because her identity was so strongly linked into her role as daughter and fulfilling her Mother's worship. Her value comes, when we remember her as a messenger of empowerment through the practice of witchcraft and as a divine messenger of the ancient Moon Goddess, Diana, sharing her mother's traditions and acting as a daughter and Priestess of the Moon

Etruscan Maiden Goddess, she is the Magick woman, the Strega, bringing the gifts of sorcery. She comes into your life at this moment to awaken your inner Goddess and liberate your inner, sovereign priestess. She avails herself to whatever we may need her help with and becomes a great source of empowerment and freedom from hopelessness. She is the embodiment of magick; a great teacher and guide. She reminds us that nature is our ally (within us and all around) to protect and heal us; to lend us their infinite wisdom. Her energy comes to offer the opportunity for occult knowledge, lineage, and ancient respected traditions of the Craft. With Aradia, we acquire the empowering practice of magick and the gift of the priestess. It is time to connect with the powers of the moon, and the strength of the night. How do you empower yourself with your spiritual allies, magick and occult knowledge? How do we reverently employ magick and the sacredness of nature to propel ourselves forward?

STREGHERIA

"True Magick is neither black nor white. It is both, because Nature is both, loving and cruel...all at the same time. The only good or bad is in the heart of the Witch. Life gives a balance of its own..." The movie, "The Craft"

Although Stregheria shares many similarities to Wicca, it is arguably not a form of Wicca. It prides itself in being a revival of an archaic religion that dates back, probably further than the once presumed fourteenth century. It is an ancient spiritual religion, akin to an early form of Shamanism, steeped in Tuscan cultural history and Italian folklore. Like most archaic religious practices, there are numerous, conflicting stories of its origins, but there is also much that confirms its validity, birth and existence.

Etymologically, *"Stregheria"* is the archaic Italian word for witchcraft. It is sometimes referred to as *"La Vecchia Religione"* which means in English, "The Old Religion". The word, *"Strego,"* means to enchant and in Italy, the word *"Strega,"* refers to a female witch, while the word *"Strogone,"* refers to a male witch. Stregoneria is a common Italian word used now when referring to witchcraft, but you might also find the archaic Italian word, Stregheria, more commonly used.

Two distinctly different authors are attributed for unearthing and devoting further research into this long, almost forgotten hidden religion; Charles Godfrey Leland (August 15th, 1824- March 20th, 1903)and Raven Grimassi (born 1951-). **"Aradia, Gospel of the Witches"** was published by Charles G. Leland in 1899 and in 1994 Raven Grimassi published, **"Ways of the Strega."** Grimassi later published several more books on the fascinating subject; **"Italian Witchcraft"** in 2000 and in 2001 **"Heridatary Witchcraft."**

Charles Godfrey Leland claimed that this religion goes back farther than the 14th century, before Pre-Christian times. His writings reveal that this is actually an ancient Etruscan Religion that blended itself with the Tuscan peasant religious practices of the time. Charles Godfrey Leland, among his many professions, was an American writer, anthropologist, Linguist, Folklorist. Educated in Princeton University, he traveled a great deal and in the late 1800's lived in Italy, where he was studying and researching Gypsy and Italian folklores. In Tuscany, he formed a very close, special friendship with a woman by the name of Maddalena and from this relationship he acquired a great deal of knowledge about *"La Vecchia Religione..."* Maddalena proclaimed to be a Hereditary Witch with a vast knowledge of the ancient witch practices that had been passed down to her by her family. With her as his informant and her own Italian hand writings and documentations (which were later translated), Mr. Leland was able to publish with David Nutt, a small book. He had written numerous books before, but by far the one that gave him notoriety and has survived all these years was, **"Aradia; Gospel of the Witches,"** published in 1899- years after his initial meeting with Maddalena.

The book revealed a number of incantations, spells, practices, incredibly beautiful and eloquent prose and the mythos of Aradia. It presented the Maiden Aradia as daughter of the great ancient moon Goddess, Diana, and told of how she was sent down to Earth, temporarily, as a messenger to teach the art of sorcery to those who were enslaved and oppressed by the wealthy, Feudal lords of the land. Life was very different back then and these spell workings and incantations reveal how necessary magick and the craft was to the hopeless and the poor. It was their only salvation, when Christianity was victimizing and abusing them and Aradia became their personal, spiritual avatar.

According to Raven Grimassi, "Stregheria is the worship of the source of all things through the personification of the Goddess and God." *Raven Grimassi, "Way of the Strega."* Grimassi believed that the Hereditary witch cult of Stregheria became widespread due to a type of Holy Strega (Aradia) and he believed she was not just an archetype, but an actual woman who was documented as living in Tuscany in the fourteenth century, teaching the old ways that had been taught to her, by her family.

Long ago in the Tuscan Hills of a town named Arida, a woman by the name of Aradia di Toscano was born. Some documents claim she was born on August thirteenth in the year 1313. Perhaps this date is given in an effort to connect her even further with witches and the revered thirteen moons in a year or perhaps indeed this is her precise date of birth. According to Grimassi, Aradia traveled from town to town in the Roman and Tuscan hillside to share, among the rustic Italians, her aunt's teachings of the *"La Vecchia Religione."* At a time when the poor and those that lived outside the margins of "civilized" society, were being oppressed and enslaved by the rich and privileged class, her teachings were the only source of empowerment and hope. It would seem to fit the bill in fulfilling the desperate hunger of an oppressed class.

The people that lived on the hillsides, in far away remote villages, quite far removed from the cosmopolitan city centers, could not relate to the lofty Gods and the growing, oppressive religions, like Catholicism and Christianity. For those who lived so close to their land, whose livelihood was dependent on the benevolence of nature, their reverence and worshipped was relegated to those they were in communion with on a daily basis. Hence, Stregheria with its proselytization of the old ways and the worship of agricultural Gods, elemental Spirits, forest faeries, the Moon and the stars, was a religion they could easily identify with.

Aradia became affectionately known as *"La Bella Pilligrina"* for she traveled far and wide, teaching her family's ancient tradition of Italian witchcraft and as a result Stregheria became wide spread throughout rural villages, the Alban hill region, Etruscan villages, and in particular the towns near Lake Nemi, as some documents of the time period reveals. The city of Benevento as well, became particularly instrumental in flourishing *"La Vecchia Religione"* and was even attributed for later inventing an alcoholic drink, appropriately named by them, *"Strega Liquore."*

According to Raven Grimassi, Aradia became known as the Holy Strega and accumulated quite a following. Consequently, to her devotees, she became known as a highly regarded avatar and the beloved daughter of her mother, the Moon Goddess - Diana. The worship of nature Gods and Goddesses (honoring both polarities of genders) was common; with their Moon Goddess, Diana and her Consort Dianus being the two most highly regarded. There were many others like Herodias, Tana and Tanus and faeries, forest & tree spirits were also venerated.

Similar to Wicca, in their use of enchantments, incantations, amulets, talisman, hexes, poppets, oracles and divinations, theirs was an old tradition. They utilized herbalism, animal magick, fairies, incantations, magick of spell casting, and rituals. They had sky clad (nude) meetings under the full moon in groves or Boschetto (forest) amidst nature - these are all part of the Stregheria tradition. Like Wicca, there are eight holy-days or sabbats traditionally celebrated and they coincide with the change of season and the honored Nature Deities.

Their Rites traditionally focused on the agriculture and fertility of the land, hexes and protection, as well as imbuing everyday objects like Keys, scissors, knives, horseshoes, pearls, gemstones, rocks, trees, salt, clove of garlic, herbs, roots, red ribbons, statues, (to name just a few), with the energy of the Divine. For sacred rites, a High Priestess assisted by her High Priest led the group (coven) and this too is very similar to most Wiccan traditions. They also utilized a Maiden known, in Italian, as *"Dama D'onore"* and the traditional Gate keeper, known in Italian as *"La Guardia."* Altars were normally placed in the highly venerated North Quarter because it was believed to be a place of great power. Their tools of magick were everyday items like feathers, sea shells, and needles, rocks painted with a pentacles, crystals and wood branches as wands. Knives as athame, salt, sand, potions and herbal concoctions, chalice or bowls of water, sometimes candles, bells and offerings of honey, milk, wine, and spirits like "Strega Liquore."

Interesting to note that Hebrew Mysticism in the Middle ages, undoubtedly, had a great influence on Stregheria rites and practices. Masonic Lodges in the 1800's, obviously, borrowed from various traditions, not excluding, "*La Vecchia Religione*". The notorious protagonist and main contributors to Wiccan Religion; like Gerald Gardner, Doreen Valiente, Dion Fortune, Aleister Crowley are indebted to the teachings of Italian Witchcraft and "*La Vecchia Religione*". According to Raven Grimassi in his Book "The Holy Strega," Aleister Crowley studied Italian occultism and lived in Italy from 1920-1923. He was attributed to forming the "Abbey of Thelema," with licentious mural paintings of the nature deities like the Horn God, Pan and the Goddess. When the city got word of his Pagan creation, he was booted out of Sicily. Yet another well-known contributor to Wicca, Gerald Gardner, borrowed much from Stregheria and initially had learned a great deal from Aleister Crowley himself. This would explain the coincidental similarities, Wicca and Stregheria share.

Witchcraft has always appealed largely to women, with its message of female empowerment and inherent feminine divinity. It appears more matriarchal than other religious faiths. In major cities, in the fourteenth century, men were the predominant rulers during this time and one can only presume how the practice of Stregheria and the sight of a large group of women gathering for any reason, could've been seen as suspicious, bothersome and possibly a threat to their own patriarchal religions. When Stregheria found itself in danger of being banned and extinct by the patriarch, it needed to transmute itself. According to Raven Grimassi, three witch clans, a Triad, sprung forth in an effort to preserve this ancient religion and safely pass down Aradia's teachings, to future generations. The distinctly three traditions of Tanarra, Jannara, Fanarra, evolved from Aradia's ancient witchcraft teachings.

Fanarra was located mainly in Northern Italy and this was a witch tradition that was considered the keepers of the Earth mysteries. Their form of worship emphasized the land, sacred sites and places and objects found among the earth. They held true that Nature is filled with spirits that inhabits objects and places, making them sacred to witches and at our disposal for powerful magick.

Janarra, was a tradition mainly located in Central Italy and they were believed to be the keepers of the Lunar mysteries. Their form of witchcraft highly regarded the cycles of the moon and the powers inherent in our own connection to the moon. Drawing her down and regular gatherings under the Full moon *Veglione*, (Italian word for full moon rites) was part of their tradition. During this time there was also a common, indigenous belief that the souls of the dead dwelled in the moon awaiting their final resting place and in the Janarra tradition, the moon is honored as the sacred dwelling place of the feminine divine-the Goddess- as was Aradia's initial teachings.

Central Italy also became the home for the Tanarra Tradition, whose emphasis was on the Stellar Mysteries. In 1981, The Aridian Mysteries was born (named after Aradia's birthplace) and it was established in North America.The Aridian tradition is considered a direct extension of the Tanarra, Stellar mysteries. According to Raven Grimassi, it is a tradition dedicated to reviving the archaic teachings of Aradia, the Holy Strega.

There are numerous wonderful books on Italian Witchcraft, "*La Vecchia Religione*" and both the ancient and modern practices of Stregheria. I know that I have only touched the surface of this profoundly, fascinating subject here. To learn more, I encourage you to look into Charles Godfrey Leland's books and the multitude of books written by one of the leading, modern day protagonist of the Stregheria tradition, Raven Grimassi.

CIRCE

CIRCE

Circe is the beautiful, magnetic, ancient Greek Goddess of Sorcery, Magick, Incantation and Herbology. She was gifted with the art of hallucinogenic and the ability to turn men into beasts. Her name comes from the Greek word, "*Kirkoo*," which means to "secure with rings or to bind."

We know much about the Goddess Circe and her beautiful appearance, due to the numerous descriptions in the early writings of the time and the plethora of illustrations and renderings in paintings and sculptures by various talented artists throughout the centuries.

The Goddess Circe was believed to be the daughter of the Titaness, Sun God, Helios and the nymph, Perse (daughter of Oceanus). Other writings indicate that she was probably the daughter of the great Goddess of the Crossroads and Witchcraft, Hecate. She was also the recognized aunt of yet another enchantress in Greek Mythology, Medea. Circe's brother, Aeetes, fathered by Helios, was a God known also for his magical gifts, incantations and Herbology. He was the guardian of the Golden Fleece. Circe had two additional siblings; her sister, named Pasiphae, who became the wife of King Minos, in Crete, and her brother, named Perses.

Her home was noted to be on the island of Aeaea but there were also many islands connected to her Temple and worship. Her mansion on Aeaea was depicted as a magickal fortress, surrounded by all types of wild exotic creatures. It was a place where all was not what it seemed and it was enveloped by her crafted illusions and serviced by her servants.

Circe was mentioned in numerous ancient texts like; *"The Odyssey"* by Homer, *"Theogony"* and *"The Homeric Hymns"* by Hesiod, and *"Metamorphoses"* by Ovid, to name just a few. These early writings established her as the archetypal image of the Witch.

The Odyssey

She is strongly linked with the legend of the Odyssey and the brave, Odysseus and his men. According to the early writings, it was said that Odysseus's ship and his crew ended up on the shore of her Island. For three days and three nights they lay hopeless in total despair, abandoned on the shore. Then Odysseus detected smoke rising from the distance. Cautious, he decided to split his crew into two groups. He stayed behind on guard with one group of men, while sending the other group with Eurylochus to investigate the source of the smoke. Eurylochus and half of his crew ventured out to search the island for life and hopefully bring back much needed help. What they encountered was the alluring Goddess, Circe, and her illusionary magical abode.

The famished men were greeted by the powerful Goddess and her beautiful servants with much feasting and overflowing libations. Naturally, the men enjoyed themselves but, unsuspectedly, while in her abode, they were charmed and spellbound by her powerful potions. Her concoctions turned them into swines and placed them under her arrest in pigsties. After some time had passed, when the men did not return, it concerned Odysseus. Of all the men captivated and charmed by the Goddess, Eurylochus managed to escape and quickly returned to Odysseus to alert him of the shocking news about what had occurred to his crew. Determined to get his men back, Odysseus takes the great risk and ventures alone to make the trip to the home of Circe. But, before reaching Circe, he is visited by the messenger God, Hermes, who warns him and instructs him on how to secure his safety while in the presence of the great enchantress.

Odysseus confronts the Temptress, and following all of Hermes instructions, he manages to safeguard himself and befriend her. They even become lovers. All the men that had been turned into swines were turned back into men, even stronger and more handsome than they were before. According to the legend, their time in Circe's home was so full of revelry and ecstasy that they willing stayed with her, on the island, for a year. As lover and friend, Circe helped Odysseus complete the Odyssey. It is also speculated that together they had numerous offspring during the year they spent together. Some of her known children were Agrios & Latinos, as stated in Hesiod's Theogony, and Telegonos, as mentioned in Homeric Hymns. She was also mother to Nausithous and Phaunos.

The Legend of Picus

One day while out in the woods, the Goddess, Circe, fell madly in love upon catching sight of the handsome, Picus. He was the son of Saturn, according to the writings of Servius, and later became the First King of Latium. Picus was devoted to his wife, the beautiful nymph, Canens, although some writings reveal he was in love with Scylla. There are clearly different renditions of this story but needless to say, they are all reflective of Circe and her gifts as a Sorceress. When her advances to Picus were rejected, she immediately turned him into a woodpecker and her rival, Scylla, was converted into a gruesome looking monster.

The worship of the Goddess Circe extended far beyond the land of Greece but also into Roman territories. She was so beautiful and renowned that there are numerous images rendering her as this breathtaking seductress; with long flowing or braided hair, often holding her wand. Mentioned throughout a plethora of writings from ancient times to Modern literature, she is forever cemented in our collective remembrance as a beautiful enchantress; the quintessential image, created in ancient times and sustained throughout our modern era, of the Witch.

Circe is the powerful Goddess of Sorcery & Magick. She is the patron Goddess for all who seek to know the ancient mysteries of the occult; that includes but is not limited to incantations, transmutation, and Herbology. She is also clearly an expression of the independent, empowered, magick woman, who lives her life by her own rules. What she desires, she passionately endeavors to attain, and she is not shy about employing all of her inherent gifts. She is the awakener of our intuitive abilities and our inner Enchantress.

ISIS

ISIS

The ancient Egyptian Goddess, Isis, is a patron Goddess of a multitude of relevant blessings and attributes; she is of particular significance to women. She was worshipped in ancient time as a Goddess of love, fertility, healing, immortality, magick, agricultural blessings and as humanities' savioress. By far one of the earliest most venerated deities recorded in history was the Queen of Heaven, Isis. Her widespread worship and her longevity were partly due to the fact that she was worshipped among the nobility as well as the lower classes. There was an unusual approachability found within Isis that was absent among many other aloof Gods. Her worship spread across numerous lands and she was cherished by all for her great benevolence. She was known then as a Goddess who would fight for your personal cause and her worshippers believed her to be their defender and guardian.

Her worship and myths traveled across various terrains and they were often connected with her consort and twin brother, the God, Osiris. Her myths are so ancient they can be traced back to Pyramid text (late third millennium BCE). According to the ancient texts the Egyptian deities, Isis and Osiris loved each other deeply even while in the womb as twins. Upon their birth they were destined to unify as husband and wife. Their story is one of great significance and illuminates, Isis's great powers.

According to her most famous myth, Osiris had an evil brother name Seth. This brother eventually lures and traps Osiris into a wooden chest/coffin and then tosses it away in the river. This very evil act inaugurates the suffering and deep mourning of the Goddess, Isis. Her myriad of shed tears are often connected with the flooding of the Nile River and consequently the lands fertility and nourishment. In this way we see her great relevance as a Goddess of fecundity and harvest.

The wooden chest/coffin that held the lifeless body of Osiris somehow find its way to Byblos, where it gets hidden inside of a tree. This tree then becomes a pillar for the King's abode but all the while the Goddess, Isis, continues to mourn for her lost consort. She eventually learns of her lover's whereabouts, tells the king her story and he then gives her the chest with Osiris. She takes this chest/coffin, opens it, only to find her lover lifeless and dead. It is at this very pivotal moment in the story that we get a glimpse into the great power of this Egyptian Goddess. For as the story continues, Isis so loved Osiris that she was able to use her magick and her great love for him to revive him and bring him back to life. She revives his genitalia as well, has intercourse with him, and manages to conceive a child with Osiris. Together they have Horus, the Egyptian falcon headed God. Horus then eventually becomes the one to destroy Seth and avenge his father's demise, however not before another tragedy ensues related to Osiris. The wicked Seth manages to kidnap Osiris again only this time he cuts him up into tiny pieces and scatters them across the globe; purposely making it almost impossible for his resurrection. The Goddess Isis however, is no ordinary deity, as is revealed in this tale. She manages to search the globe, successfully retrieve and gather all the pieces of Osiris, except for his genitals. Because she's a Goddess of great power she is thus able to travel to the land of the dead, where eventually she resurrects her beloved consort, long enough for him to pass down his power and knowledge to his son, Horus.

Many of the ancient texts reveal numerous prayers and beautiful invocations to the Queen of Heaven. These eloquent writings depict Isis as a supreme mother deity, as an important Goddess of healing and a patron Goddess of deep love, fertility, magick and sexuality. She is a nurturing Goddess that is so intimately connected with the land and the flowing Nile River that some believe her to be the sacred land itself. She was worshipped then as she is still today as; *Regina*/Queen, *Domina*/Mistress, as *Augusta*/the Glorious One. Isis is beloved and forever remains; Queen of Sorcery and Magick, Queen of the Pharaohs, Life of the Nile, Protectress and Mother, Queen of Heaven.

"At times you have to leave the city of your comfort and go into the wilderness of your intuition. What you'll discover will be wonderful. What you'll discover is yourself. "
Alan Alda

HEKATE

When you know how to listen, everyone is the Guru...Ram Dass

HEKATE

Goddess of the Crossroads, Hekate is an Ancient chthonic deity of the Moon and the night. Hekate is better known as a Guardian and Triple Goddess of the Crossroads. She is also the Goddess of magick and sorcery and a patron Goddess for women in all stages of life. She is a protector of entrances and homes. Sometimes, she is even seen as a patron Goddess of Childbirth- as this too, is an entry way, of magickal significance, into the world of the living. Ancient Crone Goddess of the Gateway and a beloved deity among practitioners of the Craft, in ancient Greece she was just as significant then, as she remains today among Goddess women.

Her name means *"she who works from afar"* also interpreted as *"she who works her will"* and one of her primary roles was to guide the souls to the underworld. She was the only Goddess who could travel through all realms. Beloved by Zeus, she was given rule over the Underworld, but also the Earth and the Sky. She had a special relationship with Zeus because according to some, she was the only Titan that aided him during the battle of the Olympians against the Titans, but, as with all ancient deities, there are many conflicting stories about her early incarnations.

Some believe this ancient Goddess has origins in Mycenaen Greece, possibly originating in Carians of Anatolia; though she had a very large cult following in Thrace. She is said to have been a native of ancient Thrace. In Asia Minor and Thrace she had numerous followers and a very large cult following among the Eunuchs, her servants. In many Greek homes, while the hearth was Hestia's domain, the entryway was Hekate's and altars with offerings were often dedicated to her here. Offerings to Hekate were also made at cemeteries and at three way fork roads with meat, honey, goat blood or actual black dogs, being sacrificed to her.

Hekate is often depicted with three heads. Sometimes they were the heads of a snake, a dog and or a horse, other depictions portray her with just the heads of three dogs. The sound of barking dogs were said to warn you of her omnipotent presence and she was known to easily shape shift at will, into her beloved totem. Black female dogs, in particular, were sacred to her and were sometimes sacrificed in her name by her devotees. Because black dogs were her sacred animal she, herself, was also sometimes referred to as the "black bitch." The Frog was another animal connected to Hekate because of its ability to cross between two elements.

There are some conflicting stories about Hekate and her birth. She appears to be a Goddess of ancient origins with many myths regarding her manifestation. One theory, found in the Theogony, was that she was a child of the great Mother Earth, Gaia and Uranus or perhaps even a sibling of Zeus. A more accepted genealogy came from other writings by Hesiod who stated that Hekate was the daughter of the Pre-Olympian Titans, Perseus and the Star Goddess, Asteria. The sister of Star Goddess Asteria was the Goddess of Childbirth, Leto. Leto as we know gave birth to the twins; Apollo and Artemis. This would mean that Hekate was a cousin of the Maiden Moon Goddess, Artemis. Here we understand her connection as a Moon Deity and the genealogy that intimately connects her to light, most notably, the Moon's. This would also imply that their Grandmother would have been Phoebe, the ancient Titaness Moon Goddess and their Great Grandmother, the Primordial Earth Goddess- Gaia. In either case, her strong associations to light, in particular moonlight, is very clear.

Not much is known about Hekate's romantic life but we do know she had two daughters. Her union to Phorcys created her daughter, Scylla. With Hermes, the Messenger God of Magick and Science, she unites and gives birth to Circe. Circe later becomes Medea's aunt. Medea, according to the myths of her time, becomes a notoriously powerful Sorceress, Priestess and Queen of the Witches, due to the teachings from her extended family. She later becomes a devoted High priestess of her grandmother, Hekate.

Perhaps, Hekate will forever be most remembered for her involvement with Demeter and Persephone in the legend of the *Great Eleusinian Mysteries*. Remember that it was Hekate who heard the Maiden's cries, when she was abducted by Hades and it was She, who tried to console the despondent mother and offer aid in regaining her beloved daughter. Thus Hekate became known as a Goddess who was very sympathetic to the universal cries of all wommin, most notably those in great distress and in danger. Women abused or mistreated by men received her utmost protection. If called upon, she executed just retribution against those offensive men, when supplications were made by her worshippers. As a Goddess who could travel through all three realms, she was often invoked for safe journeys by those going to unknown, distant lands. In ancient times, she was often called upon by women in the midst of childbirth, a precarious delicate state for most women and as a Goddess of entryway; one can see how her presence would be compulsory for both, death and births alike. As a Goddess of the night, the dark moon and all things mysteries, she became a patron to witches and sorcerers, seeking divine occult knowledge.

Today there is a great resurgence in her cult and her worship remains strong among her growing followers. One trip to the library now will reveal an increase in the amount of books published on the fascinating subject of Hekate and her continuous worship. Her festivals, in which she was honored, were held on August 13th and the 30th of November.

There are many herbs associated with Hekate. Yew berries, Cypress, belladonna, mandrake, hemlock, opium poppy are all linked to the Goddess of the underworld. Not surprising, herbs that were hallucinogen or help alter states of consciousness are all appropriately associated with this ancient Greek Goddess.

*Ancient, immortal Goddess of the Threshold, she rules the night, death, sorcery, witchcraft and the sacred portals that lead to the underworld. She is the venerated archetype of the wise crone. Hekate brings a plate offering with our lineage and ancestry and the importance of our spiritual connection. She is the night wandered and facilitates travels through all the realms. She is the guide through all of life's various thresholds and portal of transformations.

There is much wisdom to unearth in our ancestry and in our past-lives. Hekate guides us through this realm to attain magickal knowledge and our ancestral connections. Hekate endeavors to help you connect to spirit allies and your sacred ancestors for guidance. She awakens in you other realms, other sources for support and other ways of knowing. She awakens you to your sacred role as an ancestress and your intrinsic part of your family's lineage. Ancestresses that you are already...what will you leave behind for your beloved one? This is the time to look closely at who we share this realm with, honor our Spiritual family, and the sacredness of the cycles of life and death.

ISHTAR

ISHTAR

Ishtar is the ancient Akkadian, Assyrian Goddess of Love, Sexuality, Fertility, War, and unbridled Passion. For her devoted followers, Ishtar was and continues to be a supreme ancient Goddess that rules over all areas connected to a Woman's life. Some might even consider her one of the first known, Goddesses of Love. Her presence was well documented as early as the first millennia and her worshipped crossed numerous regions and survived throughout the centuries.

Known also as; Ishara, Istar, Istara, the name Ishtar is considered a Semitic or an Akkadian name related to star. It should therefore come as no surprised that one of her sacred symbols is the eight pointed star. In Babylonian astrology, Ishtar was deemed as the personification of the planet Venus; the morning & evening star. She is also considered to be an important part to the celestial Triad representing, Life force. In this triad, she joins the Sun God, Shamash (who represents justice) and the Moon God, Sin (who represents wisdom).

Ancient Babylonian scriptures refer to the Goddess, Ishtar as, "*The Opener of Wombs,*" *The Righteous Judge,*" and the "*Exalted Light of Heaven,*" among her numerous titles. They are indicative of a highly venerated Goddess who remains linked to our gender's progress and empowerment. In ancient times she had numerous temples build in her honor and she was also embraced as a patron Goddess of prostitutes; again reflecting her powerful sexual attributes. Often depicted nude to denote her unquestionable connection to beauty and sexuality, Ishtar was also shown in robes and war armour. Holding a bow and arrow, and other weapons of war to reveal her warrior aspect; her fierceness was also symbolized by the Lion. Other symbols connected to Ishtar include, the dove, the owl, the snake, and gemstones like Lapis Lazuli and Carnelian.

As with most ancient deities there are some conflicting stories related to genealogy and because she is so often assimilated with other deities, like the Sumerian Goddess, Inanna, it's hard to know for certain. She is considered a daughter of the Uruk deities; Moon Goddess, Ningal and Moon God, Sin (Suen) but also known as daughter to Anu and the Sky god, An. She is believed to be assimilated with the Goddesses; Astarte, Lilith, Isis and of course Inanna. Most historians connect her numerous myths and depictions to be a surviving aspect of the Sumerian Goddess Inanna and later as the Semitic Goddess, Astarte. She and the Goddess, Inanna share many similarities and myths. Most noteworthy are the collection of passionate illustrative scriptures about her beloved consort, Tammuz, who appears to be similar to Inanna's consort, Dumuzi. Throughout Mesopotamia (the region mostly known today as Iraq, Syria, Kuwait, Turkey) Ishtar was exalted as one of the earliest, most important deities among the pantheon of Gods across this regions and within this beloved deity we are gifted with a supreme symbol of woman empowerment.

ATHENA

*"Opportunity is missed by most
people because it is dressed
in overalls and looks like work..."*
Thomas Edison

ATHENA

The Greek, Maiden Goddess of Wisdom, intellect and war-craft was often referred to as Grey-eyed Athena in the writings of her time. She was described as bright eye, wide eye and often depicted with her totem animal, the Owl. The Owl is a perfect representation of her wisdom and this common reference to her piercing eyes. Athena was reminiscent of the Goddesses found in ancient Minoan and Mycenaean Culture, in that these earlier deities had snakes as their sacred symbols and were regarded as protectors of cities and palaces - the way Athena was regarded as the protector of the city of Athens. On the Acropolis, the olive tree was considered Athena herself because of its ability to recover quickly from any damages and thus it was seen as a perfect symbol for this resilient Goddess. Athenians believed their Greek Goddess also took the form of her many sacred totem animals; the snake, birds and the revered owl. The more we learn of this Greek beloved Goddess, the more we see her correlation to ancient deities and how her existence and her worship goes back a lot further than originally believed.

According to Greek mythology (most of it written by men) Athena was born parthenogenesis, out of Zeus' head. As the well-known Greek mythology reveals, Zeus had been suffering from a horrible headache for days. He called on Hephaestus, the Smith God, to split his head open hoping to attain some relief from the pain. When Zeus' head was cut open, out sprang Athena. She was born fully armored, with her spear, and shield, a popular depiction of this Goddess that has survived throughout the ages. Important to note that she was born not as a child, but already as a full grown woman, ready for battle.

Athena's Mother was an ocean deity, the Goddess Metis. Not much is known or written about her mother for most literature connects Athena primarily with her father. We do know that Metis was the first consort of Zeus. We also know that she herself was the Goddess of wisdom and intelligence because her name translates as such. As can be surmised, Athena's own wisdom and great intelligence can be attributed to being born from Zeus' head but most importantly, her gifts should be attributed to having the lineage of a mother who was known as the Goddess of intelligence and wisdom. It is important to note that her intellect was not of the mystical kind. Athena was not about other-worldly wisdom or esoteric, spiritual knowledge. She was pragmatic and cherished practical, useful knowledge, cultural and historical knowledge. She was also a lover of all skills and art forms. In the myths of her time, we also learn of her impressive skills in handiworks, dressmaking, embroidery, pottery and needlecrafts among her many skills and gifts bestowed to her devotees.

In her mythologies we learn that Zeus, after being warned by oracle seer, feared that an offspring with the Goddess Metis would produce a child more powerful than himself. He tried to remedy this situation by swallowing Metis whole. However, she was already pregnant with their child. Athena thus, continued to grow and live on (now) inside of her father, Zeus. A headache soon began to overtake Zeus and when his head was cut open, out came the strong and wise Athena. Zeus fell instantly in love with his daughter and throughout literature we also see her great devotion to her father.

Athena is the beloved Goddess of the Greek city of Athens. There, she is the personification of civic law. The story of how she came to be the patron Goddess for Athens reflects her popularity and early examples of democracy. Athenians had to participate in a democratic vote to decide who would be the patron God/Goddess for the city. The choices were the God of the Sea -Poseidon or Athena, the Goddess of Wisdom and War-craft. When the ballots were counted, they discovered that all the male citizens voted for the male God, Poseidon and all the female votes were given to Athena. Because there were more female citizens at the time in Athens, Athena was the natural winner. As can be expected, the men of Athens did not like this turn of events and displayed much resistance. As a result, they imposed a series of new laws that would need to be implemented, if they were to accept a Female Deity as leader of their beloved City. The most significant new laws that manifested from this election was the replacement of matriarchal lineage by the patriarch. It meant that a child would now carry on the father's last name, instead of the traditional mother's name, according to the writings of this time. Eventually Athena was fully embraced as the patron Goddess of Athens by both, men and women.

This beloved Greek Goddess also has an ancestral connection to her people through the first King of Athens -Erichthonius. This myth is very similar to the Sun Goddess, Amaterasu and the first Imperial family of Japan. According to one myth, Athena was seduced by Hephaestus. As a virgin deity, she refused him, but interestingly enough, Hephaestus' semen falls upon her thigh. In total disgust, she takes a rag and wipes it off. She throw the rag upon the Earth and from this action a child is produced. The Earth (Gaia) then gives birth to a child, which Athena then nurtures and raises as her own. In this story we see the preservation of her status as Virgin Goddess, adopted mother and teacher. She names the boy, Erichthonius and teaches him everything, including the worship of Gods. In him she creates one of Athens' first leaders. Erichthonius fulfills her vision for Athens and succeeds in establishing civic law and governmental structure and thus Athena is directly responsible for Athens' growth and civilization as a prosperous city. There is also a direct connection between the Goddess and her ruling class descendants. Today, a trip to modern day Greece will reveal Athena is still honored and revered in her famous temple - the Parthenon, in Athens, Greece. Images of her are sold in every neighboring Greek tourist kiosk surrounding the still commanding nearby ruins and the Parthenon is an amazing site to behold.

As a Virgin deity she was never married, nor did she ever actually give birth to a child. According to Jean Shinoda Bolen, M.D. in her book *"Goddess in Everywoman, A New Psychology of Women,"* Athena perhaps refused to be linked romantically with a man for fear this would restrict her active participation and involvement with politics, war and her public life image. However, unlike other Virgin Goddesses, she does not appear to have any animosity towards the opposite sex. Quite the contrary, she seems to have great love and adoration for men and clearly uplifts, inspires and supports numerous men throughout Greek mythology. She was born from her father and clearly had a strong bond solely with him. Throughout Greek mythology she is always surrounded by various men and sometimes even disguises herself as one. She appears to be a defender and cheerleader of men in her efforts to empower them for battles. She does not express any romantic feelings, nor sexual liaisons with men for fear it would demean her or make her seem subordinate to men. In the writings of her time, she appears to enjoy competition with men and her virginity strictly assures her independence and her status as their equal. She is almost unapproachable sexually by men and her virginity and chastity, maintain her platonic camaraderie relations with men. Reckless emotions left one vulnerable in times of war and thus she was an advocate of moderating ones' emotions... something quite difficult to do in the throes of a passionate love affair.

Athena was most concerned with order, socialization, culture and institutions - Marriages falls under this category. Though she herself never married and while she was not an advocate for romantic or sexual unions, she was a promoter and protector of marriages. Marriages are social institutions and promote a valued structure and order in society, according to her specific ideologies. Athena is not a Goddess to be called upon for fertility or child birthing skills, as she never actually gave birth to a child, nor does she appear to concern herself with these things. Learning of her connection to Erichthonius, we can surmise her attributes regarding children. With children, she is more concern with their education and their socialization as future citizens and leaders of her beloved city.

As a Goddess of War-craft, she was a prudent Commander and had the gift of strategizing war. She was responsible for the skills and the weapons of war in ancient times.

Athena is about courage and inspiring that courage in Heroes and their companions on the battlefield. She encourages willingness, intelligence, and control of emotions, boldness and a will to victory. Athena was known for her cunningness and her ability to use words and her intellect in battles and debates. She was more about calm emotions, restraint, clear thinking, and not resorting to brute violence. Mindless killings did not appeal to her. This Goddess was not an advocate of killings just for the sake of the sport. In contrast to the other Gods of war, like Ares, who fights in an emotional frenzy and fury, Athena's approach to war in battle fields was calm, methodical and controlled and she always tempered her emotions. She despised anything crude, wild, barbaric, uncivilized. This Virgin Goddess does not use Aphrodite's physical, sexual charms to win, nor does she use the violent, brute force like Ares. She uses intellect to win all her battles. For Athena, war is more than just a battle of strength; it is part of what's necessary to attain specific goal or higher ideals. She was defender of social order and the prosperity of civilization. Anything that deviated from these ideals inspired her to battle. She represents rational, practicalities, democracy, and administration of justice, rhetoric and the art of persuasion. Athena is the personification of a cultured society and she was victorious in wars because of these honorable attributes.

*Greek Goddess of wisdom, skills, war-craft and intelligence. She is the embodiment of a strong mind, tempered heart and fierce leadership. She inspires greatness in all your undertakings and blesses all hand crafted projects. She is the teacher and awakens in you a drive for excellence and competence. If magick is to be defined as, changing consciousness at will, then indeed aligning our mind with our will makes perfect sense, and Athena would be a great catalyst for this procedure. All things we wish to bring to fruition must first begin with a thought, an initial vision, a plan, and the engagement of the mind, this is Athena's realm. She comes into your life now to teach you that wishes and goals are best met, first and foremost in our initial imagining and strategizing. She beckons you to tap into the power of your mind; plan, strategize, organize to achieve your goals, for this can be much stronger than sheer brute force

CHAPTER ELEVEN
COURAGE
SHE WHO FACES THE UNKNOWN

INANNA

INANNA

By far, one of the most treasured Deities found throughout Ancient Mesopotamia is the Goddess, Inanna. Known as the Queen of Heaven, she is the Goddess of Love, Sexuality, War, Leadership, Supremacy and all aspects of Femininity. She embodies all the attributes of an ancient Goddess that is of monumental importance to women. And, her prominent worship in ancient times reveals how vastly different women's role and value were then, compared to various other times in history.

She was often depicted as young, strong, assertive, independent, beautiful, very sensual, and in tuned with her gender's inherent powers. In ancient times there were many depictions of this Goddess with a lion or riding a lion to show her supremacy. It was also not uncommon to see images of Inanna with quiver and bow, or suited up in armor, to reflect her attributes connected to war. Statues of Inanna show her cupping her breast with her hands depicting nurturance but possibly also elucidating her sexual attributes, very similar to Ishtar.

Her temples and shrines were numerous in ancient Mesopotamia. Her main cult center was located at Uruk, where she was even revered among the sacred prostitutes of the temples. Many writing of the time describe explicitly her great powers of sexuality and the many rites & invocations her worshippers engaged in. At the Akitu annual Festival in Babylon, the king and queen, as well as its citizens, would re-enact the sacred union between the Goddess Inanna and her beloved consort, Dumuzi. In this common ritualistic sexual act, they believed they could help guaranteed the land's fertility.

Early Sumerian writings included Inanna as one of the seven primordial entities that would later become the foundation of other developed deities. Inanna was among, Anu, Enlil, Enki, Ninhursag, Nanna, and Utu. There are varied stories connected to her parentage as one would expect from such an ancient deity. She is believed to be daughter of the Moon God, Nanna and Ningal but also as possible daughter of the Supreme God, Anu. But she is also linked to being fathered by the God Enki, and the Air God, Enlil. Her connection to Ereshkigal, the dark Goddess of the Underworld, is depicted in ancient myths. One of the most beloved remaining poems, illustrative of Inanna and her relationship to her sister, the Goddess of the underworld, Ereshkigal, is, "The Descent of Inanna" (c.1900-1600BCE). It is the powerful story of survival, inner journeys & transformations, similar to that of the Greek Goddess, Persephone and her descent into the underworld. Another well-known work that speaks of Inanna, among many is found In the Epic of Gilgamesh (C2700-1400BCE). Here in this well-known, Sumerian Babylonian poem, the Goddess Inanna is spoken of as the Goddess Ishtar.

Like most ancient Goddesses, Inanna has several obvious, noteworthy aspects she was known for. This Goddess who was exalted by the Sumerians and worshipped as a Goddess of love, war, creation, sovereinty, healing and wisdom, could have easily been included in any of the other chapters in this book. Inanna is included in this chapter on courage because she exemplifies for us the strength and courage needed to surrender what we value most and, willingly, delve into a journey of the unknown. In her most widely known myth, "The Descents of Inanna," we learn of her frightful, dark journey into the land of the dead, where she must come before the intimidating Dark Goddess Ereshkigal and submit to her Dark Queendom. With all of her great beauty, rich robes & jewels and her brilliant lifeforce, Inanna, had to surrender these one by one to attain something greater. In this grueling process, she exemplifies for us the Courage we can tap into when we reach a point in our own personal journey that requires a frightful confrontation and a surrendering of all that we once knew and held onto so tightly, believing we couldn't survive without.

Of all of Inanna's significant aspects, she is included in this chapter as a Goddess we call upon to help us confront the unknown and conquer fears with indomitable courage.

"Discovering Goddesses and embracing the long
forgotten aspects of our gender as Divine women,
inaugurates shifts in our collective psyche that
changes everything in us;
for once we gain an awareness of our
Past Goddess existence and her stories,
only then, can we begin to walk and exist in our Divine truth...."
B. Melusine Mihaltses

MAMAN BRIGITTE

GRANDE MAMAN BRIGITTE

Maman Brigitte is a Voodoo Loa who comes to us from New Orleans, though her origins surely begin in Haiti and quite possibly Africa. She is often referred to as a new World Loa/Goddess (I mean no disrespect to the culture, but I will use the term Goddess which is so ingrained in my own personal vernacular when referring to this beloved Voodoo loa). In Voodoo, as is in most spiritual theologies fully submersed in ancient indigenous practices, the Loa is more than just an archetype or lofty deity but a personification of a living breathing spirit. Since this too is my own personal definition of a Goddess I will respectively, use both terms interchangeably.

Maman Brigitte is born as a result of the merging African slave and European influence in New Orleans, but most important to note is that she is born, like most Loa, out of a need. With the brutal rise of the African and Haitian slaves came the increase in senseless horrifying deaths. A multitude of vagrant, unidentified, displaced cadavers abound and for a people who venerated their land and their ancestors, this was a most tragic experience, to say the least. Back home, when death arrived, they were comforted in the knowledge that they would be buried in their homeland and reunited with their beloved sacred ancestors. Dragged to this new land, they couldn't even hope for this, as their customs and spiritual beliefs were challenged and nearly eradicated through the vile practice of slavery and assimilation. Clearly the need for a loa, like Maman Brigitte, becomes imperative... a fiercely protective mother who assures you, your death will not be in vain, your bones will be properly cared for upon your death and your spirit will be led to your homeland to reconnect with your sacred ancestors where you belong. This is the very least you can hope for and Maman Brigitte takes on this critical role for a people stripped of everything else.

There is clear evidence that there was a lot of mingling of cultures in this new land, and the Irish and English undoubtedly influenced the manifestation of this Voodoo loa. Grande Maman Brigit (as she is also sometimes called) is often linked to the Celtic Goddess Brigit, who was attributed to inventing the art of keening (a special funerary howl of grief), hence the similarity in their names and attributes. There are some that believe Maman Brigitte is known as a healing, matron smith Goddess, just like St. Brigit. Sometimes this Loa is even depicted as being very light skin, possibly blue eyed with reddish or white hair- the obvious genetic attributes of someone from European descent.

In some of the writings I have read about this Voodoo Loa there is sometimes reference to Maman Brigitte, as just being another aspect of the Yoruban African Goddess, Oya. I don't see this at all... I feel her in my body vastly different than Oya. I love both Goddesses and worked with Oya exclusively a few years ago and can honestly say that these two are respectively different deities. They might share in some of their well-known attributes like; being strong willed, ruling over the cemetery, and patron Goddesses to our female gender, being particularly sympathetic to women's issues, but they must be respected and worshipped as two very distinctly different deities.

Oya is a Yoruban African Orisha, an ancient Goddess very much connected to the Niger river. She is most known as a fierce elemental Goddess of drastic Change, thunderstorms, high winds, tornadoes, cyclones and the Elements; Air, Earth, Fire and Water are associated with her. She is a warrior Goddess, who often will join her consort, Chango, in battles. She appears to me very physical, willful and strong, dare I say lots of testosterone energy in a feminine package. Yet even with noted connections to various lovers and husbands, she is not terribly tied into them for she is known as fiercely independent, intelligent, autonomous, a shrewd business feminine leader and an inspirer to women to share in her gifts.

Grande Maman Brigitte, for me personally, comes as a sort of Corpse Bride. It is not surprising the Celtic Goddess Brigit (whom she is so often associated with) also has a connection with this aspect and was known as St. Bride. Maman Brigitte clearly has this very strong linked to her Spouse, Baron Samedi, together they rule the cemetery. Respectively, they are both known as father and mother to the (Ghede) dead and share many similar qualities. Writings, documenting spiritual possessions, claim that when she arrives, although she can first appear very proper, she will sometimes take on some of Baron Samedi's eccentricities. She might even choose to wear his black top hat and match his level of vulgarity with her own bawdiness and potty mouth.

For Maman Brigitte, the cemetery alone is her beloved realm. Unlike the Orisha Oya, who had originally been given dominion over the Oceans and who (as some myths reveal) through trickery, was given the cemetery to tend to forever after, (a duty she rightfully might not fully embrace). Maman Brigitte appears quite comfortable as Mistress of the Cemetery. This is in total contrast to Oya and Maman Brigitte happily appears to reside over bones and claims the cemetery as her home and here too, is another reason why I strongly believe Oya and Maman Brigitte are two very distinct deities.

I don't recall reading anything that connects Maman Brigitte to Elemental energy like; Winds, Fire and Water, unlike the Orisha, Oya. I don't see Maman Brigitte having any link or correlations to fighting wars or wielding a "machete" or sword... but maybe a long phallic shaped wand or pole to ride on during her licentious banda dancing. To me she appears so much more bawdy and lighter, it seems, in her derelict humorous nature and much too interested in getting a good chuckle than in fighting wars. Perhaps after a life of various stressors and "war- like" challenges, battled in the flesh, while living on this earth, it is in death that we can finally be liberated from such nuisances. Maman Brigitte makes it a point to remind you of the liberating freedom from these human, earthly, trifling concerns. She is not a war deity perhaps, because in death the battle is already over and done with and all that remains is a resignation to tend to your spiritual peace and happiness.

Another interesting observation is that Oya is known as the mother of Nine but it is Maman Brigitte who is known as the mother of the Dead. With all the dead being her children, (an obvious multitude) you can imagine she is a fiercely strong Goddess with some amazing matriarchal skills and when someone needs the guidance and ardent protection of a mother, she becomes the best one to invoke.

Some of the writing reveals that there is also a connection to Maman Brigitte invoked by her worshippers as a judge, like the Egyptian Goddess Ma'at. She is called upon when there are extraneous, unfair circumstances that need to be mediated and here too the loving, righteous, protective nature of a mother is almost compulsory.

To me, Maman Brigitte is indeed a New World (U.S.A.) Goddess of the Cemetery, with origins from Africa and Europe. For practitioners of Voodoo, she is the Loa of the dead, mother of the Ghede, Corpse Bride wife to Baron Samedi. She is keeper of the bones and the one who greets you upon your awakening. The first female buried in a cemetery is sacred to her and you will find Maman Brigitte near this tomb. It is my belief that she is not a Goddess of the underworld like Persephone, Ma'at, Erishgigal or so many other underworld Deities like Hades/Pluto, but rather she is ruler of entryway, doorways, and transitions. Here she resembles the ancient Greek Goddess Hekate, in this role as gatekeeper and as the one who dwells in those sacred transitory junctures. Her home IS the cemetery and her role is to help you understand you are no longer in the flesh, but of bones and then, soon enough.... of ether. It is with her help that we transition from one realm to the next and the next.

Lover of Bones, she is the gate keeper of the Cemetery and this is her realm NOT the underworld, not what I envision to be the forever after. To me, and of course this is just my personal opinion, when we first die, there might be lots of confusion and an obvious period of adjustment. For some…that period might be longer than others, but this period of adjustment is where Maman Brigitte is most needed and called upon. I suppose that is why she is known as the Mother of the dead. When you die or… find yourself in a strange, unfamiliar place, in a uniquely different circumstances and situation and lacking all that was, previously, familiar to your personhood, it is precisely at this moment when we most need "Mother." It happens upon our birth, as it happens upon our death. Maman Brigitte is the Mother who helps and guides us as we figure out how to maneuver our way in this new realm and with these new, vastly different skills.

As a growing embryo, floating and merging with uterine water, was your specialty. Upon leaving that realm, to enter into the living, you encounter a vast set of circumstances that require the nurturance and guidance of mother for your very own survival; such is the inception of every human's life. As a Corpse, I suspect you'll have a similar experience as you find yourself exiting one familiar realm to enter another, quite mysterious, perhaps just as daunting, and scary of a place, as this living realm first appeared to you. And with death comes different skills to experiment and familiarize yourself with; a metamorphosis, new form of being, a vast set of circumstances that, again, require the nurturance and guide of mother for your very own survival. It is Maman Brigitte who, according to popular Voodoo tenets, will be waiting there to help in this role.

You've probably never actually watched a human body decompose. The concept of death and its grueling intricate process in our modern day society seems so shrouded in mystery. I think in particular, in the U.S.A. now, death is more often than not, handled very privately, almost concealed and beautified for us. The old and sick, nearing death, are separated by sterile hospitals and old age homes, sometimes devalued, pushed away from society long before their actual deaths takes place. Cadavers receive beautifications via the practice of embalming and then there are some funerals that opt for a closed casket. No one appears to want to talk about it and for many Westerners, it is either not given much thought or it is simply feared. Perhaps what makes it so frightening is the inexperience and lack of knowledge of what actually happens to us when we die. And so it seems, that the process of rigamortis appears hidden from us… and most of us go to our own graves never knowing what to expect at this junction in our journey.

Unless you are in the medical field, mortuary business or a forensic scientist, you probably have little experience and knowledge in the process of a decomposing body or the process of death. Ignorance in the process of dying might make it easier to trivialize its value and sacredness, unlike in centuries past and in those indigenous cultures, where death was and still is exalted and commemorated on the same stratum, echelon as birth. I muse and wonder how vastly different our present day society would be, if there was more reverence and respect, expressed and understood, towards the process of death. Living and dying are so intrinsically linked that I imagine, a reverence for death, would naturally result in a more heightened way of living in harmony with nature and a deep rooted respect and need to live every minute aware of the Divine within and all around…

When the "Tomb" is honored, the sacred "Womb" is honored and everything in between falls harmoniously into place.

For indigenous cultures, their religion and spiritual practices are linked to the "old ways." Death and its sacred process is highly esteemed and venerated and thus, merits a

Goddess dedicated dutifully to its provision. Voodoo loa, Maman Brigitte fits that role perfectly as Mistress of the cemetery, guardian of the bones and Mother to the dead.

Long may she be respected, loved and worshipped...
Hail Grande Maman Brigitte!!!

*The Voodoo Loa Maman Brigitte is the gatekeeper, threshold guardian and beloved Ghede Mother of Bones and the dead. In the darkness of the unknown, on the threshold of life and death, we must all eventually pass through these realms; here she makes herself known to us. Maman Brigitte arrives with a rather unusual sass, lightheartedness and humor about death. Rather taboo and unconventional, she reminds us, death is not a finality but a transition and one that should be approached with love, not fear or trepidation. *"What are you afraid of, death is simply a transition and if you are free of this fear, there is very little else to be afraid of in life...."* *"After all, there is no death, only transformations, my little ones..."* She draws near and the hairs on the back of your neck are felt rising. In her bawdy style, she jokes and dances for you, while daring you to enter her realm of cemeteries. We begin to consider our very own mortality and the content of our lifetime now. She comes to remind you that your time here on earth is very limited; unlike your infinite spirit, she dares you to face this fact. And your life's purpose must be met within those physical time restraints. She arrives as a wake- up call, announcing death's unpredictability, as never too far away. Whether young or old, she awaits to reclaim your sacred bones when that time does come. *Will you be ready to relinquish your bones to her, upon your death? Will you be ready to surrender all that you've known in this physical life to enter the next stage in your development, with a Mother who will lovingly and humorously guide you into the next phase? Are you living your life mindful of the expiration of your flesh and the infinity of your spirit?* Maman Brigitte is the crone that prepares you for death and transitions, whether metaphorically or in actuality. Her energy however, is not one of doom and gloom but rather celebratory.

LILITH

Probably one of the most controversial Pagan deities and one full of conflicting, yet intriguing mythologies is the Sumerian Goddess Lilith. Lilith is a powerful archetype for any women to unearth and work with.

The Goddess, Lilith today is viewed as a Goddess of the night, Goddess of Sexual Liberation, a Goddess of revenge and retribution and anger. According to a collection of ancient writings, she could not be wild and free in God's heavenly presence in the Garden of Eden and she would not subordinate herself to her spouse, Adam. Thus, she's a

Goddess that represents independence among many other feminist ideals. She is the liberated woman who does not compromise herself and she answers to no one. She is the one who embraces the pain of solitude rather than relinquish her power to any man. Lilith represents the autonomous woman who refuses to subordinate herself or lay down beneath her oppressor. She is the women who reclaims her powers and reclaims her authentic self in a world that so persistently, only wants to control and oppress her. She is the rebellious one who refuses to play societal stereotypical roles. She is sexual liberation, delighting in her unbridled sexuality and enchanting beauty. She is flight of spirit that comes and goes as she pleases. Lilith is the opposite of the nurturing maternal Goddess, even though she is attributed for birthing a race of demonic beings; she is far from the coddling mother archetype. She is considered the shadow side of Eve; that part of her she has yet to embrace or discover, for Eve only appears to accept her limiting role as Adams' rib, created inferior to him.

We claim Lilith now as a powerful Goddess for we see her significant value and cathartic importance for modern day women, especially with the rise of Feminism, but when researching Lilith you will soon discover ancient text that reveal she was not initially viewed as a Goddess but rather as a very much feared She-Demon. Perhaps, as many Dianics claim, she was indeed initially a Goddess a long time ago, who was stripped of her crown and demoted with the rise of patriarchy. One will never really know. Despite limited resources, remnant scriptures, actual sacred text scattered about mentioning her numerous different names and a plethora of mixed, conflicting tales, she has survived into the 21st century, which is astounding, when you really think about it. Consider that her oral traditions remained strong throughout the ages and sustained her in our auric "herstory."

Lilith has often been viewed by Wiccan Feminist as a Goddess who was simply demoted, vilified as a demon because, in a patriarchal society, that is the ultimate way to control and oppress a woman; vilify her, make such a scandalous rebellious Goddess, evil, to discourage any other woman from reclaiming her own powers or even slightly considering how vastly different her world might be, if she stood up as well. Lilith's claws or talon represents her tenacity; digging her heels, refusing to surrender her ideals. Her wings represent her freedom and her red eyes represent anger of those who tried to restrain and oppress her. She is often depicted with wings, owl talon as claws for her feet, and hairy legs (for in ancient times, a hirsute woman was considered a sign of demonic association). Suspecting that Queen of Sheba was demonic, King Solomon asked to see her legs and behold he discovered that she was indeed very hairy and this led him to conclude that she was the embodiment of Lilith.

Some symbols linked to Lilith are the flower lily and the lotus as well as gemstones like the Garnet and Bloodstone. Her depictions with animals indicate that she had an affinity to wild creatures. Animals like the owl, wolves, the lion, scorpions and the serpent were accepted as her symbols and the screeching owl, a name so often used in the bible, to refer to her. The serpent in particular, was often representative of the Goddess herself. She has also been associated with harpies, sirens, mermaids, undines, nymphs and melusines, perhaps due to her close connection with water and the sea. French poet and novelist, Victor Hugo (1802-1885) even claims Lilith as Satan's eldest daughter and as a succubus, she was attributed for creating a race of vampires.

The name Lilith, which translates in the Semetic language as "Night," is also associated with the wind and the breeze. The word "Lil" or "Lilitu," meant ghost, spirit breath, wind and storm demon. What is remarkable is that the name Lilith and various derivations of her name appear throughout history in Sumerian, Kabbalistic writings and Jewish mysticism and yet, it's quite interesting that according to Kabbalah scriptures, she was the first woman God created; Lilith (night) and yet, the next woman created for Adam was consequently named Eve (again a reference to night), reaffirming a connection between woman and the night.

According to Raphael Patai, in his book, *"The Hebrew Goddess,"* he states that **Lilith or Lillu** was actually one of Four Demons, belonging to the vampire or incubi-succubae class.

Lilitu and **Lillu** (Lilith) believed to be a She-Demon
Ardat Lili (Lilith's Hand maiden) who visited men at night to procreate offspring.
Irdu Lili (male counterpart) who visited women to also proliferate, impregnate and further expand the race of Demons.

The Goddess, Lilith was originally considered to be a part of a clan of Storm Demons, due to some confusion with the origins of her name, which sometimes refers to wind, breeze, ghost and spirit of the dead. There was also around the third Dynasty of Ur, another documented Sumerian Goddess, by a similar sounding name, Ninlil. Ninlil was a known Babylonian - Sumerian Goddess of the Wind and she was also known as the Avenging Bride, perhaps there was some confusion regarding these two feminine figures or perhaps they are one the same. Clearly the myths and attributes of Ninlil and Lilith are intriguingly similar and there is no question they crossed path at some point.

Lilith was known by many names and interestingly enough, sometimes, she was referred to in the singular form as well as in the plural. She was known as Lilin, Abito, Abizo, Amo(z)rpho, Haqash, Odam, Kephido, Ailo, Tatrota, Abniqta, Shatrina, Kalubtza, Tiltoi, Pirtsha.

By far one of the most controversial Feminine figures in ancient mythology is Lilith. There are numerous conflicting and controversial references to this ancient deity. We find references to her in Jewish mysticism; Kabbalah, the Talmudic, the Zohar, even the Bible, in Isaiah 34:14. Some early writings revealed she manifested when, on the fifth day of creation, God created the Sea creatures and she was among them. Other text, like the one found in the Zohar, claims she was a soul lodged in the Abyss that finally was called down upon, to descend, only after Yahweh had created Adam. Notice in this myth she was already present before Adam's manifestation.

In the lost Midrash Abkir, Kabbalistic writings of the 10th century, Lilith, who was also named, Pizna was actually viewed as two spirits in one. She is considered Lilith and Naamah. According to this text, Adam's beauty was so radiant and irresistible that they were both enchanted by him as he slept and they mated with him, unable to restrain themselves. Together they procreate the "plagues of mankind," the demonic race of Lilim. And the name Naamah, translates as the "**charmer**" and she is known as a high ranking demon that often accompanies Lilith. In Talmudic- Midrashic mythology, Naamah is actually depicted as a human being, a beautiful enchantress, daughter of Lamech and Zillah and sister of Tubal Cain. She is clearly a descendant of Cain and in her great beauty; she is a deadly enchantress, as sadly, all dangerously, magnetic women tend to be ironically portrayed. It is believed she then becomes Noah's wife, that is according to Abba bar Kahana. However, later, in the Kabbalah she was transformed into semi-human, demonic stature and thus, an aspect or a type of Lilith.

Barely mentioned in the Bible, most of what we know today about this enigmatic female figure, Lilith, can be extrapolated from pre-Biblical writings, Jewish Mysticism, oral traditions passed down and documented in many scriptures, as well as Kabbalistic writings, preserved in the Midrashic, the Zohar and Talmudic works of Sages and Rabbis throughout history. Perhaps it's best to start from the beginning with one version of her birth and manifestation but as can be expected with such an ancient figure, there are numerous versions and theories related to her birth.

"The Alphabet of Ben Sira," written in German between the 8th and 10th century gives a complete narrative and description of one version of Lilith's manifestation and perhaps it came about to explain the confusing Biblical lore found in Genesis, which upon closer inspection does not make much sense. *"The Alphabet of Ben Sira"* was considered a satire but in reality it was more likely a surviving oral tradition that sustained itself through the ages to explain the existence of Adam's first wife. According to *"The Alphabet of Ben Sira,"* Lilith was the first woman created by God, not Eve. Although some authors like, Janet and Stewart Farrar in their book, *"The Witches' Goddess,"* suggests that Eve and Lilith are really one the same and thus Lilith is the shadow aspect of Eve.

> *"Truths banished to the unconscious do acquire talons –*
> *representing both our fear of them and their ability to tear away*
> *through the veils of hypocrisy and distortion*
> *with which we have tried to surround them.*
> *Only when we come to terms with them and*
> *integrate them with consciousness is their loveliness restored,*
> *so that their talons become feet again.*
> *Only when the night-owl is admitted to the sunlight*
> *can we appreciate the beauty of her plumage.*
> *Lilith the true Mother of All living, must be re-acknowledge –*
> *so that She and Eve can become One again*
> *For without that One, Adam is only half man..."*

(The Witches' Goddess," Janet and Stewart Farrar page 133)

In *"The Alphabet of Ben Sira,"* Lilith was created at the same time as Adam, on the fifth or sixth day of creation. And God had fashioned Adam from the earth and he used the same raw material to create Lilith probably before or at the exact same time. There are other conflicting works that claim that God picked up, not the clean earth as he did for Adam, but the filth and impurities or sediments from the earth to form woman and thus it was to be expected that she was to have an impure, evil spirit, this was according to some very patriarchal Talmudic writings. Clearly a poor attempt by patriarchy to pollute our entire gender right at the start of humanity by claiming woman is destined to be evil, since she was created from impure soil and sediment. There is yet another version of Lilith's manifestation which claims that she manifested not from God himself but from the spontaneous great supernal abyss and out of the power aspects of God; the Din and the Gevurah. God was believed to have ten mystical attributes, Serifot, and his lowest kinship with the realm of evil was referred to as the, *"dreg of wines"* and this is where both, Lilith and Samuel or Satan originated from, according to these early Talmudic writings.

Lilith and Adam were created equally from the earth as written in *"The Alphabet of Ben Sira."* One day Adam desiring to have sexual relations with his mate demanded that she lay down underneath him but Lilith, viewing this position as subordinate, refused. She demanded to know why she should lay beneath when they had both been created as equal. *"Why should I lower myself, surrender my power to you when we have been created equally?"* I imagine her asking. Adam would not have it any other way and neither would Lilith. A huge argument ensued and in this contemptuous, stressful, highly emotional moment, Lilith utters the unspeakable secret name of God, something that was forbidden in the Garden of Eden and she then flies away. Although, there are variant versions that reveal she actually lulled Adam to sleep, enchanted God to reveal his secret powerful name to her and then, she went ahead and uttered it to manifest the wings that would inevitably get her out of the Garden of Eden. Be that as it may, in this power struggle with Adam she uttered the unspeakable, effable name of God, which was not viewed favorably and upon doing this she grew the wings that would allowed her to flee her oppressors and escape from the Garden of Eden. And Lilith flew away from the light of God, paradise, and Adam and chose the notorious Red Sea; a place scandalously known for harboring fallen angels, demons and evil spirits. There is a connection at this time between the waters and demons, especially the waters of the Red Sea and it's attraction to malign entities, and evil spirits. It is stated that Lilith upon the edge of the Red Sea delighted in numerous sexual relations and she fornicated and took to unbridle promiscuity; having intercourse with a multitude of demons daily and procreating a myriads of children, a race of demons called Lilim. Three days later, Adam finally begs God to bring her back to the Garden of Eden and so God sent three angels to lure and fetch her from the Red Sea. He sent the angels; Senoy, Sansenoy and Semangelof.

When the three angels arrived they found her copulating; indulging in various sexual dalliances with numerous demons and giving birth to many offspring. According to early scripture interpretations, the angels approached her and asked her to return with them to the Garden of Eden and she refused. They threatened to drown her in the Red Sea and she seemed un-moved, almost bothered by their angelic presences and demands. The angels threatened to kill off One Hundred of her very own offspring daily and she retorted she would do the same to any children born to Eve. All of these threats and the presence of these three angels were beginning to bore her and in her efforts to get rid of them, she finally agrees to not kill any future babies that have the inscribed names of the three angels, Senoy, Sansenoy and Semangel, upon them.

"..... Let me be for I was created in order to weaken the babes:
if he is a male, I have power over him from the moment of his birth until the eighth day
of his life,that is when he is circumcised and
thereby protected, and if a girl, until the Twentieth day..."

Pg 224, The Hebrew Goddess by Raphael Patai,-Alpha Beta di Ben Sira, ed. Einstein, Otzar Midrashim, pg.47

Interestingly enough, there are other tales found in the Zohar that reveal the first humans created by God were Hemaphrodites or Androgynes, attached to each other by their backside initially. All creations were created in the image of God, according to Biblical scriptures, and thus, all contained both male and female attributes, how this later changed, remains a mystery but there is a belief that Lilith was joined with the King of demons (Samuel, Satan or Ashmodai etc..) and they were created in the exact mirror image of Adam and Eve to represent the synchronicity of, as above so below. Adam and Eve were also alleged to be Hemaphrodites or Androgynes and this couple, mirrored Lilith and Samuel, but I digress.

As was her custom, Lilith was known to tickle newborns (which explains why babies have these random, spontaneous smiles while they sleep) and she is credited for leading them to their deaths but in this myth she agreed to allow One Hundred of her own demon offspring to be killed daily by God and she makes an oath to not harm any babies that revealed the names of the three angels upon them. Much controversy surrounds Lilith as a SheDemon that kills and even cannibalistically devours children's blood and bones. There was no other way of explaining such horrific tragedies as stillborn and mysterious infant deaths except to blame a demoted deity and contribute to her fabricated, growing negative reputation. Stillbirths, miscarriages, children that mysteriously died in infancy and spontaneous abortions were all attributed to her. A plethora of artifacts found with incantations to her, supplicating her to keep away from newborns, supports this connection.

Returning to the tale of Lilith's manifestation from "The Alphabet of Ben Sira," the angels left Lilith to live in a cave by the Red Sea and now Adam, in the Garden of Eden, required a new mate and here is where the Bible begins its tale. Adam now required a new spouse and from the hidden part of Adam, his rib, Eve was crafted by Yahweh. She was to be more obedient and subservient to Adam, always beneath him, complacent, accommodating and she was to reflect the nurturing maternal attributes that Lilith so lacked. Now here is where we get some conflicting stories because according to one tale, Lilith was matched to the King of demons, Samuel, Satan, Ashmodai, Lucifer but according to other scriptures, God, fearing these two (Lilith and Samuel) would populate the earth with a powerful breed of demons, castrated Samuel, in his effort to control their proliferation of children. And because licentious Lilith was now in need of a sexual partner, she chose to sneak back into the Garden of Eden from time to time to have relations with Adam while he slept, through nocturnal emissions. The conflicting part is that some say Lilith would inevitably return to the Garden of Eden as the Serpent and in her wrath and jealousy, would eventually lead Adam and Eve into sin, by offering them the fruit from the forbidden Tree of Knowledge. There is some text however, that reveals the Serpent was really Samuel/Satan, the King of Demons himself. Samuel, exercising retribution, since his wife was taking on Adam as her nightly lover, he felt justified in now seducing Eve in the same manner. Nonetheless, both Adam and Eve had tasted of the forbidden fruit, from the Tree of Knowledge, according to Biblical lore and as a result there immortality was taken from them. They were expelled from the Garden of Eden, as we all have learned through popular Biblical interpretations.

In his remorse and disgust, Adam vowed 130 years of celibacy and self- imposed punishment, fasting and self-denial. Both he and Eve roamed the earth during this time and according to the numerous mystical writings. It was during this 130 year sojourn and because of his sin, that Lilith now had even more access to him. His very sinful nature made him vulnerable to her presence according to the writings of this time. She frequented him nightly, having sexual intercourse with him through nocturnal emissions, aka wet dreams. Eve was not spared of this either, as she too was visited nightly by the King of Demons and was impregnated daily so that she would give birth to half human and half demon, light and dark beings, just as Lilith would give birth to Adam's half demon, half human children. It is believed that through these unions between Lilith and Adam, and Samuel and Eve that the descendants of Cain, Tubal-Cain and his sister Naamah, manifested. It is also believed that when Cain, after Abel's murder, was banished by God, Lilith took him on as her lover and together they too populated the earth with the first demonic vampiric race this is according to these early Kabbalistic writings. Researching these ancient scriptures, it would appear to me that the whole of humanity is somehow connected to Lilith, Adam, Eve and Samuel as direct descendants of both human and demonic lineage.

Even older than *The Alphabet of Ben Sira*" are the numerous artifacts found displaying Lilith's name, function and revealing how she was truly viewed in ancient time by the Sumerian people. One of the earliest mentions of Lilith is found in 2000 B.C.E. on a clay tablet in which we have the Mesopotamian Epic tale of Gilgamesh, Inanna and the Huluppu (Willow) tree.

According to the Gilgamesh epic, Huluppu tree lore, the great Goddess, Queen of Heaven, Inanna, discovered the tree in the sea and brought it to her garden, planting it near the Euphrates River, where she tended to its growth and nurturance. The tree grew nice and strong and one day, lamenting that she did not have a personal throne, she saw the tree as the perfect material to make her divine throne from but when she approached the tree, she learned that it was already inhabited. There was a fierce serpent, a special serpent-dragon that could not be charmed, living at the base of this tree. She also discovered a Zu bird which had built a nest way up above, at the crown of the tree and much to her surprise, the Dark Maiden Lilith, had made her home in the trunk of this Huluppu tree. And these three obstacles sadly prevented Inanna from reclaiming her tree and thus creating her divine throne. In the tale, she calls on Gilgamesh and he's able to chop down this tree with a special Bronze axe and he saves the day by removing all the obstacles and Lilith as a result of this, abandons the tree and flies into the wilderness, the desert. Interesting to note Gilgamesh's father, a Sumerian king was known as a Lilludemon, a reference to Lilith and her Clan of demons. This epic tale reveals Lilith's early myths and her connection to the Queen of Heaven, as she was sometimes known as Inanna's Hand-maiden and some tales reveal Lilith in "Erecht", as one who gathered men from the streets, with her beauty, to come enter the Goddess Temple for ritual sex offerings.

Isaiah 34:14 "The wild –cat shall meet with the jackals and the satyr shall cry to his fellow, Yea, Lilith shall repose there, and find her rest..."

And here we have one of the only mentions of her name in the bible and it supports the Gilgamesh Huluppu tree Epic, which claims Lilith flew away to live in the desert.

In Nippur Babylonia, modern day Hilla in Iraq, there were many discovered bowl artifacts with carvings and inscriptions referring to her name. These bowls, from about 600 B.C.E., with their inscriptions, revealed how Lilith was viewed by the locals and how her myths still survived outside of academia and the scholastic researcher's domain. Sacred scriptures found in the Zohar and Talmudic writings revealed how the elite and the educated viewed Lilith and her myths but via these excavated artifacts we get a glimpse into the most precious and intimate views on this iconic female figure by the everyday people amidst their residential communities. Many of them had inscriptions, invocations with protective charms and incantations to keep Lilith away and to safeguard their offspring. In Mesopotamia and North Syria, by the eighth century B.C. E., she was clearly already known as a She-Demon in Israel. A 7th century B.C.E, clay tablet found in Northern Syria depicts her as a sphinx with an inscription...

"O, flyer in the darkness, Go away at once, O Lili..."

pg 222 The Hebrew Goddess, by Raphael Patai.

There is a medieval story preserved in Hebrew and Arabic which tells of a youth who marries the daughter of Ashmodai. He later decides he wants to be free of her and gives her a "*Get*" which is a kind of letter of divorce required back then when one intended to separate from their demonic spouse. Seems strange but this tale supports the notion that demons, in ancient times, married and intermingled with humans. It is quite a curious bizarre tale and reflective of a time when the belief of Demon attachments was so prevalent. The result of this was even more enthralling. As planned, the letter is finally delivered and as documented, the daughter of Ashmodai responds to it with a kiss of death.

Rabbi Joshua Ben Perahia, and the names of other rabbis are invoked several times and found, documented on these excavated Nippur bowls. Rabbi Joshua Ben Perahia, was a first century B.C.E. sage who was believed, by the sixth century CE, to have been a powerful exorcist of demons and often called upon with regards to exorcising a Lilith. First century teacher, Rabbi Hanina stresses the importance for man not to sleep alone in his home, less Lilith gets a hold of him via nocturnal emissions, revealing she is a Goddess men should fear because, remember, it was during Adams' 130 years of solitude and self-imposed punishment that Lilith had her way with him nightly, through these nocturnal emissions. The Rabbi warns men not to sleep alone as it will invite her presence and this caution for Jews still survives to this very day.

Early 14th century Kabbalist writer, Bahya ben Asheribn Halawa, (death-1340) reveals in his biblical commentaries that Lilith was one of four known Mother Demons. Lilith, Naamah, Igrath and Mahalath were the four wives of Esau's divine patron, aka Samuel, Ashmodai, Satan. These four women, each ruled their respective Tequfot (Winter Solstice, Summer Solstice, Vernal Equinox, Autumnal equinox). The writer Halawa also claims King Solomon had rule over them and they were considered his slave-women aka his Liliths, which he manipulated for his personal gains and invoked freely as needed.

Another tale reveals an encounter between the Prophet Elijah, Lilith and her Clan or band. The Prophet Elijah, saw Lilith and asked her where she was going and she boasted that she was going to the house of a woman in the middle of childbirth, Mercada daughter of Donna. *"....to give her the sleep of death and to take her child, which is being born to her, to suck its blood, and to suck the marrow of its bones and to seal its flesh..."* *(Page 227 "The Hebrew Goddess" by Raphael Patai.)* The prophet then recited a curse to restrain Lilith, " *with a ban from the name Yahweh, Blessed be He, be you restrained, be restrained and Be you like unto a stone.....*" and she recites back and asks to be released of the restrained placed upon her and promises not to harm them. Lilith gives a list of her sacred names and her various titles, that if she is called by these names or if she sees these names in print, she will do no harm and she will be rendered powerless. These are the names she recited to him that day; Lilith, Abitar, Abiqar, Amorpho, Hakash, Odam, Kephido, Ailo, Matrota, Abnukta, Shatriha, Kali, Taltui, Kitsha.

Hayyim Vital (1543-1620) a Safed Kabbalist , explains in his writings that there was a fallen angel, known as *"the flame of the revolving sword."* This angel was sometimes referred to as a demon called Lilith and thus it would appear that Lilith and this fallen angel are regarded interchangeably and as being one the same. According to one tale in the Zohar, when Lilith first manifested she sought companionship immediately, and soaring up high she rose to attach herself to the small boy faces of the Cherubim, which she saw surrounding God's throne. When God created man, with Adam, he detached her from the Cherubim and ordered Lilith to descend to earth. Upon seeing Adam with Eve, she felt displaced and immediately sought to return to the Cherubim but by then, they knew what she was up to and barred her from heavens, banishing her to the Sea. *Which begs the question, why is she banished to the Sea? It appears that Biblical scriptures always view the sea as containing evil and water as a place for the uncontrollable, the volatile, evil spirits, and the wicked. Yet water is closely related to the Moon and therefore to Night and somehow Woman has always been linked with these realms. I find this fascinating and it conjures up all kinds of musings, but I digress.*

Visual Depictions:

Lilith has often been depicted in numerous conflicting ways. Some claim she is wind, just a breath, nonhuman in form and yet others depict her as a woman with her lower half enflamed with roaring fires. In connection with one of her totems, the Owl, she is depicted as a screeching Owl, a winged creature in nocturnal flight. She has also been portrayed as a wise calculating Serpent, with a woman's head and a snake's slithering body. As an incubus succubus and Mother of Vampires she has been depicted as an enchanting, blood thirsty vampire. During the age of Enlightenment many artist and poets, like Dante Gabriel Rossetti, romanticized her image, depicting her as an exquisite beautiful misunderstood woman. The 1889, "La Fille de Lilith" by Rossetti, tells her tale of retribution. Goethe includes her in "Walpurgisnacht" and her likeness appears in Shaw's "Back to Methuselah" as well as Thornton Wilder's "The Skin of Our Teeth." Writer, Anais Nin, dedicated the Erotic poem, "Delta of Venus" to Lilith and there is no question that many stories and images of Lilith have inspired many artist and writers throughout the ages. Depicted in a way that our human eyes can comprehend, an old Babylonian Terra cotta, Burney relief, remains now in a British Museum and here is a visual description of this image of her;

"She is slender well shaped, beautiful and nude with wings and owl feet.
She stands erect on two reclining lions, which are turned away from each other
and are flanked by owls. On her head she wears a cap
embellished by several pairs of horns.In her hand, she holds a ring and rod combination."

(Emil G.H. Kraeling, Bulletin of the American Schools of Oriental Research 67
(Oct.1937), pages 16-18)

As an enchantress she is often describes with long flowing red hair, pale skin and red lips and blushing cheeks. Sexually inviting, her beauty is unmatched and she is so captivating that she leads men to their own death. She is often adorned with ornaments as described in the passage below.

"Her ornaments for the seduction of the sons of man are:
her hair is long and red like the rose,
Her cheeks are white and red, from her ears hang six ornaments,
Egyptian Cords and all ornaments of the land of the East hang from her nape,
Her mouth is set like a narrow door, comely in its décor;
her tongue is sharp like a sword,
her words smooth like oil, her lips red like a rose
and sweetened by all the sweetness of the world.
She is dressed in scarlet and adorned with 40 ornaments less one."

Raphael Patai's, The Hebrew Goddess,pg 233

Today Lilith is embraced by most modern day Pagans and Goddess worshipping women as a Goddess of the Night and Sexual freedom, who initially debuted as a vilified, much feared She-Demon. Lilith is understandably the saboteur of patriarchy, the one who will NOT go with the flow, will not succumb nor lay down to be ruled over. She is the rebellious one who will create her own rules to live by. Demonized by a patriarchal society, Lilith represents the most frightening aspect of femininity. She represents what patriarchy wants to control, rule over and oppress. She can be seen as the hidden subconscious, as she's connected with night, the Moon, and the Moon is connected with waters, emotions, deep hidden emotions of the murky waters. In patriarchal writings, she is classified as a harlot, a vampire, a hag, a witch, an enchantress, seductress, barren one, child killer, insatiable, blood thirsty and most of all misunderstood. She is one with no milk upon her breasts as described in ancient texts and yet, she is also considered the mother of a race of Demons and equally referred to as a maiden in her epithet. She is a virgin archetype -for she belongs to no one and experiences life by her own rules.

Lilith and even Eve, perhaps share in the traits of another deity known as Blodeuwedd, as their most negative attributes seem to have been created by men's vision and fantasy, created to serve patriarchy; to be obedient, subordinate, unrealized, disempowered, sexually confined and restricted, only to serve the "master." And yet, both (Lilith and Blodeuwedd) appear to be "punished" into Owl-hood, banished into the night for their divine awakening and refusal to play by the oppressor's rules. Representing the dark side of the unconscious, the night and the shadow, they become the scariest threat to patriarchy, and must then be ostracized, relegated, demonized into the night. How frightening must it be to a nation of self-proclaim masters to confront the true all-powerful strength of Goddess; reflected in the maiden, mother, crone, the bitch, the harlot, the warrior, the protectress mother, the seductress, sex loving, pleasure seeker, commanding, demanding, sea lover, compassionate, wise, strategic, intelligent, competent, beast lover, cave dweller, howler of the night......in each and every awakened woman/Wombmyn upon this earth!

She is Goddess and a model for those who have opened themselves up to their autonomy, great beauty, sexuality and their self-reliant strength. For those who gladly surrender the suffocating chains of complacency and stereotypical female "nice-a-ties" of a life played under the thumbs of patriarchy, she is a powerful force to unearth. Yes, she is a She-Demon, just as todays' powerful, no nonsense, feminist is classified as "the bitch" and both are... in my opinion, **Goddess.** There is no debate, in my mind, whether she is a She-Demon or Goddess, for in Lilith we come to yet another sacred aspect of the Divine Feminine. A thunderstorm, with its massive pouring of rain, can neither be classified as good or bad for in the dry desert she is everything connected to good and in the marshland she is everything connected to bad. Thus, a thunderstorm, much like the Feminine Divine, and all of Nature, is neither good nor bad.... **it just is!!!** And to deny one aspect is to only embrace and comprehend half of Goddess. Hail to you most powerful beautiful Liliatu!!!!

*The Sumerian Goddess, Lilith, is a most fascinating, yet controversial Goddess. She enters your life in a most distinctly irrefutable fashion and her influence is probably one of the most impactful on a women's life. She is the Dark Goddess that rises from the depths of our subconscious and provokes you into your own powers. When the Goddess Lilith asserts herself in your life you will feel the depths of her intense strength, energy and her intolerance for women's suppression and inequality. She is the adamant voice that will not be victimized, oppressed nor engaged in patriarchal rules. Lilith is autonomy and freedom and she will not succumb to societal pressures, no matter what names are flung at her. You can call her demon, bitch, cunt, dyke, witch, monster, whatever... but she WILL remain whole and authentically true to herself, for she will not lay herself down, beneath anyone. She will not subordinate herself for man's pathetic, sick ideologies and she soars in flight with her autonomous woman power intact throughout the ages because of it. She is brazen pleasure seeker, whole unto herself and epitomizes woman's sexual liberation and a powerful representation of Feminism.

BABA YAGA

BABA YAGA

"But Baba Yaga does not merely stand for the end of the cycle;
She is the Cycle, the black earth that closes over dead bones yet also is the fertile womb
for seedlings in Spring. Her hut turning on its chicken legs is the turning of seasons, the
endless motion of the Universe..." Rebecca Vassey, writer for SageWoman Magazine

Her imageries conjure up all sorts of frightening stereotypical, old images of the Witch, the Hag, the decrepit wicked and the near dead. With her long bony fingers and limbs, and her oversized long nose with hairy warts decorating its edge, she can appear quite frightful to our inner child. Her hunched back and the appearance of her menacing gnawing iron clad black teeth is enough to make you run for the hills. She triggers our earliest memories and terrors of heart stopping childhood fairytales that warned us about the unknown and kept us from going into secluded, distant places, like the woods. We didn't ever want to meet the child-eating witch out there and so these infantile fairy tales, with their ghastly painted pictures, certainly made us cognizant of the possible dangers in the worlds but also fed our consciousness, tenacious prejudices and negative views on the unknown, the different and the old.

Baba Yaga is the Slavic Crone. Her origins come from the Baltic region and there are hints of her in Ukrainian and Polish folklore as well. She is found in numerous fairy tales as the wicked terror-striking Hag and although there is some conflict regarding her deity status, many myth scholars and Goddess worshippers exalt her as the quintessential, and misunderstood, Crone. She is elevated from this fairytale folklore dark fearsome character, to the Black Goddess we unearth her to be, after years of patriarchal suppression. Baba Yaga, like many powerful, ancient female deities that can threaten patriarchal growing societies, has been vilified and pushed out into the outskirts of civilization, far out into the uncultivated woods. Those who are researching "herstory," connecting to the Divine in her numerous guises and seeking to reclaim lost forgotten heritage are finding it in the tales orally passed down and later documented; patriarchally altered and revised and modified to hide the sacred feminine. We are finding her again and Baba Yaga is yet another reflection of Goddess in her Crone aspect; as Grandmother Moon, as Dark Mother, as the Black Goddess. And again I must stress, as I have in my previous books, that the color Black is not viewed as negative, at least not in Goddess Spirituality. Black, the Crone and Dark Goddesses in general are not viewed as negative or something evil or bad, on the contrary, they are very strong and powerful... and necessary. Black connotes the mysteries yet discovered, like our dark womb, it is a term used to define the hidden, the shadow that which is misunderstood, what is prime and awaiting fertilization, There is much power In this.

Baba Yaga is a Goddess of death, and regeneration. She is a Goddess of monumental transformations and courageously facing our biggest fears. As her myths will reveal, she is a Goddess of initiatory characteristics, for she inaugurates for us, change that comes from knowledge and facing our truths. She is the Grandmother archetype, the wise, all knowing Crone. A Deity of prophecy and bringer of psychic and intuitive gifts, she is Goddess of our intuition and the primordial mysteries found in nature and her cyclical continuous patterns. Though her image might be frightening and at times down right gruesome, she beckons us to take courage and lift the façade, to unveil considerable wisdom and power that can positively transform our lives.

Perhaps it is best to begin by examining her name. In Russia the word for Grandmother is *Babushka*. Not surprising, some believed the name "*Baba Yaga*" originates from this sweet affectionate appellation. However when we look at the word "*Baba*" it has not only a different feel but also a slightly different meaning. In Russia the term "*Baba*" was used to describe an old woman, more specifically it was a term meant to describe a woman who is or was married and therefore non-virginal. Listening to the sound of the word "*Baba,*" it has a harsher phonetic feel, as this was a deprecating term, meant to infer the whining wife. *Baba* meant the complaining, constant yelling and nagging woman. It is a word to connote that women, once they become wives or mothers, are witch-like, hags, complainers and naggers. Therefore, the first part of her name in our modern language suggests a rather whining, bothersome, unpleasant woman and old, certainly not virginal or maiden-like. Another indication of her association as a crone deity is her nicknames. Baba Yaga was also called "Blue-nosed" and "Bony-legged" Her full name was accepted as, "*Baba Yaga Kostianaya Noga,*" which means "Baba Yaga Boney Legs" and this confirms even further her elderly status.

Connected as a Goddess of Cycles and Life and Death, it is not surprising she is Goddess of Bones but also a Goddess very much linked with the Harvest. For it is believed she plants us, fertilizes us, then prunes us and (throughout the cold Winter months) keeps us safe until we are ready to be replanted again, to bloom in the spring. Baba Yaga is the cycles of nature and the cycles of birth, life and death and rebirth, we personally experience at various points in our lives.

Described as a bony, hunchback, with numerous warts covering her face, disheveled silver hair and a bent crooked, long nose, that could reach the underside of her chin, she was meant to conjure fear in you. Baba Yaga was a frightening sight. As frail and bony as she appeared, she was a ferociously strong force to be reckoned with and she delighted in the nightly rides inside her spinning iron mortar and pestle. She would steer her pestle across the sky and make the howling sound of the fierce nightly breeze and if you listened closely enough you could hear her cackles amidst the orchestra of night. Yet it is important to note that it is our fears of the unknown; of death, of the old, that makes Baba Yaga so fearsome and ugly in our collective consciousness.

Gruesomely depicted as an ogre and known as a Hag, it is very important to understand that the term Hag had a very different meaning in olden times than it does today. In the Middle-Ages, the word Hag was often associated with nature Fairies. The word Hag often connoted something holy. It is derived from the Greek word *Hadia* or *Hagiolatry*, which means the worship of Saints. Considering this definition and Baba Yaga so often being referred to as a hag, her numerous names and titles already begin to reflect a different perception of this Dark Goddess, when we endeavor to study her more closely.

To be sent to Baba Yaga was to be sent on a journey to death but courageously facing this fact manifested into an unfathomable freedom and liberation from all things fearsome. As a Goddess of death she was known to be the Guardian of the Waters of life and death. It was believed, corpses were brought back to life with a mere sprinkled of these waters, of life-powers, to be reborn again. Baba Yaga is best viewed as a Goddess of initiation and transitions. As the midwife of death she is the sacred portals we must all bravely pass through.

The brick oven, which plays a prominent role in her Baltic myths as the place where she lures and bakes her victims before devouring them, has often long been associated with the sacred womb. In its capacity to heat up and transform grains into nurturing bread, it is reminiscent of the pregnant Mother/Goddess birthing new life. In this same manner we are invited to consider that Baba Yaga's myth reveals her powers of actually taking us through this process of womb-like transformation, as we face our biggest fears, allow them to be devoured, buried, then transformed and reborn again. She is thus, in this way, a midwife of death and powerful initiations.

Often we think of three archetypal stages for women but really one may consider there to be four and the fourth one can be viewed as the afterlife or what appears after death. Baba Yaga precedes this stage and prepares us for the next, whether it does come to pass or whether a slight of hands changes our fate unexpectedly. As the Maiden precedes the Mother and the Mother precedes the Crone, it seems likely that the crone prepares and precedes what comes next, until the cycle is repeated once more. This is Baba Yaga's domain. They say she eats humans, especially children but it is really our inner child that she devours and transmutes in preparation for the next stage of life. In this way she is indeed the perpetual alchemist who transforms our fears and pain into our ultimate strengths. She leads women into transformational states, into this sort of new, second stage; a new age of Woman, one in which she is no longer suffocatingly bonded to the role of maiden (daughter to her parents) nor mother to her offspring. In this new stage of her life, her new role affords her to taste freedom and this allows her to better serve her community and herself. As with other ancient deities presented in this book, it becomes clear that Baba Yag, with her numerous divine attributes can offer us many different themes to explore. She could have easily been included in the chapter on leadership and community, as well as, the chapter on Liberation. Here, she is offered in a chapter that touches upon the subject of taboo and included in that theme are the issues related to sex, death, fear and power.

The crone is ultimately the one who births herself and, as a wise-woman, she offers the opportunity to receive and re-view the world through different eyes; wiser, all knowing eyes, that can reflect back to a long life filled with experiences and monumental reference points that shed invaluable spirit filled wisdom. Yes, she is indeed a midwife and the real labor unfolds as she reflects back at the culmination of her life experiences and looks forward to birthing the space for this new era as she enters into herself and the archetype of the Crone.

More of Baba Yaga and her Dark Goddess stature is memorialized in the famous popular Russian tale of "**Vasilisa the Beautiful**" There are numerous versions of this Russian tale that introduces us to Vasilisa and Baba Yaga. The story of Hansel and Gretel also comes to mind as well as a Spanish folktale named, *"Don Octavio"* and "Pedro and the Witch," coming from the Philippines. Below I will try to capture one version of the famous Russian tale as best I can.

"Vasilisa the Beautiful"

Most of the various versions of her tale begin in the same way...

There was once a man and his lovely wife who lived together in a home with their exquisite child, named Vasilisa but one day the wife became very ill and unexpectedly died leaving the man a mournful widower. On her death bed, right before dying, the mother asked to see her daughter. She handed her daughter a tiny wooden magickal doll. She spoke to her daughter about the importance of this doll imbued with love and how it had been passed down to her from her mother. She instructed Vasilisa that the doll would protect and help her in times of need and that she should keep it safe and hidden. In times of distress, she should feed the doll and heed its counsel. The crying Vasilisa took the doll with both hands, trying to logically comprehend her mother's last words. She then embraced her dying mother for the last time before death snatched her away. Many mournful years passed for her before Vasilisa even remembered the doll, her mother's instructions or the doll's intended purpose.

Life without his wife became very difficult for Vasilisa's father. He was required to make numerous business trips and eventually he realized he needed to find a new wife to help with the maintenance of his home and rearing his beloved only daughter. At the time, there weren't too many available women in their village. He didn't have much of a selection to choose from, but he took on a widower who already had two daughters that were older than Vasilisa. The news of her father's engagement was dreadful to Vasilisa, especially because he would be marrying the well-known village's shrew, named Lilya, but she tried to accept this turn of events. In time her father remarried Lilya and brought the daughters along with his new bride to move into their home with Vasilisa. Life changed drastically for Vasilisa as a result of this marriage. This new wife did not look too kindly to her stepdaughter, as Vasilisa was beautiful and well-loved by everyone in the community. It was hard to find potential suitors for Lilya's aging daughters, as every young man that came by the home only wished to see and court the young and beautiful Vasilisa. As time progressed the stepmother grew more frustrated, resentful and intolerable of her stepdaughter. Daily she showed preference for her own children while slowly denying her stepdaughter a mother's care and affection. Often she would yell at her and order her around the house to do various harsh and laborious chores but Vasilisa, with her blessed wooden doll, was well protected. This doll, when petitioned with a small morsel of food, would often comfort her and magickally do the entire chores for Vasilisa. When Vasilisa felt alone and mistreated, she often found comfort in the little wooden doll her mother gave her. It repeatedly made things right and assured her she was truly still loved.

Resentment and disdain for her stepdaughter grew as Lilya could not compete with Vasilisa's beauty and popularity. The thought of getting rid of her became ever more prevalent in Lilya's wicked heart and one day she crafted a plan that would surely get rid of the child.

Vasilisa's father was often absent from the household, away on long business trips and one day he had to take an exceptionally long trip away from home. When Vasilisa was told of this impending trip she begged her father to stay and tried to convince him of the cruelty she was experiencing in the hands of her stepmother and stepsisters but the father had to meet his work obligations. He assured his beautiful daughter that all would be right and perhaps it was all in her mind and that she needed to try to get along with everyone. Despondently, she accepted her father's request and watched as he left. As one would have expected, the abusive cruelty towards Vasilisa escalated as soon as her father left. Even the nosy neighbors now made notice of how cruel Lilya and her daughters were treating the beautiful Vasilisa. And though they tried to intervene to help the young maiden it only made matters worse as the stepmother began to lie and publicize that Vasilisa's father had abandoned them and would never returned.

Unbeknownst to anyone, the stepmother decided that they would move to the countryside in the middle of the night. She had hoped they would move close enough to the forest, where the infamous old hag, who loved to kidnap and eat children, would surely catch and devour the young Vasilisa. Lilya's plan was revealing itself, as she had hoped to feed her to the old Hag of the Forest, Baba Yaga.

Vasilisa during this painfully abysmal time relied on her magick wooden doll and it reassured her that her father loved her and had not abandoned her at all and thus she stayed hopeful and happy. Although she was sent often to work and fetch things in the deep frightening forest, she always returned safe and sound, much to her stepfamily's chagrin. Unbeknownst to anyone, the wooden doll her mother gave her, kept her well protected and safe during these frightening sojourns. One night however, the wicked stepmother and stepsisters orchestrated a plan to get Vasilisa eaten by the ill-reputed Baba Yaga once and for all. Late at night, when the last candle had been blown out in the household, the sisters sent Vasilisa out to the nearest neighbor, to Baby Yaga's hut, claiming a need for a source of light (candle) so that they may fulfill their mother's wishes and chores. Vasilisa was frightened but as always, she found comfort and strength in her mother's wooden doll. Close to her heart she carried it and asked for its counsel and guidance. She was assured that all would be well on the journey, so she continued onward towards the forest.

Vasilisa headed out into the deep dark forest and she walked for what seemed like eternity until she felt hopeless and lost. There was nothing in sight, except for darkness and she began to feel a gripping terror. She walked further deep into the forest and then discovered the house, passed a clearing. It was a wooden hut strangely elevated on chicken legs, with eyes for windows, and a mouth as its door. It was a house strangely animated; appearing as if it had its very own personal soul and entity. The frightened Vasilisa looked around and spied a plethora of scary bones and bright red eyed skulls all around the property and the fence that was made up of corpses. There were animals too; a black cat, vicious geese-swan and a hungry looking dog. Then all of a sudden, she heard the thundering hooves of a horse approaching, it was getting louder, then flying above her, as it went passed Baba Yaga's entryway. She saw the Black Horseman disappearing into thin air as he entered the hut. Eventually she would also see a Red Horseman flying through Baba Yaga's entryway and in the morning she would again hear the hooves of horsemen and watch as a White Horseman would appear to fly into her hut and disappeared into thin air. Vasilisa would later learn that these were Baba Yaga's servants. They were her brightest Dawn, her Red Sun and her Black Dark Night. Vasilisa would also learn that Baba Yaga shared her home with her "Soul friends" and "trusty servants," the herdsman named Koshchey and three magickal hands that would grind the grain for her breads and press the oil from her Poppy seeds.

Standing in the dark of night, Vasilisa finally encounters the bony, hideous looking Baba Yaga as she flew in her spinning mortar and pestle, back to the elevated chicken leg held hut. She utters an incantation to make the hut turned to her, lowered itself, and welcome the hag inside but not before smelling the scent of a Russian nearby. Baba Yaga smelled the child near and confronted her. Terrified at the numerous ghastly sights before her, Vasilisa finds the strength to speak to Baba Yaga and tells her why she is there. Baba Yaga immediately puts the child to work, telling her she will get what she needs and will not get devoured by her, if she completes a number of tasks. Secretly, with her doll in hand, Vasilisa is again comforted and protected by her mother's blessing, as all the daunting tasks the hag had demanded from her were magickally completed by nightfall. Baba Yaga returned from her daily rides on her spinning mortar and pestle to find her house had been cleaned and a large meal prepared for her by the young girl. The old Hag devoured the meal, fit for ten men and laid herself out, dissatisfied that she had nothing to complain about. She gave Vasilisa another series of task for the next day with the same threat, that if she wanted to survive in her hut, she needed to complete these tasks. Baba Yaga indicated that her Poppy seeds needed to be cleared of any signs of the earth and Vasilisa was again required to complete some of the most hideously daunting tasks to gain her freedom. With her wooden doll however, she was able to magickally complete these demands. The poppy seeds were cleaned and now pressed by Baba Yaga's trusty servants, the three magickal hands that had prepared the grain for bread the night before.

When all was done and Baba Yaga had finished her colossal feast she asked the child to finally speak. Vasilisa asked the crone about the three different horsemen she had seen outside. Then Baba Yaga asked how she managed to get these impossible tasks done and the intimidated girl replied simply, with her mother's blessing. This revelation of Vasilisa's mother's blessing sent Baba Yaga into a tiff. *"I cannot have a child blessed by her Mother in my home, away with you..."* I imagine her saying. Baba Yaga claimed that Vasilisa's mother's blessing was actually hurting her bones and she needed to swiftly get out of her hut. Vasilisa hastily tried to get out of the house as quickly as possible but she had not yet received the source of light she was obligated to bring back home. Quickly Baba Yaga pulled one of her red-eyed glowing skulls, propped it on a stick and gave it to the child to give to her stepmother and stepsister for light. Then swiftly the young girl proceeded to get herself out of there and, in darkness, find her way back to the house.

Vasilisa tried to hurry as fast as she could but the journey was long and arduous. She walked for eternity it seemed without any clue or evidence if she was even on the right path but she persevered. The red glowing eyes of the skull, given to her by Baba Yaga, helped shine a light for her but its light went out a few time throughout the long journey, only to come back on as she finally arrived to the doorsteps of the house. When she arrived back home, she found her stepmother and stepsisters looking rather sickly, crouched in a corner in the dark. They had not eaten nor had any form of light since Vasilisa had first left on her journey. Somehow they were unable to maintain a consistent source of light in their house in her absence and they looked horrible. When Vasilisa presented them with Baba Yaga's gift they dismissed and ridiculed it. They poked fun at the maiden for taking so long to return. Then, unexpectedly, the red eyes of the eerie looking skull began to glow brightly and it stared right back at the ungrateful women. Within minutes Lilya and her two daughters caught sight of the skull's enchanted stare and they quickly burned; disintegrating into ashes. Vasilisa, with her pure heart and protected by her mother's love was unscathed by Baba Yaga's final tool of enchantment.

The Russian tale ends with Vasilisa returning to her old home in the village and happily finding her father there awaiting her return. Some claim she would become the love target of the Tzar and later agree to become his loving bride but that goes into yet another fascinating Russian folk tale.

BABA YAGA MUSING & MEDITATION

"...She has a way of showing certain mountains up
for the relatively insignificant molehills they often are..."

Rebecca Vassey, writer for SageWoman Magazine

The Dark Goddess, Baba Yaga, is the shadowy, hidden ugliness that one must admit to before arriving at our destination. She is the test! The painful confrontation of all that paralyzes and scares you is encapsulated in her frightful cackles. She is a mirror to our deepest fears and reluctancies. In the end, she reveals and exemplifies a fearlessness and courage based on simply her truths, for she doesn't sugar coat the battle scars we are expected to courageously endure, if we dare. She is the old crone who has earned the right to tell it like it is without any filters, fears or concerns and this is very scary for most in our society; as the unpleasant is always disguised and relegated to the far off regions of mainstream society. Our fears of the unknown; of death, monstrocities, the sick and the old, is what makes Baba Yaga so fearsome and ugly in our collective consciousness. Her ways are viewed as harshly abrasive or negative, even evil, to those uninitiated, because she doesn't have to make her message pretty, nor acceptable to our esthetic. Our modern day society, that so often likes messages to be delivered neatly in veiled illusions, is ill-equipped to handle the uncensored power of the bold, fearless Crone, who is untamed and immuned to societal manipulations. She stands in her truth, unadorned, alone and sovereign, for she has lived a long life that has garnered her unfathomable gifts. Her eyes pierce through all realms and her lips reveal truths marinated in her oozing rawness and timelessness. She does not need to be ornamented, laced up in pretty pinks or enchanting youthfulness, for those days of endured entrapment have long gone.

Baba Yaga has lived, it seems many lives and played many conventional and unconventional roles and I bet she has also sacrificed a lot in her lifetime in order to survive for so long. And Baba Yaga has seen, experienced and witnessed much in her unnaturally long life. Unnatural...for how many people are able to live many years and outlive their families, communities and even survive being marginalized and relegated to the irrelevant and invisible realm of the near silence.

Her bony, disheveled, hunchback physique is a testament to all she has endured in her lifetime and her frightfully mangled body reflects numerous wounds (emotional, mental, spiritual and physical) as well as the years of battle scars that have rewarded her with wisdom. She has earned the right to be...simply be, in her truth; whether nice or gruesome, clean or disheveled, unadorned, alone and in rags. She is not invested in impressing you or society at large. She simply is and this state of being intimidates many who are unaware, unconsciously living, and many who dare not dream of unearthing their own authentic voice.

You need to meet her to confront that which appears ugly, threatening and downright frightening.... Let the rest of the world stay in sad states of delusions, self-deceptions, states of unconsciousness, complacency and ignorance and paralyzing fears.... You know your life is a Soul journey, cyclical and ever evolving. You have embraced that your life is approaching a major turning point and these are the fires you must now confront to proceed forward. This is the dark forest you must travel through. She is your test and passage of initiation, for you have arrived at the sacred threshold, the edge of her forest. You are ready to be free of all hindrance. And in her spinning mortar and pestle you will find the liberation to just be and fly. Her wisdom expands far beyond your self-imposed limited reality and she will not save you, nor spare you of the truth. Heed her tasks, heed her counsel and she will lead you though the labyrinth of darkness, pain, destruction, rebirth and ultimately into the conquerable. Be prepared to know, what it is you seek and why you must stand before her now.

The journey to her chicken leg elevated, wooden hut is monumental. Beginning the journey alone through this dark forest is an admirable feat, in and of itself, but it is not enough. Arriving at her door steps and courageously demanding to be let in, to face her and your deep rooted fears, is only the beginning of this journey. Come face to face with Baba Yaga and bring your purest of hearts encased within. Come with your sincerest endeavor to know, to heal, to unearth truth, her wisdom, to be guided and to somehow find the spark of light within the darkness. Meet her eye to eye and come with reverence for the one who has immeasurable wisdom and insight to guide you through even the darkest of Labyrinths. Come and confront the archetype of the Crone and welcome Baba Yaga's ancient wisdom.

"Why do you come here?
What do you seek to know from me?" you hear her ask.

"..... Baba Yaga, I am scared... I am scared of failing but most of all, I am scared of succeeding. Oh my... oh dear...I am scared of actually succeeding, it hadn't dawned on me but I am scared of actually achieving my biggest brightest childhood dreams. I am scared of being fully fulfilled, happy and completed. I am scared of meeting myself as this brilliant, talented, well-loved being. It has been such a long time on this expansive, self-defeating road. I've gotten so accustomed to feeling loneliness and failure that they have become comforting familiar friends. Anything else to feel and experience would send me to a frightful place and awaken the intense anxiety so entangled in my self-worth. And I fear the self-sabotaging entity that always seems to creep up at the most expertly orchestrated moments. I need to say goodbye to past failures and ideals that no longer serve me and release the comfort of the painfully outworn. I wish to singe the scripts of the past so that I may be liberated to rewrite new ones..."

"How do you prepare your bones for death, most holy, old wise one? I fear I will die...I will surely die. I know I will... She who has placed herself in the hermitage coffin, the orphaned, the isolated island, the frightened, secluded, lonely one will die and I fear her death. I fear the consequences of her death. I fear the metamorphosis in her absence... I fear what she will demand of me next...I will have nothing to hold on to, nothing to blame for this life and the choices I've made and the ones I was too scared to make. I will have nothing holding me back....no more excuses, for the wings will be exposed and Baba Yaga will say...."*Fly!!!!"* And I will say, "**but...I, I have no wings**" and she will point to the ones that have always been on my shoulders; dusty, neglected, abandoned so long ago. "*FLY*!!!!!" she commands, as she pushes me off her spinning mortar and cackles away..." **"Fly...."**

*She is the archetype of the old, wise crone. She is the Slavic hag and Dark Goddess, who frightens our inner child with her distinctly, gruesome appearance. Her bony hunchback body, her wild silver hair and long warty nose and her shrieking cackles are a frightening depiction of our worst nightmare. She is not someone we typically want to encounter, not the way patriarchy has defined her but she is a force to be reckoned with. Baba Yaga is the crone, a most imperative, crucial invaluable aspect of the Goddess. She is meant to dare you to take a daunting step towards growth and transformation, by initially first confronting her nightmarish appearance. She represents that which is frightening and unknown, as the start of the winter months so often brings a tangible fear of what the frigid weather may bring. We wonder if our harvest will last throughout the next four months and will we confront death and survive. All that we fear but must confront is represented in the hag and she comes into our realm to challenge and build up our courage.

CHAPTER TWELVE
LIBERTY
SHE WHO EMBRACES HER FREEDOM
"Freedom lies in being bold..." Robert Frost

ARTEMIS

*"There is a powerful driving force inside every human being that,
once unleashed, can make any vision, dream, or desire, a reality." Anthony Robbins*

ARTEMIS

ARTEMIS

Virgin, maiden, whole unto herself, Artemis is the Greek Goddess of the Crescent New Moon. She is the Huntress, known in Rome as Diana-Artemis. She is Goddess of the wilderness, Goddess of Archery and the Hunt. Artemis was considered a leader to the Amazons and a patron Goddess to all wild animals, women and children. She is the immortal spirit of the wild, free maiden and her name is derived from the Greek word, *"Artemes"*, which means, healthy and energetic and a reference to strength and vitality –all attributes she exemplifies.

As Lady of Ephesus, she was depicted with a multitude of breast and worshipped more as an ancient, pre-Olympian, Mother Goddess. In Rome she was known as Diana-Artemis, mother of Aradia, and thus, Goddess of the Witches, according to Charles Godfrey Leland.

The Greek Huntress Artemis is associated with the crescent new moon and was often depicted wearing a short tunic and a circlet of the crescent moon upon her brow. Artemis was sometimes viewed as the maiden aspect of Hekate. There are numerous variations of this trinity, but a common one makes Hekate, the crone, symbolized by the dark moon, Selene (a Titaness moon Goddess) as the mother, symbolized by the Full moon, while Diana-Artemis, as the maiden, was symbolized by the crescent.

As a lunar Goddess she shares some characteristics with Hekate and their connection is undeniable. Some text reveals that Hekate was actually a cousin of Artemis because her mother's sister, Asteria, was mother to Hekate. In this cosmology, their great grandmother was the primordial Goddess, Gaia, and their grandmother was the ancient Moon Goddess, the Titaness, Phoebe. Phoebe, interestingly enough, translates as *"light-bearer"* and this is an attribute that all her familial descendants possess.

Artemis was the daughter of Zeus and the Goddess Leto and she was a twin to Apollo-The sun God. Though she herself, as a Virgin deity, never gave birth, she was considered the Goddess of Childbirth, and often called upon by women in the midst of labor. She was immortalized in the writings of her time as the young one who was immediately employed to be her mother's midwife, as the birth of her twin brother proved to be difficult.

According to the well-known myths, documented in the Callimachus, and the Homeric hymn, Artemis was born on the Greek Island of Delos, also known as Ortygia, Isle of Quails. Perhaps this is one reason why she is also known by the name of Cynthia, a reference to her birthplace on Mount Cynthus, in Delos. According to one account, her mother searched tirelessly to find a safe place to birth her children, away from Hera's jealous wrath. Zeus's wife, Hera, had decreed that Leto would not be allowed to give birth anywhere upon the earth, but with some divine intervention, the Greek island of Delos emerged from deep within the sea, as an enchanted island, immuned to Hera's curse. Although there are some variations to this story, Artemis was first born and witnessing her mother's distress and struggles to birth her twin brother. She wasted no time in immediately helping her beloved mother and easing her labor pains. This is one reason why she is so often associated with women and childbirth and the practice of midwifery. In this capacity she is known as, *Kourotrophos*, the nurse for the young and as *Locheia*, the Goddess of childbirth.

Throughout mythology, this maiden Goddess was often seen coming to her mother's aid and protecting various women in distress. She became known as the protector of the hopeless, the vulnerable and the defenseless, such were at the time; children, women, young girls, animals beast, babes. In the tale of Niobids, the Queen of Thebes made the grave mistake of boasting about her fourteen children and comparing her rather fertile birthing abilities, as more superior than that of the Goddess Leto, who had only given birth to one male and one female. For Artemis and Apollo, who loved their mother dearly, this was gravely offensive. They spared no time in defending their mother's honor and succeeded at killing the Queen's children by shooting at them with poisoned arrows. The father, Amphion, completely distraught, killed himself upon witnessing the tragic death of his sons. The Queen, Niobe, and her remaining children were quickly turned to stone by Artemis as they mourned the tragic, demise of their family. It becomes clear in this tragic tale, and numerous other Greek lore, that Artemis, while very protective of the vulnerable and defenseless, could also be just as fierce, unapologetic in her defense and quick to retaliate if offended. A Goddess of swift action, there were many men, as well as women, in Greek mythology that fell victim to her volatile wrath when they dared to fail her expectations.

The Cypress and Laurel wreath were sacred to her, as were the mountains, wilderness and the raw powers found in nature. Here is a Goddess who perfectly exemplified this wild, untamable, raw power. All wild beasts, in her beloved forest, fell under her love and care. Artemis was sometimes known as the stag lover and some of her sacred animals were the deer, bears, horses, hare, and like Hecate- the hounds. She was often associated with bears, perhaps because she too, exemplified the same fiercely, protective nature towards the young, as bears do with their cubs. In many artistic depictions of the Moon Goddess we see her holding her bow and arrows, surrounded by stags, hare, wild beast and dogs. She was indeed the huntress, but engaged in this sport with great reverence. The act of killing an animal, for mere pleasure, was sacrilegious to this Goddess and resulted in her unforgiving retaliation.

All forest animals were under her protective domain, as were young girls. Young maidens were expected to dedicate themselves to her. Traditionally, her devotees would spend a year in her service, prior to marriage. Some of the text of the time reveals interesting rituals young girls performed in her honor, like wearing yellow tunics and mimicking animals in a special bear dance. Numerous priestesses took vows of chastity and exemplified the virtues and attributes of Artemis in their service to her. She was depicted as pure and chaste and demanded her priestesses to also live their lives in the same manner, devoted to her. Her numerous temples were found in Sparta and the town of Brauron and the largest, in Delos, her birth place. At Ephesus in Ionia (Turkey) her temple became one of the Seven Wonders of the World. Her Temple of Ephesus was built around 323BC and therafter; updated and rebuilt numerous times throughout history.

Artemis is the Goddess of the Hunt. Her Archery skills were unmatched and her aim and focus unsurpassed. She did not back down to any man and proudly display her archery skills at every opportunity. It was also apparent, she preferred the company of women, over men. Greek lore reveal that she probably was once in love, with a mortal hunter named Orion, but she vowed never to love again when that love ended tragically and of course, there are various accounts of this tale. Her brother, who was also a fine, competitive archer, engaged her in a little competition one day, which subsequently resulted in her arrow killing the love of her life. According to one myth, Apollo loved his sister greatly and perhaps was jealous of the relationship she was forming with Orion, but some speculate, that he also wanted to protect his sister's chastity. One day he challenged his competitive sister to see if she could hit a shiny target, far away in the distance, near a lake. Artemis, lover of challenges and never one to miss her target, aimed… and unbeknownst to her, she shot the arrow that would inevitably kill Orion – the man she loved.

Although she interacted very little with men, she had an extremely close relationship with her brother, but it becomes apparent through some of the Greek literature of the time, that she also had a special relationship with her father, Zeus. Artemis was always confident, focus, strong willed and very decisive. She displayed these strong attributes at a very young age too. According to the popular Greek writings of the time, by her third birthday she already knew precisely what she wanted as a gift and made her request known to her beloved father, while sitting upon his lap. Without hesitation, Zeus conceded to his bold, confident birthday girl and provided her with the desired bow & arrows, sixty nymphs, as well as stags and hounds, just as she requested at age three. She wanted to be chaste and free of the confinements of marriage and she wanted a silver bow and arrow, like her twin brother. According to the legend, at this tender age, she let it be known that she wanted to reside among the wild, in the mountains and Zeus was only too pleased to comply. The Hellenic Goddess didn't want to wear the traditional attire that women of her time wore. She wanted a short tunic as her hunting attire, which gave her maiden legs freedom to run. She wanted to bring light into the world, in the same way her twin brother did, as God of the Sun, and she was not at all interested in the distractions of love and thus, she was given immunity from Aphrodite's charms.

In Artemis we see the roots of feminism, leadership, sisterhood and the spirit of independence. She embraced being a leader to her clan of nymphs and amazons, yet the young Artemis passionately valued her freedom and those moments of solitude. She fiercely defended her privacy and there are numerous tales of her retaliations on those who dared violate her privacy, especially if they were men.

Artemis was known as a maiden, virgin Goddess because she belonged to no one. The term Virgin, was a title in ancient time, referring to societal position – not necessarily sexual and more than anything it pointed to her autonomy. The Hellenic Goddess was never married and had no known children and thus, she was considered whole unto herself, belonging to no one. In mythology we see how she was fierce and impulsive, if pushed to anger. Often men and some women fell victim to her wrath, if they failed to meet her expectations. Still, this immortal Greek

Maiden Goddess is a champion of women/wommin and exemplifies for us; autonomy, strength and the power inherent in our focus and passionate will. She awakens us to our inner confident maiden; embracing our physical strength, competitiveness, athelitism and the freedom to exist in the world, not by societal standards but by our very own defined tenets. Artemis demanded to live her life on her own terms, unconventionally, not conforming to the traditional roles of women of her time. She is quite a force of empowerment for today's modern women and feminist alike.

*The Greek Maiden Huntress, Artemis is the Goddess of our untamable, wild inner child. Artemis arrives to remind you of your effervescent youth, your inner maiden, running freely and the power intrinsic in youth's fearlessness. Do you remember running as a child, do you remember how it felt....? The Huntress awakens in you the gift of a Maiden's willpower and energy. She stirs your heart to a special connection to the beloved creatures that inhabit the forest. Connect to her exeburant leap, as she beckons you to move, run, jump, dance, engage in a comepetitive sport, and connect to your sacred body no matter your age. The perpetual Maiden, connects you to the value of your physical body unrestrained and liberated, wild & free. The archer's supreme, intense focus begins to take hold now. She is the Divine huntress, whose archery skills and keen focus are unmatched. As her mother's biggest defender, she was also very protective of all women and thus promotes the importance of establishing strong, positive relationships with women within our family and our communities, while also maintaining our freedom and the equally important spirit of Independence.

LESSON ON ARTEMIS

- **Known as:** The GreekVirgin Maiden Goddess Artemis
- Goddess of the Hunt, Goddess of Archery, Goddess of the New Moon, Goddess of the Amazons.
- Patron Goddess to Women, Children, Animals.
- Her name also translates as "protector/safety"
- Virgin meaning: whole unto herself and no one else. It was a word referring to a societal position –not sexuality. She was never married, no known children.
- She was also known in Rome as Diana, Diana Artemis, multi- breasted Lady of Ephesus.
- **Birthplace:** Born on the Greek Island of Delos, she was daughter of Zeus & Goddess Leto (Goddess of Child birthing). She was twin to Apollo-The Sun God. Thus she shares a lot of characteristics with her brother, such as being a light bearer. When she was born, as mythology reveals, she was immediately employed as midwife to assist her mother, who was having a difficult time birthing her twin brother. This is one reason why she is often associated with women and childbirth and is the Patroness of midwifery though she, herself, never had any known children.
- **Her Symbols:** Associated with the Crescent new moon and is often seen as the maiden aspect of Hekate and part of that trinity (maiden, mother, crone). Selene, Hekate, Diana-Artemis many variations on this trinity like Demeter, Kore & Hekate etc... She is Light bearer sharing similar characteristics to Hekate.
  - She became known as the protector of the hopeless and defenseless, which at the time were; children, women, young girls, animals beast, babes etc. Young girls would often dedicate themselves to Artemis and she had numerous priestesses and temples.
  - Her sacred animals were the Stag, Rabbits, Bears, and like Hekate, Dogs, all wild beast and offspring were sacred in her beloved forest. The mountains and the wilderness were sacred to her. Perhaps because she was the known defender & protector of women and the defenseless, she became the Goddess of the Witches as her Roman counterpart, Diana.

- **Her Mythology/stories:** When her mother was ready to give birth she ran into trouble trying to find a safe place to deliver her twins due to Hera's wrath- no one dared assist the pregnant Leto. A magical island (the Greek island of Delos) was made available and there she was able to give birth to Artemis.
  - Through out mythology she was often seen coming to her mother's aid and defending and protecting her, along with other women.
  - Artemis was confident, even at the early age of three, she knew she wanted; her bow & arrow, sixty nymphs, hunting dogs. She wanted to reside among the wild in the mountains. She knew she didn't want to wear traditional dress and wanted her hunting costume as her attire; she wanted to bring light into the world. She did not want the distractions of love and thus she wanted immunity from Aphrodite's charms.
- **Her Gifts:** She was seen as pure and chaste and she expected her priestesses to live in the same way. Artemis valued her freedom and could be quite fierce if angered. She loved her time in solitude but also being a leader, to nymphs and to her clan of Amazons. She was very competitive and no one could match her aim & focus as an Archer; she backed down to no man. The beautiful Callisto was her known, beloved companion. Artemis was self-confident, strong, decisive and loved the company of women.

ARTEMIS

"Authentic freedom is actually the freedom of knowing who you are, why you are here, your purpose in life, and where you are going when you leave here..." Wayne Dyer

IRIS

"It is difficult to free fools from the chains they revere..." Voltaire

IRIS

Iris is the Greek messenger for the Gods, similar to Hermes and Mercury. The Goddess Iris traveled between the earth and the other realms freely to execute her role as Divine messenger. She was often depicted as a winged young maiden. Rainbows are particularly of great significance to her and she is known as a patron Goddess of protection, peace and freedom. Connect to the Goddess Iris to awaken your inner freedom loving, adventuresome, youthful spirit. Delve into your inner maiden with Iris and consider taking a trip to a far off land. The rainbow is a powerful symbol of hope, after surviving dark turbulent storms. Spend some time reflecting on the imagery of a colorful bright rainbow (you may even paint one) and note what emotions it conjures up. The Goddess Iris can sometimes be seen as the personification of the rainbow; bringing us hope, freedom and peace.

*"The task ahead of you is never greater than the strength within you."*Anonymous

"Take care of your Body. It's the only place you have to live..." Jim Rohn

"There's no greater freedom
than the freedom to be yourself.
Give yourself that gifts and choose to surround yourself
with those who appreciate you exactly as you truly are... "
Doe Zantamata

ERZULIE-DANTOR

Erzulie-Dantor is part of an assemblage of powerful iconic Voodoo Lwa, known as Erzulies. They are loa, also known as Mysteres that dedicate themselves to the realm of love, sex and the arts. There are numerous Erzulies in Haitian Voodoo but for the time being we will focus on Erzulie-Dantor and occasionally make mention of her sister Erzulie-Freda who is very much a part of her history and folklore.

In Voodoo, there are the Loas, spirits, Gods, (and forgive me for I will tend to use these term interchangeably, as I address loa as Gods and mean no disrespect by doing this). I understand the Loa in Voodoo are viewed as mysteres and living spirits and since this too is my definition of Goddess and Gods I will often use the term in regards to loas. The loa are divided into nanchons (nations) or groups. There are several Voodoo nanchons like the Ghede, Nago, Djab and the two we'll speak about here are the Rada Loa and the Petwo or Petro Loa. Some make the mistake of viewing these two nanchons as good and evil or light and dark but (according to author and Houngan, Kevin Filan) it is probably most effective to view them as Hot and Cold spirits or pantheons.

The Rada, which contains the loa; Erzulie-Freda, La Sirene, Atibon Legba, Dambhala Wedo, Agwe Tawayo are considered cold, balanced, stable and beneficent. They are sometimes related to royalty and are familiar in nature. Their lineage is traced to West Africa; sometimes Dahomey, which is now considered Benin, Africa. The Petwo Loa are considered hot, spicy, volatile, warrior-like, and become aggressive and quick to take actions. They are connected to military and also foreigners. Erzulie-Dantor, Ogou, Maynette and Ti-Jean loa fall under this nanchons. Red is their color and there is no question of their mars-like intensity. They are even honored on a day ruled by Mars, Tuesday. The Petwo loa's origins are found in some parts of Africa, like the Congo, and the New World (Americas), which is why so many of them retain some of their slavery attributes. Erzulie Dantor's origins would therefore be linked to Africa but more obvious is her connection to the new World, in Haiti.

Erzulie Dantor (Dantor, Danto, Ezili-Danthor, Ezili-Dantor etc...) is embraced as the Patron Loa/Goddess of New Orleans and the one who protects the newly initiated Priest/Priestess (Mambo and Houngan) in Voodoo. She is also considered to be a part of the Orthodox practice of Voodoo. She is a Warrioress, fierce Mother, protectress of women and children. As a Loa of the Petwo type, she is so strong and aggressive, sometimes even feared for her boldness, that some have even labeled her as a loa from the "Djab," which translates as Devilish or connected with sorcery and magick. Others can view this reference to her as simply that she is a fierce loa/Goddess, who exemplifies the "bitch" and is not one to be trifled with or approached haphazardly. She is known to exercise retribution when supplicated by her worshippers and she is a great defender of those women who have been abused or betrayed by their lover.

Erzulie Dantor's manifestation is linked and attributed to a very important historical period in Haitian history, as has been documented by numerous sources. It is believed that the Haitian Revolution began with Erzulie Dantor's manifestation at a Voodoo ceremony taking place in Bwa Cayman (Bois Cainman), Cainman Forest in 1871. There are some minor conflicting tales regarding the details of this night, for some say it was the spirit of Ogou that manifested, but a more popularly accepted belief among Voodoo practitioners is that Dantor was the spirit that made herself known on that fateful night.

At this particular time in Haiti there was much political unrest, resentment and anger among the citizens of the French Colony, known then as Saint-Domingue before the revolution. The land was one full of riches; producing sugar, coffee, cocoa, tobacco, indigo, cotton, sisal, fruits and vegetable to its mother land, France. Although it was a rich, fertile land, it was France and its greedy royalty that was benefitting distastefully due to Slavery. Citizens of Saint-Domingue were white, European, black African slaves, mulattoes, maroons (escaped slave blacks), free blacks, white slave owners as well as blacks and there was a lot of anguish and hostilities towards Europe's control on this rich land and its multi-raced people. It is important to note that the French Revolution (1789) and the dethroning of Marie Antoinette and Louis XVI must have also influenced this capricious, turbulent period in Haitian history.

These were unpredictably volatile and unstable times. Many Haitian slaves of African descent were being abused and even killed by their masters without any retribution or just consequence. There was mounting frustration, anger and resentment by the growing number of Blacks who were actually beginning to outnumber white citizens. It would not take much effort to push something that was clearly already on the edge of transpiring. Although the Haitian Revolution is documented as occurring from 1791 till 1804, its inception clearly began much earlier, but one particular documented event, catapulted Haiti's metamorphosis and eventual liberation.

Many disgruntled citizens; blacks, African descendants, slaves and maroons, were already gathering regularly trying to organize themselves but with little success. The evening of August 14, 1791, a Petwo loa Voodoo ceremony was taking place at Bois Caiman, (Alligator woods) led by the maroon Houngan, Dutty Boukman. At this particular ceremony, according to legend, a priestess drew down the spirit of Erzulie-Dantor. As Dantor rode her serviteur she took her favorite form of offering, a Black pig, slit its throat and proceeded to have all participants' drink of its blood, while simultaneously inciting courage and the warrior's energy and confidence to these otherwise oppressed citizens of Saint-Domingue. Most present at this ceremony were of African descent, brutally suffering at the hands of European enslavement and Erzulie-Dantor ridding her serviteur rallied them to fight...fight for their freedom, fight for their humanity, banish the French and establish for themselves, the "Free Black Republic of Haiti." A week later, on August 21st, 1791, the Haitian Revolution had begun with unspeakable acts of courage and violence, massive killings, incineration of Haiti's lush land and a horrific revolution that would last for thirteen years before Haiti could declare itself the victor and finally free of France. It is only the second colony, next to the U.S.A. that was able to successfully free itself from the tyrannical, oppressive restraints and enslavement of a European country; its connection to Erzulie-Dantor is considerably monumental. Dantor can be seen as the liberator and mother of the "Free Black Republic of Haiti."

The Revolution is also attributed to Dantor being mute. There are two different stories explaining how she became a mute. One claims that her own people cut out her tongue in fear that she would divulge their secrets if caught, captured and tortured to speak up by the enemy and it was a necessary sacrifice to protect and maintain their spiritual practices. Others say that she was indeed a victim of the Revolution and that the opposition abducted her and she was brutally tortured by these soldiers. They mutilated her by chopping off her tongue for being a part of that ceremony and instigating this civil war. The "Ke, ke, ke, ke, ke, ke, ke," clicking of her tongue is the only sound you'll hear from her when she rides her serviteur nowadays in Voodoo rites. She is also known to spit out and vomit blood from her mouth, when she is in possession of her horse, her serviteur. This can be quite frightening for the uninitiated to witness but there is an explanation for it.

According to one Haitian Lore, Dantor was a savvy Business woman who actually sold Black Pigs (native to Haiti) at the marketplace in Port-Au-Prince. One day, she was attacked by a man and legend has it she was stabbed seven times, which is why you will find references to her being stabbed seven times in many of her songs, invocations and poetry. There is also a belief that her spitting or vomiting of blood is, again, related to the torture she underwent by the hands of the French. For each of the seven stabs she endured by the hands of her captors, she spat blood at them.

Set kout kouto, set kout pwenya,
Prete m dedin a pou m al vomi sang mwen,
Set kout kouto, set kout pwenya,
Prete m dedin a pou m al vomi sang mwen,
Sang mwen ape koule.

Seven stabs of the knife, seven stabs of the dagger,
Lend me the basin, so I can vomit my blood,
Seven stabs of the knife, seven stabs of the dagger,
Lend me the basin, so I can vomit my blood,
My blood is pouring down...

This very revealing and well known Haitian song is about the Petwo Iwa, Dantor and it is included in VoodooMystic's website page created by Bon Mambo Racine Sans Bout Sa Te La Daginen as well as the Book, "Mama Lola: A Vodou Priestess in Brooklyn," by Karen McCarthy Brown, University of California, 2001

*"As the spirit of light in darkness she comes to break the chains of those
who live in the prison of unconsciousness and
restores them to their true home...*

"The Cult of the Black Virgin, by Ean Begg." Page 134,

Despite the numerous tragedies surrounding her manifestation and her life, she is far from being a victim and instead is worshipped as someone who exemplifies strength and opens the gateway to our own inner strength and endurance capabilities. She awakens in us the fighter, the warrioress, the survivor that she herself is. In such an impoverished country, where daily living presents so many obstacles and challenges to ones very own precious livelihood, Erzulie-Dantor is a remarkable loa/Goddess of fierce hope, determination and strength. Many say that she is a mystere who will fight for you with all her heart and soul and that she doesn't require much in exchange, unlike other loa. She only requires that you not pity yourself and crawl away in fear but rather, to take action, when action is needed, and value yourself enough to fight... fight for what is yours... just as she incited Haitians to fight for their country and re-claim it as theirs. She want you to embrace your worth and take action. She is a fierce mother, a warrioress and protectress, who is particularly protective of all women and children; especially women who have been raped, violated and abused by men and single mothers trying to provide for their children.

Impoverished conditions in Haiti requires many men to travel far to find work, sometimes even forced to leave the country (going to U.S.A. and the adjoining country Dominican Republic) to find ways to generate income. This creates a society brimming with numerous abandoned wives (or mates, as actual marriage ceremonies were not as popular, nor necessary in Haiti). This creates a society filled with single mothers left alone with their children, having to find a way to carry on and feed their kids during their father's absence. Erzulie-Dantor is therefore one who is very sympathetic to the struggles of woman, especially financial and she is quite moved to defend women and become invested in women's issues, especially those unique issues plaguing mothers and their children in today's day and age.

Erzulie-Dantor herself is known to have seven children. One of her daughter's, "Anais," is her personal translator and interpreter since she is mute. Anais is often depicted being carried in her mother's arms, holding a book, in a very popular Black Madonna depiction. Erzulie-Dantor also has a son, named Ti-Jan with one of her spouses, Ti-Jean. And some within Voodoo make her and her husband, Ti-Jean, the beloved respective mother and Father of the Petwo Loa nation. She actually had two known husbands; however, they were Simbi Makaya (a Magician) and Ti-Jean (the Herbal magician). Baron Samedi the Lord of the dead and cemeteries and Ogou, the warrior, are also two other lovers, Erzulie-Dantor is often linked with.

Some say she is a Patron Goddess of Lesbians, though there is no mention of her being one, except that she is very bold, strong, aggressive and, again, exclusively very sympathetic to women's struggles and issues. I suppose these can be viewed as the perfect marker for a Goddess embraced by the Lesbian community, but certainly it is not a requirement to worship her.

In contrast to her sister Erzulie-Freda, Erzulie-Dantor is not as Frilly in pink, ultra-feminine nor overtly romantics. She is a warrior Goddess, loa, mystere, who concerns herself with survival, strength, passion, sex, and the empowerment of women. You will find her dressed, not in the pink lace Chantilly that her Sister Erzulie-Freda donnes, but in the blue denim dresses (known as karabel in Haiti) of the common folks. She will also sport on her head a calico "moushwa" (headscarf) or a red handkerchief and always carries a dagger, as she has a great passion for knives, swords and daggers. Any altar dedicated to her would not be complete without displaying some sort of dagger for her.

Images of Erzulie-Dantor always reveal her cheeks scarred with two slashes, also known as "Twa mark" (three marks) even though only two slashes are visible. There are some conflicting stories behind these noticeable brutal scars on her face. Some say they are probably just indicative of the common sacred scarification that identifies certain African tribes and these scars might connect her to her roots in the Congo. Others note how similar these scars are to the warrior face painting that most indigenous tribes, like the Tainos, would wear prior to going into battle and since she is a warrioress this makes perfect sense. However, a more common explanation for these scars can be found in Haitian folklore that would also explain the rivalry between her sister, Erzulie-Freda.

According to one lore, Erzulie-Dantor and Erzulie-Freda both fell head over heels in love with the charismatic warrior Loa, Ogou. These scars are the result of an intense fight where

Erzulie-Dantor took her dagger and stabbed her sister through the heart (which explains Freda's popular image as the Mater Delarosa) and Erzulie-Freda in turn then took her dagger and slashed her sister's face a few times. This fight would also explain why many Voodoo Priest, Houngan/Mambo stress the importance of having separate peristyle (ritual spaces or rooms) for these two powerful loa. It is not wise to serve or worship these two Sisters together, as they do not get along and your wanga (magick) will suffer as a result, according to Voodoo practitioners. Their respective Veve are also reflective of this connection with swords and daggers and the heart. One of Dantor's veve is a Heart with two daggers piercing through it.

Regarding the origins of the scars there is also a legend related to the original icon of the Black Madonna of Czestochowa, which is one of the most popular depictions of Erzulie-Dantor. It is alleged that a while back, in Poland, where this venerated icon was maintained, vandals caused damaged to the face of the painting of the Black Madonna and it resulted in these noticeable slashes upon the holy image of her right cheek. Despite numerous restorations the scars would always miraculously reappear and so to this day, when her image is reinterpreted and recreated authentically, those slashes are always revealed for they are a part of her lore and history.

While Erzulie Freda is often depicted as white or light skinned, Dantor, however, was often depicted darker; either as a mulatto woman or black, as in the numerous Black Madonnas, found scattered throughout history. Commonly accepted images of her can be found in the Mater Salvatoris, Our Lady of Perpetual Help, Santa Barbara Africana, Our Lady of Mount Carmel and Our Lady of Czestochowa. Erzulie Dantor as a patron Loa of New Orleans is also connected to Our Lady of Lourdes, since she too, is patron Saint of New Orleans in the U.S.A. There are some lore that also connects her to heavy rainstorms, hurricanes and natural disasters and this is slightly reminiscent of the Orisha, Oya, worshipped in Santeria.

The Black Madonna of Our Lady of Czestochowa is a beloved image often associated with Erzulie-Dantor. It reveals a dark skinned woman dressed in a dark blue robe, crowned as the Virgin Mary along with her child. She is holding her baby who has a book in her left arm. This image of the Virgin holding baby Jesus is believed to be Erzulie-Dantor with her daughter, not the baby Jesus so evangelized by Christians. And this image has been highly venerated in Poland since the late 1300's. Perhaps this holy image arrived to Haiti's shores when Polish soldiers came to fight with and against the French, alongside with the Haitians during the Revolution. Haitians immediately recognized in this image their beloved Loa, mama Dantor.

"It is, however, no longer shocking, to suggest that the images
represent a continuation of Pagan Goddess- worship,
and that some may have once been idol concentrated to Isis or other deities.
It is also undeniable that a remarkably high proportion
of Madonnas over 200 years old, that are credited
with miraculous powers, are Black,
as are the traditional patronesses of nations provinces and cities."

"The Cult of the Black Virgin, by Ean Begg" Page 130

August 15th is the Asumption day-The Virgin Mary is celebrated and
July 16th is Erzulie-Dantor's Feast Day
The Black Madonna of Czestochowa's feast day is on August 26th

The origins of this famous icon are mysterious but according to several sources the Byzantine icon was originally painted by St. Luke the Evangelist, who lived during the same time period as the Christian, Virgin Mary. He painted her likeness on a cypress table top alleged to have been owned by the holy family and handcrafted by Jesus himself when he was a carpenter and an apprentice to Saint Joseph.

Research reveals that the icon was kept hidden in Jerusalem by the disciples during the Roman's reign, fearing it would be destroyed but around 326 A.D. the icon was found again by St. Helena, mother of Constantine the Great, who took it to Constantinople. She then either gives it to her son or delivers it herself to Constantinople, where a special shrine is built for it among several other relics. It eventually went through various different owners and was housed by many, including the prince of Ladislaus of Opole. When his fortress was invaded by Tartars and their arrows had pierced and damaged the throat region of the painting, he sought to save and preserve it immediately. Some even claim he was guided by angels in dreams to have the precious icon safely sent to Czestochowa, Poland. He surrendered the painting to the Pauline monks and had it moved to Czestochowa, where it arrived on August of 1382 and remains to this day in Jasna Gora (translated as Bright Hills). In 1383 the Jasna Gora monastery was created by Pauline monks, who had originally hailed from Hungary, and had been invited to create this special monastery by Wladyslaw, Duke of Opole.

In 1430, when the church of Czestochowa was invaded by looters, although many sources claims it was the Hussites that ransacked the Pauline monastery where the holy icon was being stored, the painting received more damage. According to one legend, the thieves ended up slashing the cheek region on this painting twice and there is a renowned folklore that tells of the severe punishment they experienced, as they tried to steal this icon and further damaged it with an unsuccessful third slash. According to popular folklore, the robbers fell to the ground, writhe in severe agony and quickly met their death. Another legend tells that the painting of the Madonna started to bleed actual blood at the place where the gashes had been executed. It was enough to scare the robbers and eventually spread the word of her great powers.

The icon of the Black Madonna of Czestochowa, is so often associated with Erzulie-Dantor, has garnered a reputation throughout the centuries for performing all kinds of miracles. To this day people make holy pilgrimages to visit and view this icon reputed to answer prayers and bring about all kinds of documented miracles.

In 1656, after frightening the Saracens from invading the land, Poland finally declared the Black Madonna as their Queen. In a ceremony held at the Cathedral of Lviv, the Black Madonna was there finally crowned and formally declared as Queen protectress of Poland, on April 1, 1656, by the King of Poland, Jan Kazimiertz.

The Song; Black Madonna,

> There is a recess on this earth,
> Where everybody wants to come back,
> Where reigns Her face,
> On the face – two cut scratches,
> Eyesight has sorrowful, anxious,
> Like She wanted to ask you,
> You to entrust yourself to Her Protection.

Madonna, Black Madonna,
How it is good to be Your child,
O, allow, Black Madonna,
To be hidden in Your arms.

In Her arms you will find peace
And you will be protected from evil,
Because for all of Her children,
She has loving heart and she will protect you,
When you give Her your heart,
When you will repeat these words:

Madonna, Black Madonna,
How it is good to be Your child,
O allow, Black Madonna,
To be hidden in Your arms.

Today, when trouble is around us,
Where a person can hide herself,
Where a person should go,
If not to the Mother,
who will give consolation.
So, we are beseeching , O, Madonna,
Direct eyesight on Your children
And hear, when we are singing , asking you:

Madonna, Black Madonna,
How it is good to be your child,
O allow, Black Madonna,
To be hidden in Your arms.

From; www.catholicculture.org/culture/library/view.cfm?recnun2996, www.marypages.com/czestochowa.htm, www.Czestochowa.pl/welcome *and*

www.jasnagora.com, *www.enwikipedia.org/wiki/Black_Madonna _of Czestochowa,*

(I don't know the original author of this poem to the Black Madonna but it fits perfectly for Dantor....It was attained from http://www.Marypages.com/Czestochowa)

Her Worship, Offerings and Altar Set Up

    Serving Erzulie-Dantor is quite simple as she is a Loa that welcomes her vodouisant/worshippers and, unlike her sister Ezulie-Freda, who loves all things pink; her preferred colors are Navy Blue and Gold or yellow. Sometimes red is added because, after all, she is a Petwo Loa. Her colors reflect her beloved connection to the Revolution and to Haiti's independence and thus, she shares in their flag color of blue, red and gold. And because she is a hot Petwo loa, it is suggested to first begin all workings for her with a goblet of cool water to keep her from getting too hot. An altar decorated with her sacred colors, via various altar cloths, flowers, candles, even the food (like the icing on a cake offering) can display her favorite colors. Practitioners of Voodoo spare no expense when it comes to their exquisite altars and rites and they really lay out ostentatious spreads for their loas. Erzulie Dantor's altars should have daggers as these are sacred to her, as well as maraccas or calabash, dolls and silver jewelry, as this is her preferred metal of choice. She also enjoys the perfume Reve D'Or and Kleren or Aguardiente. And of course, no Voodoo altar would be complete without some Florida water on hand, as this is reputed to bring on spiritual possessions.

Food offerings, which are an important part of Voodoo rites, are also offered to Erzulie-Dantor. She is particularly fond of cane liquor, sweet potatoes and among her preferred offerings are the Griyo (fried pork). She loves unfiltered cigarettes, grilled pork, and rice, red or black beans. Cakes, with blue and yellow frostings, would also be appropriate on an altar dedicated to her. Black pigs are incorporated in rituals to her in Haiti, perhaps due to her folklore connection to this animal and the tales surrounding that infamous Voodoo Rite that started the Haitian Revolution. She is also noted for appreciating the offering of a spicy Haitian Dish made with marinated fried Pork cubes. Other common offerings to her are pan fried corn with pepper, fried bananas, black rice made with mushroom (also known as Riz Djon-Djon). And of course, serve her rum, red wine or honey with cinnamon and pepper, for as you can see, a hot Petwo loa requires hot spicy food offerings. Brown Grain Breads can be used in place of animal offerings if you are a vegan and opposed to these meat offerings according author and Houngan, Kevin Filan and Sallie Ann Glassman but I feel it's best to respect the culture and their lore and serve the loa what they would appreciate regardless of your own personal dietary preferences.

When preparing your food offerings for the Loa it is suggested to first lift up the food (or food dish) over your head in a sign of offering, then lower it to your lips, breathe on the actual food, pouring your essences over it. Then elevate it to your forehead, then to your heart chakra and finally to your root chakra or pubic region to bless it. Next, one should pour three drops of crème de cacao on the ground and then place your food offerings to Erzulie-Dantor and verbalize your gift to her. Light your Voodoo candles around these food offerings. Allow your offering to surround your Voodoo candles and let it melt over it, burning all night if possible. The next day gather all remnants and these should be disposed of at a crossroad or wilderness, where hopefully it will not be disturbed by humans and will become compost for the earth.

Interesting to note, early Voodoo ceremonies allowed food offerings to be given to the animals whose blood would eventually be sacrificed to the Gods. This prepared and consecrated the animals for the Divine.

To begin your Voodoo rite to Erzulie-Dantor, begin by calling on your highest Divine deity. Most in Voodoo will begin by reciting the Lords'prayer (the Our Father) and the Hail Mary. Afterwards, as no loa can cross the threshold into this realm without the help of Legba, the guardian of the Crossroads, you would be wise to invoke him and respectfully ask him to open the gates so that spiritual communion may take place. Be sincere in your petition and present an offering to him on the earth. Papa Legba will open the gates and allow for divine interaction to bless your rite from this moment onward.

The center of the peristyle (the Voodoo ritual room) holds a large erect pole at the very center. It is considered a Divine axis, the sacred pole, which is reminiscent of the ancient Canaanite Asherah; this center pole is the axis. It is through this pole that heaven and earth meet and we can begin to have access to the spirits/Loa, for it is believed they travel through this pole to grace worshippers (vodouisants) with their presence. Spiritual possession, which is a common occurrence in Voodoo, is encouraged and very much a part of all Voodoo rites.

Erzulie Dantor, as a patron and protectress of those first initiated into Voodoo, is often invoked during a Kanzo, this is a special Petwo rite of initiation. She is also the patron of the "paket," which is a special power object made under the guidance of the Hougan/Mambo for the newly initiated Voodoo Priest/Priestess. "Bat guerre" or "Bat Ge" is the ceremony that comes before the initiation or Kanzo Ritual and it is the opening ceremony of a Voodoo initiation rite. All these rites fall under her domain as a Petwo Loa and this also includes the creation of the "paket."

Other Rituals for Erzulie Dantor

For a Voodoo money ritual, a website called "Roots without End" suggests putting your candle within a boiled sweet potato, pour Crème de Cacao and let it burn. It is also suggested to offer frenetic dances to Dantor, as she greatly appreciates movement and dance as a form of worship. There is another simple ritual incorporating a request to the Warrioress loa, written on a sheet of blue and gold decorated paper. Fold this paper with your written wishes and then, with your dagger or special knife, stab it seven times in her name and declare your wish done!

Musing

Erzulie-Dantor exemplifies for us the spirit of the true protectress and fierce warrior. She elevates the spirit of humanity with inspiration and confidence to go into battle, wherever those battles may be; whether in a country facing turmoil and fighting for its independence or in the privacy of ones' home, while asserting liberties and basic human rights. Her validity and importance for us today, is just as relevant as it was centuries ago and yet, her aggressive, "hot" energy is so often feared by women who have yet to unearth this aspect within themselves.

Some that may fear her but remember she is a fierce protective mother, first and foremost, to her vodouisant and worshippers, who so often even endearingly refer to her as Mama Dantor. Consider the nature of a Mama bear with her cub, consider your own interactions with those you most love and cherish, what wouldn't you do for them....? Approach her with this view as a protectress mama bear and you will see your fears turn into reverence, great love and appreciation for someone so lovingly invested in your own wellbeing. You are her cub. She would rather bestow to you magickal abilities and wealth but not the lavish, superfluous riches that her sister Freda is so often connected with. She rather bestow to those who serve her, the many opportunities to create riches of all kinds, through jobs and other means. Dantor opens the way to help you make your own fortunes and resolve challenges in unexpected fashion. In this way, she is loa, and yes, a Goddess, who opens the way to reveal opportunities, liberation, strength, courage and confidence to do more than survive but to thrive in pursuit of your most cherished goals.

> *"Our ancient, battered, much –loved, little –understood, Black Virgins*
> *are a still-living archetypal image that lies at the heart*
> *of our civilization and has a message for us.*
> *The Feminine Principle is not a theory but real and it has a will of its*
> *own which we ignore at our peril..."*
>
> The Cult of the Black Virgin, Ean Begg page 134

*Liberator, Erzulie-Dantor, is the awakener of our desire for freedom. In Voodoo, Dantor is the spirit of the revolutionist who incites our courage to stand for what is right and just. She is the Voodoo Loa Mother, who defends her offspring at all cost. She is the fierce, machete/dagger wielding energy of the Dark Goddess. Protectress and defender of women and children, she will go into battle when the only way to be emancipated is to finally fight back. When wars need to be fought she incites the heart with strength and when we must face our abusers and oppressors, she equips us with the courage. Yes, she is a love Goddess like her sister Erzulie-Freda but her energy has a ferocious passion that will bring about monumental changes. She is an advocate for your emancipation and lures you into a transformative journey towards true freedom.

SHINA TSU HIME

Shina Tsu Hime is a Japanese Shinto Goddess connected to the winds and sailing ships. She is the Goddess of Freedom, Movement, Playfulness, and the Fulfillment of Wishes. Her connection to playfulness and the wind explains why rituals involving kite flying are performed in her honor.

Sailors have been known to petition her protection and blessings upon their voyages and because of her many known gifts. Farmers called upon her to bring rain and blow fertile seeds upon their land. She is also known to thwart negative winds and blow away evil. She can almost be seen as the personification of the morning breeze or the one that parts the clouds and scatters the morning fog away. In this way, we see her as the one who allows the light into our world; the bringer of the morning sun. She liberates the sky of darkness so that the light comes forth. It is a beautiful metaphor for our exploration of freedom in this chapter.

Partnered with her consort, Shina Tsu Hiko, she is venerated at the Shinto Temple of Ise Jingu but their main temple can be found in the small Japanese town called, Yamamoto.

"I raise up my voice not so I can shout but so that those without a voice can be heard, we cannot succeed when half of us are held back" Malala Yousafzai

FERONIA

FERONIA

Feronia is the ancient Roman Goddess of Abundance, Fertility, Wilderness, Vitality, and Freedom. In ancient times she was petitioned to grant freedom to slaves most notably during her annual festival, the **Feroniae Festival,** held November 13th.

In Latin, the word, "*Ferus*" means the untamed, crude or, of the field, and uncultured. It is interesting to note that many of her ancient shrines were found in places that would've been considered away from the general population and in the wild, untamed remote parts in nature. Therefore, it is not difficult to see her connection to the wilderness.

As a Harvest Goddess, she received the first fruits in order to guarantee an abundant crop for the year; this was customary for most Harvest deities in ancient times. She had one Temple at the base of Mount Soracte, near Capena and many others near water springs, which is indicative of the types of rites offered to her. She had many known cults and shrines, many of them found near groves and remote areas. Two notable Temples of Feronia were in Aquileia and in Terracina.

Beloved by Plebeians and Freedmen, a surviving inscription at one of her sanctuaries indicates why she is a patron Goddess for Civil Rights and the enslaved. It is said that there is a surviving stone at her Temple in Terracina which states, "*Let deserving slaves sit down so that they may stand up free...*" this according to Roman historian, Titus Livius Patavinus.* *Wikipedia* There is also a reference by an ancient writer, Servius, who documents that there was a Roman Goddess of Liberty named, Feronia or Fidonia. Here we find several supporting evidence that connects Feronia as a Patron Goddess of Freedom. The Roman Goddess Feronia thus becomes a wonderful deity to work with in this chapter as we explore the theme of liberation.

****

GODDESS WOMYN INSPIRED INDEX

*"Character cannot be developed in ease and quiet.
Only through experience of trial and suffering can the soul
be strengthened, ambition inspired and success achieved..." Helen Keller*

**"The World is round and the place which may seem like the end
may also be only the beginning." Rebecca West**

GODDESS and the WOMYN INSPIRED INDEX

ARADIA, HEKATE, HINA, CIRCE
Womyn who follows her intuition

HATHOR, PELE, APHRODITE, LILITH, OSHUN, ERZULIE-FREDA
Womyn who values her Pleasure

ERESHKIGAL, SEKHMET, KALI, MA'AT, DANTOR, SEDNA, THEMIS,
Womyn who seeks retribution and justice

SUPERWOMAN, DURGA, OYA, MACHA, DANTOR, SEDNA, ARTEMIS, KALI, MAUVE
Womyn who unearths her courage

KALI-MA, SEKHMET, OYA, PELE, DANTOR
Womyn who must detonate and destroy to rebuild

UZUME, HATHOR, ERZULIE-FREDA, OYA
Womyn who dances into ecstasy

GAIA, BRIGIT, SARASWATI, NU-KUA,
Womyn who honors her inner Creatress

BRIGIT, HESTIA, HYGIEA, HINA, SEDNA
Womyn who commits to healing

ARTEMIS, SKADHI, UZUME, AMAZONS
Womyn who honors her physical body

HESTIA, HYGEIA, ARTEMIS, SUNNA
Womyn who prioritizes Health and self-care

PELE, EMPOWERED WOMEN, OYA, SEDNA
Womyn who invites change

SEKHMET, KALI, PELE, DANTOR, DURGA,
Womyn who roars and honors her voice

KWAN-YIN, GREEN TARA, YEMAJA, MOTHER-MARY, SOPHIA,
Womyn whose heart flows with compassion

TARA, LIBERTA, ARTEMIS, MACHA, IRIS, DANTOR, FERONIA, IX CHEL, HINA
Womyn who relishes her Freedom

KWAN-YIN, YEMAJA, GREEN-TARA, RHIANNON
Womyn who offers herself the gift of forgiveness

VENUS, APHRODITE, HATHOR, INANNA, ISIS, PELE, LILITH, OSHUN, ERZULIE-FREDA
Womyn who honors her sexuality
Womyn who explores self-love

HINA, HESTIA, IX CHEL
Womyn who values her home and sanctuary

ARTEMIS, SIF, ERESHKIGAL,
Womyn who values community

ARTEMIS, AMAZONS,
Womyn who longs for sisterhood

MOTHER MARY, HESTIA, INANNA, HINA, TARA, KWAN YIN
Womyn who is prayerful and devoted to her spirituality

ARTEMIS, ASHERAH, BOVINIAN, LILITH
Womyn who embrace her wild, primal nature

ODUDUWA, GAIA, NU-KUA, ASHERAH
Womyn who taps into her power as mother and Creatress

WONDERWOMAN, ATHENA, DURGA, KALI, SEKHMET, MACHA
Womyn who taps into her inner warrioress to fight for herself

ATHENA, ARADIA, CIRCE, HEKATE
Womyn who champions her intelligence and cerebral gifts

(Con't)

GODDESS and the WOMYN INSPIRED INDEX

LAKSHMI, ATHENA, ERESHKIGAL
Womyn who is devoted to her financial autonomy

LAKSHMI, VENUS, APHRODITE, BLODEUWEDD, ERZULIE-FREDA
Womyn who sees and values her inner and outer beauty

ATHENA, SKADHI, MACHA, OYA, ERESHKIGAL
Womyn who is goal oriented and embraces working hard

SIF, HINA, CORN-MOTHER, SELU, HESTIA, PERSEPHONE, DEMETER
Womyn who sacrifices for the greater good of all

CORN-MOTHER, SELU, SIF, DEMETER, HAMBODIA, PERSEPHONE
Womyn who nurtures and feeds herself and others

HEKATE, BABA-YAGA, ERESHKIGAL, ISIS
Womyn who embraces the sacred cycles of life and death

LAKSHMI, AMATERASU, HATHOR, ERZULIE-FREDA, OSHUN
Womyn who knows she is worthy of more

ARADIA, HEKATE, HINA, INNANA, CIRCE
Womyn who connect to her Spirituality

BLODEUWEDD, ERESHKIGAL, MEDEA
Womyn who explore her shadows and taboos, Rule breaker

BABAYAGA, HEKATE, MAMAN BRIGITTE
Womyn who recognizes her inner Crone

KALI, DURGA, BABA-YAGA, OYA
Womyn who faces her fears

SUNNA, IRIS, UZUME, KORE
Womyn who dances with her inner child

PERSEPHONE, BLODEUWEDD, SEKHMET, KALI-MA
Womyn who balances her dark and light aspects and the cycle of life

IRIS, SUNNA, UZUME, KORE/PERSEPHONE
Womyn who remains hopeful and optimistic
Womyn who is ready for an adventure

DURGA, OYA, SIF, FREYA
Womyn who is multi-dimensional nature.
Womyn who embraces & shares all of her gifts

RESOURCES & BIBLIOGRAPHY

AINE

Aine - Wikipedia.com Free Encyclopedia

Ancient Mirrors of Womanhood, a Treasury of Goddess and Heroine Lore from Around the World by Merlin Stone

Love Magic, The Way To Love through Rituals, Spells, and the Magical life by Laurie Cabot

Goddess In World Mythology, a Biography Dictionary by Dorothy Myers Imel and Martha Ann

365 Goddess, a daily guide to the magic and inspiration of the Goddess by Patricia Telesco

AMATERASU

Circle Round, Raising Children in Goddess Tradition by Starhawk, Diane Baker and Anne Hill

Goddess Mirror, Visions of the Divine From East and West by David Kinsley

The Book of Goddesses, Past and Present: An Introduction to her Religion by Carl Olson

The Goddess Path, myths, invocations and rituals by Patricia Monaghan

The Goddess Oracle, A Way to Wholeness Through The Goddess and Ritual by Amy Sophia Marashinsky and Hrana Janto

Nihonghi -translated by W.G. Aston

SageWoman No.# 54 Summer 2001, Reclaim Your Power...and Find inner Peace, Too! by Lady Moondance

SageWoman No. #65 Truth and Beauty, Calligraphy lessons by Kela Vaeltaja

Wikipedia internet free encyclopedia

APHRODITE

Ancient Mirrors of Womanhood, A Treasury of Goddess and Heroine Lore from Around the World by Merlin Stone

Ariadne's Thread, a Workbook of Goddess Magic by Shekhinah Mountainwater

Goddess in Every Woman, a New Psychology of women by Jean Shinoda Bolen, MD.

Goddess Mirror, Visions of the Divine from East and West by David Kinsley

Grandmother Moon, Lunar Magic in our Lives by Zsuzsanna E. Budapest

Grandmother of Time by Zsuzsanna E. Budapest

The Goddess Path, myths, invocations and rituals by Patricia Monaghan

The Witches' Goddess, The Feminine Principle of Divinity by Janet and Stewart Farrar

Wikipedia.com

ARADIA

Aradia; The Gospel of the Witches by Charles Godfrey Leland

Grandmother Moon, Lunar Magic in our lives by Zsuzsanna E. Budapest

Hereditary Witchcraft, Secrets of an Old Religion by Raven Grimassi

Italian Witchcraft -the old religion of Southern Europe by Raven Grimassi

The Book of the Holy Strega by Raven Grimassi

The Holy Book of Women's Mysteries by Zsuzsanna E. Budapest

The Witches 'Goddess, The Feminine Principle of Divinity by Janet and Stewart Farrar

Stregherie.com

Witchcraft for Tomorrow by Doreen Valiente

ARTEMIS

An ABC of Witchcraft from Past and Present by Doreen Valiente

Ancient Mirrors of Womanhood, A Treasury of Goddess and Heroine Lore from Around the World by Merlin Stone

Ariadne's Thread, a workbook of Goddess Magic by Shekhinah Mountainwater

Goddess in Every Woman, a New Psychology of Women by Jean Shinoda Bolen, MD.

Grandmother Moon, Lunar Magic in our Lives by Zsuzsanna E. Budapest

Grandmother of Time by by Zsuzsanna E. Budapest

SageWoman No.#57 Spring 2002, One of Then Thousand: Goddess Lore and Ritual article-Artemis, Hunting The Moon by Diana L. Paxson

The GoddessGift.com Artemis

The Holy Book of Women's Mysteries by Zsuzsanna E. Budapest

The Mythic Image Moon Maiden: Young Diana by Wynter Rose Stiles

The Goddess Path, Myths, Invocations and Rituals by Patricia Monaghan

Witches, Investigating an Ancient Religion by T.C.Lethridge

Women's Mysteries Ancient and Modern by M. Esther Harding

ASHERAH

Ancient Mirrors of Womanhood, a Treasure of Goddess and Heroine Lore from around the World, by Merlin Stone, Beacon Press, Boston, Massachusetts, 1979

Goddesses in World Mythology, a Biographical Dictionary, Martha Ann and Dorothy Myers Imel, Oxford University Press, New York 1993

The Book of the Goddess Past and Present, an introduction to Her Religion edited Carl Olson, The Cross Road Publishing Company, New York, New York, 1987

The Hebrew Goddess by Raphael Patai, Wayne State University Press, Detroit Michigan,1990-third enlarged Edition Internet: http://en.wikipedia.org/wiki/Asherah

Internet: "Asherah, the Tree of Life and the Menorah" http://wwww.asphodel-long.com/htm1/Asherah.htm1

Internet: The Goddess in Judaism www.asphodel-long.com/htm4goddess

Internet: "Asherah, the tree of Life" http://www.asphodel-long.com/htm1/asherah.html

Internet: Classical Hebrew.com - http://blog-en.classicalhebrew.com/tag/asherah

ATHENA

Ancient Mirrors of Womanhood, A Treasury of Goddess and Heroine Lore from Around the World by Merlin Stone

Grandmother of Time by Zsuzsanna E. Budapest

Goddess in Every Woman, a New Psychology of Women by Jean Shinoda Bolen, MD.

Goddess Mirror, Visions of the Divine From East and West by David Kinsley

SageWoman No.# 35 Autumn 1996, 10th Anniversary, One of Ten Thousand; Goddess Lore and Ritual- Athene, The Reconciler of Opposites, Article by Diana L. Paxson

The Goddess Path, Myths, Invocations and Rituals by Patricia Monaghan

The Holy Book of Women's Mysteries by Zsuzsanna E. Budapest

Wikipedia.com a free Encyclopedia

BABA YAGA

Baba Yaga – The Ambiguous Mother of the Russian Folktale by Andreas John ($28) 2004, Isbn#13-9780820467696

Balkan Traditional Witchcraft by Radomir Ristic

The Goddess Oracle, a Way to Wholeness Through the Goddess and Ritual, Amy Sophia Marashinsky, Illustrated by Hrana Janto, Element Books, Inc, Rockport, MA, 1997

365 Goddess, a Daily Guide to the Magic and Inspiration of the Goddess by Patricia Telesco, HarperSanFrancisco, a Division of Harper Collins Publishing, 1998

Internet: www.realmagick.com/700 BabaYaga article by Freya

Internet: www.examiner.com/article by Juliet Friette

Internet: www.matrifocus.com/ SAMO/BabaYaga,Susun Weed Article

Internet: www.orderwhitemoon.org

Internet: www.healingwayofrabbit/BabaYaga Part I and Part II

Internet: www.helium.com

Internet: wwww.Blueroebuck.com

Internet: www.7yearoldwitch.blogspot, BabaYaga 2009

Internet: www.Mythling.com

BAUBO

Goddess In World Mythology, a Biography Dictionary by Dorothy Myers Imel and Martha Ann

Goddessgift.com Article on the Greek Goddess of Mirth- Baubo

365 Goddess, a daily guide to the magic and inspiration of the Goddess by Patricia Telesco

Reconnect With Your Inner Goddess.com byAnita Ryan Revel-2000

The Yoni, Sacred Symbol of female creative Power by Rufus C. Camphausen

Wikipedia.com Free Encyclopedia

BENZAITEN

Goddesses in World Mythology, a Biographical Dictionary, Martha Ann and Dorothy Myers Imel, Oxford

365 Goddess, a daily guide to the magic and inspiration of the Goddess by Patricia Telesco

BLODEUWEDD

Goddess Afoot, practicing Magic with Celtic and Norse Goddesses by Michelle Skye, Llewellyn Worldwide Publishing, Woodbury, Minnesota, 2008

Goddesses in World Mythology, a Biographical Dictionary, Martha Ann and Dorothy Myers Imel, Oxford University Press, New York 1993

The Goddess Oracle, a Way to Wholeness through the Goddess and Ritual, by Amy Sophia Marashinsky, Massachusetts, Element Books, 1997

The White Goddess, a Historical grammar of Poetic myth, by Robert Graves, International Authors, N.V. Farrar, Straus And Giroux, New York1948

365 Goddess, a Daily Guide to the Magic and Inspiration of the Goddess by Patricia Telesco, HarperSanFrancisco, a Division of Harper Collins Publishing, 1998

Internet: www.orderwhitemoon.org/goddess/Blodeuwedd2.html

Internet: www.goddessrealm.com/goddess-of-the-moment/16

Internet:: www.mysticwicks.com

Internet:www.paganpages.org/contenttag/blodeuwedd

BRIGIT

Circle Round, Raising Children in Goddess Tradition by Starhawk, Diane Baker and Anne Hill

The Goddess Path, Myths, Invocations and Rituals by Patricia Monaghan

The Wheel of The Celtic Year.com chalice centre.net/imbolc

The Witches ' Goddess, The Feminine Principle of Divinity by Janet and Stewart Farrar

Pan Gaia Exploring the Pagan World No #20 Summer 1999, Brigid in Ireland; Discovering the Magic by Diane Conn Darling

SageWoman No.#46 Summer 1999, One of Ten Thousand: Goddess Lore and Ritual article -Brigit, Inspiration Upwelling by Diana L. Paxson

Wikipedia.com a free Encyclopedia

CIRCE

Pagan Anger Magic, Positive Transformations From Negative Energies by Tammy Sullivan

Goddesses in World Mythology, a Biographical Dictionary, Martha Ann and Dorothy Myers Imel, Oxford

INTERNET: Http: www.Maicar.com/GML/CIRCE.HTML

INTERNET: Http: www.Greekmythologydotcom

INTERNET: Http: www.Theoi.com/Titan/Kirke

DANTOR (ERZULIE-DANTOR)

Gathering for Goddess, a Manual for Priestessing Women's Circles, by B. Melusine Mihaltses.Publisher; Feminine Divine Works, Schertz, Texas, 2012

Mama Lola: A Vodou Priestess in Brooklyn, by Karen McCarthy Brown, University of California, 2001

Secrets of Voodoo by Milo Rigaud, City Lights Books, San Francisco, CA 1969, 1985

The Cult of the Black Virgin, by Ean Begg Chiron Publishing, Wilmette, Illinois 2006

The Haitian Vodou Handbook, Protocols for Ridding with the Lwa by Kenaz Filan (Houngan Coquille du Mer), Destiny Books, Rochester, Vermont, 2007

Vodou Love Magic, A Practical Guide to Love, Sex, and Relationships by Kenaz Filan), Destiny Books, Rochester, Vermont, 2009

Internet:www.Voodoomystic.com, website page created by Bon Mambo Racine Sans Bout Sa Te La Daginen

Internet:www.squidoo.com

Internet:www.widdershins.org

Internet:www.Mysticvoodoo.com

Internet:www.rootswithoutend.com

Internet:www.vodoureligion.com

Internet:www.Qualiafolk.com

Internet:www.webster.edu/-corbetre/haiti/history/revolution/revolution1.htm,
Internet:http://www.travelinghaiti.com/history_of_haiti/slave_rebellion.asp,
Internet:http://wikipedia.org/wiki/Haitian_Revolution
Internet:www.catholicculture.org/culture/library/view.cfm?recnun2996,
Internet:www.marypages.com/czestochowa.htm, www.Czestochowa.pl/welcome
Internet:www.jasnagora.com, www.enwikipedia.org/wiki/Black_Madonna _of Czestochowa,

DEMETER

Ancient Mirrors of Womanhood, A Treasury of Goddess and Heroine Lore from Around the World by Merlin Stone

Circle Round, Raising Children in Goddess Tradition by Starhawk, Diane Baker and Anne Hill

Goddess in Every Woman, a New Psychology of women by Jean Shinoda Bolen, MD.

The Goddess Path, Myths, Invocations and Rituals by Patricia Monaghan

The Mythic Tarot, a New approach to the Tarot Cards by Juliet Sharman-Burke and Liz Greene

The Witches 'Goddess, The Feminine Principle of Divinity by Janet and Stewart Farrar

DURGA

Goddess Grimoire Journal, a Collection of Simple Prose and Spells, by B. Melusine Mihaltses, Publisher; Feminine Divine Works, Schertz, Texas, 2012

Hindu Goddesses, Visions of the Divine Feminine in the Hindu Religious Tradition, by David R. Kinsley,University of California Press, Berkeley and Los Angeles California, 1988

Hindu Gods and Goddesses by Swami Harshananda, The President, Sri Ramakrishna Math, Mylapore, Madras

Pagan Anger Magic, Positive Transformations from Negative Energiesby Tammy Sullivan, Citadel Press, Kensington Publishing Corp. New York, NY 2005

The Book of the Goddess Past and Present, An introduction to Her Religion, edited by Carl Olson, The Crossroad Publishing Company, New York NY, 1987

The Goddesses' Mirror, Visions of the Divine from East and West, by David R. Kinsley, State University of New York Press, Albany New York, 1989

Twenty-Four Aspects of Mother Kali by Babaji Bob Kindler, SEV Associations, Honoka'a, Hawaii, 1996

Internet: www.philhine.org/uk/wrting

Internet: www.Dollsofindia.com

Internet: lotussculpture.com/Durga.htm

Internet: www.Womeninworldhistory.com

Internet: www.srimatham.com/storage/docs/arjunas-hymn-to-durga

Internet: www.dipika.org.za/index.php?option...hymn...durga

Internet: www.shivashakti.com/durga.htm

Internet: www.hinduism.com

ERESHKIGAL

Inanna, Queen of Heaven and Earth, Her Stories and Hymns from Sumer by Diane Wolkstein and Samuel Noah Kramer, 1983 First Edition

Goddess In World Mythology, a Biography Dictionary by Dorothy Myers Imel and Martha Ann

Goddess Grimoire Journal, a Collection of Simple Prose and Spells, by B. Melusine Mihaltses, Publisher; Feminine Divine Works, Schertz, Texas, 2012

Pagan Anger Magic, Positive Transformations from Negative Energiesby Tammy Sullivan, Citadel Press, Kensington Publishing Corp. New York, NY 2005

The Book of the Goddess Past and Present, An introduction to Her Religion, edited by Carl Olson, The Crossroad Publishing Company, New York NY, 1987

INTERNET: Http: www.Ancient pagesdotcom

INTERNET: Http: www.Ancient dot eu by Joshua J. Mark

INTERNET: Http: www.Mrpsmythopediadotwikispacesdotcom/Ereshkigal

ERZULIE-FREDA

Erzulie, Everyday better living.com by Judi Singleton

Pan Gaia, A Pagan Journal for Thinking People No. #36 Summer 2003 Erzulie Freda,

Mistress of Love by Kevin Filan

Rituals and Spells of Santeria by Migenez, Gonzalez-Wippler

Secrets of Voodoo by Milo Rigaud

Spellmakererzulie.love.com

The Book of Goddesses, Invoke the Powers of the Goddess to Improve Your Life by Roni Jay

The Book of Goddesses, Past and Present: An Introduction to her Religion by Carl Olson

The Haitian Voodoo Handbook, Protocols for Ridding with the Lwa by Kevin Filan

365 Goddess, a daily guide to the magic and inspiration of the Goddess by Patricia Telesco

FERONIA

Goddesses in World Mythology, a Biographical Dictionary, Martha Ann and Dorothy Myers Imel, Oxford

365 Goddess, a daily guide to the magic and inspiration of the Goddess by Patricia Telesco

INTERNET: Http: www.wikipediadotorg

FLORA FLORA

Goddesses in World Mythology, a Biographical Dictionary, Martha Ann and Dorothy Myers Imel, Oxford

365 Goddess, a daily guide to the magic and inspiration of the Goddess by Patricia Telesco

https://www.Britannica.com -Flora-Roman Mythology

https://www.thaliatook.com —Flora, Roman Goddess of Flowers

FORTUNA FORTUNA

Gathering for Goddess, a Manual for Priestessing Women's Circles, by B. Melusine Mihaltses.Publisher; Feminine Divine Works, Schertz, Texas, 2012

Goddesses in World Mythology, a Biographical Dictionary, Martha Ann and Dorothy Myers Imel, Oxford

365 Goddess, a daily guide to the magic and inspiration of the Goddess by Patricia Telesco

FREYJA FREYJA

Goddesses in World Mythology, a Biographical Dictionary, Martha Ann and Dorothy Myers Imel, Oxford

365 Goddess, a daily guide to the magic and inspiration of the Goddess by Patricia Telesco

The Goddess Oracle, A Way to Wholeness Through The Goddess and Ritual by Amy Sophia Marashinsky and Hrana Janto

Norse-mythologydotnet/Freya-goddess-of-love

Northernpaganismdotorg/shrines/Freya/who-is-freya

Scandinavian Mythology, by H R Ellis Davidson

The Cassell Dictionary of Norse Myth and Legend by Andy Orchard

Poems of the Elder Edda, Trans. P Terry

Poetic Edda, Snorri Sturluson, Trans A. Faulkes

GAIA

Ancient Mirrors of Womanhood, A Treasury of Goddess and Heroine Lore from Around the World by Merlin Stone

Circle Magazine, Celebrating Nature, Spirit and Magic Issue 87 Spring 2003 Earth and Spirit: Mother Gaia by Jesse Wolf Hardin

Gaia; A New Look At Life on Earth by J.E. Lovelock

Goddess In World Mythology, a Biography Dictionary by Dorothy Myers Imel and Martha Ann

Green Egg a Journal of the Awakening Earth Vol. 30 No #125 November-December 1998, Gaian Ministry; Reclaiming Earth and Spirit by Jesse Wolf Hardin

People of the Earth, The New Pagans Speak Out by Ellen Evert Hope and Lawrence Bond

Persephone Unveiled, Seeing the Goddess and Freeing Your Soul by Charles Stein

The Book Of Goddesses, Past and Present: An Introduction to her Religion by Carl Olson

The Goddess Path, myths, invocations and rituals by Patricia Monaghan

The Encyclopedia of Magical Herbs by Scott Cunningham

Wikipedia.com a free Encyclopedia

GEFJUN GEFJUN

Goddesses in World Mythology, a Biographical Dictionary, Martha Ann and Dorothy Myers Imel, Oxford

365 Goddess, a daily guide to the magic and inspiration of the Goddess by Patricia Telesco

Scandinavian Mythology, by H R Ellis Davidson

The Cassell Dictionary of Norse Myth and Legend by Andy Orchard

Poems of the Elder Edda, Trans. P Terry

Poetic Edda, Snorri Sturluson, Trans A. Faulkes

INTERNET: Http: www.Norsemythologydot org

HATHOR

Ancient Mirrors of Womanhood, A Treasury of Goddess and Heroine Lore from Around the World by Merlin Stone

Egyptian Gods and Goddess- 4 from Ellie Cystalinks.com

Egyptian Mythology by Veronica Irons

Grandmother Moon, Lunar Magic in our lives by Zsuzsanna E. Budapest

Hathor, the Goddess of Love, Music, Beauty.com by Caroline Seawright

The Book Of Goddesses, Past and Present: An Introduction to her Religion by Carl Olson

The Goddess Oracle, A Way to Wholeness Through The Goddess and Ritual by Amy Sophia Marashinsky and Hrana Janto

The Goddess Path, myths, invocations and rituals by Patricia Monaghan

365 Goddess, a daily guide to the magic and inspiration of the Goddess by Patricia Telesco

Who is the Goddess Hathor? Pyramidcompany.com On the Internet by Rhiannon Barkemeijer de Wit

Wikipedia.com free Encyclppedia

HEKATE

Pagan Anger Magic, Positive Transformations From Negative Energies by Tammy Sullivan

The Witches' Goddess, The Feminine Principle of Divinity by Janet and Stewart Farrar

The Theogony by Hesiod

Homeric Hymn

Grandmother of Time by Zsuzsanna E. Budapest

The Holy Book of Women's Mysteries by Zsuzsanna E. Budapest

Hekate Soteira, a Study of Hekate's Role in the Chaldean Oracles by S.I. Johnston

Who is Hekate? from WitchVox.com by Helena Domenic

SageWoman No.# 39 Autumn 1997, One of Ten Thousand; Goddess Lore and Ritual Article by Diana L. Paxson Hekate Guide of the Soul

HESTIA

Ancient Mirrors of Womanhood, A Treasury of Goddess and Heroine Lore from Around the World by Merlin Stone

Goddess in Every Woman, a New Psychology of women by Jean Shinoda Bolen, MD.

Goddess In World Mythology, a Biography Dictionary by Dorothy Myers Imel and Martha Ann

The Goddess Oracle, A Way to Wholeness through The Goddess and Ritual by Amy Sophia Marashinsky and Hrana Janto

365 Goddess, a daily guide to the magic and inspiration of the Goddess by Patricia Telesco

Wikipedia.com free Encyclopedia

HINA

Goddess In World Mythology, a Biography Dictionary by Dorothy Myers Imel and Martha Ann

Hawaiian Mythology by Martha Berkwith

Hina Adventures.com

Hina, the Woman in the Moon from Legends of Maui, a Demi-God of Polynesia

by W.D. Westervelt also on Sacred text.com

Many Moons, the Myth and Magic, Fact and Fantasy of our Nearest Heavenly Body,

by Diana Brueton

The Order of White Moon Gallery.com presents, The Goddess Hina by Leigh Hall

365 Goddess, a daily guide to the magic and inspiration of the Goddess by Patricia Telesco

The Hawaiian Oracle, Animal Spirit Guide from the Land of Light, by Rima A Morrell, PhD

INANNA

Inanna, Queen of Heaven and Earth, Her Stories and Hymns from Sumer by Diane Wolkstein and Samuel Noah Kramer, 1983 First Edition

Goddesses in World Mythology, a Biographical Dictionary, Martha Ann and Dorothy Myers Imel, Oxford

Goddess Grimoire Journal, a Collection of Simple Prose and Spells, by B. Melusine Mihaltses, Publisher; Feminine Divine Works, Schertz, Texas, 2012

Pagan Anger Magic, Positive Transformations from Negative Energiesby Tammy Sullivan, Citadel Press, Kensington Publishing Corp. New York, NY 2005

The Book of the Goddess Past and Present, An introduction to Her Religion, edited by Carl Olson, The Crossroad Publishing Company, New York NY, 1987

The Goddesses' Mirror, Visions of the Divine from East and West, by David R. Kinsley, State University of New York Press, Albany New York, 1989

ISIS

Egyptian Gods and Goddess- 4 from Ellie Cystalinks.com

Egyptian Mythology by Veronica Irons

Goddesses in World Mythology, a Biographical Dictionary, Martha Ann and Dorothy Myers Imel, Oxford

The Book of the Goddess Past and Present, An introduction to Her Religion, edited by Carl Olson, The Crossroad Publishing Company, New York NY, 1987

The Goddesses' Mirror, Visions of the Divine from East and West, by David R. Kinsley, State University of New York Press, Albany New York, 1989

ISHTAR

Inanna, Queen of Heaven and Earth, Her Stories and Hymns from Sumer by Diane Wolkstein and Samuel Noah Kramer, 1983 First Edition

Goddesses in World Mythology, a Biographical Dictionary, Martha Ann and Dorothy Myers Imel, Oxford

Goddess Grimoire Journal, a Collection of Simple Prose and Spells, by B. Melusine Mihaltses, Publisher; Feminine Divine Works, Schertz, Texas, 2012

Pagan Anger Magic, Positive Transformations from Negative Energiesby Tammy Sullivan, Citadel Press, Kensington Publishing Corp. New York, NY 2005

The Book of the Goddess Past and Present, An introduction to Her Religion, edited by Carl Olson, The Crossroad Publishing Company, New York NY, 1987

The Goddesses' Mirror, Visions of the Divine from East and West, by David R. Kinsley, State University of New York Press, Albany New York, 1989

IRIS

Goddesses in World Mythology, a Biographical Dictionary, Martha Ann and Dorothy Myers Imel, Oxford

365 Goddess, a daily guide to the magic and inspiration of the Goddess by Patricia Telesco

IRENE

Goddess In World Mythology, a Biography Dictionary by Dorothy Myers Imel and Martha Ann

INTERNET: Http: www.Theoigreekmythologydotcom

INTERNET: Http: www.Goddessguidedotcom

INTERNET: Http: www.Greekmythologydotcom

INTERNET: Http: www.Wikipediadotorg

IX-CHEL

Ancient Mirrors of Womanhood, A Treasury of Goddess and Heroine Lore from Around the World by Merlin Stone

Grandmother Moon, Lunar Magic in our lives by Zsuzsanna E. Budapest

Librarythinkquest.org

Ix Chel Wisdom, Seven Teachings from the Mayan Sacred Feminine by Shonagh Home

Mayan Healers-Daughters of Ix Chel by Rozanna Herrera

365 Goddess, a daily guide to the magic and inspiration of the Goddess by Patricia Telesco

The Goddess Oracle, A Way to Wholeness Through The Goddess and Ritual by Amy Sophia Marashinsky and Hrana Janto

SageWoman No. #57 Spring 2002, Coming across The Great Goddess Ix Chel by Bethany Walsh Smith

Wikipedia.com the free Encyclopedia

KALI KALI

Pagan Anger Magic, Positive Transformations From Negative Energies by Tammy Sullivan

The Goddess Oracle, A Way to Wholeness Through The Goddess and Ritual by Amy Sophia Marashinsky and Hrana Janto

365 Goddess, a daily guide to the magic and inspiration of the Goddess by Patricia Telesco

The Cult of the Black Virgin, by Ean Begg Chiron Publishing, Wilmette, Illinois 2006

Goddess Grimoire Journal, a Collection of Simple Prose and Spells, by B. Melusine Mihaltses, Publisher; Feminine Divine Works, Schertz, Texas, 2012

Hindu Goddesses, Visions of the Divine Feminine in the Hindu Religious Tradition, by David R. Kinsley,University of California Press, Berkeley and Los Angeles California, 1988

Hindu Gods and Goddesses by Swami Harshananda, The President, Sri Ramakrishna Math, Mylapore, Madras

Pagan Anger Magic, Positive Transformations from Negative Energiesby Tammy Sullivan, Citadel Press, Kensington Publishing Corp. New York, NY 2005

Twenty-Four Aspects of Mother Kali by Babaji Bob Kindler, SEV Associations, Honoka'a, Hawaii, 1996

KUAN-YIN

Goddesses in World Mythology, a Biographical Dictionary, Martha Ann and Dorothy Myers Imel, Oxford

The Goddesses' Mirror, Visions of the Divine from East and West, by David R. Kinsley, State University of New York Press, Albany New York, 1989

Https://www.Holymtn.com-Legend of Quan Yin

https://www.Goddess.ws

LAKSHMI

Healing Mantras, Using Sound Affirmations for Personal Power, Creativity and Healing, by Thomas Ashley-Farrand, A Ballantine Wellspring Book- The Ballantine Publishing Group, New York, New York, 1999

Hindu Gods and Goddess by Swami Harshananda, printed in India; Sri Ramakrishna Math Printing Press, Mylapore, Madras

The Book of Goddesses, Invoke the Powers of the Goddess to Improve Your Life by Roni Jay, A Quarto Book, Baron's Educational Series, Inc. Hauppauge, New York, 2000

The Book of the Goddess Past and Present, an introduction to Her Religion edited Carl Olson, The Cross Road Publishing Company, New York, New York 1987

The Goddesses' Mirror, Visions of the Divine from East to West by David Kinsley, State University of New York Press, Albany, New York 1989

The Goddess Oracle, a Way to Wholeness through the Goddess and Ritual, by Amy Sophia Marashinsky, Massachusetts, Element Books, 1997

Internet: Goddess Lakshmi by Bansi Pandit at wwwkousa.org/Gods/God6.html

Internet: Lakshmi Goddess of Wealth and Beauty, by Subhamoy Das, About.com

Internet: www.freemeditationinfo.com

LILITH

Ancient Mirrors of Womanhood, a Treasure of Goddess and Heroine Lore from around the World, by Merlin Stone, Beacon Press, Boston, Massachusetts, 1979

Goddess Grimoire Journal, a Collection of Simple Prose and Spells, by B. Melusine Mihaltses, Publisher; Feminine Divine Works, Schertz, Texas, 2012

Inanna Queen of Heaven and Earth, Her Stories and Hymns from Sumer, by Diane Wolstein and Samuel Noah Kramer, Harper and Row Publishers, New York, New York, 1983

Pagan Anger Magic, positive Transformations from Negative Energies, by Tammy Sullivan, Citadel Press, Kensington Publishing Corp. New York, New York, 2005

The Case of Lilith, 23 Biblical Evidences, identifying the Serpent as Adam's first failed wife in Genesis, by Mark Wayne Biggs, Published by ReligionBookMix, 2012

The Cult of the Black Virgin, by Ean Begg Chiron Publishing, Wilmette, Illinois 2006

The Goddess Oracle, a Way to Wholeness through the Goddess and Ritual, by Amy Sophia Marashinsky, Massachusetts, Element Books, 1997

The Hebrew Goddess by Raphael Patai, Wayne State University Press, Detroit Michigan,1990, -third enlarged Edition

The Witches' Goddess, the Principle of Divinity by Janet and Stewart Farrar, Phoenix Publishing Inc. Custer Washington, 1987

Internet:Embracing the Dark Goddess by Dominae

Internet:www.flutterbywings.com/goddess /Lilith.htm, "I am Goddess, Worship me" Nov. 2008

Internet:Sumerian Legend of Lilith, translated by Charles Alexander Moffat from The Lilith Gallery

Internet:An Order of the White Moon, "Lilith –Child of Light, Daughter of Darkness

Internet:Lilith; A Romance by George MacDonald, 1985

Internet:The Lilith Shrine by Dante Gabriel Rosetti, "Collected Poems," London 1906

MA'AT

Ancient Mirrors of Womanhood, a Treasure of Goddess and Heroine Lore from around the World, by Merlin Stone, Beacon Press,Boston, Massachusetts, 1979

Egyptian Paganism for Beginners, bring the Gods and Goddesses of Ancient Egypt into Daily Life by Jocelyn Almond and Keith Seddon, Llewellyn Publications, St.Paul, Minnesota, 2004

The Book of Goddesses, Invoke the Powers of the Goddess to Improve Your Life by Roni Jay, A Quarto Book, Baron's Educational Series, Inc. Hauppauge, New York, 2000

The Gods of the Egyptians; studies in Egyptian mythology- Vol.I, by E.A. Wallis Budge, Dover publ.1969

The Goddess Oracle, a Way to Wholeness through the Goddess and Ritual, by Amy Sophia Marashinsky, Massachusetts, Element Books, 1997

The Witches' Goddess, the Principle of Divinity by Janet and Stewart Farrar, Phoenix Publishing Inc. Custer Washington, 1987

365 Goddess, a Daily Guide to the Magic and Inspiration of the Goddess by Patricia Telesco, HarperSanFrancisco, a Division of Harper Collins Publishing, 1998

Internet: Themystica.org/mythical-folk/articles/maat.html

Internet: From http://en.wikipedia.org/wiki/Maat

Internet: Egypt.idolhands/maat/intro.html

Internet: Crystalvaults.com/pages/goddess_maat.php

Internet: Paganwicca.about.com/od/egyptiandeities/p/maatprofile.htn

Internet: www.Daughterofmaat.hubpage

Internet: www.touregypt.net/godsofegypt/maat2.htmCaroline Seawright

Internet: ancient-egypt.info/2012/03/maat-egyptian-goddess-and-blinding-of.htm

Internet: In existence since the old kingdom, pyramid text of Unas (CA2375 BCE and2345 BCE)

Egyptian religion by Siegfried Morenz, translated by Ann E. Keep page 275, 1992

Cornell University Press, l

SageWoman Magazine no. #78, Spring 2010- Finding our Balance,

"One of Ten Thousand: Goddess Lore and Ritual' by Diana L. Paxson page 36-42

MACHA

Goddess Afoot, practicing Magic with Celtic and Norse Goddesses by Michelle Skye, Llewellyn Worldwide Publishing, Woodbury, Minnesota, 2008

Goddess In World Mythology, a Biography Dictionary by Dorothy Myers Imel and Martha Ann

The Goddess Oracle, A Way to Wholeness Through The Goddess and Ritual by Amy Sophia Marashinsky and Hrana Janto

365 Goddess, a daily guide to the magic and inspiration of the Goddess by Patricia Telesco

Whitemoondotcom/goddess/Macha

MAIA

Goddesses in World Mythology, a Biographical Dictionary, Martha Ann and Dorothy Myers Imel, Oxford

365 Goddess, a daily guide to the magic and inspiration of the Goddess by Patricia Telesco

Powers of the Orishas by Migenes Gonzalez-Wippler

365 Goddess, a daily guide to the magic and inspiration of the Goddess by Patricia Telesco

MAMAN BRIGITTE

http://members.aol.com/racine125/index1.html website by Bon Mambo Racine Sans Bout Sa Te La Daginen internet

www.Meta-Religion.com world religions/voodoo/ancestors.htm internet

SageWoman Magazine, Autumn 2008- issue 75 -Surrendering and Awakening-One of Ten Thousand; Goddess Lore and Ritual (page 31-37) Article- Maman Brigitte, Priestess of the Tomb, by Diana L. Paxson

www. Sosyetedumarche.com/html/b...te.html -internet

www.Thaliatook.com/AMGG/mamanbrijit- Thalia Took Oracle website

The magical buffet.com/blog½...cemetery internet

Secrets of Voodoo by Milo Rigaud

Wikipedia.com free Encyclopedia internet

MAUVE

Goddesses in World Mythology, a Biographical Dictionary, Martha Ann and Dorothy Myers Imel, Oxford

365 Goddess, a daily guide to the magic and inspiration of the Goddess by Patricia Telesco

The Goddess Oracle, A Way to Wholeness Through The Goddess and Ritual by Amy Sophia Marashinsky and Hrana Janto

INTERNET: Http: www.celticlifedotcom

YouTube Channel: Society of Antiquaries of Scotland, Lecture 5, the Goddess of Sovereignty

YouTube Channel: 3rd Coast Celtic, Beyond Green Beer

YouTube Channel: Celtic Notes, Ronnie Drew – Mauve & the Bull of Cooley

NIKE

GoddessGift.net

Hesiod's Theogony

Homeric Hymns

Loggia.com

Orphic Hymn 33 to Nike Translated by Taylor (Greek Hymns C3rd B.C. to 2nd A.D.)

Theoi.com Project

Wikipedia.com free encyclopedia

NU-KUA

Chinese Mythology, Irene Dea Collier, Enslow Publishers, Inc. 2001

Chinese Mythology: An Introduction by Anne Birrell

Goddesses in World Mythology, a Biographical Dictionary, Martha Ann and Dorothy Myers Imel, Oxford University Press, New York 1993

Handbook of Chinese Mythology (Handbook of World Mythology) Lihui Yang, Deming An, with Jessica Anderson Turner, Oxford University Press, 2005

The Goddess Oracle, a Way to Wholeness Through the Goddess and Ritual, Amy Sophia Marashinsky, Illustrated by Hrana Janto, Element Books, Inc, Rockport, MA, 1997

365 Goddesses, a Daily guide to the magic and inspiration of the Goddess, Patricia Telesco, Harper SanFrancisco,1998, Nu Kwa- Feb 13

Internet: www.Mysticwicks.com

Internet: www.Wikipedia.org/wiki/N%C3BCwa

Internet: www.chinavoc.com/history/ancient/myth_nw.htm

Internet: www.squidoo.com/nukuagoddess

Internet: From WIKI http://en.wikipedia.org/wiki/N%C3%BCwa

Internet: http://www.Chinavoc.com/history/ancient/myth-nw.htm

Internet: http://www.thaliatook.com/AMGG/nukua.html

ODUDUWA

Jambalaya , the Natural Woman's Book of Personal Charms and Practical Rituals by Luisah Teish

Ritual and Spells of Santeria, by Migene Gonzalez-Wippler

The Handbook of Yoruba Religious Concepts, by Baba Ifa Karade

Goddesses in World Mythology, a Biographical Dictionary, Martha Ann and Dorothy Myers Imel, Oxford

Mama Lola: A Vodou Priestess in Brooklyn, by Karen McCarthy Brown, University of California, 2001

Secrets of Voodoo by Milo Rigaud, City Lights Books, San Francisco, CA 1969, 1985

The Cult of the Black Virgin, by Ean Begg Chiron Publishing, Wilmette, Illinois 2006

INTERNET: Http: www.Awonifadotcom/orishas

INTERNET: www.the Yoruba.com

INTERNET: www.theOrisha.com

YouTube: Moses781 Youtube

YouTube: Orisha Yoruba, Chief Yuya Vlog

OLWEN

Goddess Afoot, practicing Magic with Celtic and Norse Goddesses by Michelle Skye, Llewellyn Worldwide Publishing, Woodbury, Minnesota, 2008

Goddess In World Mythology, a Biography Dictionary by Dorothy Myers Imel and Martha Ann

The Goddess Oracle, A Way to Wholeness Through The Goddess and Ritual by Amy Sophia Marashinsky and Hrana Janto

365 Goddess, a daily guide to the magic and inspiration of the goddess by Patricia Telesco

https://www.Wikipedia.org-Olwen

OSHUN

Mama Lola: A Vodou Priestess in Brooklyn, by Karen McCarthy Brown, University of California, 2001

Secrets of Voodoo by Milo Rigaud, City Lights Books, San Francisco, CA 1969, 1985

The Cult of the Black Virgin, by Ean Begg Chiron Publishing, Wilmette, Illinois 2006

The Haitian Vodou Handbook, Protocols for Ridding with the Lwa by Kenaz Filan (Houngan Coquille du Mer), Destiny Books, Rochester, Vermont, 2007

Vodou Love Magic, A Practical Guide to Love, Sex, and Relationships by Kenaz Filan), Destiny Books, Rochester, Vermont, 2009

OYA YANSA

A Ritual For Change, The tribal tradition Omnipresent Oya.com By Heathwitch

Carnival of the Spirit, Seasonal Celebrations and Rites of Passage by Luisah Teish

Jambalaya, The Natural Woman's Book of Personal Charms and Pracitical Rituals by Luisah Teish

Oya; in Praise of the African Goddess by Judith Gleason

Powers of the Orishas by Migenes Gonzalez-Wippler

The Blue Roebuck.com and A Primer in Dianic Witchcraft by Bendis also known as Deanne Quarrie founder of the Apple Branch

The Goddess Oracle, A Way to Wholeness Through The Goddess and Ritual by Amy Sophia Marashinsky and Hrana Janto

The New Book of Goddesses and Heroines by Patricia Monaghan

Paganwiki.com

SageWoman No. #47 Autumn 1999, Petition to Oya, a letter offering from a reader by Juniper in Colorado

SageWoman No.#55 Autumn 2001, One of Ten Thousand: Goddess Lore and Ritual article- Oya, Lady of Change by Diana L. Paxson

SageWoman No. #65 Truth and Beauty, Masks for the Goddess by Lauren Raine

Santeria, the Religion by Wippler, Migenes Gonzalez

PELE

Cofeetime.com by Betty Fullard-Leo

Goddess Mirror, Visions of the Divine From East and West by David Kinsley

MythicRealm.com

Pagan Anger Magic, Positive Transformations From Negative Energies by Tammy Sullivan

SageWoman No.# 54 Summer 2001, Reclaim Your Power...and Find inner Peace, Too! by Lady Moondance

Tales of Hina Online By Lana's Aumakua

The Goddess Oracle, A Way to Wholeness Through The Goddess and Ritual by Amy Sophia Marashinsky and Hrana Janto

365 Goddess, a daily guide to the magic and inspiration of the Goddess by Patricia Telesco

White Moon Gallery.com

Wikipedia.com free Encyclopedia

PERSEPHONE

Circle Round, Raising Children in Goddess Tradition by Starhawk, Diane Baker and Anne Hill

Goddess in Every Woman, a New Psychology of women by Jean Shinoda Bolen, MD.

Greek Goddess of innocence and Queen of the underworld. http://www.goddessgift.com/goddess-myhths/greek-goddess-peresphone.htm

Persephone Unveiled, Seeing the Goddess and Freeing Your Soul by Charles Stein

The Goddess Path, Myths, Invocations and Rituals by Patricia Monaghan

The Meaning of Persephone's name-m.anthony, http://quantum-witch.com/theos/w/p-name.htm

The Myth of Persephone- Greek Goddess of the Underworld by Laura Strong, PhD., http://www.mythicarts.com/writing/persephone.html

The Mythic Tarot, a New approach to the Tarot Cards by Juliet Sharman-Burke and Liz Greene

The Witches 'Goddess, The Feminine Principle of Divinity by Janet and Stewart Farrar

Wikipedia.com a free Encyclopedia

RHIANNON

Ancient Mirrors of Womanhood, a Treasure of Goddess and Heroine Lore from around the World, by Merlin Stone, Beacon Press,Boston, Massachusetts, 1979

Goddesses in World Mythology, a Biographical Dictionary, Martha Ann and Dorothy Myers Imel, Oxford University Press, New York 1993

365 Goddess, a Daily Guide to the Magic and Inspiration of the Goddess by Patricia Telesco, HarperSanFrancisco, a Division of Harper Collins Publishing, 1998

The Goddess Oracle, a Way to Wholeness through the Goddess and Ritual, by Amy Sophia Marashinsky, Massachusetts, Element Books, 1997

The (Mabignon) Mabinogi translated by Patrick K. Ford, Berkeley: University of California Press. 1977

Internet: www.mabinogion.info/Rhiannon.htm

Internet: www.paganwiccan.about.com

Internet: www.goddessgift.com/goddessgallery/Rhiannon.html

Sagewoman Magazine, Issue 73. Rhiannon the Mare Mother, One of Ten Thousand: Goddess Lore and Ritual regular Column by Diana Paxson (pages25-33)

SARASWASTI

Chakra Workout, Balancing your Energy with Yoga and Meditation by Mary Horsley

Goddess In World Mythology, a Biography Dictionary by Dorothy Myers Imel and Martha Ann

Grandmother Moon, Lunar Magic in our lives by Zsuzsanna E. Budapest

Healing Mantras, by Thomas Ashley-Farrand

Hindu Gods and Goddess by Swami Harshananda

SageWoman No.#46 Summer 1999, The Great Goddess Saraswati; Flowing River of Creativity, Inspiration and Joy by Suzin Green

SageWoman No. #64 Prayer and Invocation, One of Ten Thousand: Goddess Lore and Ritual- Article, Sarasvati, Word of Wisdom by Diana L. Paxson

The Book of Goddesses, Invoke the Powers of the Goddess to Improve Your Life by Roni Jay

365 Goddess, a daily guide to the magic and inspiration of the Goddess by Patricia Telesco

SEDNA

365 Goddess, a daily guide to the magic and inspiration of the Goddess by Patricia Telesco

The Goddess Oracle, A Way to Wholeness Through The Goddess and Ritual by Amy Sophia Marashinsky and Hrana Janto

Goddesses in World Mythology, a Biographical Dictionary, Martha Ann and Dorothy Myers Imel, Oxford University Press, New York 1993

INTERNET: www.polarlife.ca>traditional

INTERNET: www.Goddessgift.com>goddess-myths

INTERNET: www.dltk-teach.com

INTERNET: www.wikipedia>wiki>Sedna_(mythology)

INTERNET: Franz Boas' (1888, Monograph)"The Central Eskimo"

SEKHMET

Egyptian Paganism for Beginners, bring the Gods and Goddesses of Ancient Egypt into Daily Life by Jocelyn Almond and Keith Seddon, Llewellyn Publications, St.Paul, Minnesota, 2004

Pagan Anger Magic, Positive Transformations From Negative Energies by Tammy Sullivan

The Goddess Oracle, A Way to Wholeness Through The Goddess and Ritual by Amy Sophia Marashinsky and Hrana Janto

365 Goddess, a daily guide to the magic and inspiration of the Goddess by Patricia Telesco

The Cult of the Black Virgin, by Ean Begg Chiron Publishing, Wilmette, Illinois 2006

SELU/CORN MOTHER

365 Goddess, a daily guide to the magic and inspiration of the Goddess by Patricia Telesco

The Goddess Oracle, A Way to Wholeness Through The Goddess and Ritual by Amy Sophia Marashinsky and Hrana Janto

http://www.michellemays.com

Song: "Selu awa do li"

Corn - myth encyclopedia-mythology , god, story, names, world, creation, people, children, fire

http://www.mythencyclopedia.com/corn

http://www.abaxion.com/sz02.jpg

http://www.dovercards.com

http://www.rainewalker.com/selu.htm

Corn mother's gift by Chrity Salo

The story of Corn-History detective-in the beginning

http://www.campsilos.org/mod3/students/c-history.shtml

http://www.witcvox.com/music/bardic Circle-Michelle Mays;

The story of Selu, Michelle Mays

SIF

Dictionary of Northern Mythology, byRudolf Simek

Goddess Afoot, practicing Magic with Celtic and Norse Goddesses by Michelle Skye, Llewellyn Worldwide Publishing, Woodbury, Minnesota, 2008

Myth and Religion of the North, by Turville-Petre

Norse Magic by D.J. Conway, Llewellyn Publications, St. Paul Minnesota, 1997

Northern Mysteries and Magick: Runes and Feminine Powers by Freya Aswynn, published in 1998 by Llewellyn

Poems of the Elder Edda, Trans. P Terry

Poetic Edda, Snorri Sturluson, Trans A. Faulkes

Sagewoman Magazine, Issue 62, Courage, A Circle is Cast, Column, by Sage women readers. Autumn Equinox Ritual by Gallina Krasskova page 73-76

Scandinavian Mythology, by H R Ellis Davidson

The Cassell Dictionary of Norse Myth and Legend by Andy Orchard

The Goddess Oracle, a Way to Wholeness through the Goddess and Ritual, by Amy Sophia Marashinsky, Massachusetts, Element Books, 1997

The Rites of Odin by Ed Fitch 1990, Llewellyn

365 Goddess, a Daily Guide to the Magic and Inspiration of the Goddess by Patricia Telesco, HarperSanFrancisco, a Division of Harper Collins Publishing, 1998

Internet: http://www.sodahead.com/unitedstates/sif-norse-goddess-of-the-grain/question-1596261

Internet: http://www.mysticwicks.com

Internet: http://www.thorshof.org/sif.htm.

Internet: http://ancienthistory.about.com/od/norsemyth/a/aa081799Norse.htm

Internet: en.wikipedia.org/wiki/sif

Internet: http://www.Valkyrie tower.html.com/sif

Internet: http;//www.Mistress of EnchantmentBlog.com:Sif- 2010

SHINA TSU HIME

Gathering for Goddess, a Manual for Priestessing Women's Circles, by B. Melusine Mihaltses.Publisher; Feminine Divine Works, Schertz, Texas, 2012

Goddesses in World Mythology, a Biographical Dictionary, Martha Ann and Dorothy Myers Imel, Oxford

365 Goddess, a daily guide to the magic and inspiration of the Goddess by Patricia Telesco

SKADI

Ancient Mirrors of Womanhood, a Treasury of Goddess and Heroine Lore from Around the World by Merlin Stone

Llewellyn's 2005 Magical Almanac; Article; "Skadi, Norse Goddess of Winter" by Lily Gardner

pg 64-65 St. Paul Minnesota, Llewellyn Worldwide 2005

Norse Magic, by D.J. Conway, Llewellyn Publications

The Elder Edda, translated by Lee Hollander, Texas, USA, University of Texas, 1986

Skadi - Wikipedia.com free encyclopedia

SUNNA

Goddess Afoot, practicing Magic with Celtic and Norse Goddesses by Michelle Skye, Llewellyn Worldwide Publishing, Woodbury, Minnesota, 2008

Goddess In World Mythology, a Biography Dictionary by Dorothy Myers Imel and Martha Ann

The Goddess Oracle, A Way to Wholeness Through The Goddess and Ritual by Amy Sophia Marashinsky and Hrana Janto

365 Goddess, a daily guide to the magic and inspiration of the Goddess by Patricia Telesco

Scandinavian Mythology, by H R Ellis Davidson

The Cassell Dictionary of Norse Myth and Legend by Andy Orchard

TARA

INTERNET: www.Crystallinks.com> Tara

INTERNET: www.En.m.wikipedia.org> Tara

INTERNET: www.Religionfacts.com>Tara

INTERNET: www.Sacredwind.com>Tara

INTERNET: www.Hologramthoughts.com>Buddhism

Goddess in World Mythology, a Biographical Dictionary by Martha Ann Dorothy Myers Imel

Hindu Goddesses, Visions of the Divine Feminine in the Hindu Religious Tradition by David R. Kinsley

Hindu Gods and Goddeses by Swami Harshananda

Siddhartha by Hermann Hesse

The Book of Goddesses, Invoke the Powers of the Goddess to Improve Your Life by Roni Jay, A Quarto

The Goddess Oracle, A Way to Wholeness Through The Goddess and Ritual by Amy Sophia Marashinsky and Hrana Janto

Twenty –Four Aspects of Mother Kali by Babaji Bob Kindler

365 Goddess, a daily guide to the magic and inspiration of the Goddess by Patricia Telesco

THEMIS

Goddess In World Mythology, a Biography Dictionary by Dorothy Myers Imel and Martha Ann

INTERNET: Http: www.Theoigreekmythologydotcom

INTERNET: Http: www.Goddessguidedotcom

INTERNET: Http: www.Greekmythologydotcom

INTERNET: Http: www.Wikipediadotorg

TYCHE

Goddesses in World Mythology, a Biographical Dictionary, Martha Ann and Dorothy Myers Imel, Oxford

365 Goddess, a daily guide to the magic and inspiration of the Goddess by Patricia Telesco

UZUME

Ancient Mirror of Womanhood, a Treasury of Goddess and Heroine Lore from around the World, by Merlin Stone, Beacon Press, Boston 1984 edition

Gathering for Goddess, a Manual for Priestessing Women's Circles, by B. Melusine Mihaltses.Publisher; Feminine Divine Works, Schertz, Texas, 2012

Handbook of Today's Religions- by Josh McDowell & Don Stewart

The Book of the Goddess Past and Present, an Introduction to Her Religion Edited by Carl Olson, The Crossroad Publishing Company, New York 1987

The Goddess Oracle, a Way to Wholeness Through the Goddess and Ritual, Amy Sophia Marashinsky, Illustrated by Hrana Janto,Element Books, Inc, Rockport, MA, 1997

365 Goddesses, a Daily guide to the magic and inspiration of the Goddess, Patricia Telesco, Harper SanFrancisco,1998, Nu Kwa- Feb 13

Shinto, a Celebration of Life by Aidan Rankin, OBooks, Winchester UK, Washington, USA, 2010

Internet: www.uwec,edu/philrel/shimbutsudo/uzume.html

Internet: www.greenshinto.com

Internet: Kojiki Records of Ancient Matters transl. B.H. Chamberlain

Internet: Religion in Japanese History, Joseph M. Kitagawa

Internet: www.1000questions.net/en/religion/shinto.html

Internet: en.wikipedia.org/wiki/Ame-no-Uzume-no-Mikoto

Internet: www.Goddessgift.com/goddess/Japanese_goddess_Amaterasu.htm

Internet: www.Pantheon.org.>Areas>Mythology>Asia>Japanese mythology

Internet: www.Bukisa.comReligion & Spirituality

Internet: www.Ancient history.about.com/od/uzumemyth/

Internet: www.Land of wisdom.com

YEMAJA

Goddesses in World Mythology, a Biographical Dictionary, Martha Ann and Dorothy Myers Imel, Oxford

Jambalaya, The Natural Woman's Book of Personal Charms and Pracitical Rituals by Luisah Teish

OTHER RESOURCES

A Guide to Mystic Faerie Tarot by Barbara Moore

Easy Tarot Guide by Marcia Masino

Feminine Divine Works Intuitive Oracle, A Powerful Tool for Daily Insight and Inspiration by B. Melusine Mihaltses ISBN#978-0-9851384-9-3

Feminine Divine Works Intuitive 70x Oracle Deck

Gathering for Goddess, A Complete Manual for Priestessing Women's Circles by B. Melusine Mihaltses ISBN#978-0-9851384-4-8

Goddess Grimoire Journal, A Collection of Simple Prose and Spells by B. Melusine Mihaltses ISBN# 978-0-9851384-3-1

Living Goddess Spirituality, A Feminine Divine Priestessing Handbook by B. Melusine Mihaltses ISBN#978-0-9851384-7-9

Major Arcana Goddess Living Tarot, A Feminine Divine Works Creation by B. Melusine Mihaltses ISBN#978-0-9851384-8-6

The Mystical Tarot, a Step-by-Step Guide to the Tarot's Ancient and Mysterious Symbols by Roasemary Ellen Guiley

The Mythic Tarot, a New Approach to The tarot Cards by Juliet Sharman-Burke and Liz Greene

The Morgan –Greer Tarot Deck

The Spellcrafting Coach, A Metaphysical Guide to Revamp your Life by B. Melusine Mihaltses ISBN#978-0-9851384-0-0

The Tarot, Art, Mysticism, and Divination by Sylvie Simon

INTERNET: www.presentlove.com

INTERNET: www.laughteronlineuniversity.com

INTERNET: www.ancienthuna.com

**** For a more comprehensive Reference and Bibliography of helpful Goddess books check out the author's first book; "Gathering for Goddess, A Complete Manual for Priestessing Women's Circles," -Isbn#978-0-9851384-4-8

B. Melusine Mihaltses is a Certified life coach, a Published author, intuit artist, Yoga teacher, priestess, and a Woman's group facilitator. She is also a classically trained singer; holding both a Bachelors and a Masters of Music in Vocal Pedagogy. From an early age she expressed and exemplified a passionate creative, artistic soul and her spirituality has always been steeped and deeply intertwined in her numerous creative expressions. She is a Goddess priestess, dedicated to the intense study of various goddesses from around the world and her commitment to understanding their positive influence on women is undeniable. As founder and priestess of, **Grove of the Feminine Divine**, one of the few, at the time, all-women's Goddess group in Texas, she has been an active promoter of woman's empowerment and an advocate for women reclaiming their power; returning to their Goddess gifts. She Coaches her private clients and organizes beautiful gatherings in her home temple to encourage sisterhood, commemorate the changing seasons and honor various notable deities significant in every woman's journey. These celebratory gatherings are a testament of love and devotion to her gender's empowerment and the Sacred Feminine. Her first book, **"Gatherings for Goddess, a Complete Manual for Priestessing Women's Circles,"** holds her priestessing journey, invaluable lessons and precious experiences throughout the creation, nurturance and sustenance of this group. It is a treasure trove of insight for anyone heeding the call to promote community, women's Circles and Goddess Spirituality. Other known noteworthy publications by this prolific author are; **"Goddess Coaching Companion, a Woman's Guide to Magick, Protection and Empowerment.",** "Goddess Grimoire Journal, a Collection of Simple Prose and Spells," "Living Goddess Spirituality, a Feminine Divine Priestessing Handbook," and "The Spellcrafting Coach, A Metaphysical Guide to Revamp your Life." She continues to share her vast research on Goddess mythologies, Metaphysical tools, artistic creative expressions, inspiring words and her unique journey. She is also the creator of a beautiful 70x card Oracle deck & guidebook that features her own unique artworks titled, **"Feminine Divine Works Intuitive Oracle,"** and she also created the **"Major Arcana Goddess Living Tarot"** with its accompanied colored guidebook. All of her creations are available on Amazon, her FeminineDivineWorks Etsy page and you can also learn more on her website, **http://www.femininedivineworks.com**

As a Goddess Gathering Women's group Facilitator, Yoga teacher and Life Coach, she incorporates her training, experiences & education to be of service to others. Her mission in life is to fully co-create and help women reshape their lives and reclaim their inherent gifts through a more Feminine exalting tradition found in Goddess Spirituality.

Growing up in New York City afforded her many opportunities for Spiritual growth and knowledge. She was exposed to numerous learning venues, women's circles and greater opportunities to further her Metaphysical studies. In these numerous women circles, B.Melusine unearth great magick, empowerment, healing, sisterhood and an ancient way of being that resonated deeply with her core beliefs. A student at The Source of Life and at the New York Open Center, she studied tarot with renowned psychic/tarot reader Patti Canova. She also participated in numerous seminars on spiritual matters, drumming circles and rituals. She participated in open Sabbat rituals held by thealogian Susan Marie Hellerer, DMIV, lectures by Margot Adler, author of *"Drawing Down the Moon"* and Phyllis Currott, author of *"Book of Shadows"* & *"Witch Crafting"* and HP of Temple of Ara. At the Learning Annex she took classes on traditional magick, tarot and participated in lectures and rituals held by Donna Limoge, co-author of *"Sexual Bewitchery and other Ancient Feminine Wiles."* She was part of a yearlong Pagan Grove study, at New York City's emblematic "Enchantments, Inc." and at the Zodiac Lounge, on the upper Westside, she was a member of The Zodiac Lounge Women's Circle, an all-female Goddess centered group. At "Crystal Quilt," in Manhattan, NewYork, She participated in a weekly, all female circle, advocating the tradition of –"Wise-Woman Healing Ways" and it was facilitated by Robin Rose Bennett; a well-known Herbologist, student of Susun Weed, Green-Witch and author of *"Healing Magic; A Greenwitch's Guidebook."* It was in these early precious Women's circles, amongst some of the most amazing powerful teachers and sisters (*"all of us were hungry for wisdom, healing and knowledge,"* she remembers) that her life started to shift in ways she had not anticipated. These circles along with the numerous female centered Goddess literatures she was being exposed to like; Shekhinah Mountainwater, Z. Budapest, Marion Weinstein, Ffiona Morgan, Diane Stein, all sparked a greater interest in Women's spirituality. These early Goddess and women centered groups enriched her life greatly and in the presence of such great teachers, facilitators and priestesses, she was privileged to learn a great deal about how to formulate groups and circles that nurture Women's spirituality.

Mrs. Mihaltses was a part of several Goddess Gatherings sojourns; traveling to San Jose California, to attend the **2008 Z.Budapest Goddess Gathering**, where she finally met and was initiated by beloved founder of the Feminist Dianic Wiccan tradition, Z. Budapest. The following year, she traveled to Madison, Wisconsin to attend another critical Dianic event.This time, B.Melusine partook of Dianic Author and songstress, **Ruth Barrett's Daughter of Diana Festival.** She attended this annual Goddess Gathering and here, she continued to expand her ritual experiences & knowledge of Goddess Spirituality.

As a presenter, B.Melusine Mihaltses was offered a chance to share her works in various venues and workshops. In the autumn of 2013 she was a presenter at the **First, "Goddess Spirit Rising International Goddess Conference**," held in Malibu, California. Early summer of 2013, B. Melusine Mihaltses was the recipient of **"The Shift Network Team Scholarship"** for additional studies on Women Leadership and Spirituality. This scholarship was offered to her for participation and further course studies in the, *"Soulful Women Rising, Living your Soul's calling to Co-create a New World,"* taught by Devaa Haley Mitchell and Elayne Kalila Doughty, the founders of, "Inspiring Women Summit." With this training she intends to enhance her work as a writer, artist and Life coach and hopes to be of greater service to her Spiritual community.

In 2020, she became a Registered Yoga Teacher with Yoga Alliance, completing her 200hrsYoga teacher Certification and published her 9th book titled,"**Revamped Goddess, Coaching Yourself to a Better Life.**" The previous year she was hard at work completing the exhaustive cataloguing process of her Art creations, resulting in the publication of her Colored Art book titled, **"Goddess Inspired, Artistic Offerings to the Sacred Femine."** Currently, she is working on her 10th book titled, **Sixty-Four Goddesses, Reflections of Sacred Identity & Female Empowerment,"**a compilation of various noteworthy Goddeses to be released in 2024. To learn more about the author and her numerous creations check out **http://www.femininedivineworks.com or http://www.GoddessWomyn.com**

www.ingramcontent.com/pod-product-compliance
Lightning Source LLC
Chambersburg PA
CBHW080952020726
47505CB00009B/2172